KEN SANCHEZ

Stormweaver (Willowbrook Book Two)

Contents

1

Glimmer's Secrets

Dominic

Dominic swirled the mop across the bakery floor, lost in the rhythmic dance of cleaning. The soft hum of the refrigerator and the scent of freshly baked pastries created a cocoon of peace around him. His goofy grin stretched ear to ear until the entrance bell jingled, shattering the tranquility.

In walked Gary, a menacing presence that turned the bakery into a nightmarish arena. Dominic's goofy smile contorted into a scowl as he faced the unwelcome visitor.

"We're not open. Get out," Dominic barked, his tone sharper than the knives neatly arranged on the counter. The air crackled with tension as Gary, the menace, smirked in response.

"Open or not, I'm here for a little chat with Benjamin. Where is he?" Gary's voice, low and menacing, echoed through the bakery like a distant thunderstorm.

Dominic's eyes narrowed. "I don't know where Benjamin is, and even if I did, you're not welcome here."

Gary's laughter, a sinister symphony, resonated through the bakery.

"You're hiding something, Dominic, and I don't like secrets." He cracked his knuckles, a sound like thunder in the confined space.

A surreal energy enveloped the room as Dominic and Gary locked eyes. "I told you, get out! I don't want trouble," Dominic pleaded, his demeanor replaced by a surreal determination.

But Gary had no intention of leaving peacefully. With a sudden lunge, he aimed a punch at Dominic, who, in a surreal twist, summoned the power of the weather. Lightning crackled around Dominic's fingers as he defended himself with a stormy rage.

"You think you can just waltz in here and demand answers? Well, prepare for a storm, Gary!" Dominic exclaimed, his weather magic spiraling into a tempestuous display.

Thunder roared, and rain poured from nowhere as Dominic fought to repel the menacing force. The bakery transformed into a surreal battleground of magic and malice. Lightning clashed with Gary's relentless blows, creating a chaotic spectacle that defied reality.

Despite Dominic's best efforts, the surreal storm wavered, and the menace prevailed. Gary's punches landed with surreal force, each blow punctuated by a burst of thunder. Dominic's goofy resilience waned as he struggled to withstand the tempest of violence.

"I'll find Benjamin, one way or another," Gary sneered, his voice cutting through the storm. Dominic, battered and bruised, could only muster a defiant glare.

With a final, overwhelming surge, the surreal storm collapsed, leaving Dominic on the bakery floor, defeated and broken. Gary loomed over him, a triumphant menace, as the tempest faded into an eerie calm.

"You should've cooperated, Dominic. Now, remember this lesson," Gary warned before disappearing into the surreal shadows, leaving Dominic alone in the wreckage of his once-peaceful bakery.

Gasping for breath, Dominic surveyed the surreal aftermath of the encounter. The scent of pastries lingered, but the tranquility was shattered, replaced by the echoes of a surreal battle. Dominic, still defiant in spirit, vowed to rebuild, his goofy determination undeterred by the menace that had temporarily cast a shadow over his bakery.

Dominic Reed woke up gasping. That nightmare again. He was getting real tired of it. Ever since Gary attacked him in his bakery, he'd been messed up. Sounds or stuff would remind him of that awful day and he'd freak out.

His buddy Ben wanted him to see a therapist. Dominic wanted to, but between the bakery and his coven duties, he didn't have time. But he promised Ben he would when he could.

"Get it together, Dominic," he muttered.

He brushed his sweaty hair off his face and got out of bed. The cool morning air raised goosebumps on his skin as his feet hit the hardwood floor. He shivered slightly, rubbing the sleep from his eyes.

Padding to the bathroom, he caught a glimpse of his disheveled reflection in the mirror. Dark circles under his eyes spoke to his restless nights. He splashed some cold water on his face, which helped wake him up.

Dominic ran his fingers through his hair in an attempt to smooth down some of the wild bedhead he was sporting. The chestnut brown waves were going every which way from tossing and turning all night. He grabbed a brush and managed to get it looking reasonably neat.

The hot shower felt soothing on his sore muscles. Letting the water cascade down his back, Dominic took some deep breaths to start the day calmly. The vanilla scented soap filled the bathroom with a warm, comforting aroma.

After getting dressed in his usual jeans and a soft flannel shirt, Dominic made his way to the cozy kitchen. He opened the faded blue curtains covering the window above the sink, letting the morning sunlight stream in.

Leaving his family didn't hurt like he thought it would. He only missed his father. His mom died giving birth to him. From his father's stories, she sounded great. They were close until his father met Lina.

When Dominic first moved out on his own, he was worried he might feel lonely or homesick. But he quickly embraced the freedom of having his own space. No more tense family dinners or arguments with his stepmom. Dominic took comfort in the quiet solitude of his little house. He could come and go as he pleased without criticism.

Though Dominic didn't miss the dysfunction of his family home, he did still long for his old relationship with his father. They used to stay up late talking by the fire, going fishing on weekends, working together in the garden. His father taught him so much and gave him cherished childhood memories. His stories made Dominic feel connected to the mom he never knew.

But when Lina came into the picture, his father changed. He grew distant, cold, dismissive of Dominic's concerns about Lina. It was like he was under some kind of spell, no longer the caring father Dominic once knew. Lina clearly despised Dominic, though he wasn't sure why. She turned his father against him. Dominic knew in his gut she was manipulating his father somehow, but he struggled to prove it.

Living alone was better than constantly fighting at home. Yet Dominic still missed the good old days with his father, before Lina's toxic influence took hold. He hoped to one day get to the bottom of whatever scheme Lina was brewing, and free his father from her clutches. For now, Dominic took solace in his little quiet home, independent at last despite the sadness of losing his father's love.

What made the situation even more troubling was that Dominic's father was the longtime leader of their local witch coven. He was well-respected among the witch community. But now who knew how his leadership might change. Dominic hated seeing his father's legacy tarnished this way. He worried what Lina might influence him to do with the coven under his control.

Humming quietly, Dominic cracked a few eggs into a bowl and whisked them with a fork. He chopped up some veggies from the fridge - onions, peppers, spinach. After melting a pat of butter in the cast iron skillet, he poured the eggs in and cooked up an fluffy omelet filled with all the fixings.

The familiar sizzle and aroma was soothing. Dominic had taught himself to cook, and he thought of her mother every time he was in the kitchen. He wished she could be here to give him advice and comfort about his father. For now, at least he had her pans to cook with.

He was in the middle of eating when his phone started to ring. He looked at the caller ID and saw that it was Benjamin. He dropped the spoon that was already half-way to answer the call.

"Hey Ben, what's up?"

"Oh, nothing. Just checking on you," Ben said.

Dominic checked his watch. "This early? What's really going on?"

Ben sighed. "Okay, fine. Adrian and I were thinking, and we want to help you with therapy. Adrian knows someone who could help. Want to give it a shot?"

Dominic knew that Ben still felt bad about what happened. But they couldn't change the past and even thought he was starting to get annoyed with people asking if he was okay it still warmed his heart that Ben was there for him. He told Ben more than enough times that it wasn't his fault but his friend still worried about him.

"I appreciate it, but I gotta do this myself, on my timeline," Dominic said.

"I know, I know. We just wanna help, Dom."

"I'll think about it, but no promises," Dominic replied.

Ben squealed. Dominic held the phone away until he was done.

"Thank you! That's all we ask," Ben said.

Dominic smiled. Little things made Ben happy.

"You coming to the bakery today?" Dominic asked.

"Yep, bringing Adrian. He's been cranky and craving your bear claws."

Dominic laughed. "Awesome, see you later then?"

"Yeah, see ya," Ben said before hanging up.

Dominic placed the phone down finished eating. He stood up and took the dishes to the sink and cleaned them before taking off.

Before he he walked out the door he turned around and sighed. At times like these, he envied Benjamin who found someone in the form of Adrian Belmont.

He shook himself out of it before taking his hat and coat from the rack and left the house.

Early morning sunlight filtered through golden leaves as Dominic strolled the familiar sidewalks. He breathed deep, savoring the crisp autumn air. This was his favorite time to amble through Willowbrook undisturbed.

The peaceful streets showed no signs of the magical activity this early in the morning but it was normally filled with magic and fun mischief.

The different kind shifters, vampires, witches, and more recently, a dragon disguised in the form of Adrian. Somehow they all coexisted harmoniously here.

The sunlight warmed Dominic through his coat as he continued on his way. Leaves of gold, red and brown rustled gently overhead. He soaked up the tranquility, breathing deep the crisp scent of fallen leaves.

When he reached his Bakery, Dominic stopped and admired the hard work that he had put in his business.

When Dominic opened Glimmer, he drew inspiration from his childhood to make the exterior warm and welcoming. Sunny yellow walls recalled his grandma's kitchen. The stone and shingled roof gave it an old-fashioned cottage look, while inside was sleek and modern. Flower boxes overflowing with blooms hung below the windows, like his mother's garden.

Dominic chose elegant script for the signage and had it illuminated at night. Bare Edison bulbs hung over the entryway, beckoning customers inside. He built Glimmer from cherished memories - the flowers for his mom, the yellow walls for his grandma's cooking.

Glimmer welcomed everyone, human and supernatural alike. Dominic hoped the cozy, nostalgic exterior would make people feel at home. When he unlocked the green door each morning, the bakery felt familiar and inviting. Vanilla and cinnamon scents drifted out the windows, promising comfort. Glimmer reflected Dominic's history and his inclusive hopes for the future.

The scent of cinnamon and sugar welcomed Dominic as he unlocked the front door of Glimmer. Click went the lights, illuminating the sleek white counters and ratan cafe chairs. Dominic inhaled deeply. His favorite time of day.

He went through his usual morning ritual, prepping the bakery for its daily dose of warmth and sweetness. The ovens rumbled to life as Dominic popped in trays of croissants and muffins. Measuring cups clinked gently as he mixed up fresh icing. The lemon verbena soap filled the air with a crisp, clean aroma as he tidied the front.

This was Dominic's happy place. For him, baking was therapeutic. Measuring, mixing, kneading - it soothed his soul. And a little extra charm never hurt. He smiled as he added a pinch of secret magical spice to his scones for an extra mood-boosting quality.

But lately, it had all become a bit much. Between the bakery's popularity and his other obligations, Dominic was overwhelmed. As much as he loved it here, he needed help.

The 'Help Wanted' sign had only been up a week when Lyra flounced in, resume in hand. She was young, bubbly, a little sarcastic. Totally unlike Dominic. In other words, perfect.

The bell jingled right at seven in the morning am. In walked Lyra, wearing a pink apron and chatting on her phone.

"Okay, okay, I gotta go. I'll tell you all about it at lunch. Okay, love you too. Byeee." Lyra tucked her phone in her back pocket. "Heyyy, Dominic!"

Dominic looked up from the bear claws he was glazing. "Well hey there, good morning! Ready for your first day?"

"Born ready," Lyra grinned, tying her curly blond hair up in a bandana. "This place is so cute. It smells amazing!"

"All thanks to my grandma's secret recipes. Here, let me show you around."

Dominic demonstrated the espresso machine, ovens, and cash register. Lyra picked it up quickly. By the time Dominic unlocked the front door, she was raring to go.

Their first customers trickled in. The morning rush was heating up. Lyra chatted warmly with everyone while taking orders. Dominic shuffled around behind the counter, filling coffee cups and packing pastries into bags.

"How's the new girl working out?" asked Mrs. Abernathy, their favorite regular.

"Fantastic," Dominic said. "It's only been an hour, but I think she was meant to work here. Customers love her already."

"Well, she's just darling," Mrs. Abernathy replied. "What a ray of sunshine to start the day."

The morning hours zoomed by. Dominic and Lyra's teamwork was surprisingly seamless for her first day. During a brief lull, Dominic showed her how to make his famous chocolate croissants.

"The secret is folding the dough just so, to get the perfect flakiness," he explained as Lyra watched closely.

Just then, Dominic heard a familiar voice at the counter that made his stomach drop.

"Well, well, if it isn't my baby brother Dominic," the voice drawled.

Dominic looked up to see his stepbrother Lee smirking at him. Great. Just what he needed.

"Hey Lee," Dominic mumbled. "What can I get you?"

"Oh I think you know what I want, little brother," Lee sneered.

Dominic gritted his teeth. Ever since their father married Lina, her twin sons Lee and Austin had bullied Dominic relentlessly. He tried to rise above their taunts and cruelty, but it was difficult.

Lee scanned the bakery, looking for ways to needle Dominic. "Cute little shop you've got. Baking cupcakes not manly enough for you though?"

Dominic ignored the jab. "Did you want to order something?"

"Yeah, how about a black coffee and a grow a pair?" Lee laughed.

Just then, the bell jingled at the door. In walked Dominic's friends Ben and Adrian. Thank god.

"Hey, we got your text about the bear claws, we came as fast as - oh," Ben stopped short, seeing Lee.

"Well hey there fellas, you're just in time for the show," Lee snickered.

Ben stood taller. "I think you should leave, Lee."

"Ooh, scary," Lee pretended to shudder. "Looks like you've got your own little bakery boys to defend you now, Dominic. Pathetic."

Dominic's face burned hot with anger and embarrassment.

"Time for you to go," Adrian said firmly, stepping between Lee and Dominic.

"Alright, fine, I'm going," Lee said, rolling his eyes. He snatched a coffee off the counter. "This place is lame anyway. Smells like old lady perfume."

And with that final insult, Lee strode out the door. The bakery was silent for a moment.

"Dominic, are you okay?" Lyra asked gently.

"Yeah, I'm fine, he's just a jerk," Dominic muttered, busying himself with cleaning the espresso machine.

"I'm really sorry you had to deal with that," Ben said. "Let me know if he bothers you again."

Dominic gave a small smile. "Thanks man, I appreciate it."

He was grateful for friends who had his back. Adrian clapped Dominic on the shoulder supportively.

"Forget about him. We came here for bear claws and dang it, that's what we're going to get," Adrian said.

Dominic laughed, the tension starting to dissipate. "Coming right up!"

He grabbed a pair of tongs and picked out two perfect bear claws, golden and glistening with glaze. Adrian took an enthusiastic bite of one.

"Mmm! So worth the drive over," he mumbled through a mouthful.

"Yeah, nothing like a Dominic original bear claw," Ben agreed.

The sweet, buttery flavor helped shake off the bitter encounter with Lee. Dominic was relieved to have his friends there. He tried not to let his stepbrothers ruin his passion for baking. This place was his happy escape.

The afternoon flew by in a blur of cookies and lattes. Before Dominic knew it, closing time was approaching at Glimmer Bakery.

He untied his flour-dusted apron and called over to Lyra.

"Hey, we're winding down here. How was your first day overall?" Dominic asked.

Lyra finished wiping down the front counter. "It was amazing! I had so much fun meeting all the customers. And I feel like I learned a ton already."

"You were a natural on the register and with the baking. I'm impressed," Dominic said.

"Well, I had a great teacher showing me the ropes," Lyra replied with a wink.

Dominic laughed. "Happy to pass on my grandma's secrets. Baking is my passion."

Lyra grabbed a broom to sweep up. "I can tell. Everything is so cozy and charming here. You've created something really special."

"Aw, thanks," Dominic said, touched by her praise. "That means a lot. I wanted this to be a warm, welcoming place for people."

They chatted casually as they closed up shop. After just one day, Dominic knew Lyra was a perfect fit for Glimmer. Her cheerful presence gave the bakery an extra spark.

Dominic handed Lyra her share of the day's tips. "Get home safe, and thanks again for an amazing first day."

"No, thank you! I'll see you bright and early tomorrow," Lyra said, waving goodbye.

Dominic stood alone in the quiet bakery. He took a deep breath, taking in the lingering scents of sugar and cinnamon. Working here brought him so much joy. He wished he could stay all night.

But eventually he had to lock the door and head home. Dominic's shoulders slumped as he walked to his car. He really didn't want to go back to his little house. Lately his nights there had been plagued by horrible nightmares.

Ever since he got attacked that day in the bakery, Dominic hadn't felt safe. His anxiety spiked at night. The dark shadows in the corners of his bedroom took on lurking shapes. And his dreams were filled with terrifying replays of the attack.

Dominic knew it wasn't healthy to spend every night dreading sleep. But opening up about his feelings didn't come naturally to Dominic. Easier to just bury it all under mounds of work.

As he arrived at his house, Dominic let out a groan. The thought of lying awake in bed for hours in the dark made his stomach churn with dread. He trudged up to the front door like a condemned man.

Resigned to his fate, Dominic went through his bedtime routine robotically. He brushed his teeth and changed into pajamas. As he crawled under the covers, the familiar fear welled up in his chest. Sleep meant surrendering to the terror of his own mind.

Dominic lay rigid, eyes fixed on the dark ceiling above him. It was going to be another long night.

2

The Vampire's Dilemma

Christian

Christian Belgrade was in the middle of working as a bartender in his own club, Midnight. Even though he owned it, he still loved working there so he could lurk around and watch the mingling supernaturals and humans alike. Though, this evening it was one of their feeding nights.

During feeding events for vampires, the bar transformed into a wall full of drinks mixed with high quality blood from the nearby blood center. The humans involved came voluntarily - most benefited from being fed on by a vampire, since it halted their aging. Everything at Midnight was consensual.

Dawncreek used to overflow with all kinds of supernaturals. But eventually most moved away, leaving only vampires and some humans. At first, Christian struggled to understand why. Over time he realized vampires started running the town like they created it. His coven alone kept order and peace. That's why some stayed, his sire explained.

Christian was making drinks when his senses picked up a familiar presence. He finished serving patrons before turning to see Elvira

Greene, an elder vampire from the Greene coven. Stunning as ever with dark skin and a bright personality, she was also his best friend.

"Chris, darling! Lovely to see you," Elvira said.

Christian smiled. "Elvira, it's been too long! How have you been?"

"Oh fine, fine. My sire called me back to town," she explained.

"I've missed you. Give me a moment." Christian asked the other bartender, "Matt, can you take over for a bit?"

"Of course, Elder," Matt replied.

Matt was a new vampire Christian took under his wing. So far he was doing well, though Christian monitored his bloodlust. New vampires struggled to control their intense cravings.

Christian removed his apron and joined Elvira, embracing her warmly. They sat together at the bar.

"The fledgling seems to be thriving," Elvira remarked, glancing at Matt.

"He is, thankfully. I hope it continues," Christian said.

Elvira sipped her drink. "So how are things around here?"

Christian sighed heavily. "As good as they can be. I feel my sire is hiding something. It worries me."

Matt delivered their drinks. After he left, Elvira asked, "Does the whole coven sense it?"

"No, they're oblivious. But the other elders feel something's wrong."

"Even Eros?" Elvira raised an eyebrow.

He saw Eros Grim as he first was - an ambitious young vampire, turned only a decade before Christian. Eros took Christian under his wing when he was still a fledgling learning to control his powers. The elders of their coven favored Eros for his cunning and skill.

In those early nights, Christian admired Eros greatly. He learned ruthlessness and strategy at Eros's side, as they dominated the coven's political games. But Christian also tempered Eros's cruelty with his own compassion.

Their sire, Augutus Belgrade, was especially impressed by Christian's gifts. Though younger, Christian soon matched Eros in rank and authority. This is where the resentment took root. Eros saw Christian as a rival usurping his rightful role.

Over the decades, Christian gained prominence in the coven. His even-handed leadership was valued in volatile times. Eros's penchant for brutality fell out of favor as mortal rule gained civility and sophistication.

Christian shook his head. "Eros avoids me these days. Ever since…" His voice trailed off.

Elvira touched his arm comfortingly. She knew their history of violence and betrayal.

Christian took a long drink before continuing. "I wish I knew what troubled our sire. He's withdrawn from all of us."

"Have you tried confronting him directly?" Elvira asked.

"No. I fear making demands would only drive him further away," Christian admitted. "He was always so wise and strong. Now he seems…diminished."

Elvira considered this, sipping her drink. "Diminished how?"

Christian lowered his voice. "His power - it's unstable. He tries to hide it, but I've seen signs. And he looks weary in a way I've never seen before."

"You think he could be ill?" Elvira asked, frowning.

"I don't know," Christian sighed. "He insists it's nothing when I ask. But I saw him stumble the other night, and a chair flew across the room when he lost his temper."

Elvira's eyes widened. "That doesn't sound good at all."

"No, it doesn't," Christian agreed gravely. "Something is draining him. I've pleaded with him to seek help from the Council, but he refuses."

Elvira shook her head sadly. "Well, that certainly complicates matters."

Christian nodded grimly. He understood his sire's disdain for the Vampire Council. Christian had experienced their cruelty and hypocrisy firsthand.

As a young vampire, he had respected the Council's aim to bring order among their kind. But his faith in them eroded over centuries of observing their politics and petty power plays.

"They claim to uphold our laws, but show no mercy," Augustus would say. Christian now knew his sire was right.

When the Council refused rights to Augustus's newest fledglings, Christian saw their callousness himself. They saw only volatile beasts, not scared newcomers needing guidance.

By shunning the Council's summits, Augustus took a stand. Christian admired his bold defiance of their arrogant dictates. Who were they to undermine a wise elder's leadership?

When they arrived in Dawncreek, the Council demanded Augustus report on local covens. Christian supported his sire refusing such an insult.

"They want only to extend their reach," Augustus declared. Christian concurred - the Council sought influence, not stability.

Christian regretted not speaking against them more vocally. Their broken bond had isolated Augustus in illness. The Council's only concern was neutering threats to their power, not legitimately helping vampires.

"I wish he could see that the Council cares only for control, not cooperation," Christian told Elvira.

"Forcing help on the unwilling rarely works," she replied. "Patience and discretion may prevail where demands fail."

Christian knew she had a point. Augustus would reject the Council's strong-arming. But Christian would also no longer encourage concession or compromise with those hypocrites.

Some called Augustus stubborn and proud. But Christian now recognized his sire's wisdom in rejecting the Council's hollow overtures. They offered thin veneers of aid, but through gritted teeth.

Christian would support his sire fully, without reservation. To restore Augustus's vitality, they needed no venomous Council. Together their coven would find its own way, beyond the Council's grasp.

There could be no reconciliation with those despots. Christian saw that now. His sire's instincts had been right. The Council cared only for increasing its power. Christian hoped one day to see their corrupt regime crumble.

But for now, he would focus on helping his sire recover, on their own terms. Patience, discretion and loyalty - those would mend this rift, not crawling back to the Council.

His thoughts that threatening to spiral was broken when Elvira spoke again.

Elvira considered this news, swirling the blood and whiskey in her glass. "I wish I knew what to tell you, Chris. But if he won't accept help, what can you do?"

Christian ran a hand through his hair in frustration. "I keep hoping he'll confide in me. But he still sees me as the young upstart."

"Have patience. He took a chance on you once. He knows your worth, even if he won't admit it," Elvira said.

Christian glanced around the crowded club, taking comfort in the lively atmosphere. "I hope you're right. This coven needs him. I'm not ready to lead."

"Oh hush, you'd make a fine leader," Elvira chided.

"Maybe someday. But not yet, not like this." Christian finished his drink, troubled.

Sensing his mood, Elvira changed the subject. "On a lighter note, have you heard about the new bakery in Willowbrook?"

Christian managed a small smile. "Ah yes, the human Dominic's place. I've been there a couple of times."

"His pastries are divine," Elvira gushed. "The lemon tarts are my favorite."

"Well now I'm thoroughly intrigued," Christian laughed.

They passed the next hour cheerfully discussing local gossip and reminiscing about their travels. Elvira's presence lifted Christian's spirits like always. She had a gift for pinpointing just what troubled him, and knew when distraction was the best remedy.

As midnight approached, the club began emptying out. Christian bid Elvira goodnight with a fierce hug.

"Thank you for listening," he told her. "It helped ease my mind."

"Anytime. And do let me know if I can help with your sire," Elvira said.

After she left, Christian tidied up behind the bar, lost in thought. He decided he would stop by the bakery soon to introduce himself to Dominic. associating with mortals always reminded him what truly mattered - human lives, with their brevity and vibrancy. It heartened him to walk among them.

Matt finished wiping down tables and came over. "Elder, I wanted to thank you again for taking me under your guidance. I hope I can prove myself worthy."

Christian smiled and put a hand on his shoulder. "You're off to an excellent start. Get some rest, you've earned it."

Pride swelled in Matt's eyes. Christian was glad to be a mentor to him. Patience and understanding were required to guide a young vampire. Recalling Eros's mentorship all those years ago, Christian mused on how far they had drifted. He could not change the past, only keep striving to improve their future.

After Matt left, Christian did a final walkthrough and locked up for the night. Stepping outside, he took an unnecessary breath of the cool night air. The streets were finally still.

Christian pondered the uncertainties ahead. His sire's health, Eros's lingering hatred, training Matt…

But he had faith things would work out, with time. As an immortal, time was his ally.

For now, he would focus on what was in his power - supporting his sire, leading his coven, and connecting with the human community that depended on their protection.

Christian set out on foot back to the estate. Despite lingering concerns, he felt his usual sense of purpose restored. No matter what storms arose, he would steer his coven to safe harbors. They would endure, together.

Christian was on his way home when a vampire from his coven suddenly appeared before him - Igor, one of their scouts. As usual, his face was impassive.

"Master Augustus requests your presence," Igor stated flatly.

Christian was surprised but tried not to show it. "Tell him I'll be there soon. Did he say what he wants to discuss?"

Igor simply shook his head before dashing off into the night. Christian felt uneasy as he continued walking. Augustus summoning him like this was highly unusual. He wondered nervously what it could be about.

When Christian arrived at his manor, he quickly changed into a crisp suit, wanting to look presentable for his sire. Examining himself in the mirror, he neatly combed his short blond hair and straightened his jacket. Satisfied with his appearance, he set out for the coven's grand mansion hidden deep in the Dawncreek forest.

Approaching the intimidating stone facade, Christian steeled himself before entering through the heavy double doors. Inside, the atmosphere was hushed and somber. The mansion had always seemed cold to him, even after all these years. He much preferred his own smaller home.

This grand gothic structure served as the gathering place for the Belgrade coven, hidden deep within the remote Dawncreek forest. An ancient magic shrouded the mansion, shielding it from unwelcome eyes. Only those permitted by Augustus could penetrate its illusion and find the entrance.

Stepping inside, Christian felt the familiar chill creep over his skin. No natural light penetrated the stone walls or stained glass windows. Elaborate iron chandeliers holding flickering candles provided the only illumination. Their pale light flickered across the faces of past Belgrade leaders gazing sternly from their portrait frames.

The floors were polished obsidian, reflecting the candles' glow eerily. Christian's soft footsteps seemed to echo uncomfortably loud in the cavernous space. He quickened his pace, wanting to escape the heavy hush that shrouded these halls.

As Christian walked by, ancestral weapons and arcane relics watched silently from their perches and cases. The coven's storied history weighed on him here. He felt out of place, too modern for these shadows of the distant past.

Turning a corner, he nearly collided with a marble statue of Augustus's long-dead sire. Christian muttered an apology, feeling foolish. He would never grow fully accustomed to the ancient grandeur here.

Heavy velvet drapes lined the corridors, muffling sound. Christian imagined generations of vampires gliding silently through these halls, whispers barely penetrating the oppressive quiet. No signs of life existed here - no lingering scents of food, no discarded books or coats. Just ornate, outdated opulence.

The coven itself now convened in a more modern annex added decades ago. But Augustus inhabited the original manor, seeming more ghost than vampire at times. He ruled over this monuments of past glory, seldom emerging.

To Christian, the cold perfection of the decor reflected Augustus himself - cultured and imposing, but devoid of intimacy or warmth. He dwelled here alone but for servants, refusing change. His sole leniency was permitting Christian's minimal renovations to his own chambers.

Christian much preferred mingling with vibrant, chaotic humanity. Yet duty called him back often to these lifeless halls that time had forgotten. He hoped to gently lead the coven toward a more enlightened future, shedding some of this severity.

Arriving at Augustus's elaborate doors, Christian paused, steeling himself before knocking firmly. A muffled voice bid him enter. Christian turned the ornate handle and stepped inside.

Heavy antique furnishings occupied the large chamber, all gilded wood and leather. Books, candles, and scrolls cluttered every surface. It suited Augustus perfectly. The scent of aging paper and wax permeated the room.

At the far end before a massive desk sat Augustus. And already deep in discussion with him was Eros, shooting Christian a scowl as he entered. Suppressing a sigh, Christian moved to join them, leaving the door slightly ajar.

He felt Eros's resentment hitting him in waves. They had never trusted one another since the Paris Catacombs incident decades ago. But Christian had tried to mend things between them, for the sake of the coven.

Now it seemed Eros would always view him as a threat, no matter how Christian tried to reassure him. He clung tightly to past slights and power struggles. Here in this cheerless manor, ghosts of old grudges found fertile ground.

Christian wished Eros could see how little he cared for authority - he only wanted peace. But darkened halls bred suspicion, leaving no room for trust.

"What is he doing here?" Eros demanded impatiently.

Augustus waved a dismissive hand. "I asked you both here. Please, sit." He gestured to the chairs before his large wooden desk.

Eros sat reluctantly, glowering at Christian. Christian gave a polite nod to his sire. "You wanted to see me?"

"Yes. Tea?" Augustus offered.

"Thank you." Christian accepted the delicate cup and took a sip of the fragrant herbal tea, hoping it would calm his nerves.

Augustus settled back in his high-backed leather chair and appraised the two vampires before him.

"I have given this much thought," he began. "And I believe it is time for new leadership for this coven."

Christian tightened his grip on the teacup, eyes widening. Beside him, Eros visibly tensed.

"What exactly are you saying, My Lord?" Eros asked slowly.

Augustus clasped his hands on the desk. "I have decided to name Christian as my successor. Upon my retirement, he shall lead the Belgrade Coven."

Christian froze in shock. At his side, Eros shot to his feet, face contorted in rage.

"This is outrageous!" he shouted. "I am next in line to lead! Not this impertinent whelp." He jabbed an accusing finger at Christian.

Augustus remained calm, but his power crackled through the room. "You forget your place, Eros. I have made my choice."

Eros trembled with fury. "Choose me, My Lord, I beg you! I swear I shall not fail you as leader."

Augustus rose to his full height, eyes blazing. "Enough. Leave us."

The command in his voice made Christian shiver. Eros had no choice but to bow his head in acquiescence and depart. But the venomous look he gave Christian left no doubt this was far from settled.

Alone now, Christian turned to his sire, still reeling. "Why me?" he asked simply.

Augustus regarded him thoughtfully. "You possess compassion and wisdom beyond your years, Christian. This coven needs a leader who values justice as well as strength."

Christian stared at the floor. "Eros has guided this coven for centuries. The others respect him deeply. I'm still seen as young and untested."

"And that is precisely why you must lead them," Augustus said, not unkindly. "Your fresh vision is needed in these times of change."

Christian struggled to accept this. "I fear I lack the experience required for such a role."

Augustus smiled and put a hand on his shoulder. "I too felt unprepared when I first became leader. But you are ready, Christian. You need only trust in yourself as I do."

Looking into his ancient sire's eyes, Christian saw faith there - and exhaustion. The extent of Augustus's fading power suddenly dawned on him. He needed rest. Christian may not feel ready, but he could not refuse his sire's request.

"If this is your wish, then I humbly accept this duty," Christian pledged solemnly.

Augustus nodded approvingly. Then he leaned in and spoke in a low tone. "I must confess, I have had suspicions lately that Eros has been employing his powers of influence upon me."

Christian's eyes widened in surprise. Eros was gifted with subtle mental manipulation. Christian had wondered if Eros was possibly exploiting this against their sire.

Augustus smiled wryly. "Oh yes, I am quite certain he hoped I did not notice. But I know Eros well. The failed persuasions, the implanted doubts - his tricks are not so potent against me."

Christian frowned. "That is deeply troubling. To use his gifts against you…"

"Indeed," Augustus said seriously. "It only affirms I have chosen correctly in you, Christian. Eros is ruled by ambition, as I said."

Christian felt conflicted. While disturbed Eros would manipulate Augustus, Christian hesitated to think the worst of him. They had history together, after all.

Augustus seemed to sense his hesitation. "Do not despair for him. Discipline and guidance will cure Eros of this envy in time. But you, Christian - your integrity is untouched. That is why you must lead."

Reassured, Christian bowed his head gratefully. "I am honored by your faith in me. I will strive to prove it warranted."

Augustus nodded, looking well pleased. "You shall make an excellent leader, my son. Never doubt that." He squeezed Christian's shoulder warmly before withdrawing his hand.

Christian took a deep breath. "What of Eros? He will openly challenge this, I fear."

Augustus waved this off. "Eros is ruled by ambition, not wisdom. He must accept my judgment, or face consequences." His tone made clear Eros's fate should he defy his sire again.

They spoke a while longer about the transition before Christian took his leave, reeling with this new destiny. Upon returning home, he found Eros waiting for him.

"Reconsider this folly!" Eros demanded. "I am meant to rule our coven."

Christian sighed. "The choice is not mine. I did not ask for this."

Eros sneered. "Always so humble and dutiful. It disgusts me." He stormed off into the night.

3

Invitations and Intrigues

Dominic

ominic just finished closing up the Bakery. He normally closes early at this time of the week even though more people come in due it being a day before the weekends. The people who were loyal to his bakery understood that he needed some time for himself and friends.

It was a breezy afternoon as Dominic made his way through the quaint town of Willowbrook on the way to his favorite local diner. As a weather witch, he felt intrinsically connected to the seasonal shifts in the air. The early spring air still held a faint winter chill that tingled against Dominic's skin. Fallen leaves from past seasons blanketed the sidewalks and streets, crunching under Dominic's boots as he walked.

Though the trees were still bare from winter, the pale afternoon sun hinted at warmer days ahead. Dominic closed his eyes and turned his face up to the sunlight, feeling its glowing warmth seep into his spirit. The light caught swirling dust motes in the air, almost like tiny glowing embers adrift on an invisible wind. Dominic sensed the winds were ready for a change, carrying the scent of renewal.

Dominic breathed in the fresh, grassy scent of the coming spring. Here and there early daffodils poked up along garden beds and window boxes, a cheerful sign of the changing season. The cool air mingled with traces of warm earth and new flowers. Dominic's own magic quickened in resonance with nature's rebirth.

As Dominic ambled down the main street, shopkeepers could be seen sweeping away the last remnants of salt and sand from their stoops. The town was waking up from its winter slumber and starting to stretch its limbs. Dominic passed familiar faces on the sidewalk exchanging hopeful greetings. He shared in their relief at winter's end.

The glowing windows and smells of home cooking drifting from the diner up ahead kindled a warm sense of anticipation in Dominic's stomach. The changing weather and sunlight lifted his mood and energy. Happy to be here in his waking hometown, Dominic stepped inside the diner, in tune with the season and ready to welcome spring.

Dominic found his friends Sloan and Ben waving at him from a booth. He smiled, happy to see the two people he loved spending time with most. Dominic went over and gave them both quick hugs before sitting down.

"How've you guys been? Feels like forever since we hung out," Sloan said.

Dominic and Ben knew Sloan's job as the town's veterinarian kept him super busy these days. But they understood why he hadn't been around much.

"I'm doing great," Ben replied. "Adrian and I have actually been thinking of adopting a kid."

Dominic and Sloan wore matching shocked expressions.

"Whoa, that's big. What are you guys leaning towards?" Dominic asked.

Ben grabbed a menu and handed them out as he spoke. "We can't decide. Adoption would be amazing, but we also talked about getting a surrogate."

"Either way, you two will make incredible parents," Dominic said supportively. "You're so good with kids, Ben. And I can already picture grumpy Adrian chasing after a little rascal."

Sloan chuckled. "Yeah, exactly! Just take your time deciding. That baby will have an awesome life no matter what."

Ben smiled gratefully. "Thanks, guys. We know it's still early, but we're feeling hopeful about our options."

The waitress Gem came by for their orders. After she left, Ben looked at Dominic with concern. "How about you, man? Getting any sleep lately?"

Dominic sighed. He should've known that question was coming. "I'm sleeping fine," he lied, hoping to appease their worries. "Trying to keep busy at the bakery and keep things light, you know?"

His friends nodded, though they didn't seem fully convinced. Sloan leaned forward with a playful grin. "So Ben told me about this mystery guy that's been coming into the bakery…"

Dominic felt his face get hot. The tall, handsome blonde stranger had starred in all his recent daydreams.

"There's nothing going on," he mumbled, suddenly shy. "I don't even know his name. Just that he's from Dawncreek."

"But you like him, right?" Sloan prodded. "Come on, give us the details!"

Dominic hesitated, but finally admitted, "Okay, yes, he's cute. And he's always really nice and polite. But it's not a big deal."

"I don't know, I think you should go for it," Ben encouraged. "Maybe ask him out the next time he comes in or something."

Dominic fiddled with a paper napkin, considering it. The idea made him nervous, but also a little excited.

Sensing his indecision, Sloan said, "No pressure, man. Gotta do what feels right. But you miss every swing you don't take, you know?"

Dominic blushed deeper and changed the subject. "So, what's new with you, Sloan? How's work at the clinic?"

"Oh man, you should have seen this huge Mastiff that came in last week," Sloan chuckled. "Big old friendly guy but not the brightest bulb. Ate an entire bag of his dog food in one sitting!"

Dominic and Ben laughed. "That's too good," Ben said. "Did he end up okay?"

"Oh yeah, we just had to give him some meds for an upset stomach," Sloan replied. "But he was back to his happy self in no time."

The conversation flowed easily between the three old friends. As omega Arctic fox shifters, Sloan and Dominic had a natural rapport. And Ben never treated them any differently, which they appreciated.

As they polished off their burgers, Sloan's expression turned a bit more serious. "So, my dad's been on me again about settling down," he said. "You know, marrying some nice fox from a prominent skulk and having pups."

Dominic nodded sympathetically. As a shifter, Sloan was under pressure to make a good match and grow his skulk. But Sloan hated how it limited his choices.

"What did you tell him?" Ben asked.

"Same thing as always - that I'll find my own mate when I'm ready," Sloan said firmly. "I don't care about status or skulk politics. I want to follow my heart."

Dominic smiled supportively. "That's really brave, Sloan. Your happiness should come first."

"Exactly," Sloan agreed.

As they dug into their burgers and fries, Ben suddenly perked up like he remembered something. "Oh hey, I was just thinking of heading over to that club Midnight tonight. It's over in Dawncreek. You guys should come with!"

Sloan nodded, chewing his bite of burger. "Yeah, could be fun! I've heard good things about that place."

They both looked expectantly at Dominic. He hesitated, uncertain. "Uh, I don't know…I have to open the bakery in the morning."

"Aww, come on Dom! Live a little," Ben cajoled. "It's been ages since we all went out together."

Dominic wavered. A night out did sound nice. And the idea of visiting Dawncreek intrigued him even though he didn't know why. But late nights weren't his forte these days.

Seeing his reluctance, Sloan chimed in. "How about you think on it? No pressure if you can't make it."

Dominic smiled, grateful for the understanding. "Yeah, I'll let you guys know. Maybe I can meet up for at least one drink or something."

"Works for us!" Ben said. "It'll be a good time no matter what."

The conversation moved to other topics, but Dominic's mind lingered on the possibility of a night out in Dawncreek. He realized part of him hoped maybe he'd run into the mysterious bakery customer again. What were the odds? But he couldn't deny he was curious about the handsome stranger. An evening out might be just what he needed.

The three friends didn't linger long at the diner. Merin joined them at the very end, having been busy serving customers. The hulking, red-haired seer rounded out their little band of misfits.

After, Dominic headed to the grocery store. He realized that morning he was running low on ingredients, which always put him in a grumpy mood. A grumpy Dominic was not ideal.

The store, Willowmart, wasn't the most creative name. But it carried everything one could need and then some. The owner, Mr. Lidel, was a kindly elf who'd fallen in love with a local resident and settled in Willowbrook.

Dominic entered the supermarket, the automatic doors swooshing open. The produce section up front assaulted him with its riot of colors and smells. Mr. Lidel looked up from stacking apples and waved in greeting.

"Dominic! Good to see you, my boy," he said warmly. He had a slight lilting accent from his native Elf homeland.

"You too, Mr. Lidel," Dominic replied. "How are the fruits and veggies today?"

Mr. Lidel grinned. "Oh, perfect as ever. I have a new shipment of Shimmer Berries in from the realm. You simply must try one."

He handed Dominic a glossy pink berry. It popped juicily between his teeth, the sweet tangy flavor bursting onto his tongue. Dominic's eyes widened.

"Wow, that's incredible! I'll take a pint," he said. Mr. Lidel chuckled, clearly pleased.

As Dominic shopped, he and the grocer chatted amiably. Over the years, they'd become good friends, given Dominic's near daily visits for bakery ingredients. Mr. Lidel always had special stock just for him.

At the flour display, inspiration struck Dominic. "Mr. Lidel, would you happen to have any of your elf-made baking flour? I'm working on a new creation."

Mr. Lidel's eyes twinkled. "But of course! Right this way."

He led Dominic to a storeroom in back. With a whispered word in Elvish, a shimmering doorway appeared in the otherwise solid wall. Beyond it lay an enchanted pantry lined with magical goods and rare spices. Dominic followed Mr. Lidel inside, eyes wide with awe.

The space was far larger than should have been possible. Magic had warped the dimensions somehow to fit an endless number of overflowing shelves. The air itself tingled with energy. Strange colorful powders, vials of glowing liquid, and jars of mystical herbs filled the room.

Dominic's senses were overloaded by the barrage of exotic scents

- cinnamon and cardamom mingled with fairy nectar and crushed moonstones. He reached out to touch a sack labeled 'Stardust' but paused and looked questioningly at Mr. Lidel first.

"Go ahead, have a feel and smell," Mr. Lidel encouraged with a twinkle in his eyes.

Dominic sank his hand into the glittery powder. It was impossibly soft, and it shimmered as it slipped through his fingers. The scent was sweet and slightly metallic, making his mind swim.

Further in, hangs of dried flowers and vines cascaded down, brushing Dominic's shoulders. He recognized some plants - ginger, lavender, elderberries. But others were totally foreign, twisting in alien shapes and colors.

Glass jars on the shelves contained liquids that churned, glowed, or gave off plumes of perfumed smoke. Countless small drawers hid who knows what mysteries. Dominic longed to open every container and uncover its secrets.

"This is incredible," he murmured in hushed awe. "It's like…magic come to life."

Mr. Lidel beamed. "Most mortals never get to glimpse such wonders. But I believe you have the spirit to appreciate it."

"Thank you for showing me this place." Dominic said.

Dominic knew he was seeing something incredibly rare. His own magic seemed to hum just being near such potent mystical energies. He hoped one day to be worthy of Mr. Lidel's trust and learn to harness the enchantment surrounding him.

"I don't often share this place, but for you, anything," Mr. Lidel said graciously.

Dominic spent some time selecting items, giddy over the prospects of these magical ingredients. His inventive mind whirled thinking up new recipes.

As they exited the secret pantry, Mr. Lidel peered closely at Dominic with a concerned frown. "Your spirit seems troubled lately…are you quite well?"

Dominic hesitated before shrugging. "Oh, you know. Just the usual stuff."

Mr. Lidel's expression softened with understanding. "I have just the thing." He disappeared into his office, returning with a pendant on a silver chain. The teardrop charm glowed gently.

"This amulet channels healing energy. Keep it close, and it will aid you when you most need it," he explained, pressing it into Dominic's hand.

Dominic stared at the charm, overcome with gratitude. "Mr. Lidel… thank you. This means a lot."

"Of course, my dear boy." Mr. Lidel squeezed his shoulder warmly. "Now, let's ring you up!"

At the counter, he tallied Dominic's items, including the secret ingredients. Dominic tucked the pendant safely into his pocket, the small weight both foreign and comforting.

After paying, he thanked Mr. Lidel again profusely. "Seriously, I appreciate everything. You always take such good care of me."

"It brings me joy, Dominic," Mr. Lidel replied sincerely. "I hope your new creations are a delight!"

Carrying his grocery bags, Dominic walked home feeling contemplative but content. The necklace in his pocket seemed to radiate soothing energy. Everything Mr. Lidel did came from a place of care and compassion. Dominic wished he could be so openly generous.

As Dominic approached his house, anxiety prickled through him. His front door was slightly ajar. He hadn't left it that way. Steeling himself, Dominic reached inward for his magic and felt it hum gently in response.

Shifting the grocery bags to one hand, he reached out and slowly pushed open the door. Dominic prepared to unleash his magic in defense if needed. Instead, he sighed in irritation at the sight of his stepbrother Austin sprawled on the couch drinking Dominic's whiskey.

"Make yourself at home, why don't you," Dominic muttered.

He tamped down his magic and headed to the kitchen to unload his groceries.

Austin wandered in, whiskey in hand. "What, no warm welcome for your big bro?" He smirked, clearly trying to get a rise out of Dominic.

Dominic kept his back turned, putting away ingredients. "What do you want, Austin?" He was tired of these petty power plays.

"Ouch, that's cold," Austin taunted. "What, Daddy not teach you any manners?"

Taking a slow breath, Dominic faced him. "Seriously, why are you here? If you have something to say, then say it."

Austin's smile faltered briefly. He shrugged and took a long swig of whiskey before speaking. "Fine, if you must know, father and mother wants to see you."

Dominic tensed. Nothing good ever came from summons by his father and stepmother. "Did they say what they want this time?"

"Nope. I'm just the messenger," Austin said casually, poking through Dominic's cupboards.

Dominic's patience wore thin. He snatched the whiskey bottle back from Austin.

"Tell them if they want something, they can come to me themselves," he said firmly. "I'm not jumping through hoops for them anymore."

Austin raised his eyebrows. "Oooh, little brother's getting bold. Careful, that type of attitude won't fly with Dad."

"I don't care," Dominic snapped. "I'm done being manipulated. They only contact me when they want something. I'm not playing these games."

For a moment Austin looked taken aback. Then his usual cocky expression returned. "Hey man, don't shoot the messenger. Just passing along the request." He sidled past Dominic toward the front door. "But you know, you should really watch that temper of yours. Could get you into trouble someday." With a taunting wink, he sauntered outside.

Dominic slammed the door behind him, pulse racing. How dare Austin violate his space and drink his alcohol? And acting like Dominic was in the wrong for standing up for himself.

Dominic paced the kitchen, trying to calm his nerves after dealing with his stepfamily. Part of him wondered if he should've kept quiet. But the necklace against his chest radiated warm reassurance.

On impulse, he grabbed his phone and called Ben. "Hey, is that offer to go to Midnight tonight still standing?"

"Absolutely!" Ben said. "I can pick you up in an hour if you want."

Dominic nodded even though Ben couldn't see him. "That sounds great. I could really use a night out."

After they hung up, Dominic went to get ready, suddenly buzzing with anticipation. A few hours ago, he'd been uncertain about going out. But now, the thought of loud music and drinks with friends was exactly what he needed to forget the day's tensions.

In his bedroom, Dominic scanned his closet for something party-worthy. He wanted an outfit to make him stand out in a nightclub. He decided on slim black pants and a silky burgundy shirt that hugged his torso. After some debate, he added a subtle smokey eye and mussed his hair artfully.

Checking the mirror, Dominic nodded in approval and gave himself an encouraging thumbs up. He felt sexy and ready for a fun adventure. The necklace rested comfortably against his chest, giving him an extra boost of confidence.

Right on time, the doorbell rang. It was his friend Merin, towering form filling the doorway. "Hey Dom, looking good! The guys are waiting in the car."

They drove over the bridge into Dawncreek, heading for the industrial area downtown. Dominic gazed curiously out the window, taking in the grittier vibe so different from his quaint hometown. He wondered what kind of place this Midnight would be.

The club itself was tucked away in a side street off the main drag. A bold neon sign cast a purple glow over the entrance. Dominic could hear the thumping bass from outside. A line of eager patrons waited to get in.

Ben led them straight past the line to the bouncer up front. After checking their IDs, he unhooked the velvet rope and waved them through.

Stepping inside, Dominic was overwhelmed by the dark, chaotic energy - so unlike his cozy bakery with its scent of cinnamon rolls and sunlight streaming through the windows. The cavernous space throbbed with distorted rhythms and frenetic lights in dizzying patterns.

Patrons laughed and shouted at the bar, trying to be heard over the music's brain-rattling decibels. Out on the crowded dance floor, bodies gyrated and jumped recklessly as if in a frenzy. Strobes blinded, smoke choked, lasers seared through the artificial fog.

Dominic blinked, struggling to adjust to the relentless sensory assault. He wasn't sure he'd be able to relax in such an intense environment. But he was determined to try for his friends' sake. Still, an uneasy inkling lingered that something here was not as it seemed.

After grabbing drinks, Dominic chatted with his friends, taking in the unusual clientele around them. He noticed several patrons whose pale skin, intense gazes and graceful movements reminded him oddly of predators stalking prey.

Before he could consider it further, a group of three intimidating figures approached them, cutting off their path. Two men and a woman, clad in black leather and chains. Their pale skin seemed to glow under the purple lights. Dominic instinctively moved closer to his friends.

"Well well, look what we have here," one said, a tall man with jet black hair in a long ponytail and cold grey eyes. "Seems we don't often get your kind visiting our little establishment."

The other man, bald and hawk-nosed, circled them slowly, eyeing them up and down. "Do you think they know where they are, brother?" he asked with a cruel smile.

The woman tossed her long auburn hair. "Mmm I bet they just came for a fun night out in the big bad city." Her voice dripped mockery.

Dominic exchanged wary glances with his friends. Their faces reflected his own dawning sense that they were very much out of their depth here at Midnight.

4

Revelry and Recognition

Christian

Christian sat in his office, trying to focus on the paperwork in front of him. As mundane as it was, he enjoyed the human feeling of drudgery it brought. It distracted him from the endless stretch of immortal days.

Leaning back, he glanced at a framed painting on the wall depicting him as a human with his parents. That long ago life came rushing back...

He had been Christian Picard then, born in a small village in England centuries past. His family was not wealthy, but respectable. Parents Karina and Ludwig were kind and generous, known to all in the village.

Christian had helped his father in the fields from a young age. Ludwig would ruffle his hair and praise his strong work ethic. In the evenings, Karina would hum softly while mending clothes by the fire, the picture of domestic comfort.

When Christian turned sixteen, his father secured him apprenticeship with a local blacksmith. Christian reveled in shaping metal, feeling he had some mastery over his environment. The soot and sweat felt honest. At day's end, he would collapse into bed bone tired but fulfilled.

On Sundays, the family dressed in their one set of fine clothes to go to chapel. Christian fidgeted through the lengthy sermons, but enjoyed the communal singing. Afterwards, they would share meager lunch with neighbors. Laughter filled their cottage as village children came scampering around.

Then the plague came, and everything changed.

It started as whispered rumors from the coast - a terrible fever that wiped out whole villages in mere days. As it crept inland, fear walked with it. People shuttered windows and doors. Masked doctors filled carts with the dead under the cover of night.

When the first case struck their village, the church bells tolled incessantly. Christian's family sequestered themselves inside, hoping to be spared. But soon Karina's wracking cough signaled the sickness taking hold within their own walls.

Ludwig begged the doctor to bleed her, but the treatments were futile. A week later, Karina breathed her last, cradled in her weeping husband's arms. Christian could only stare helpless, feeling his childhood end with her final rattling breath.

The doctor led Christian's father away. "Burn anything she touched - it spreads through the air," he warned. Christian swallowed hard and turned to the terrible task. The stench of burning sheets mingled awfully with his grief.

Sleepless, Christian waited for the first sign of fever in himself or his father. When Ludwig began coughing violently, Christian's heart sank knowing the battle was already lost. He tended his increasingly delirious father, keeping watch through the long night.

By morning, Ludwig was gone too. Christian was alone in the world at seventeen. He dug their graves himself, tears wetting the mask over his face. Friends averted their eyes, avoiding contact. The church bell kept tolling, tolling, tolling.

That evening, a tall stranger named Augustus came knocking. "I can take you someplace safe from this," he offered. Christian knew of no such place, but latched onto this frail hope. They rode through the night to Augustus' isolated manor.

There Augustus made his proposal - an end to sickness and death, strength and speed beyond imagining, eternal life…if only Christian would accept him as sire. In his grief, Christian grasped at this second chance. Anything to escape the wasteland his life had become.

And so Christian Picard died, and was reborn as Cristian Belgrave, immortal child of Augustus. The sacrifice was profound, but at least he was no longer utterly alone. And he need never fear loss in the same way again.

The painting returned Christian to that simpler time of humanity, now impossibly distant. He wondered sometimes what his parents would think of the creature he became. But he could not undo Augustus's gift. The only way was forward.

With a heavy sigh, Christian turned back to his paperwork. Lingering on the past accomplished nothing. He had duties in the present that needed attention. The club awaited his visit later. For now, he focused on balancing the books, taking refuge in the ordinary.

Someday he might pass the business to another, when the mundane felt more burden than comfort. Immortality afforded him infinite possible futures. But this was his life for the moment. Christian had learned to find peace in acceptance, and make the most of wherever the years led him.

Nostalgia had its place, but could not change reality. His human family was centuries gone. Augustus and the coven were his kin now. He would carry the memories while making this new life meaningful.

Christian finished his paperwork and headed out to the main floor of his club. As he stepped through the staff door, the pulsating music and hypnotic lights washed over him. The crowded dance floor was a sea of gyrating bodies and floating hands. At the bar, laughter punctuated shouted conversations.

Though Christian had seen this a thousand times before, it never failed to energize him. After the stillness of his office, the vibrant chaos was invigorating. He nodded in satisfaction as he glanced around, ensuring everything was running smoothly.

Christian wove through the crowds, exchanging greetings here and there. A trio of young vampires waved eagerly, hoping to catch his eye. Immortality didn't make one immune to flattery. Christian gave them a good-natured wink before moving on.

Nearing the bar, he was surprised to spot a familiar face - Dominic, the kindly bakery owner. Christian had grown fond of visiting his shop, comforted by the sweet mortal routines. But Dominic seemed out of place here amid the frenetic energy and hidden terrors.

Christian moved closer, frowning. Dominic was with three other men, looking around warily. His body language screamed discomfort. As Christian watched, a group of three vampires approached Dominic's group, preventing them from leaving.

Christian tensed, ready to intervene as the vampires threatened Dominic's group. Before he could react, Dominic's friend summoned a glowing quill-shaped staff, generating a shimmering shield around them.

Christian halted in surprise. Celestial magic users were exceptionally rare. He studied the dark-haired man with new fascination. But there was no time for curiosity as the confrontation intensified.

"Is this little spell supposed to scare us? How adorable," the lead vampire taunted, baring her fangs. Her companions hissed with laughter. In a blur, one grabbed the staff, wrenching it from his grip.

The staff clattered to the floor. The vampire seized the mage by the throat, smirking as he struggled in her iron grip. "Let's see what wizard boy's blood tastes like," she purred.

As the other two vampires closed in, the mage choked out a spell. His eyes flashed white and he thrust out his palm. An invisible force hurled his captor backward. She crashed into a table, splintering it into pieces.

The other vampires hissed in fury. Moving almost too fast to track, one kicked the mage's legs out from under him. He hit the floor hard. The vampire pinned him down, claws extending from her fingertips.

But before she could strike, the red-haired man alongside Dominic raised his hands. The air seemed to shimmer around the vampires, solidifying into shackles of light binding their limbs. They howled in outrage, straining against the glowing bonds.

"Nice one, Merin!" The man with the staff yelled. He scrambled to regain his dropped staff. The vampires growled, pulling against their magical restraints.

As Christian edged closer, ready to put an end to this, he noticed Dominic hanging back protectively near a petite looking man who seemed unnerved by the magical chaos. Interesting…

He heightened his hearing senses to hear what's being said.

"Should I shift?" The man behind Dominic said.

Dominic shook his head. "Stay human, we got this. Just watch our backs."

The vampire who had crashed into the table was back on her feet, blood dripping from her temple. With preternatural speed, she charged the hulking red head. But she collided with an invisible barrier, staggering back with a shocked hiss.

The red head, Merin gave a little smirk, hands still raised maintaining the shield. "You're not getting through here, fang face."

The vampire struck the shield again and again, face contorted in a ferocious snarl. Merin's smirk faltered. Sweat beaded his brow from the effort of holding the barrier against the powerful repeated impacts.

Seeing his friend faltering, Dominic stepped forward, brow furrowed in concentration. He swept his arms in a wide arc. The air pressure dropped sharply and a fierce wind whipped up, forcing the vampires back a step.

Dominic made a pulling motion and the wind condensed into a small swirling vortex that snatched the vampire's dropped staff up off the floor. With a flick of his wrist, Dominic sent it spinning through the air back to the grateful mage's hand.

The vampires scowled, regrouping for another attack. But suddenly the fire sprinklers on the ceiling burst to life, spraying them with water mixed with drops of blood from their wounds.

They cried out in confusion and outrage as the crimson liquid stung their eyes. Dominic gave a satisfied nod at his handiwork. The vampires clawed at their faces, hissing in pain.

Seeing them blinded, the mage slammed his staff down forcefully. A shockwave exploded out, crashing into the vampires and flinging them backwards across the room, where they lay bruised and dazed in a heap.

Deciding it was time to step in, Christian pushed his way into the middle of the confrontation.

"Enough!" he commanded, voice slicing through the noise. "Release them, now!"

The vampires surrounding Dominic's group froze, eyes widening in dismay.

"E-elder Belgrave," one stammered nervously. The one holding the mage quickly released him.

Dominic and his friends looked equally shocked. Christian met Dominic's gaze briefly before turning a stern eye back on the chastened vampires.

"You know the rules - no force or threat of harm toward my patrons," he said sharply. "Consider your access here permanently revoked."

He beckoned his head bouncer over. "Scott, please see these three out and get their sire's name. Their conduct requires discipline."

"You got it, boss," Scott rumbled, grabbing two of the troublemakers by their collars. They wisely didn't resist as he led them away. The third one trailed shamefacedly behind.

Christian turned to Dominic's group after dismissing the vampires. The mage was rubbing his throat, glowering.

"My apologies for that unpleasantness," Christian said sincerely. "Are you all unharmed?"

Dominic's eyes widened in sudden recognition. "It's you - from the bakery!"

Christian smiled. "Yes, we've crossed paths before. I'm Christian Belgrave, pleased to make the acquaintance." Christian sighed then continued. "Unfortunately, some of our youth lack manners," Christian said regretfully. "This is your first visit to Midnight?"

"Yeah, we wanted to check out the clubs, but I think this scene is a bit too much for us," Dominic said with an embarrassed laugh.

Christian studied him thoughtfully, sensing an alluring aura beneath the anxiety. "Well, allow me to make amends with some drinks, on the house of course."

Dominic exchanged looks with his friends, then nodded. "Um, okay. One drink couldn't hurt."

Christian smiled, leading them to the bar and signaling for his best vintages. He spent the next hour chatting before discreetly taking his leave, wanting Dominic's group to relax. But he kept a watchful eye from afar, intrigued by the promising mortals. What a fortuitous encounter this was turning out to be.

As the night wore on, a nagging thought weighed on Christian's mind. Dominic stirred something in him, a profound instinct he'd only heard about in lore. Could this kind, unassuming baker actually be...his true mate?

Christian had always been skeptical such a thing existed. Vampires took lovers as they pleased, bound by desire not destiny. But since that first meeting in Dominic's bakery, Christian felt drawn to him in ways he couldn't explain.

It began with the scent - warm vanilla mingled with fresh rain on pavement. An earthy sweetness that spoke to ancient parts of Christian he'd forgotten. Stepping inside the little shop, Christian was struck by the feeling of coming home after years wandering alone.

He watched Dominic knead dough, brow slightly furrowed in concentration. Christian imagined those strong hands massaging the tension from his shoulders. He ached to tangle his fingers in Dominic's chestnut waves. When their eyes met, something resonated deeply, beyond logic or reason.

Christian began visiting the bakery every morning, craving even casual proximity. The brief exchanges over coffee sustained him. Dominic's goodness called to Christian's long-buried humanity. And his smiles sparked inexplicable joy.

But Christian resisted the notion they could be true mates. Dominic was mortal - such a pairing was unthinkable. It must be mere infatuation. Christian refused to indulge fanciful notions and endanger Dominic with the perilous shadow world.

Now, seeing Dominic here tonight roused a protectiveness in Christian bordering on primal. He burned to shield Dominic from all harm. But was that mere chivalry? Or the mate-bond making itself known? The implications were dangerous and profound.

This phenomenon was whispered about but scarcely verified among vampires. True mates were two souls destined for union, the lore said. Upon meeting, they were drawn together by an undeniable force. Doubting only risked grave damage to them both. For immortals, true mates were their only chance at true belonging.

But the pragmatic Council scorned such tales as antiquated fantasy. Christian himself had been skeptical. Now, he could no longer ignore the palpable energy between Dominic and himself. His cynicism crumbled before the power of fated love recognizing its missing half.

Christian shook his head slowly at the impossibility of it. A mortal baker, his eternal soulmate? It was madness, and yet he could not bring himself to deny this mystical joining. Fate clearly had a twisted sense of humor.

Even contemplating embracing Dominic as his mate broke countless vampire codes and taboos. The Council would seek to "correct" this aberration if discovered. But how could something meant to be be wrong? Christian would not reject this gift because of archaic constraints and politics.

Across the crowded club, Dominic laughed at something his friends said, brown eyes crinkling with mirth. Christian's unbeating heart ached. He yearned to make Dominic laugh like that every night for the rest of their days, mortal and immortal. A stunning promised glimpsed then snatched away.

No, he must proceed cautiously. Revealing too much, too soon could push Dominic away and put him at risk. But neither could Christian ignore destiny's call. He would find a way, even if it took patient years coaxing Dominic to trust him. They were bound, and Christian would let nothing sever that sacred bond.

For now, he was content watching Dominic enjoy a carefree time with his friends. The future stretched before them, unwritten. Christian need only follow the compass pull of their hearts entwining. In time, all would unfold as fated. This astonishing night was just the first step on the journey.

Standing here, Christian felt the axis of his existence tilting. Once the mate-bond manifested, there was no return from it. Doubts could not change what the soul already knew. He both feared and thrilled at choosing this unpredictable path with the unexpected mortal who was his everything. The only way led forward.

Suddenly, Elder Eros appeared soundlessly at his side, scowling. Christian tensed. In his preoccupied state, he'd let his mental defenses slip, forgetting Eros could pluck surface thoughts from unwary minds. There was no telling what Eros may have gleaned about Dominic in those unguarded moments.

"Well, well. Our illustrious leader seems...distracted tonight," Eros remarked, his tone mocking.

Christian smoothed his features to impassivity. "Merely observing our guests, as is my duty."

Eros stepped uncomfortably close, searching Christian's face intently with his chilling silver eyes. "I wonder...anything in particular catch your interest?"

When Christian stayed silent, Eros pressed on. "Or should I say, anyone?" He glanced pointedly toward Dominic's departing figure.

Christian clenched his jaw, cursing internally. Clearly Eros had glimpsed enough to suspect Christian's fascination with the mortal. He would use this vulnerability against his rival without hesitation.

"Ah yes, I thought so," Eros purred, seeing he'd hit a nerve. "Doesn't take a mind-reader to know that look in your eye. You always were a slave to your impulses." His lip curled in disgust.

"My personal affairs are none of your concern," Christian said tightly.

Eros let out a mocking laugh. "Oh, I beg to differ. When the coven leader's judgment becomes compromised, it concerns us all." He lowered his voice to a vicious whisper. "Let me make this clear - do not pursue this folly with that mortal. Or you will come to profoundly regret it."

Christian bristled, hands clenching into fists. "Do not presume to dictate my actions. You overstep."

"For the good of this coven, I must," Eros retorted. "Have you forgotten the code we live by? Our kind and humans do not mix in such ways. Or need I remind you what happened with your dear Celeste when you forgot your place?"

Christian flinched, stung by the verbal blow. Eros knew just how to exploit old wounds. His relationship with Celeste over a century ago had ended in tragedy thanks to the bigoted Council.

Seeing that his barb hit home, Eros twisted the knife deeper. "This little infatuation will only end the same. Tragically. You would risk everything for a fleeting fancy?" His lip curled in scorn. "Pathetic."

Christian's reply was icy. "As I said, my affairs do not answer to you."

But inwardly, doubts took root like creeping tendrils of poison. Eros was cunning - he knew just how to uncover and exploit vulnerabilities. Was Christian being reckless, risking so much for attachment to a mortal?

Eros leaned in close, his voice a viper's hiss. "Mark me - nothing good will come of this. The Council does not take kindly to such... deviance. Do not drag the coven down with you."

With that last venomous warning, he melted back into the crowds, leaving Christian shaken and torn. Could he really endanger Dominic and his coven by selfishly pursuing this bond? The stakes were far higher than just his lonely heart.

Brooding, Christian retreated to his office, poured himself a drink with unsteady hands. Eros had voiced his worst fears - that Christian might repeat past sins, allowing desire to lure him into disaster.

Perhaps keeping Dominic at arm's length was safest for now. Christian could not rush into this and gamble with his beloved's life so carelessly. But the thought of letting Dominic go tore his ancient soul asunder. Surely their love was not wrong, when it felt so profoundly right?

Fate had gifted Christian something precious and rare. Yet fate could also be cruel. Eluding Eros's malice and the Council's harsh decrees would require utmost caution and cunning. Christian rested his head in his hands with a heavy sigh. Why must something so beautiful be so fraught with peril?

For now, he decided, it was best to proceed slowly with Dominic. Learn more about his gifts and temperament before revealing their bond. Guard his emotions against Eros's telepathic spies. With wisdom and patience, they would find a way. Christian only prayed his hesitation would not cost them everything.

But he could not dwell on doubts. What mattered was keeping his mate safe. All else would follow in time, once the forces aligned against them were properly understood and disarmed. This was but the first of many trials along love's thorny route. Faith would see them through the burdens ahead. Of that, Christian had to stay convinced.

Someday he and Dominic would look back on this as the night when fates intertwined. A new era would dawn for them both, and the shadow world. Change always brought growing pains. Tonight Christian's eyes had opened to the difficult road destiny placed before him. But at its end waited the ultimate reward - a love everlasting.

5

Echoes of the Past

Dominic

Dominic awoke feeling like death warmed over. His head was absolutely pounding from last night's shenanigans. But despite the pain, he didn't totally regret going out. After the vampire attack, the rest of the night ended up being pretty great.

Still, he had no idea why those vamps went after them in the first place. Just weird. Anyway, it was over now. Time to move on.

For the first Saturday in forever, Dominic actually felt motivated to get out and about. He wanted to reintroduce himself to nature and cleanse out all the negative juju. A hike sounded perfect.

Dragging himself out of bed, Dominic slipped on his comfy house shoes and shuffled to the shower. The hot water helped wake him up, but did nothing for his raging hangover headache. Ugh.

After drying off, Dominic checked his closet for something hiking appropriate. "Well hello there," he muttered, unearthing his old gear. "Wonder if you still fit me, it's been a minute."

He was right to be skeptical. Dominic had gotten pretty built in recent years. He grunted and tugged to get his clothes on. Tight squeeze, but they'd do. "Beauty is pain," he sighed.

Before leaving, he checked his pockets for the necklace Mr. Lidel gave him. Strange, it wasn't there. Then again, he had gone out last night. He must've left it on his nightstand or something. Oh well.

Grabbing his phone and wallet, Dominic headed to the kitchen to start some coffee. As it brewed, he phoned his assistant Lyra.

"Hey bossman, what's up?" Lyra answered brightly. In the background, a baby could be heard wailing at high volume.

Dominic chuckled then winced as pain stabbed through his skull. "Is that a tiny human I hear screeching? Please tell me you didn't have a secret baby."

Lyra laughed. "Nah, just my bratty baby bro refusing his nap. Little demon." The crying intensified as something crashed off screen. "Robbie! No, bad!"

"Yikes, sounds like I called at an inconvenient time," Dominic said apologetically.

"No worries, what can I do for ya?" Lyra asked, voice slightly muffled as she wrestled her brother.

"Any chance you can open the bakery today? I know that's not really your specialty…"

"Sure thing, no problem!" Lyra said. "I'll just get one of your baking staff to come assist. Damian, right?"

Dominic sighed in relief. "You're the best, Lyra. I'll swing by with the keys before my hike. Seriously, thank you for this."

After they hung up, Dominic downed some painkillers with his coffee. As the bittersweet drink warmed him, his mind drifted back to last night at the club. He grappled with a mix of conflicting emotions about the bizarre encounter.

Dominic was shocked to discover the polite, elegant man and the brooding vampire were one and the same. He never imagined his mysterious regular with the seductive voice was immortal.

Dominic didn't have anything against vampires as a whole. But knowing this intriguing individual was not human still gave him pause. There were many old prejudices and misconceptions to overcome regarding such deadly creatures.

Dominic knew he should keep his distance - Christian represented everything forbidden and dangerous. He commanded lethal vampires with a snap of his elegant fingers. Power and mystique surrounded him like a dark aura.

Yet Dominic could not deny that Christian defied stereotypes so far. He had shown Dominic and his friends only grace once tensions cooled the previous night. And Dominic sensed a profound sadness and weariness in Christian, unlike the soulless monsters from scary stories.

Not to mention, Dominic didn't have the best track record when it came to risky relationships. Past heartbreaks had left him wary of entangling with unpredictable, charming men. His scars ran deeper than even his closest friends knew.

Perhaps engaging with him would help dispel lingering falsehoods, easing the tensions between their kinds. If only Dominic could silence the warnings screaming this was foolish, reckless. But he had never been able to resist the pull of the unknown.

Christian appeared sincere about making amends and welcoming newcomers to experience Dawncreek's secret splendors. His eloquent words painted vivid pictures of a hidden world both beautiful and terrifying. Dominic was captivated in spite of himself.

As they talked over drinks, Christian's smooth voice soothed Dominic's rattled nerves. In the dim club, cloaked in leather and mystery, he was devastatingly handsome. Dominic indulged in subtle glances when Christian's gaze roamed the crowds.

But he checked himself sharply - this road only led to heartache. Christian was an immortal predator. Dominic, a small-town baker.

They existed in different realities. This silly fixation would pass in time, Dominic told himself. All he had to do was keep perspective.

Dominic decided he would judge Christian based on his actions, not old biases. Their kinds weren't so different deep down. Dominic knew the loneliness of mortality well - it was its own heavy burden.

As if conjuring him, a knock suddenly sounded at the front door. Dominic froze - who could be visiting so early? He reached out magically, sensing no ill intent from the person on his doorstep. Still cautious, Dominic went to investigate.

Swinging open the door, he stared in shock at the elegant, imposing figure of Christian Belgrave. Dominic's brain short-circuited momentarily.

"H-how are you here?" he stammered. "Shouldn't sunlight, you know…vampires…" He cringed at his blundering attempt to ask about the deadly sun taboo.

But Christian just chuckled, looking unfairly perfect as always in a tailored gray suit. "Your wards are quite adept. May I come in? I mean no harm." His voice was smooth and earnest.

"Uh, yeah, of course," Dominic mumbled, remembering his manners. "Come on in." He stepped aside and let Christian cross the threshold.

Safely inside, away from the bright morning sun, Christian visibly relaxed. Dominic tried to play it cool, but his thoughts were in overdrive. What was Christian doing here at his house completely unannounced?

"Apologies for the intrusion," Christian said politely. "But I wished to return something you dropped last night during the…unpleasantness at my club."

He held out his hand. Sitting on his palm was the tear-shaped pendant from Mr. Lidel that Dominic thought he had misplaced. Relief flooded him.

"My necklace! Oh my god, I can't believe you found it," Dominic said gratefully as he took it. "Seriously, thank you for returning this, it means a lot."

"Of course. Couldn't have something so precious getting lost." Christian's hand lingered a moment as their fingers brushed.

"Here, allow me." Before Dominic could react, Christian gently took the necklace and stepped behind Dominic to clasp it around his neck.

Dominic shivered as Christian's cool fingers grazed the sensitive skin at the nape of his neck. Fastening the clasp, Christian smoothed the chain, his touch sending tingles down Dominic's spine.

Standing so close, Dominic caught Christian's subtle, intoxicating scent - parchment, spice, and something uniquely him. It was maddeningly perfect.

Flustered, Dominic muttered a thank you when Christian came back around to face him, looking unfairly elegant as always. The necklace settled into place over Dominic's racing heart.

He had to get some distance,Dominic thought desperately. Christian's proximity was overwhelming his senses, making his pulse flutter and skin buzz in a way that was as frightening as it was exhilarating.

Trying to break the sudden tension, Dominic asked, "So, um, not to be rude, but how are you up and about? Isn't sunlight risky?"

Christian's eyes glinted with subtle amusement. "Older vampires can endure sun temporarily before it becomes…uncomfortable. I simply woke early to catch you."

"Ah, got it. And exactly how old are you?" Dominic asked before he could think better of it.

"A gentleman never tells." Christian gave him a playful, devastating smile that made Dominic's brain short-circuit again. "Let's just say I've been around a while."

Dominic laughed awkwardly. "Yeah, dumb question. Anyway, thanks again for this." He waved the necklace. "And for stopping by. Can I get you something to drink, or…?"

Christian regarded him thoughtfully. "I appreciate the offer, but should leave you to enjoy your day. I only wished to see your pendant returned." He gestured at the hiking clothes Dominic wore. "Heading on an outdoor adventure?"

"Oh yeah, going to hit the trails for some fresh air," Dominic said, suddenly self-conscious. Why did Christian make him feel so flustered?

"Well then, I shall let you get to it." Christian smiled and Dominic's knees nearly buckled. "I'm glad it was merely misplaced, and now back where it belongs."

Was Dominic imagining a subtle double meaning there? He tried to ignore his racing pulse as he showed Christian out. This was just an odd, chance encounter. Christian was only being chivalrous by returning the necklace.

Pausing on the doorstep, Christian gave Dominic a searching look that made his mouth go dry. "I don't suppose…would you care to join me for dinner tonight?" he asked, hope tingeing his honeyed voice. "Strictly as friends, of course."

Dominic's eyes widened. Was the vampire asking him out? He knew he should politely decline. Instead, some reckless part of him blurted out, "Yeah, dinner sounds great."

Christian's pale features lit up. "Wonderful. I'll pick you up at twilight, then." He raised Dominic's hand and brushed his knuckles lightly with his lips, peering up through dark lashes. "Until tonight."

Then he was gliding away down the street with preternatural speed and grace. Dominic stood frozen on the doorstep, skin tingling where Christian's cool lips had grazed it. What had he just agreed to?

Dazed after Christian's visit, Dominic grabbed his gear and headed out. But the vampire's unexpected proposal occupied his thoughts. Dominic still couldn't believe he had agreed to what was essentially a date.

With an intimidating immortal predator, no less. What had he been thinking? Christian was dangerous, commanding forces beyond Dominic's comprehension. At best, he would break Dominic's heart. At worst…well, Dominic tried not to imagine the gruesome possibilities.

Even if Christian seemed sincere so far, he was still a relative stranger from a shadowy world. Not exactly boyfriend material. Dominic must have lost his mind, trusting him so recklessly.

But he had to admit, part of him thrilled at the prospect of getting to know the fascinating vampire better. That gravitational pull between them was undeniable, defying all reason and self-preservation. Dominic couldn't resist wanting to understand its power.

He was shaken from his turbulent thoughts when he arrived at Lyra's house. She answered the door looking frazzled, with a wailing baby on her hip.

"Oh my god, Dominic, you're a lifesaver," she said in relief as he handed over the bakery keys. "I don't know the difference between a whisk and a spatula, but I'll make it work."

Dominic smiled sympathetically. "Don't stress. Call Damian if you need help with anything baking-related. You'll do great."

After giving her a few last pointers, Dominic set off to clear his head in the Willowbrook Forest. Out here among the birdsong and breeze, he could think through this new twist rationally.

The familiar wooded trails soothed his rattled nerves. Dominic followed the dancing sunlight through the canopy, leaves rustling gently overhead. His magic hummed contentedly, recharged by the earth energy.

Drawing from the ancient oak and whispering wind, Dominic considered his situation logically. This dinner with Christian was likely just an isolated incident, a momentary lapse of reason.

Once they spent more time together, Dominic's senses would return and the novelty would fade. Immortals and mortals ran in very different circles for good reason. Christian would soon realize that too.

Dominic simply needed to keep perspective until this passing fascination cooled. By giving Christian a chance, perhaps they could find common ground between their kinds. If the vampire continued defying expectations, barriers between their worlds might gradually dissolve.

One dinner together could plant the seeds of goodwill. Dominic had to believe Christian's interest was benign. People often feared what they didn't understand. With open minds, they could dispel lingering falsehoods.

As Dominic hiked the familiar forest trails, he noticed something amiss. The ambient magic permeating the air felt disturbed, subtly wrong. Brow furrowing, Dominic gently released his own magic to mingle with the breeze and investigate.

It responded in concerning whispers, brushing phantom fingers that beckoned Dominic off the path toward a small clearing among the oaks. As he stepped through the underbrush, Dominic gasped—the space was utterly drained of life.

Brittle leaves disintegrated to ash under his boots. The trees surrounding the clearing stood stark and bare, skeletal limbs clawing a too-bright sky. Their bark was bleached bone-white, with no birdsong or rodents rustling within.

The air itself felt stale, devoid of magic's usual gentle thrum. Not a whisper of wind stirred the oppressive silence. Dominic shuddered as his inner magic recoiled instinctively from the unnatural void. It was fundamentally wrong, an open wound in the living tapestry of the forest.

Kneeling slowly, Dominic placed his palm flat against the barren earth, preparing to commune with it magically. But as his senses delved deeper, he jerked back in dismay.

The soil itself was utterly desiccated, all trace of vitality leeched away. It crumbled sickly under his touch into a fine, pale dust that clung to his skin. No worms burrowed, no roots held firm anchorage - only parched remains.

Dominic shuddered at the unnatural void. The rich loam, teeming microbes, and seedlings' determined quest for sunlight…gone, all gone. It was a wasteland in miniature.

Exploratory tendrils of his magic prodded gently, seeking answers, but met only absence - like reaching into a lightless abyss devouring all in its path. No nourishing water or moisture remained, only this chilling void where once abundant life had thrived.

Dominic withdrew his hand quickly, wiping the unsettled earth from his skin. His magic recoiled instinctively from the unnatural silence. This alien scar carved into the living tapestry of the forest had to be cleansed, or risk infecting all it touched. The land's delicate balance depended on it.

Whatever malevolent force was at work here, Dominic knew with chilling certainty that it had to be stopped at all costs. The forest's delicate magic depended on it.

"It is the mark of forbidden magic, I fear."

Dominic whirled, startled by the unexpected lilting voice behind him. A tall, slender man with silver hair falling to his shoulders stood watching Dominic intently. His refined features and archaic red coat seemed strangely out of place in the wild forest.

"Did you do this?" Dominic asked warily, slowly standing. If this stranger was practicing illicit arts, he could be dangerous. Dominic gathered his magic, preparing to defend himself.

But the man held up his hands placatingly. "Peace, friend. I mean no harm, only seek answers like yourself." His voice was heavily accented in a way Dominic couldn't quite place. "I am Ciaran, a druid. I come investigating dark forces plaguing this land."

Dominic's eyes widened in surprise and curiosity. "A druid? I thought your kind had died out ages ago." The ancient pagan magicians were shrouded in mystery and myth. Dominic only knew fragments about them from old folktales.

As he studied the silver-haired man before him, Dominic could practically feel the arcane energy radiating from him. The forest itself seemed heightened around Ciaran, bending to meet him.

His crimson coat bore elaborate sigils stitched in gold thread. Dominic sensed they held power, though their meanings were obscure. Probably spells and wards masterfully woven into the fabric over centuries.

Ciaran's sharp eyes glinted with ancient wisdom and secrets. Dominic wondered how many generations of mortals those eyes had watched over, guarding these woods unseen.

The druids were said to wield primal magics tied to plants, animals, and the seasons. They conversed with spirits, manipulated light and shadow, even shapeshifted into beasts. Their knowledge spanned millennia.

Dominic glanced around the lifeless clearing. If the legends were true, Ciaran could likely restore the damaged land with little more than a wave of his hand. The power to rend and mend nature itself.

This druid was clearly no mere mystic hobbyist like Dominic. Everything about him spoke of ages communing with forces beyond Dominic's comprehension. His experience could prove invaluable against this insidious threat.

Despite the danger, Dominic felt a thrill at crossing paths with a living relic from antique myths. Here was real magic - ancient, potent, and wonderous. He hoped to learn a fraction of Ciaran's wisdom, to better safeguard Willowbrook's mystical spirit. There was so much he might yet discover.

Ciaran smiled enigmatically. "Perhaps we merely became more selective in revealing ourselves. But never mind such trifles now. Might I have the honor of your name?" He gave a courtly bow that seemed straight out of a fairy story.

"Oh, I'm Dominic. Dominic Reed." Pushing past his questions, Dominic remembered the task at hand. "Ciaran, do you know what caused this unnatural blight?" He gestured around the lifeless clearing.

The druid's fair features darkened. "I suspect rogue magic. My Circle sensed a malignant power brewing, slowly leeching life from the land. We could no longer ignore such wickedness."

Dominic nodded gravely. "Is there any way to stop it and heal the damage?"

"The source must be found and quelled," Ciaran mused. "But these woods are vast. I have only begun searching for clues that might lead to the shadow's lair."

On impulse, Dominic made an offer. "I know Willowbrook well. Please let me help keep watch for anything unusual. Your Circle shouldn't have to carry this burden alone."

Ciaran studied him thoughtfully before inclining his head. "Very well. Your compassion does you credit. I reside in a hidden cottage nearby. We will join forces illuminating the darkness."

With a flourish of his hand, Ciaran conjured a weathered wooden door shimmering with azure runes in the middle of the clearing. Dominic watched in awe as he disappeared through it without a backward glance. Just like that, he was gone.

Alone again amid the eerie silence, Dominic frowned down at his hands. His magic sense was raw and unsettled, like a storm gathering pressure on the horizon. Whatever evil was brewing here, he feared they were running out of time to stop it.

6

Visions

Christian

Christian arrived home shortly after seeing Dominic, still reeling. If he'd had any lingering doubts that Dominic was his true mate, they had vanished after meeting him. Holding him, Christian's every sense came alive. His vampire instincts screamed to keep Dominic near, to claim what was his.

But Christian resisted those possessive urges - he would not let his vampiric nature sabotage this fragile bond. Dominic's mortality made this pairing unprecedented enough without adding such complications. Christian had to proceed with wisdom, not reckless haste.

Approaching his estate, Christian's head abruptly started spinning before consciousness fled completely. When he came to, he found himself in an unfamiliar void. Having visions was one of Christian's two rare extra abilities, beyond what most vampires could manifest. But never like this while awake.

Most vampires gained one extra skill at most. Christian's sire theorized one ability came from their human life, amplified by the transition. The other remained a mystery. Just one more aberration marking Christian as strange and apart, even among his kind.

His first talent emerged after being turned - prophetic dreams foretelling danger. After his turning, these visions grew in strength and frequency. His sire helped him hone this "harbinger" gift over the decades. Though unpredictable, it had proven invaluable through the centuries.

Decades after becoming a vampire, Christian discovered his second inexplicable talent - though "gift" was far too benign a word for it. This ability was an uninvited burden that filled him with dread and self-loathing when it first manifested. Even now, he regarded it as a curse to be contained, not celebrated.

Not only did Christian develop a second power, it proved volatile and sinister. He had pleaded in vain with his sire to purge this profane energy from his body and spirit. But not even Augustus could undo what blood and darkness had wrought.

When this newfound force first erupted, Christian was devastated. Plagued dreams returned, showing loved ones' faces contorting in terror of him. He withdrew entirely, terrified of harming someone during those early unpredictable months. The ability felt like a cancer metastasizing through his soul.

Even now, after centuries honing control, Christian still recoiled recalling those early days. The destructive potential at his fingertips appalled him. Keeping this power contained and dormant filled most of his waking moments. He would not become the monster it wished him to be.

Only Augustus knew the full extent of what Christian now harbored. His sire helped him erect inner barriers and focus the volatile energy safely inward. But Christian still tasted its seductive potential when his control slipped. Those lapses shamed him deeply.

So Christian had mastered the art of restraint when it came to this profane second talent. He shared its existence with no one, made excuses when it strained to unleash itself. This was his private, unending battle. And someday when vigilance failed, Christian knew with cold certainty that it would be his end. For now, he contained the monster. But darkness called to darkness relentlessly.

Never had his dream gift manifested while awake until today. As Christian took stock of the empty space surrounding him, he wondered if it portended something momentous approaching, powerful enough to pierce his waking barriers. The timing following his encounter with Dominic felt significant.

Christian surveyed the death and destruction around him. The scorched earth reeked of decay and misery. Before him stood an intimidating man in an expensive suit, casually leaning on a cane topped with a gleaming golden dice.

"Such ravishing beauty, isn't it, Christian?" the stranger mused, gazing at the hellish vista. His refined voice held an icy undercurrent that raised the hairs on Christian's neck. This was a dangerous entity.

Christian was shocked the man somehow knew his name and spoke so casually across the veil. The power it implied was immense.

"Who are you?" Christian demanded, masking his unease with anger. "How do you know me? Did you cause this?"

The man didn't turn, just kept staring at the burning horizon. "Curiosity killed the cat, or so they say." His tone held a subtle warning. "But satisfaction brought it back, so perhaps answers will come in time, Christian Belgrave."

Christian frowned, uneasy. "Enough riddles. Just tell me plainly what you want." If this being meant harm, Christian had to know.

The man tutted condescendingly at Christian's questions. "Demanding answers is rather discourteous, don't you think? We've only just met." He tapped his cane idly as Christian fumed. "In due time, matters will become…clearer. But allow an old man his diversions."

"I grow tired of your games," Christian said sharply. "Speak plainly or begone."

"Temper, temper. One would think immortality would breed patience." He inclined his head thoughtfully. "Since you insist, let me pose a question, Christian Belgrave - do you believe in fate?"

Christian hesitated, wary of revealing too much. "Fate is capricious at best in my experience."

"Is that so?" The man smiled. "Because I believe we all play destined parts in the grand design, whether we see the script or not."

He turned slightly and Christian glimpsed a familiar glittering object in his hand - a tear-shaped pendant on a silver chain. Shock jolted through him.

Noticing his reaction, the man continued, "Your role is intertwined with the witch, you realize? His choices will ripple through us all."

Christian's fists clenched. "You know nothing of Dominic."

The man laughed coldly. "Oh, but I know a great deal about his potential, just as I see yours, vampire. Crossroads approach. The question is, which paths will you take when destiny calls?" He tapped his cane once more. "We will speak again soon on these matters. I advise you reflect on where your loyalties truly lie."

With that cryptic warning lingering in the air, the man turned and stepped through a shimmering portal. Christian stared after him long after he disappeared, more shaken than he cared to admit.

The hellish vision collapsed, returning Christian abruptly back to reality. He found himself standing dazed outside his estate. Nearby, his dear friend Elvira shook his shoulder, her beautiful face etched with concern.

"Christian! Thank goddess, you've returned," she cried, embracing him in relief. "You went rigid, staring into nothingness. I could not rouse you."

Christian quickly reassured the distraught Elvira that he was fine, just momentarily lost in thought. But inwardly, his mind spun with the vision's dark implications. That stranger had clearly wielded frightening power to ensnare Christian so easily across the veil. And he possessed impossible knowledge about Christian himself.

Elvira helped Christian inside the house and guided him to the living room sofa, where he sank down gratefully. The ordeal had drained him. She handed him a glass of water and sat close beside him.

"You had a vision, didn't you?" she asked. "I haven't seen one strike you while awake before. What did you see?"

Christian recounted the bleak, burning landscape and his ominous encounter with the refined stranger. Elvira listened intently, brow creased in concern.

"He spoke as if he knew me, knew private things," Christian continued uneasily. "And he indicated our paths will cross again soon."

Elvira considered this carefully. "Did he give any clues to his identity or motives?"

Christian shook his head. "Only vague warnings and prophecies. He seems obsessed with destiny and believing we all play fated parts." He hesitated before adding, "And he mentioned...Dominic." Speaking Dominic's name aloud made his heart clench painfully.

Elvira's eyes widened in surprise. "Dominic? What did he have to do with this?"

Christian stared down at his hands. "I don't know. But I believe...he is my true mate."

"Your mate?" Elvira gasped. "Christian, that's...incredible! I didn't think such a thing was real."

Christian gave a small, helpless shrug. "Neither did I. But from the moment we met, I felt this bond between our souls. There is no denying what my heart knows."

Elvira shook her head in wonder. "I can scarcely believe it. After all these centuries alone. Tell me about this Dominic!"

Christian smiled softly. "He has a light within that draws all near him. A kindred spirit, though human. I've never felt such an immediate, profound connection."

Elvira took his hand, eyes shining. "I am so unspeakably happy for you, Christian. This changes everything!"

Her smile faltered. "Does Dominic know yet that you are fated to be together? Have you told him?"

Christian looked away. "No, not yet. We are still getting to know one another. I didn't want to alarm him by coming on too strongly."

Elvira nodded thoughtfully. "Of course. It's much to process." She touched his arm. "When the time feels right, he will understand in his heart, as you did."

Christian frowned. "I hope so. Assuming my reckless actions don't sabotage this gift before it can truly bloom."

Elvira gave him a stern look. "None of that now. This is destiny - it's beyond doubt or fear. Have faith."

Slightly buoyed by her certainty, Christian managed a wan smile. "Thank you, my friend. I shall try."

Elvira's expression grew serious again. "And this man - he knows things he should not. You must be cautious, Christian."

"I know," Christian sighed. "I need answers about him and his interest in Dominic. But he only speaks in riddles." He stood and paced restlessly before the fire. "Something dangerous looms over the horizon. But this stranger taunts me with clues, not facts."

Elvira rose and touched his shoulder. "Easy. The future is never carved in stone. Focus on what you can control - keeping Dominic and your people safe. The rest will follow."

Christian placed his hand over hers gratefully. Elvira always knew how to ground him when his mind spun too fast. For now, she was right - he should stay present and vigilant.

Seeking distraction, he turned to her with a tired smile. "Enough brooding over shadows. How was your trip visiting Ravenwood coven?"

Happy to see him sounding more himself, Elvira launched into an amusing account of her travels, skillfully turning the conversation lighter. They passed a pleasant hour this way before she had to take her leave.

"Try not to worry," she counseled at the door. "One way or another, we'll get to the heart of these mysteries. But don't let them steal today. This time is precious."

After she left, Christian stood gazing out the window at the dark grounds, pondering her words. The future was never guaranteed, for immortal or mortal alike. He resolved to heed Elvira's wisdom - be vigilant, yes, but not let ominous prophecies cloud the gifts right in front of him.

Dominic was real, not abstract portent. The stranger's interest in him gave Christian even more incentive to keep his beloved safe. But he refused to let foreboding visions poison the joy of finding his true mate against all odds.

Perhaps their union could be a catalyst for change beyond themselves, mending old divisions. Dominic's light called to Christian's long-buried humanity. Together, their resonating souls might heal splits both within and around them.

This was not the time for hesitation or fear. Fate offered Christian hope in the form of a kindhearted mortal full of magic and wonder. He would confront the shadows as they came. But Christian also dared trust destiny had brought Dominic into his sphere now for good reason.

Let the stranger and his machinations come, Christian thought resolutely. Whatever was written in the days ahead, he had found his true mate, his match in every way. Nothing could diminish the radiance of that undeniable knowledge. The rest was just mist and distant thunder. This precious moment was all that mattered.

After speaking with Elvira, Christian decided dwelling on the ominous visions wouldn't get him anywhere. Checking his watch, he saw it was time to go pick up Dominic for their date. Pushing aside his worries for now, he went to get ready.

Christian's usual refined suits wouldn't do for a casual night out with Dominic. He opted instead for a comfortable cashmere jumper and dark jeans. Vampires didn't have to only wear formal clothes, despite the stereotypes. After centuries, even suits could get tiring. Tonight was about relaxing and having fun with Dominic.

Studying himself in the mirror, Christian ran a hand through his blond hair, lightly styling it with product. A bit of stubble shaded his jaw - the "designer scruff" look suited him, he thought. Finally satisfied with his appearance, Christian grabbed his keys and headed out.

The drive to Dominic's home in Willowbrook was peaceful. Christian rolled the windows down, enjoying the warm evening breeze. It carried scents of pine and honeysuckle undercut by engine exhaust and hot asphalt - the mingled perfume of country town and city outskirts.

He stopped along the way to pick up a bouquet of roses and baby's breath that he'd ordered ahead. Their rich fragrance filled the car. Christian hoped they might bring a smile to Dominic's handsome face.

Pulling up outside Dominic's little house, Christian took an unnecessary breath to settle his sudden nerves. After so many years alone, these new feelings stirred up by Dominic delighted and overwhelmed him. He tugged at his collar, mouth abruptly dry.

The door swung open, and Christian's unbeating heart would have skipped a beat if it could. Dominic looked stunning in a buttery leather jacket over a tight white t-shirt that showed off his muscular arms.

His legs looked endless in dark skinny jeans. Christian longed to tear those clothes off and have Dominic all to himself...

But no, he had to control himself and take this slow. Christian swallowed hard and willed away the heat rushing through him.

"Good evening," he managed, holding out the flowers. "These are for you."

"Wow, thanks! You really didn't have to," Dominic said, looking pleased and slightly flustered. He took the roses, their fingers brushing. Christian fought another urge to grab him close.

"You look very nice," Christian offered sincerely. "That jacket is quite becoming on you."

Dominic ducked his head with an embarrassed laugh. "Oh, thanks. Um, you too." Their eyes met and something electric passed between them.

Clearing his throat, Dominic asked, "So, where are we off to tonight?"

Christian held out his elbow. "It's a surprise. Allow me to escort you to the chariot, kind sir," he joked playfully.

Dominic rolled his eyes but took Christian's arm, grinning. "Chariot, huh? You vampires sure do know how to live it up."

They made their way out to Christian's sleek Italian car. He opened the door for Dominic with a little bow before sliding into the driver's seat. Soon they were off, windows down and Dominic's hair blowing in the breeze. Pop music played low on the stereo. Despite his nerves, Christian felt lighter than he had in ages.

They chatted comfortably about light topics as the city lights came into view. Dominic's smile made Christian's chest ache with a pleasant sort of pain. He wanted nothing more than to spend every night driving along dark roads with this man by his side.

Christian pulled up near the glittering riverfront. "I thought we could start with dinner at a restaurant I enjoy here with an amazing view. I hope that sounds agreeable?"

"Definitely! This is such a beautiful area," Dominic said, looking out at the waterfront. The lights reflected off his brown eyes, making them shine.

Inside, the restaurant was sleek and modern with floor-to-ceiling windows looking out over the river. City high-rises glittered across the waterway. Christian gave his name and they were quickly shown to a secluded table by the windows.

Soft jazz music played as a waiter handed them menus and took their drink orders - wine for Dominic and a Bloody Mary for Christian. He caught Dominic trying to discreetly read the cocktail section listing various "red beverages." Christian hid a smile, finding his curiosity endearing.

"Have you been here long?" Dominic asked after they ordered. "In Dawncreek, I mean."

"Since the town was founded," Christian replied. "My...coven moved here for a fresh start after some time abroad. The change of scenery was overdue."

Dominic nodded. "It seems like an interesting place. Very different vibes than my hometown."

Christian smiled. "Yes, Willowbrook has a certain charming wholesomeness. But variety keeps life intriguing for...someone like me."

"Can I ask..." Dominic hesitated. "How old are you actually? If you don't mind me asking."

Christian laughed. "No offense taken. Let's simply say I've seen my share of history unfold."

Their food arrived, temporarily distracting Dominic from his immortal inquires. They lingered over the meal, chatting and laughing softly together as the river traffic lazily floated by. Christian was intoxicated by Dominic's presence. Everything else fell away outside this private bubble.

After dessert, they strolled leisurely along the riverwalk hand in hand. The breeze carried Dominic's bright citrus and sea salt scent. Christian breathed it in, imprinting this memory deep in his mind. The night felt enchanted.

Pausing to lean on a railing, Dominic said, "Hey, thank you for all this. I'm having a really great time." He gently squeezed Christian's hand.

Christian's breath caught at the tenderness in those beautiful brown eyes. "So am I," he replied, heartbeat quickening. Unable to resist, he reached out and tipped Dominic's chin up, slowly leaning down…

Their lips met, soft and seeking at first. Dominic tasted of chocolate and wine and something indefinably him. Then the kiss deepened hungrily. Christian slid his hand around Dominic's waist, pulling him closer. Heat coursed through him everywhere their bodies made contact.

Too soon Dominic drew back, breathing hard. His pupils were huge, lips kiss-swollen. Christian imagined laying him down right here…

"Wow, um…" Dominic blinked, looking dazed. "That was nice."

Christian stroked his cheek. "You take my breath away," he murmured. Dominic bit his lip, blushing deep red. It took all Christian's willpower not to kiss him again.

"What do you say we continue exploring?" Christian suggested thickly. Dominic nodded, lacing their fingers together once more. The night was still young.

They caught an artsy foreign film at a downtown theater before grabbing cocktails at a hip lounge. Dominic's inhibitions lowered after a few drinks, and their flirtatious banter turned heated. Christian was intoxicated by this charming, sexy mortal.

On the drive back, he kept stealing glances at Dominic in the passenger seat. His shirt had ridden up just enough to reveal a tempting strip of skin above his jeans. The car suddenly felt far too small and hot.

"Hey, we're here," Christian said reluctantly as they pulled up outside Dominic's place. He didn't want this magical night to end.

Dominic turned to him, eyes dark, and licked his lips. "Want to come in for a bit? I have this really great bottle of - mmph!"

Christian cut him off, mouth crashing onto Dominic's hungrily. Dominic responded just as fervently, fingers tangling in Christian's hair. They kissed with escalating passion under the muted glow of the streetlamps. Christian was lost, consumed by desire.

With heroic effort, he wrenched himself away, breathing hard. "We should stop, before I lose all semblance of control…"

Dominic looked beautifully debauched, lips swollen, shirt askew. "Oh. Right, yeah. Slow is smart." He dragged a hand through his mussed hair, laughing shakily. "Totally got carried away there."

They composed themselves, then Christian walked Dominic to his door. Taking both his hands, Christian met those gorgeous brown eyes with sincerity. "Thank you for an exquisite night. I cannot recall ever feeling such joy."

Dominic smiled, shy again. "Me too. I had an amazing time with you." He hesitated, then leaned in and kissed Christian softly. "Goodnight, Christian."

"Goodnight, my dear Dominic." Christian watched him go inside before returning to his car on air. The rest of the world had fallen away tonight. He wanted Dominic by his side for every night eternal. But for now, the sweet anticipation of their next encounter would sustain him.

The drive back to his manor felt dreamlike. Christian replayed every laugh, glancing touch, and smoldering kiss with Dominic on loop in his mind. How was it possible to fall so hard and fast? He yearned to lose himself completely in Dominic's embrace.

Yet unfamiliar anxiety tempered Christian's euphoria. He had avoided intimacy for so long, the vulnerability now scared him. Love could uplift life to poetry…or leave wastelands from careless missteps.

Though Christian's heart belonged irrevocably to Dominic, old instincts urged caution. Casual trysts were safe. But genuinely opening up risked profound hurts. Christian's damaged soul shuddered thinking of enduring loss again.

And beneath the soaring emotions ran an undercurrent of possessiveness that felt unsettling. Christian wanted to whisk Dominic away, keep him all to himself for eternity. Of course he would restrain these urges, but their strength overwhelmed him.

Was this just infatuation clouding his judgment? Christian had lived so long in solitude, the novelty of a true connection might blind him to red flags. The wise course was proceeding with care and communication. But patience was difficult when every fiber of his being burned for Dominic.

Approaching the manor grounds, Christian sensed he was not alone before he reached the grand front doors. Someone had breached his sanctuary, triggering silent protective wards. Christian tensed, ready to defend his territory.

Stepping inside cautiously, he followed the prickling sense of intrusion toward the east wing lounge. Christian threw open the heavy doors, prepared for confrontation. But he went still seeing who awaited him.

"Eros. To what do I owe the pleasure?" Christian kept his tone neutral, guard up. Eros's unexpected presence here boded ill.

"Don't worry, I announced myself to your servants," Eros said lazily from where he lounged by the fireplace, swirling a glass of Christian's finest Scotch. "They know me well, after all."

Christian remained wary. "Perhaps. State your business, it's late."

Eros's smile was sly. "I wanted to chat about things going on lately.

There are concerning rumors circulating that we should discuss." He stood gracefully and approached Christian, searching his face. "Specifically, whispers about you supposedly getting very close with a certain human. Please tell me that's not accurate."

Christian bristled, mind racing. Clearly his outings with Dominic had drawn attention, despite his discretion. "My personal life is my business. I'll have to ask you to go now."

But Eros did not back down, eyes glinting dangerously. "I'm afraid this does impact me too, friend. Relationships like that create…issues." His emphasis made the thinly-veiled threat clear.

Christian's hands clenched into fists. "Watch yourself, Eros. You've no right to police my relationships."

"Don't I?" Eros moved even closer, voice softening. "I'm looking out for an old ally who seems confused. This fling could ruin everything."

Ruin everything. The implication hung heavy between them. Eros aimed to create doubts and prevent Christian embracing Dominic as his mate. His motives were surely self-serving, not caring.

Eros was clearly still bitter that Augustus had chosen Christian over him as successor for High Elder. He wanted to undermine Christian's judgment and isolate him. Their ancient rivalry blinded Eros to unity's potential. He saw only a threat to his ambition.

Yet Christian could not simply disregard Eros's standing or valid concerns. As future High Elder, Christian had duties beyond himself. He inhaled slowly. "You're out of line. But I acknowledge your worries aren't entirely baseless."

Eros nodded, looking smugly relieved. "I'm glad you're being reasonable. We can't afford more…distractions." He moved to place a hand on Christian's shoulder. "It was only ever out of care for - "

Christian stepped back sharply, eyes flashing. "I said I grasp the risks. But I make my own choices. Question them again at your peril."

Eros appraised him coolly before inclining his head. "We shall speak again soon, once you have…perspective restored." With that ominous warning lingering, he vanished into the night.

Alone again, Christian poured himself a drink with a shaking hand. Eros's impromptu confrontation revealed cracks forming in the coven's foundation. Things were shifting as Christian's destiny with Dominic came to light.

Eros clearly remained intent on keeping Christian isolated and under this thumb. Their ancient grudge blinded Eros to the potential for unity Dominic represented. He saw only a threat to his influence.

Christian sighed, suddenly exhausted. Navigating the coven's toxic politics would require finesse. He must toe the line between duty and desire. Dominic's love was his destiny, but with it came grave new obligations and dangers.

Was he being selfish, inviting Dominic into his chaotic world? Perhaps keeping a distance would be safest, no matter how it wounded them both. Loving an immortal was complicated under the best circumstances.

Brooding into the dying fire, Christian warred with himself. His instincts screamed to clutch this unexpected joy with both hands against all obstacles. But wisdom urged prudence and patience. He would be no good to Dominic if they moved recklessly.

Tomorrow Christian would seek Augustus's counsel in private. His sire had mellowed with age and might see new paths forward. There had to be a way to gradually unify, not divide, their troubled community. It started with living openly by his true nature, not Eros's machinations.

Upstairs in his chambers, Christian gazed at the empty half of the bed that he now wanted desperately to share. Tonight he savored the memories alone, Dominic's kiss still lingering on his lips. But he vowed they would someday retire wrapped in each others' arms until the sun forced them to part. It was written.

For now he had hope renewed. The future was unclear, but Dominic was his light in the gathering darkness. Whatever betrayals tried to tear them apart, Christian would fight for their Bond with his last breath. They were meant to walk this path side by side.

7

Family

Dominic

I t had been a week since Dominic's unbelievable date with the intriguing vampire that was Christian. His mind kept drifting back to that night whenever his thoughts wandered.

Dominic still could hardly believe it had really happened.

Walking through the park with his best friend Benjamin, Dominic smiled to himself remembering how dashing Christian had looked picking him up. The kiss they'd shared - his first in far too long - still made Dominic's pulse quicken.

"Soo, are you gonna give me any juicy details or what?" Benjamin prodded, interrupting his reverie. "You've been holding out on me all week! I need the scoop about this mystery guy."

Dominic chuckled, shoving Benjamin's shoulder playfully. "And I told you, a gentleman doesn't kiss and tell."

"Ugh come on, that's so lame," Benjamin groaned dramatically. "At least give me something here! Was he a good kisser? Are you going out again?"

"Alright, alright!" Dominic laughed, putting his hands up in surrender. "It was…nice. He was really charming and cool. We just clicked right away."

Benjamin nodded eagerly for him to continue.

Sighing, Dominic obliged. "And yes, the kiss was…wow. Definitely wasn't expecting that on a first date. Sparks were flying all over the place. I can't get it out of my head."

Dominic smiled softly, thinking back over the past week. He and Christian had been talking and texting almost daily. Just casual check-ins and light flirting, but each message made Dominic's heart flutter.

The morning after their date, Dominic had woken up to a sweet voicemail from Christian saying what an incredible night it was and how he couldn't wait to see Dominic again soon.

Dominic must have replayed it twenty times, giddy as a schoolboy with his first crush.

Since then, they had fallen into an easy rhythm - chatting briefly in the mornings and for longer at night when Christian was up and about. He would ask charming questions about Dominic's day, tell funny stories, and compliment Dominic in ways that made him blush.

Dominic would share photos from the bakery, details of new recipes he was trying, mundane anecdotes that Christian seemed to find fascinating. Their conversations flowed so naturally, it was like they had known each other for years rather than days.

"You should hear the way he says my name with that accent of his," Dominic added dreamily. "And don't even get me started on his laugh. Ugh, I've got it bad, Ben."

Benjamin grinned knowingly. "I'm telling you, this one's special. When are you seeing him again?"

Dominic shrugged, trying to play it cool, but unable to keep a giddy smile off his face. "We're playing it by ear. But I think I'm really starting to fall for him."

It felt cathartic to say out loud. This captivating vampire had utterly enthralled him, and Dominic didn't care who knew it.

"I knew it!" Benjamin exclaimed. "See, you never put yourself out there, and look what happens when you finally do - magic!"

Dominic smiled, but felt his mood dim slightly. "Yeah, he's pretty special. But we barely know each other. I don't want to dive in too quick and mess this up."

Sensing his hesitation, Benjamin said reassuringly, "The best things take time to build. No need to rush what's meant to happen. Just trust your heart."

"Ever the wise romantic," Dominic said, bumping Benjamin's shoulder. "For now we're taking it slow, seeing where this unpredictable journey leads."

They walked in comfortable silence for a bit, crunching autumn leaves underfoot. The fresh air and sunshine lifted Dominic's spirits again. It was a beautiful brisk Saturday.

After a few minutes, Benjamin glanced over curiously. "So any ideas what your family wants from this visit? Seems weird they're so insistent out of the blue."

Dominic sighed. "Your guess is as good as mine. But Lee and Austin have been pestering me nonstop to come see them this week. Figured I should just go and get it over with."

"Man, families are the worst sometimes," Benjamin commiserated. "What do you think the odds are they actually want to mend fences and not just give you a hard time?"

"Ha, I'd say less than zero," Dominic said wryly. "But might as well see what they're on about. Otherwise they'll never stop nagging."

Benjamin shook his head sympathetically. "Well hey, call me after and we can get a beer or something if you need to vent."

"You're a good friend, Ben," Dominic said appreciatively, bumping his shoulder. "Speaking of, any chance you and Adrian are free tomorrow morning? There's something weird I came across while hiking last week that I want to get your take on."

"Ooh, mysterious," Benjamin said, intrigued. "We're in, just say when and where to meet up."

Dominic quickly gave him directions to the strange barren clearing he had discovered with Ciaran, the mysterious druid. Though Ciaran preferred secrecy, Dominic trusted Benjamin and Adrian to know when to be discreet.

"It looks like something magically drained all the life force from that spot," Dominic explained. "Ciaran said it's some kind of dark forbidden magic, which has me worried."

Benjamin's expression turned serious. "That doesn't sound good at all. Of course we'll come take a look and see if we can help figure out what's causing it."

"Thanks, I appreciate it," Dominic said. "The more eyes on this thing the better. I want to stop it before the damage spreads."

They parted ways soon after, Dominic heading for the train station with a sense of dread. Time to get this unpleasant family visit over with so he could focus on the real issue.

The coven manor looked pristine and imposing as ever when Dominic arrived. He steeled himself before walking up to the massive front doors. The sooner he got this pointless meeting done, the better.

The sprawling Victorian estate sat on a wooded hill just outside Willowbrook. It had been in Dominic's family for generations, passed down through the lineage of coven leaders. There was no way his traditional father would ever consider selling it.

Dominic felt strange returning after so long away. The manor held memories both fond and painful. Intricate wards shimmered over the imposing stone walls, allowing entry only to those sharing the coven's blood or invited through by a member.

Inside, the air hummed with centuries of magical energy soaked into the furnishings and walls themselves. The place made Dominic's skin prickle. He much preferred his little modern house.

Upstairs was the ritual chamber where new members were brought into the fold. Usually eager young witches hoping to tap into the coven's ancient power under the guidance of elders.

The initiation ritual involved slit palms pressed together as the oaths of loyalty were spoken. Then their mixed blood was used to inscribe the initiate's name in the massive leather-bound Book nestled in an altar alcove.

Only by binding their blood and magic to the coven's could they pass through the manor's wards unimpeded. The Book tethered all members mystically, stretching back through every generation since the coven's foundations.

Dominic had always felt uneasy about the initiation ritual. Binding new witches to the coven in blood felt archaic and wrong to him somehow. He hoped someday they could find a more welcoming, less invasive way to bring members into the fold.

The Book in particular gave Dominic the creeps - all those generations of witches tied eternally, their free will compromised. He avoided so much as looking at the massive tome shrouded in the altar alcove. The scent of dusty parchment and iron made his stomach turn.

Dominic had stalled for years on oathing new members with his own blood. He claimed it was because their numbers were solid, which was true. But his distaste for the rituals played a big role.

Unfortunately, his father and the coven elders saw Dominic's hesitation as him shirking his duties. Just another disappointment to add to their list of perceived failings. But he refused to perpetuate practices that felt so unethical, no matter the backlash.

Being back in the manor brought all Dominic's misgivings to the surface. He wanted to modernize how the coven operated, move past medieval notions of magical fidelity sealed in blood. Their gifts should bring them together, not oaths and mystic tethers.

For now, he had to endure this visit and the cloying sense of bygone generations whose notions and grudges haunted these halls. But someday Dominic would see the coven transformed into a welcoming place for all witches who sought community and knowledge without binding ties. He had to believe that change would come, no matter how gradually.

Dominic entered the manor and was immediately greeted by his arrogant stepbrother Lee.

"Oh. It's you," Lee said disdainfully.

Dominic rolled his eyes. "I'm here, as requested. Now let's get this over with. Are they here?"

Lee smirked. "It's about time you showed up. Father and Mother are pissed."

"When aren't they?" Dominic muttered under his breath as he followed Lee out to the back garden.

There he found his father and stepmother Lina sipping tea and chatting with a hulking man Dominic didn't recognize. The stranger's eyes lingered on Dominic with an unsettling intensity. After shaking Lina's hand, he strode past Dominic with a knowing smirk that made his skin crawl.

Suppressing a shiver, Dominic approached his family. "You wanted to see me?"

Lina set down her teacup with a tinkling sound. "Yes, Dominic. Please have a seat." Her tone was polite but frosty.

Dominic sat cautiously. He and his father exchanged tense greetings but little else. Their relationship had been strained for years now. Lina had driven a wedge between them that seemed insurmountable.

"I'll get right to the point," Lina began crisply. "It's come to our attention that you cavorted with vampires recently in Dawncreek. You know such…liaisons are forbidden by our coven."

Dominic tensed but kept his voice neutral. "Is that so? And who exactly have I been 'cavorting' with?"

Lina's eyes flashed with irritation at his evasiveness. "Don't play coy. The vampire Elder Christian Belgrave, among others. It must cease at once."

Dominic felt anger kindling but fought to stay calm. "Our outdated prejudices against vampires accomplish nothing. I'll associate with whomever I please."

"Rules exist for good reason," Lina snapped. "Or have you forgotten our bloody history with those monsters?"

Dominic met her icy stare evenly. "I won't judge an entire race based on the misdeeds of some long ago. The past is done - clinging to old hatreds only breeds more."

Lina's lips curled derisively. "Yet fraternizing with vampires remains forbidden by our coven. With good cause, I might add."

Dominic took a slow breath, willing himself to be patient. He knew mingling with vampires was frowned upon by the coven due to the violent clashes of the past. But he refused to perpetuate those antiquated biases.

"Times have changed," he responded evenly. "Vampires and witches shouldn't have to remain enemies till the end of days. We can move beyond the history we inherited."

Lina let out a sharp laugh. "Always the naive idealist. You know nothing of what it took to forge a fragile peace with those monsters."

Dominic shook his head adamantly. "I won't discriminate blindly against an entire race for past crimes. The only way forward is through open minds and diplomacy. Our hatred will just breed more of the same."

When Lina interrupted again, Dominic clenched his fists, tamping down a flare of frustration. This stubborn refusal to see beyond prejudice was exactly what kept barriers firmly in place between their kinds, he thought bitterly.

Lina leaned forward, eyes narrowed, she purred. "Let me be blunt then. End this foolishness with Belgrave or face consequences."

Dominic glanced at his father, who looked away uncomfortably under his son's accusing gaze. Turning back to Lina, Dominic asked in a low voice, "And what might those consequences entail?"

A cruel smile played about her lips. "Oh, just a minor magical binding to realign that rebellious nature of yours. It's for your own good, you know."

When his father remained silent, Dominic felt his simmering anger spike. "Are you just going to sit there while she threatens your own son?" he demanded. "Have you no will of your own anymore?"

His father shifted guiltily. "Rules exist for a reason, Dominic. I don't make them. My hands are tied here."

Dominic scowled, seeing the cowardice and weakness in his father once again. Ever since marrying Lina, he had slowly surrendered his free will and backbone to her manipulations. Dominic had lost all respect for him.

"Don't make excuses," he spat bitterly. "You're as much to blame for her cruelty toward your family." Dominic turned his glare back on Lina. "But I won't cave to your bullying tactics or hollow threats."

Dominic trembled with rage, hands clenching into fists at the thought of them invading his mind and magic. The previously sunny sky began to roil as dark thunderheads suddenly formed overhead, responding to his inner turmoil.

Ominous rumbles sounded as unnatural winds whipped Dominic's coat violently around him. The air grew heavy with magical charge, sending a prickle across his skin.

When Lina glanced up uneasily at the blackening heavens, Dominic saw a flicker of fear in her icy eyes for the first time. She took an instinctive step back from some primal threat she sensed in him.

Dominic made no move to restrain the tempest brewing within and around him. This was primal magic responding to his anger, but he embraced it. Let them reap the storm they had sown.

"You will stay out of my affairs and away from my magic," Dominic stated, voice deathly calm despite the growing winds. "I won't warn you again."

As Lee cautiously moved toward him, electricity split the sky with a deafening crack. A blinding bolt tore through the air and struck the ground just in front of Lee's feet, spewing dirt and molten glass. Lee recoiled with a curse, eyes wide.

The winds rose to a fever pitch, whipping Lina's dress violently as she shielded her face. The storms swelled, echoing the chaotic maelstrom of Dominic's emotions. But underneath he felt only icy purpose taking hold.

Turning on his heel, his coat swirling violently around him, Dominic strode away. At the door, he half-turned and in a terrible voice unlike his own said, "Do not interfere again."

Outside, he reined in the tempest with effort until the skies cleared. Dominic was shaken - he had never called a storm of that magnitude before. Raw power still crackled at his fingertips. What had awakened in him today?

But those concerns were secondary. He had shown his family he would not be controlled or intimidated any longer. If they dared threaten him again, they would discover just how much magic flowed untapped in his veins.

Dominic had embraced his peaceful nature for too long - this was a wakeup call. No more fear or weakness. His magic bubbled just under the surface, ready to obey his commands to protect those he cared for from all who meant them harm. For his loved ones, he would gladly unleash the tempest again.

No more weakness or fear in the face of those who sought to control him. His magic simmered just below the surface now, ready to obey his commands and protect those he cared about from all who meant them harm. For his loved ones, Dominic would gladly unleash the full tempest again.

Approaching his street, Dominic pulled out his phone to call Christian. He quickly explained what happened with his family and asked if Christian could come over later that evening, once it was safer for him to travel.

"Of course, I'll be there," Christian reassured, concern evident even through the phone. "I'm just finishing up a meeting with my sire presently. Are you alright?"

Hearing Christian's voice instantly soothed Dominic's lingering agitation. "I'm okay now. And I...I missed you," he confessed shyly.

He could hear the smile in Christian's voice when he replied gently, "And I you, my dear Dominic." The warmth and affection in those few words gave Dominic hope. Everything would be fine as long as they had each other.

They reluctantly ended the call, with Dominic promising to update Christian on the situation when he arrived later. As Dominic approached his house, lost in thought, a sudden movement caught his eye.

Beneath the big oak tree in his front yard, a huge black puppy was curled up napping. As Dominic drew nearer, its eyes opened, watching him approach with curiosity. The pup stood, giving itself a shake.

It was one of the biggest dogs Dominic had ever seen, nearly up to his waist already. Maybe some kind of wolf-dog hybrid, with shaggy fur and perked triangular ears. But its eyes were intelligent and alert, almost preternaturally so.

Dominic crouched down a safe distance away and held out a hesitant hand. "Well hi there, fella. Where did you come from?" The pup woofed softly in response, tail wagging. It seemed friendly enough.

On closer look, Dominic saw the pup had no collar or tags. "Are you lost, buddy? Or just hanging out here?"

At the sound of Dominic's soothing voice, the dog padded over trustingly and gave his hand an enthusiastic lick.

Laughing, Dominic gave it a good ear scratch. "I'll take that as a yes to some water, hmm?"

The pup followed happily as Dominic headed inside, nails clicking on the hardwood floors.

After gulping down two bowls of water, it tore into a plate of leftover chicken Dominic offered. Clearly the poor thing was half-starved. But it had a sweet, intelligent nature about it that drew Dominic in.

"What should I call you?" Dominic mused as the pup licked the plate clean. Those wise amber eyes studied him as if it understood every word. On impulse, Dominic said, "How about Vale? It means strength." The newly christened Vale gave a little "woof" of approval.

Dominic had a good feeling about this curious encounter. He would put up flyers about finding a stray dog, but wouldn't be surprised if no owner came forward. For now, it seemed meant to be that Vale had found his way into Dominic's life when he needed companionship most.

After a quick stop to walk and feed Vale again, Dominic headed to the bakery for the afternoon. His thoughts kept drifting back to the enormous but gentle pup now sleeping on a blanket in his living room. And to Christian's impending visit later that night. Despite the day's stresses, Dominic felt optimistic.

Closing up shop as twilight fell, Dominic stopped by the market for a few groceries, then hurried home to clean himself up a bit before Christian arrived. He smiled seeing Vale's huge head pop up from his bed excitedly when Dominic entered.

"Hey boy, did you miss me? I got you a big tasty bone for being so good today," Dominic cooed, petting Vale's head. The massive pup was quickly melting his heart. He took it as a good omen that Vale had arrived just when Dominic needed him most.

Soon there was a knock at the door as the last of the sun's light faded. Taking a breath to calm his nerves, Dominic opened it to find Christian waiting, perfectly elegant as always. The very sight of him eased the day's tensions from Dominic's body. He was simply happy to have Christian here. Everything else could wait.

8

Bonds of Blood

Christian

Christian was in the midst of changing into an elegant suit when his phone lit up with Dominic's number. Even through the phone, he could hear the strain in Dominic's voice as he briefly explained needing to see Christian tonight. Christian's unbeating heart ached - had he come on too strong after their date?

He tried to reassure Dominic gently that of course he would come over later, after his meeting with Augustus concluded. Hanging up, Christian sighed, running a hand through his hair anxiously. Overthinking things would get him nowhere. He would see Dominic soon and they would work through whatever was troubling him together.

Glancing at his watch, Christian saw he was nearly late for the his meeting.

Christian quickly dressed and called his assistant Miya to clear his schedule for the day. She had been with him for centuries, and he trusted her implicitly to handle things in his absence.

As the phone rang, he hurried out to his car, thoughts still consumed with concern for Dominic.

"Christian, how nice to hear from you," came Miya's melodic voice.

Though centuries had passed, she still retained hints of her native Japanese accent.

Christian pictured her delicate features and piercing dark eyes as he slid into the driver's seat. "Miya, apologies for the late notice, but something pressing has come up. Please cancel my appointments today."

"Of course, I will handle it," Miya replied smoothly.

Though he could hear notes of surprise and concern in her tone. Christian seldom disrupted his meticulous schedule so abruptly.

"Thank you, Miya." Christian said.

"Is everything alright?" she ventured cautiously. "You sound… distressed. Can I assist with anything?"

Despite the dire revelation about his past, Miya's steadfast devotion brought Christian a small smile. "I'm quite fine, no need to worry. Just an urgent personal matter."

He still recalled their first meeting vividly, when she had been a lady-in-waiting to a visiting Japanese princess at one of Augustus's grand balls centuries ago. Christian had been captivated instantly by her quick wit, artful beauty, and compassionate spirit.

Luckily, she had found his pale foreign looks and somber demeanor intriguing in turn. It was the height of impropriety, but they stole moments together whenever they could. The princess had been outraged when Miya requested to stay behind, but love recognizes no borders.

"If you're certain," Miya said gently, pulling Christian back to the present. "I will keep your schedule clear and attend to all critical affairs. Focus on what you need to."

Christian felt a rush of gratitude. "Thank you, truly. I knew I could rely on you."

After exchanging goodbyes, he sped off toward the coven manor, heart buoyed by Miya's stalwart support despite troubling revelations ahead.

The drive to the coven manor was a blur. Christian's thoughts kept drifting back to the defeated tone in Dominic's voice. He hoped he hadn't unconsciously done anything to hurt Dominic or make him feel pressured. Christian would have to keep his instincts in check and let Dominic set the pace for them.

Inside the imposing stone mansion, a human servant informed Christian that Augustus awaited him in his private chambers upstairs. Christian ascended the grand staircase two steps at a time, anxious to make sure his sire was well.

Knocking firmly on the heavy oak door, Christian entered at Augustus's muffled command. He found his sire standing pensively by the wide bay windows overlooking the manor grounds. Even from behind, Christian could see Augustus's usual strength was waning.

"Sire, is everything alright?" Christian asked with concern.

Augustus turned, attempting a wan smile. "Yes, quite. Come and sit, I have something important to discuss. But you wanted to see me first - what is on your mind?"

They settled in comfortably by the fire, but the familiar setting did nothing to calm Christian's unease. Augustus appeared deeply troubled, his stoic visage cracked with uncharacteristic vulnerability. Christian's earlier worries suddenly felt quite small.

"It's Eros," Christian began hesitantly. "His resentment toward me has worsened since you named me successor. I fear he may become dangerous."

Augustus nodded solemnly. "I suspected Eros would not accept being passed over gracefully. He has always thirsted for power and prestige." Sighing, he continued, "I have contingency plans should Eros become openly defiant. But I have faith in you, my son. You shall lead this coven well when I retire as the head of the coven."

Christian stared at the flames, uncertainty gnawing at him. "I still feel unready for such responsibility. Perhaps Eros would be better—"

"Christian." Augustus's sharp tone made him fall silent. "You underestimate your capabilities and wisdom. Self-doubt is natural, but you must look past it."

Chastened, Christian simply nodded. Augustus smiled and squeezed his shoulder. "Now, tell me of happier matters. How fare things with the lovely mortal Dominic?"

At the mention of Dominic, Christian's expression instantly lightened. "He is extraordinary. I am now certain he is my destined mate, though I have yet to tell him."

"A true mate?" Augustus asked, intrigued. "Fascinating. You seem quite smitten already."

Christian laughed. "I am. He complements me perfectly in every way. I look forward to you meeting him someday."

They talked warmly about Dominic a while longer. But eventually, Augustus's expression grew serious again as he segued into the real reason he had summoned Christian here today.

"What did you want to talk about?" he prompted gently after Augustus was silent for a long moment, staring into the flames. "I am always ready to serve, whatever you require."

Augustus placed a hand on his shoulder. "Your loyalty heartens me, Christian. But what I must tell you now may test even your bounds of grace." He took a heavy breath before continuing. "I have learned the true circumstances behind the plague that claimed your family. It was no ordinary illness - the devastation was conjured by a vampire."

Christian stared at him, stunned. "What? But how...why?" This revelation turned his understanding upside down.

Augustus' expression was grave. "A ruthless ancient who revered death as the highest art. He violated every code in his vile experiments to create what the mortals came to call the 'plague'."

Shaking his head bitterly, he continued, "I discovered the truth too late. The damage was beyond measure."

Christian rose and paced in agitation, overcome. Augustus had given him flight from the wasteland the plague had made of his mortal life. To learn one of their own kind was behind that unfathomable suffering…

"You knew this all along, didn't you?" Christian demanded, wheeling on Augustus. "Yet you shielded the monster's identity all these years?"

Augustus met his gaze unflinchingly. "I believed ignorance would spare you needless torment in your fresh grief. But you have long proven yourself above vengeance."

Christian passed a trembling hand over his eyes. This revelation changed so much of what he thought he understood. His family were not just casualties of happenstance, but victims of unforgivable malice.

"Does this butcher still live?" Christian asked through clenched teeth, dreading the answer.

Augustus nodded gravely. "Yes. Once I learned the truth, I hunted him unsuccessfully for decades. He is cunning and elusive beyond measure. But I have never abandoned the chase."

Christian exhaled shakily. To know that vile creature yet walked free was almost too much to bear. But he would not shirk from this difficult truth any longer.

"Then we shall hunt him together, and not rest until he is ended," Christian declared. Augustus's secrets wounded deeply, but justice awaited, however delayed.

Christian was not the young, grief-stricken mortal Augustus had turned so long ago. He saw now his sire had meant to shield him out of wisdom and care, not duplicity. This knowledge opened raw old wounds, but did not fundamentally alter who Christian had grown to become.

Kneeling before Augustus's chair, Christian bowed his head. "I cannot fault you for sparing me such pain when I was still so vulnerable," he said, voice thick with emotion. "You gave me new life. That gift transcends all else."

Augustus placed both hands on Christian's shoulders. "You do me great honor. But know I regret the necessity of deception, however benevolent my aim."

They took comfort in the silence and familiarity, letting turbulent emotions settle. The past could not be changed, but the future awaited reshaping. They would proceed together in truth's harsh light, their bond weathering this revelation as it had so many storms before.

As soon as Christian exited his sire's chamber, he bumped into Matt, one of the newer vampires under his mentorship. Matt had opted to reside at the coven manor for now, while he gained more control over his intense bloodlust urges.

"Good evening, Elder Belgrave," Matt greeted him respectfully. Though still in his first decade as a vampire, Matt showed great promise and aptitude. Christian was happy to guide him through the challenging transition.

"Matt, good to see you," Christian replied. "How goes your training and studies lately?"

Matt's youthful face lit up proudly. "Excellently, thank you. Each night brings new mastery of my skills." His enthusiasm revived Christian's own jaded spirits somewhat.

"Wonderful to hear. You're applying yourself diligently," Christian praised. An idea struck him then. "Speaking of training, would you care to join me for some sparring practice? I could use the exercise."

Matt's eyes widened eagerly at the invitation. "Absolutely! I would be deeply honored."

Christian clapped him on the shoulder. "Excellent. Let us proceed downstairs to the gym."

The two vampires made their way through the labyrinthine manor to the coven's vast basement training complex. Christian always found physical exertion helped clear his mind and focus restless energy. And he enjoyed mentoring talented young vampires like Matt.

Once changed into lightweight training clothes, they entered the spacious gym. Christian gazed around appreciatively as he stepped onto the padded sparring mats, memories washing over him.

The gym was equipped as lavishly as everything else in the ornate manor. One wall was covered in polished wooden weapon racks full of stakes, swords, axes - both real and practice variety. Targets and archery ranges occupied another area for honing precision skills.

The floor was sprung hardwood, ideal for traction. Thick mats created cushioned areas for full-contact sparring. One corner housed a small boxing ring, though vampiric fights required more space. Mirrors lined one wall, so techniques could be self-critiqued and improved.

Breathing deeply, Christian could still faintly detect the leathery scent of generations of vampires training here, honing their predatory skills and deadly grace. He vividly remembered his own earliest sessions here with Augustus centuries ago.

His sire had put him through endless drills to master reading an opponent's minute cues and responding with lightning instinct. Christian had been a quick study at both armed and unarmed combat. Training together also strengthened the bond between sire and progeny.

Now Christian enjoyed passing on hard-won skills to young vampires like Matt when he could. Seeing their gratitude and progress reinvigorated Christian's own dedication to mastery. This historic room saw the cycle of knowledge continue as it had for ages.

Eager to begin, Matt practically vibrated with nervous excitement across from his mentor on the mats. With an encouraging smile,

Christian beckoned him forward. The night's lesson was about to start for his dedicated student. Returning Matt's bow, Christian settled into a ready stance, feeling centered and focused.

"I'll try not to thrash you too harshly," Christian joked lightly, hoping to relax the tension.

Matt laughed. "I'll try to provide you some worthy challenge at least." Christian smiled, pleased to see Matt gaining confidence.

After bowing respectfully, they spent the next couple hours sparring vampiric-style. Their blows came in a rapid blur, enhanced by preternatural speed and reflexes. To a human observer it would have looked like a fight choreographed for film, too fast to track.

Christian was impressed by how much Matt's skills had progressed. The eager student landed several clean strikes that would have temporarily paralyzed a lesser opponent. A few times he even managed to catch his mentor momentarily off guard with advanced counter maneuvers.

"Excellent form," Christian praised as Matt executed a flawless leg sweep combo. "You've improved remarkably."

Matt grinned and helped him up. "Thanks, but I'm still no match for you."

"Give it time. You have tremendous potential," Christian encouraged.

Partway through their session, they switched to wooden swords, the clack of the blades echoing as they sliced through the air. Matt was less familiar with weapons combat, but he quickly adapted his footwork and incorporated the disarming and trapping techniques Christian demonstrated.

"Loosen your grip, you'll have more control," Christian instructed after disarming Matt.

Matt adjusted his hands and nodded. "Got it."

Soon their practice blades were just blurs slicing through the air.

Matt narrowly dodged Christian's strikes using his quick reflexes. Their fight ranged all over the mats, even up the walls at times.

After hours of intense effort, they were both happily exhausted. Matt glowed under his mentor's guidance.

"Your skills are extraordinary for one so young," Christian told him sincerely. "Keep this dedication, and you will go far."

"Thank you, elder. This means everything coming from you," Matt said. "I won't waste the wisdom you've granted me."

Christian clapped his shoulder warmly. "Use it to make our kind's future better. That will be thanks enough."

By the end, both vampires were thoroughly spent but energized by the competitive camaraderie. Matt glowed under the praise and tutelage from his idol. Christian felt his own burdened spirit lightened after the invigorating contest. He lived for these moments passing on hard-won skills to promising students like Matt. It gave him hope for the future.

It was quite late when Christian and Matt finally finished their intensive sparring session. Matt mentioned he was scheduled to work at Christian's club, Midnight, that evening. Since Christian intended to head there briefly anyway, he offered Matt a ride over so they could go together.

The club was Christian's refuge when things got stressful or overwhelming. The blaring music, chaotic crowds, and nonstop sensory stimulation kept his perpetually wandering immortal mind occupied. And he wanted to check in and ensure everything was running smoothly in his absence.

As they drove downtown, Christian turned to Matt and asked, "What are your thoughts on potentially opening another Midnight location at some point?"

Matt looked surprised Christian valued his opinion. "Oh, well...I'm probably not the best person to ask. But from what I've seen, this place already draws big crowds most nights."

Christian nodded for him to continue. "That's true. I'm interested in your perspective."

"I guess having a second club could be good for reaching more people," Matt said thoughtfully. "I know you get a fair number of patrons already coming over from Willowbrook and the suburbs."

"Excellent observations," Christian praised. "I appreciate your honesty. I have been weighing the positives and negatives. For now we will stay focused on making this Midnight the peak of what our guests desire."

Matt smiled, looking proud to have provided his mentor useful insight. Soon they pulled up to the club's back entrance and headed inside. The muffled bass beat made the walls vibrate.

Christian did a quick walk through to check on things. The dance floor was already packed with gyrating bodies bathed in hypnotic lights. A line stretched down the block outside, hoping to get in. The bar staff was scrambling to keep up with demand. Christian nodded, satisfied with how busy it was.

Christian's sharpened vampire senses were suddenly on high alert, detecting a subtle shift in the energy around him. The noise and pulsing lights seemed to fade as he focused every fiber of his being into searching for what had triggered this instinctual reaction.

Slowly sweeping his gaze across the sea of oblivious revelers, Christian's eyes finally landed on a shadowy alcove at the back of the club. Half-hidden in the darkness, a pale man with black hair raised a glass in silent mocking toast when their eyes met.

Before Christian could react, the stranger vaporized back into the shadows as partygoers walked between them, breaking the connection. Christian was left tense and unsettled. Had he imagined the silent confrontation? But every preternatural instinct screamed something was very wrong.

He reached out with his thoughts, trying to psychically trace wherever the figure had disappeared to. But the stranger's presence had vanished like smoke on the wind. Christian shook his head, troubled. For now, he had no choice but to let it go. But he vowed to get to the bottom of this unnerving encounter.

Probably just his restless mind playing tricks, he decided.

Checking his watch, Christian saw it was nearly time to leave for Dominic's. As much as he would have liked to linger and have a drink here, he had to stay sober for the drive to Willowbrook. With mixed anticipation and nerves, he headed out to his car.

The whole way, Christian tried to plan what to say to Dominic. He sensed something was deeply troubling the mortal. But Christian also longed to confess that his own unbeating heart now irrevocably belonged to Dominic. He hoped the revelation would not destroy their delicate bond.

But was it wise to burden Dominic with the pressures and dangers of being a vampire's mate? Perhaps Christian should keep his volatile emotions concealed. He was adrift, torn between selfless wisdom and reckless desire.

By the time he pulled up outside Dominic's little house, Christian was no closer to deciding on the right course. He had to trust his instincts in the moment. This astonishing mortal had awakened feelings in Christian that transcended caution or reason.

Steeling himself, Christian walked up and knocked firmly on the weathered front door. He had brave new worlds to discover at Dominic's side, if only he had the courage to take that step into the unknown. Whatever this night held, Christian knew their paths were meant to converge here and now. With an unnecessary breath, he waited for his love to open the door.

9

Mates

Dominic

Dominic sat trying to make some "Found Dog" posters for
Vale, though he was having second thoughts. After just
barely a day together, he had already grown incredibly
attached to the giant stray pup.

When Vale started happily chewing Dominic's phone charging cable,
Dominic didn't have the heart to scold him. The puppy looked so cute
and delighted, even as he destroyed Dominic's electronics. Chuckling,
Dominic went over to gently take the slobbery cable away and scooped
Vale up into his arms.

"No chewing on cables, you little monster," Dominic chided affectionately. Vale simply responded by giving him a big sloppy lick across
the face.

With a sigh, Dominic said, "I wish you could talk like Benjamin's
cat Jimmy. Then I could just ask if you belonged to someone before
bringing you home."

Jimmy was part magical familiar, which explained his ability
to converse. Dominic knew regular animals tended to be lower

maintenance pets for witches, if harder to have conversations with.

Carrying Vale into the living room, Dominic turned on an episode of his favorite baking show for them to watch, settling the giant puppy comfortably in his lap. As Dominic slowly stroked Vale's soft fur, he felt his nerves about Christian's upcoming visit finally start to settle.

Between the cozy room, the sounds of the TV, and Vale's comforting warmth and steady breathing, Dominic's eyes soon fluttered closed without him even realizing. The next thing he knew, a shrill beeping jerked him awake.

Blearily taking stock, Dominic realized it was his proximity ward alert going off, triggered by someone approaching the front steps. That meant Christian had arrived. Dominic also noticed Vale had flopped over and was drooling heavily on his leg as he slept. Some guard dog he was shaping up to be!

Hastily wiping the dog slobber from his pants, Dominic carefully extricated himself from underneath Vale and went to greet Christian. Sure enough, the vampire's tall silhouette was visible through the frosted glass of the front door. Dominic suddenly felt self-conscious about his rumpled clothes and bedhead.

Opening the door, he managed a shy smile. "Oh, uh, hi! Come on in."

As usual when faced with Christian's elegance, Dominic felt his tongue tie itself in knots. Christian's answering smile was warm and broad.

"Hello Dominic. Thank you for having me." His voice instantly put Dominic at ease again. He ushered Christian inside to the cozy living room.

"I see you have a new companion," Christian remarked, crouching down by where Vale was still snoozing. At the sound of a new voice, one amber eye cracked open inquisitively.

Dominic gave a little self-deprecating laugh. "Yeah, that's Vale. I only found him today, but we're already best buddies." He quickly relayed the giant stray pup's sudden appearance and how he'd adopted Vale on the spot.

By now, Vale was awake and sniffing Christian with great curiosity. Apparently satisfied that the visitor passed muster, Vale gave Christian's hand an enthusiastic lick of approval. To Dominic's delight, the imposing vampire proceeded to laugh and vigorously scratch Vale behind the ears.

"You, my friend, are a magnificent creature," Christian informed Vale, who wagged his tail proudly at the praise.

Dominic just shook his head, grinning at the charming scene. He never imagined he'd see the day such a scary immortal doted on a puppy.

Clearing his throat after a moment, Dominic asked, "I was about to make some tea, would you like some?"

Christian glanced up. "That would be lovely, thank you." He effortlessly hefted Vale up into his arms as he stood. "I'll keep this fellow entertained in the meantime."

Heading to the kitchen, Dominic felt a warm glow at seeing Christian so at home here already, bonding with Vale. He put the kettle on and leaned against the counter, wondering how to even begin delving into the turbulent events that had prompted his call to Christian earlier.

When the tea was ready, Dominic carried the mugs back out to the living room. He found Christian sitting on the couch with Vale sprawled happily across his lap. Dominic almost hated to interrupt the cozy scene, but he and Christian had important matters to discuss.

Settling into the armchair across from Christian, Dominic took a sip of chamomile tea before meeting Christian's thoughtful gaze.

"Thank you again for coming," Dominic began earnestly. "I'm sorry I was so vague on the phone. It's just...a lot happened since I saw you last. My family confronted me, and things escalated, and now I'm doubting so much…"

Dominic swallowed hard. He was normally so reserved when it came to personal struggles. But he needed to trust Christian with the full truth.

Taking a steadying breath, Dominic explained everything - his tense meeting with his father and Lina, her cruel threats against his magic, and how his powers had erupted out of his control. Saying it aloud brought back the maelstrom of emotions.

Throughout the whole story, Christian listened attentively, his ancient eyes full of compassion. His presence gave Dominic the courage to delve even deeper.

"There's something else," Dominic continued hesitantly. "They… they ordered me to stop seeing you. Us being together defies their old prejudices."

Dominic glanced up nervously to gauge Christian's reaction. The vampire's brow was furrowed but he remained silent, waiting for Dominic to continue.

"How they even found out about you so fast, I have no idea," Dominic went on. "Lina said our 'association' had to end immediately. And they'd use force if necessary." He looked down, ashamed. "I'm so sorry to drag you into my family's dysfunction. I don't expect you to get involved in their bigotry and threats."

Christian reached out and gently turned Dominic's face back up to meet his eyes. "Do not apologize," he said firmly. "I am here because I choose to be. Your battles are my own."

Dominic blinked back grateful tears. "Even if it puts you at risk?"

Christian gave a dismissive laugh. "I assure you, I am rather adept at handling threats." His expression softened again. "Whatever comes, we will face it together. Our bond transcends their narrow minds."

Despite the dangers ahead, Dominic felt hopeful for the first time in ages. With Christian, he wasn't alone anymore against his family's cruelty. Side by side, they could overcome anything.

"How do you think they found out about us so fast?" Dominic wondered aloud.

Christian's jaw clenched. "I have my suspicions. Trouble is afoot in the shadows. But that is a matter for another time." He squeezed Dominic's hand. "Tonight, nothing matters but being here with you."

"I just don't know what to do anymore," Dominic finished in a pained whisper. "My own family sees me as a disappointment, and I can't see us ever finding common ground again. It's like I lost my father the day he married Lina."

Dominic stared down at his now-cold tea, embarrassed by the tears stinging his eyes. A part of him wanted to apologize for unloading so much on Christian. But when he glanced up hesitantly, Christian reached out and took Dominic's hand in his gently.

"You have endured such pain, and with such grace," Christian said solemnly. "I am honored you chose to share these burdens with me. Whatever lies ahead, I am here for you."

His simple words lifted the weight off Dominic's chest. Finally confronting these wounds with someone who offered only compassion was profoundly cathartic. He gave Christian's cool hand a grateful squeeze.

They still had much to navigate in this unlikely relationship between immortal and mortal. But Dominic knew with sudden clarity that he could trust this empathetic soul with his own. That was a start. The rest they would unravel together, one day at a time.

Dominic and Christian gazed into each other's eyes, the air suddenly heavy between them. Wordlessly, Christian leaned in and met Dominic's lips with his own. The kiss began soft and searching, then rapidly deepened into passion.

Dominic's heart pounded as Christian's cool hands came up to cradle his face. He leaned into the dizzying kiss, tangling his fingers in Christian's silky hair. This growing heat between them felt at once frightening and exhilarating.

Caught up in the intensity of the moment, they stumbled to the bedroom, shedding clothes along the way. Dominic's nerves fluttered even as his body responded eagerly to Christian's touch. He wanted this, wanted Christian, with an intensity that stole his breath.

Yet a small voice of warning remained in Dominic's mind, making him hesitate. Sensing this, Christian drew back and met his eyes questioningly.

"Are you certain this is what you want, my dear Dominic?" Christian murmured. "There is no need to rush. We have all the time in the world to explore these feelings between us."

Dominic's pounding heart swelled at the tender care in Christian's voice. Here was someone who saw him, truly saw him. In answer, Dominic pulled Christian back down into a searing kiss conveying all his longing and trust.

Their bodies entwined, bare skin against bare skin. With reverent touches and gasping breaths, mortal and immortal came together at last, consummating the profound bond awakened between their souls.

Later, enveloped safely in Christian's arms, Dominic traced abstract patterns on his lover's marble chest as he sank into contented exhaustion. The world around them was still uncertain, but here in this moment, he had found his refuge. Together they would face whatever lay ahead. This night was theirs.

Moonlight filtering through sheer curtains cast the bedroom in a soft glow. Dominic traced abstract patterns on Christian's bare chest as he luxuriated in the feel of their entwined bodies. Christian's skin was cool to the touch yet set Dominic's nerve endings alight.

Dominic sighed contentedly, still floating in a haze of satiation. Moments ago ecstasy had crashed over him in waves as they came together at last, consecrating the bond awakened between them. It had been tender yet passionate, an affirmation of the depth of their feelings.

Propped up on one elbow, Christian gazed down at him, emerald eyes warm with affection. He brushed a stray lock of chestnut hair off Dominic's forehead and smiled. "Comfortable, my dear?"

Dominic nodded, snuggling closer. "Very. I don't know if I can move, actually."

Christian's chuckle rumbled low in his chest. "Well, we have all night. And you'll need your strength for what comes next."

Dominic quirked an eyebrow. "Oh? And what exactly did you have in mind?"

"This." Swift as a cat, Christian rolled on top of him and dug his fingers into Dominic's ribs.

Dominic yelped, then dissolved into breathless laughter as Christian tickled him without mercy. "No! Stop, I give up!"

With a playful growl, Christian finally relented and collapsed next to Dominic. Their mingled laughter filled the shadowed bedroom. As it faded, Dominic marveled again at how perfectly content he felt in this moment. It seemed almost surreal that only months ago, Christian had been just a friendly acquaintance at the bakery.

Yet their connection had taken root and flourished rapidly. Christian made him feel understood, made him feel complete, in a way he'd never imagined possible.

Dominic studied Christian's chiseled profile as he reclined against the pillows. His pale skin seemed to glow faintly in the darkness. Dominic still struggled to wrap his mind around the fact that this extraordinary man wasn't human at all, but rather an ancient and powerful vampire.

Perhaps sensing his gaze, Christian turned to look at him.

"What is it, my heart?" Christian's melodic voice held a thread of concern.

Dominic shook his head, offering a reassuring smile. "It's nothing, just thinking about everything that's happened since we met. About how you make me feel." He trailed his fingers down Christian's arm. "I've never been happier than I am with you."

The corners of Christian's eyes crinkled with his answering smile. "Nor I with you, my Dominic." He captured Dominic's hand, bringing it to his lips for a tender kiss.

A comfortable silence settled between them. Dominic's eyelids grew heavy as he drifted toward sleep in the cocoon of Christian's arms. Just as he was sinking into slumber, Christian's hushed question jolted him awake.

"Dominic, what do you know of vampires and true mates?"

Dominic blinked up at him. "True mates?"

Christian nodded, his expression carefully neutral.

Dominic furrowed his brow, trying to recall the lore he'd learned. "Well, I know bonded mates used to be more common among vampires. But they're rare now, right?"

"Yes, very rare indeed," Christian agreed somberly. "Our kind has dwindled since the Great Hunts. Those remaining mostly keep to themselves to survive."

Unease trickled down Dominic's spine. He pushed upright, searching Christian's face. "Why are you asking about this now?"

Christian hesitated before answering slowly. "Because you need to understand, Dominic. You are my true mate."

Dominic sat stunned, pulse thundering in his ears. Gradually he found his voice. "But…how can you know for certain? We've only been together a short while."

Patiently, Christian explained. "It began that first time I saw you in your bakery. Our auras resonated, and a preliminary bond formed though I knew you felt it not. It has only grown stronger since." His expression softened. "Our souls are intertwined, Dominic. Of this I am certain."

Dominic's thoughts raced. "What does this mean for me? For us?" A trace of fear crept into his voice.

Hastily Christian grasped his hands. "It changes nothing you do not wish, my dear. I swear it. A mate bond bestows some of my abilities, including immortality should you desire it. But you need not accept the full transformation."

Dominic searched Christian's face. "This is a lot to take in."

Christian lifted Dominic's hands to his lips. "I know, my heart. Take all the time you need. The bond between us is not yet permanent; it will settle only if we both accept it completely. For now, just know that I am yours, in whatever way you will have me."

Overwhelmed, Dominic let Christian gather him close, resting his head against the steady drumbeat of his heart. Christian pressed a kiss to his hair and murmured, "Rest now, my Dominic. Tomorrow's worries can wait."

Lulled by Christian's embrace, Dominic soon slipped into dreams.

Mop sweeping. Calm.
Bell ringing, shattering the peace.
Gary entering. Dark energy surrounding him.
Dominic gesturing angrily. Gary smirking coldly.
Clenched fists. Knuckles cracking like thunder.
Tension swirling. Building.
Gary striking suddenly. Dominic summoning magic in desperation.
Lightning at his fingertips. Storm exploding within confined space.
Rain pouring. Thunder crashing. Chaos.
Dominic striving to withstand the endless blows. Slowly faltering.
Figure watching from shadows. Grinning.
Though he fought with desperate determination, Gary gradually battered

through Dominic's defenses. Dominic struggled vainly to withstand the onslaught.

In the shadows, a figure watched, smiling.

With a final surge, Dominic's storm collapsed. Spent, he crumpled to the floor as the magic faded.

Gary towered over Dominic, promising he'd find Benjamin. Then he vanished into the darkness.

The sudden grip on his shoulder jolted him awake. Heart hammering, he thrashed against the tangled sheets.

"Dominic! It's me. Just breathe." Christian's melodic voice cut through his panic.

Dominic stilled, focusing on the familiar silhouette hovering anxiously over him. "Christian? What...I was dreaming..."

Christian smoothed back Dominic's sweat-dampened hair. "I know. You cried out in your sleep. It sounded like a terrible nightmare." His cool fingers trailed down Dominic's cheek. "Are you well?"

Dominic slowly sat up, the sheets pooling around his naked waist. He scrubbed a hand over his face. "Yeah. Yeah, I think so. Just shaken up."

Christian wrapped a supportive arm around his shoulders. Dominic focused on the comfort of that touch, anchoring himself in the present. His frantic pulse gradually slowed to match Christian's steady rhythm.

After long moments, Christian pressed a kiss to his temple. "Would you like to discuss it? The dream?"

Dominic sighed, dropping his head against Christian's shoulder. "It was the bakery again. Gary. Fighting him with my magic." He shivered. "It always feels so real."

Christian made a low, soothing noise, pulling Dominic closer. "Just a dream. You are safe here with me."

Dominic nodded, but doubt nagged at him. He hadn't told Christian about the frequency of the nightmares. It seemed trivial; Christian already worried so much about threats from his own kind. Dominic's strange dreams were a burden he needn't bear.

Pushing the thoughts away, Dominic took in their surroundings. Dawn's rosy light filtered through the curtains. He realized with some surprise that Christian lay tucked against the headboard in the shadows, not beside him as usual.

Following his gaze, Christian gave a rueful smile.

"Apologies, my heart. The sun crept higher than I anticipated." Christian gestured at the light angling across the rumpled sheets. "Its touch holds less danger than once it did, thanks to our bond, but prolonged exposure still taxes me."

Dominic curled his fingers around Christian's where they rested atop the comforter. "Here I was sleeping away without a care while you were stranded. I'm sorry."

Christian lifted Dominic's hand to brush a kiss over his knuckles. "No need for sorrow. Watching over your rest is no hardship." His lips quirked. "And the view was most appealing."

Heat rose in Dominic's cheeks at the realization he'd kicked off the covers at some point. With a half-hearted glare, he swatted Christian's shoulder, then leaned in to capture his mouth in a lingering kiss. Christian eagerly responded, thumb tracing delicate patterns on Dominic's bare skin.

By unspoken agreement, their kisses remained soft, unhurried. Dominic eventually settled with his head atop Christian's chest, listening to the steady thump of his heart. Christian toyed idly with the ends of Dominic's hair.

"What are your plans for today?" Christian murmured. "The shop, I presume?"

Dominic groaned theatrically. "No, Benjamin and Adrian wanted to see what's going on in the forest." He tilted his head up to meet

Christian's eyes. "Unless you want to come with us?"

"Nothing could keep me away." Christian leaned down to steal another quick kiss. "But for now, rest a bit longer. Dawn has only just broken; the day holds no urgency yet."

Dominic hummed agreeably, already drifting toward sleep in the sanctuary of Christian's arms. Yet a thought nagged at him, chasing away his drowsiness.

He sat up abruptly. Christian regarded him quizzically. "Dominic? Is something wrong?"

"No, just..." Dominic turned to face him. "You've given up so much to be with me. Your preferences, your nature as a vampire. The least I can do is make sure you're comfortable and can go where you wish."

Christian's expression softened. "You owe me nothing..."

But Dominic was already sliding from the bed, heedless of his nudity. He hurried to his wardrobe that held his most precious possessions. Throwing open the doors, he shifted aside spellbooks and crystals until he found the velvet pouch tucked in the back corner.

Dominic caressed the embroidered rune symbolizing his mother's coven before loosening the drawstring and shaking the contents into his palm. The slim silver band glittered in the low light.

Christian came up behind him, curiosity etched on his face. "What are you doing?"

Dominic smiled over his shoulder. "Just a little surprise." He squeezed Christian's hand, then moved to the window, brow furrowed in concentration.

Dominic reached deep inside himself, seeking the spark of power that connected him to the natural world. As a weather witch, he held dominion over storms, wind and sky. But some blessed with his gifts could harness the very elements that comprised all creation. While not truly manipulating the building blocks of nature, under the right circumstances, tiny changes could be coaxed.

Dominic sent a tendril of magic into the streaming sunlight, probing delicately at the unique properties of the rays. There - the subtle wavelength that caused the vampires' affliction. With careful tweaks, he filtered it out, gathering the adjusted light into the ring to emit its new benign influence.

Brow damp with exertion, Dominic slid the ring onto his finger and turned to Christian, uncertainty swirling in his chest. "Here. See if this helps."

Christian took his hand, examining the band. Brow furrowed, he angled their joined hands into the sunlight. When no pain or discomfort resulted, his eyes widened in wonder.

"Dominic…how did you accomplish this?" Christian asked.

Dominic shrugged self-consciously. "Just a little trick I have under my sleeve. Manipulating elements in small ways." He squeezed Christian's hand. "So it helps? You can tolerate the light?"

Joy suffused Christian's face. He surged forward to sweep Dominic into a fierce embrace. "My clever, generous mate," he whispered into Dominic's hair. "However did I get so lucky?"

Dominic hugged him back just as tightly. "I'm the lucky one."

When they finally drew apart, Christian lifted Dominic's hand to brush a fervent kiss over the ring. "A piece of your magic I can carry always. I shall treasure it." His emerald eyes were overly bright.

Dominic blinked back a suspicious wetness from his own eyes. Overcome by the moment, he pulled Christian down into a kiss, seeking to convey all the feelings swirling within him. Christian responded ardently, arms winding around Dominic to eliminate any space between them.

Eventually they parted just far enough to catch their breath. Dominic traced his fingers over Christian's sharp cheekbones, marveling anew at this extraordinary man who was his mate in every way. He cherished their closeness in this perfect moment.

A grin stole across his face as a thought struck him. Taking Christian's hand, he gave an impish look over his shoulder as he backed toward the still-rumpled bed.

"Since we're awake already, and you have nowhere to run off to now..." He winked playfully. "How about we enjoy the morning properly? We'll need our rest for the busy day ahead."

Christian's eyes crinkled with his answering smile. "Far be it from me to refuse such an enticing offer."

He allowed Dominic to pull him down onto the sheets, their laughter intertwining joyfully. Golden sunlight bathed their entwined forms as they came together once more, christening the gift Dominic had given.

Later, Dominic drifted in sated contentment, watching motes of dust dance through the warm sunbeams. The steady rhythm under his ear was a soothing reminder of the abiding connection they now shared.

10

Druid

Christian

Dominic had gifted him something extraordinary. Witches weren't meant to access death magic, yet somehow Dominic had harnessed and manipulated it to make the light safe for Christian. It was an impossible gift, yet also deeply symbolic of their bond. Dominic had found a way to bridge their two worlds.

Staring at his mate over the rim of his coffee cup, Christian felt his unbeating heart swell with emotion. Dominic met his eyes and smiled, hazel depths warm with understanding. He knew how momentous this was for Christian.

Hand in hand, Christian and Dominic strolled down the sun-washed street. Christian still marveled at the gift of walking freely in daylight after endless nights in the shadows. Now they could share simple joys without fear of harm to him.

Glancing sidelong at his mate, Christian felt his unbeating heart swell. Dominic's hazel eyes sparkled with laughter at some shared quip. After centuries alone, Christian had found the one meant for him. No other would take his place at Christian's side.

Such a love was rare among vampires, most relationships transient and superficial. But what he felt for this remarkable witch transcended mortal bonds. They were two halves of one soul, perfectly matched.

Across his long existence, Christian had opened his heart to love only to have it shattered time and again. He would fall for someone deeply, believing they were the one.

When he finally worked up the courage to reveal his vampire nature, expecting acceptance, initial reactions were always reassurance and vows not to be afraid.

But as the reality settled in, fear would take root. His lovers would withdraw behind excuses, unable to reconcile their image of him with the truth.

No matter Christian's gentleness and devotion, the monster mythology prevailed. The final stinging betrayals as they fled into the safety of denial became almost routine.

He learned to expect nothing more. Relationships were temporary mutual enjoyments, feelings kept carefully shallow.

Until Dominic. This remarkable witch saw Christian fully, unflinchingly. And chose to love all of him - the man and the vampire alike.

With Dominic, those old wounds could finally heal. Christian need never hide pieces of himself again. They had found perfect understanding, a love eternally unconditional.

As if sensing his pensive mood, Dominic bumped their shoulders affectionately. "Penny for your thoughts?"

Christian lifted Dominic's hand to brush a kiss over his knuckles.

"Just reflecting on how incredibly fortunate I am to have found you, my heart. You have given me gifts beyond measure." Christian said.

Pink tinged Dominic's cheeks, but his eyes softened. "Right back at you." He nudged Christian playfully. "Now come on, we've got a busy day ahead!"

They continued down the sidewalk, bantering lightly as they went.

Dominic was recounting a hilarious childhood mishap involving a temperamental goat that had Christian grinning.

"So the goat starts chewing right through the fence, I mean full on chomping wood chunks. And I'm just frozen watching this unfold," Dominic chuckled.

Christian laughed. "A true jailbreak. That would've been a sight."

"Oh you have no idea. Meanwhile the kids responsible are panicking, trying to wrangle this thing. It breaks through and makes a beeline right for the food stands, crashing through tables and tents!"

"That is an epic rampage," Christian said appreciatively. "Please tell me you have photos."

"Sadly no, but the memories alone," Dominic sighed nostalgically. "What about you, any wild animal encounters growing up?"

Christian thought back with a smile. "Well, once I accidentally spooked a skunk that proceeded to spray directly into my father's open mouth."

Dominic snorted with laughter. "No way! Did he keep his mouth open that entire time?"

"I know! You'd think instinct would kick in to close it," Christian grinned. "But nope, he just stood there gaping and took a direct hit. Had to gargle tomato juice for a week."

They both dissolved into laughter at the absurd image. As their chuckles subsided, Dominic asked "Ever get any bad haircuts as a kid? I'm picturing a pretty unfortunate bowl cut on little Christian."

Christian groaned dramatically. "Ugh yes, the dreaded bowl cut. My mother thought it was 'cute'. I begged her to let it grow out."

"You were an adorable little bowl-headed rascal, I'm sure," Dominic teased.

"Oh absolutely. The buzzcuts weren't much better," Christian lamented. "Let me guess - you rocked some pretty fly mullet action?"

Dominic snorted. "Hey now! It was more of a...floppy surfer look," he protested. They grinned at each other, both envisioning the tragic hairstyles of childhood.

Their lighthearted banter carried them all the way until the cheerful awning of The bakery came into view. The scent of fresh coffee and baking bread wafted over them.

"We have arrived," Christian declared happily. "Ready for that red velvet cupcake now?"

Dominic smiled and laced their fingers together. "With you? Always." Laughing together, they headed inside to enjoy some well-deserved treats.

His first visits here had been furtive, shrouded in darkness. Now he took in every sun-lit detail with wonder. Tables dotted with regulars enjoying their morning rituals. Display cases gleaming with flawless pastries. A welcoming sanctuary, vivid and warm in a way Christian had almost forgotten mortal spaces could be.

Dominic led Christian back to the bakery's kitchen, their flirtatious banter echoing off the gleaming counters and racks of fresh ingredients. With the morning prep complete, the space was now blissfully empty and theirs alone.

Dominic hopped up to perch on the central wooden table and fixed Christian with a playful grin.

"Well, fancy pants, ready to see how the common folk bake?" Dominic teased.

Amused, Christian moved closer, hands coming to rest on Dominic's hips. "I accept your challenge, sir. Show me what miracles you can produce in this kitchen."

Laughing, Dominic grabbed a sky blue apron and tossed it dramatically at Christian, who caught it and swiftly donned it.

"This color really brings out my eyes, don't you think?" Christian fluttered his eyelashes comically.

Dominic snorted. "Oh yes, very fetching. Though not quite as stylish as my salmon pink one." He struck an exaggerated pose.

"Obviously. No one can compete with such bold fashion choices," Christian said seriously.

Giggling, Dominic guided him through mixing up batches of cookie dough and muffin batter, keeping up a stream of good-natured teasing all the while.

"No no, you have to sift gently," Dominic chided as puffs of flour went flying. "We can't have you manhandling the ingredients."

"My apologies, I don't know my own strength," Christian said sheepishly, further mussing his floury hair.

As a tray went into the oven, Christian twirled Dominic jokingly across the floor in an impromptu dance. Dominic laughed and responded by booping Christian's nose with frosting, leaving him cross-eyed.

Christian retaliated by smearing a streak of chocolate down Dominic's cheek. "Whoopsie, you had a little something there," he said innocently.

Soon they were both breathless and doubled over with laughter, covered head to toe in baking ingredients. Their playful antics had completely eclipsed any actual work being accomplished.

Finally, wiping tears of mirth from his eyes, Dominic gasped "Okay, truce! This baking battle is getting out of hand."

Christian grinned and pulled him in for a quick kiss, heedless of the mess. "But so much delicious fun!"

"You are such a dork." Dominic said.

Seizing the chance, Christian snaked an arm around Dominic's waist, pulling him close.

"Never out of hand with you." He leaned in under pretense of cleaning a smudge of frosting from Dominic's lips and stole a swift kiss.

Pulling back, he arched a teasing eyebrow. "Consider it a preview.

We will revisit this cooking lesson later." His gaze turned heated. "I believe you mentioned making a master chef of me?"

Dominic's eyes softened and he drew Christian into a deeper, languid kiss. When they finally parted, Dominic murmured, "We have an eternity for that."

A beep drew their focus back to the ovens. With shared rueful chuckles, they turned their attention to extracting perfectly baked goods.

As they transferred the finished pastries onto cooling racks, Dominic bumped Christian's shoulder affectionately. "Not bad at all. You're on your way to master baker status."

Christian stole another swift kiss. "All thanks to an excellent teacher." He glanced around the now spotless kitchen. "Shall we see how the front fared without you?"

Entwining their fingers, they pushed through the swinging doors into the warmer, yeasty atmosphere of the front. Christian inhaled contentedly, marveling again at being part of Dominic's everyday world.

They had only moved a few steps when Dominic halted abruptly, almost colliding with an approaching figure.

"Whoa! Pardon me," laughed the young woman, deftly sidestepping. "Didn't mean to surprise you."

"Lyra! Hi." Dominic ran a self-conscious hand through his hair. "Sorry, we were just...never mind." He flashed a smile. "Lyra, meet my partner Christian. Christian, this is our new hire, Lyra."

Lyra and Christian exchanged polite greetings. Her keen gaze flicked between them, no doubt taking in traces of flour on their clothes. But she just smiled warmly. "Wonderful to officially meet Dominic's mysterious Christian."

Dominic gave her a grateful look before adding, "I'll be in later today if you need anything. Just had to show him the workings of the kitchen."

"No worries! I've got this covered." With a little wave, Lyra breezed off to handle an incoming customer.

Dominic and Christian walked back to Dominic's house after their morning at the bakery. Dominic wanted to drive to Willowbrook Forest to meet up with some friends.

When they arrived at the parking lot, a sleek black car pulled up blasting alternative rock music. Out stepped two guys around Dominic's age and one that he could sense older than the two by centuries..

"Christian, meet my buddies Adrian, Ben and Merin" Dominic said.

Christian smiled warmly. "Nice to meet all of you ."

Ben had artfully tousled raven black hair that fell over one eye. He had a slim, almost delicate build. But his stylish outfit of a graphic t-shirt, leather jacket and ripped jeans gave him an edgy look.

Adrian was tall and muscular with bulging biceps and broad shoulders straining against his shirt. His dark hair was cropped close to his head in a no-nonsense style. Christian noticed Adrian wore cargo pants and boots - clearly ready for action. Christian could tell from his powerful physique that Adrian worked out intensely.

Merin was a hulking red head and looked liked a lumberjack. Christian remembered him from the night of the incident at the bar.

The three contrasting guys made an interesting trio. But the easy camaraderie between them showed a strong bond.

The five of them headed into the forest, following a winding dirt trail that led deep into the shadowy woods. Christian could hear a babbling stream nearby and birds chirping overhead. The fresh, earthy scent of moss and pine trees filled the air.

Christian hung back a bit on the trail with Adrian while Dominic, Ben and Merin laughed and joked around up ahead. Their cheerful banter echoed between the tall trees. Christian smiled, taking in the dappled sunlight dancing across Dominic's face. It made his undead heart swell to see Dominic looking so carefree and happy among his friends.

As they walked deeper into the ancient forest, the trees grew thicker, filtering the sunlight into scattered beams. Christian inhaled deeply, catching the musty smell of decaying leaves and rich soil. In the shade, the air felt cooler against his skin.

Looking around, Christian saw shimmering cobwebs strewn between crooked branches and a pair of squirrels chasing each other around a mighty oak's trunk. Flowers and mushrooms sprouted up around moss-covered rocks and fallen logs. The forest was teeming with life.

Up ahead, Dominic and Ben's voices faded into the natural background music of chittering crickets, a honking goose flying overhead, and the gentle gurgle of the winding stream. Christian tuned his sharp ears to take in every sensory detail. For a tranquil moment, he felt totally connected to the primal essence of the forest.

Adrian gave Christian a thoughtful look. "So how are you able to walk in sunlight? I can sense you're a vampire."

Christian showed him the ring on his finger. "Dominic put an enchantment on this ring so I can go out during the day without burning up."

"Handy trick," Adrian replied.

"So how did you and Ben meet?" Christian asked.

"At a masquerade ball," said Adrian. "And ever since then we've been inseparable."

"What happened after?" Christian asked. "I've heard parts of what happened with the warlock but didn't really dive into it more." He continued.

"You see, I was cursed. Cursed for wanting to bring back someone that I used to love. So a powerful enchantress cursed me into turning everything that I touch into ice and turn me into an ice dragon. Ben only wanted to help break my curse but by doing so helped the warlock - Malachite - to get what he wanted, the Libranomicon. We had to get it back and in return the enchantress took away my curse by fusing my dragon's soul and my own together." Adrian said.

"So what you're saying is that you can still turn into an ice dragon and still have your sorcerer magic?" Christian asked.

"Yes. I was just glad that Ben was there to accept me for who I was and who I am now." Adrian said with a soft smile.

Christian's eyes went wide. He had heard some rumors but didn't know the details. "That sounds intense."

"It was," Adrian nodded. "Dominic got caught up in it all trying to help. Ben still blames himself for what happened."

"What did happen?" Christian asked.

Adrian shook his head. "You should ask Dominic. It's not my story to tell."

Christian contemplated Adrian's words as they continued through the shaded forest. There was more to the story of the warlock's defeat than Dominic's friends were willing to share. But pressing the issue would have to wait.

Their focus now was reaching the ominous site Dominic had discovered on a recent hike. He had been reluctant to describe specifics, only that a dark energy permeated the area, powerful enough to make him uneasy.

The path opened up ahead, sunlight splashing into a picturesque clearing. Yet as they stepped into the space, an instinctive chill raced down Christian's spine. The very air felt denser, bearing an unsettling charge. He shuddered to think what could affect him so as a vampire.

Dominic shifted closer, features drawn with worry. "You feel it too then? I've never encountered anything like this before."

Merin rubbed briskly at his arms, expression uneasy. "It's like a storm brewing, but the sky is clear. The whole place feels…off."

Adrian stood silent, eyes closed and brow faintly furrowed as he extended his magical senses. After a prolonged moment, his eyes snapped open, glinting with steel. "The veil separating realities has worn thin here. Something forced its way through from beyond."

Ben shook his head in disbelief. "But how? And why here?"

Crouching, Dominic trailed his fingers lightly over a patch of withered grass at the epicenter, making Christian's protective instincts flare. "Whatever came through, the damage is done. Now we have to determine the cause and whether it's still a threat."

Merin chewed his lip nervously. "I'll consult my divination tools back home. Hopefully they can provide some clarity."

Ben nodded. "I'll head to the archives, see if there are any historical records of similar mystical disturbances." His expression was grave. "Hopefully we can find answers before anything worse happens."

While they conferred, Adrian began a meticulous survey of the perimeter. As a sorcerer, he had the strongest chance of decoding the magical traces. Christian trailed him, watchful for any fresh signs of danger. This unknown entity had gotten too close to Dominic already for his comfort.

Pausing, Adrian sifted a handful of dirt through his fingers. "Interesting…" He held it out to Christian. "What do your vampiric senses detect?"

Christian accepted the earth, reaching out with his enhanced perceptions. The instant his skin made contact, a shockwave of energy slammed through his mind. His vision wavered sickeningly as fragmented images assailed him…

A battlefield strewn with fallen warriors…

Dominic silhouetted against a violet sky, robes snapping in an arcane wind…

The clearing blurred by rapid movement…

A pale hand wielding an ornate dagger…

The images fractured again, voices echoing strangely:

"The hour approaches…"

"Bind him! Now!"

"Protect…"

A high, cold laugh, sending icy fingers down Christian's spine…

With a gasp, he crashed back to reality, blinking up at the concerned faces hovering over him. Dominic helped ease him into a sitting position.

"Christian! What happened?" Dominic's eyes were wide with worry, hands clasping Christian's tightly.

Christian slowly steadied his breathing, still shaken. "I…I'm not sure. When I touched the earth, it triggered some kind of vision." He met Dominic's gaze. "Fragmented images, voices. Like memories, but none my own." He shook his head in frustration. "I can't make sense of them."

Adrian's sharp gaze focused on Christian. "Do you normally experience visions?"

Christian shook his head. "No, it's not a true ability. After turning, I developed a sense for dangers approaching, mere glimpses really."

Merin nodded. "It's common among immortals, a kind of intuition. But true prophetic visions are rare outside of those gifted, like Seers." He gave Christian an assessing look. "What you saw may hold more significance than scattered portents."

The others murmured in agreement, curiosity kindling in their eyes. Christian could sense they were all eager to know what fragmented pieces had assaulted his mind after touching the disturbed earth.

He tried to gather the disjointed images into some semblance of order to convey. "I'm not sure how to explain it yet. But I swear I'll share anything that starts to make sense."

Dominic squeezed his hand supportively. "Together, we'll unravel these mysteries." The others nodded resolutely in agreement. United, any threat could be faced.

Rising, Adrian dusted off his hands, expression thoughtful. "The soil holds residual magic - perhaps even imprints of events connected to whatever crossed over here." His sharp eyes bored into Christian. "We may have found a conduit by which to unravel this mystery."

Christian tensed at the implication, but Dominic cut in sharply. "Absolutely not. It's too dangerous." His grip on Christian tightened protectively.

As Adrian's fingers brushed the disturbed earth clean, traces of inky darkness swirled up from the grains before disappearing like mist on the wind. The very ground seemed steeped in eldritch magic, tainted by otherworldly shadows.

Adrian's brows drew together as he tracked the wisps' path. "Dark magics indeed were woven here. Their residual echoes may yet reveal hidden truths."

He made a mystical gesture and fiery sigils flared along the clearing's perimeter, sealing in the occult traces. Adrian's eyes glowed with azure light as he delved into readings beyond mortal senses.

The others watched anxiously. Adrian wielding such arcane forces stirred primal awe and unease in Christian. But Dominic's steadying presence kept foreboding at bay. Whatever mysteries the sorcerer unearthed, they would unravel together.

Eventually Adrian sagged, sigils fading as he broke the spellcraft. He accepted water from Ben gratefully. "Magics old as the earth itself were at play here," he finally pronounced. "But their purpose remains obscured."

Dominic squeezed Christian's hand, resolve steeling his eyes. "Then we keep searching until this threat is brought to light."

Christian started to nod when an ominous rumble shook the

clearing. The ground roiled as if alive, nearly knocking them off their feet. Christian steadied Dominic protectively as Adrian and Ben dropped into battle-ready stances, magic flaring in preparation.

A rending crack split the air as the earth split. Dark vapor spewed forth, coalescing into a hulking, misshapen form. Blazing crimson eyes focused on the group as clawed limbs tore free of clinging dirt.

Dominic staggered back, voice hushed with dread. "A hellbeast. But that's impossible…"

"Legends walk abroad this day." Adrian's tone was grim, eyes narrowed at the creature unfurling before them. It released a bone-chilling roar, the fetid stench of its breath scalding the air.

Muscles rippled under ebony flesh as it flexed six-inch talons. Oily shadows dripped from its frame, bespeaking eldritch magic woven through sinew and bone. Power roiled off it in palpable waves, primal bloodlust kindling in its fiery gaze.

Dominic called on the elements, conjuring violent gusts that whipped his hair and clothes. The gale-force winds slammed the creature from all sides, making it stumble. Dominic clenched his fist and lightning cracked from the skies, scorching the beast's hide in branching veins of light.

But unnatural vitality flowed through its body, repairing the damage as they watched. It was an extension of the eldritch darkness that had birthed it. Their mortal magic could only inflict temporary harm.

Gripping his carved staff, Ben traced arcane symbols that flared and hovered in the air around him. With a wordless cry, he sent the glowing sigils flying at the creature. Celestial fire erupted on impact, engulfing the fiend completely for a moment. It emerged smoking and snarling, the holy flames burning away the oily shadows shrouding it. But they had not purified deeply enough. Already fresh demonic essence suffused it, redoubling its frenzy.

The creature turned those maddened eyes on Adrian. As it charged him with uncanny speed, Adrian flung up another fiery counterstrike. But his most destructive magic detonated uselessly again, not even slowing its momentum.

Adrian braced futilely as the massive body collided with him, swiping him aside like a rag doll. He tumbled limply across the clearing.

Horrified, Christian rushed to intercept the beast's charge at Adrian's prone form. Gripping the snapping jaws, Christian strained against the monster's overwhelming physical might. This foe was far beyond them. But he would not yield.

Merin manifested a gleaming longbow wrought of pure spirit energy. Though physically slight, power radiated from him as he took aim. The spectral weapon sang again and again as he loosed arrows that exploded in bursts of purifying light against the creature's hide.

It roared in frustration as the blessed shafts seared away layers of demonic shadow shrouding its body. But Merin's gift quickly took its toll, each shot sapping more of his aura. Eyes glassy with exhaustion, he stubbornly reached for another spectral arrow.

"Save your strength!" Adrian shouted, carving fiery purple sigils into the air that rocketed at the creature. The exploding runes halted its advance, driving it back a pace.

Merin reluctantly lowered his bow, swaying unsteadily. But a determined light still burned in his eyes. "This battle is far from done."

They were outmatched, yet Christian took heart from the defiance kindling in each of them. Though vastly powerful, their enemy did not stand unopposed. Side by side, they would make it pay dearly for each inch of ground.

The hellbeast's roars rattled the clearing as their attacks proved futile. Defeat seemed imminent.

Suddenly, the forest bowed reverently as ancient power gathered.

The air thickened with primal magic as gnarled roots erupted from the earth, entangling the creature fully. It thrashed against the vines but the living wood held fast.

A mist coalesced, solidifying into a towering figure in a crimson hood. The scent of loam and cedar washed over them as he approached the bound beast calmly. Laying a weathered hand upon its brow, leafy tendrils spread across its body from his touch. The creature went still, fire in its eyes dimming.

The man's fingers carved mystical symbols in the air. Green fire followed their path, scorching away the demonic essence until only purified earth remained. He turned to the awestruck group and drew back his hood, revealing green eyes that were greener than grass.

Dominic gasped. "Ciaran!"

"Dominic. Nice to see you again." Ciaran turned and looked at the rest of them. "I am Ciaran, a Druid that was tasked to investigate what is going on here." Though power shrouded him like a cloak, his smile was benign. This was a guide, not a conqueror.

Adrian clasped Ben's hand. "We should reconvene at the manor to discuss these events." He included Ciaran and Dominic. "Will you both join us?"

Ciaran turned his ancient gaze on Dominic, who nodded after a moment's hesitation. Christian knew Dominic's history with Willowbrook's townsfolk made him wary of traveling in magical circles. But Ciaran's aid had proven him an ally worth trusting.

Adrian clapped a hand on Dominic's shoulder. "Come. Much needs unraveling this day."

As they made their way out of the forest, Christian stayed close to Dominic, letting their linked hands ground him. Adrian was right, many mysteries still lingered after the day's harrowing events. But united with those he loved around him, Christian felt ready to confront whatever revelations awaited at the manor.

11

Magical Secrets

Dominic

The ride to Adrian and Ben's manor passed in tense silence. Dominic kept his eyes fixed out the window, struggling to process the day's harrowing events. The creature had been no mindless fiend, but a calculated attack targeting him specifically.

Christian's hand on his knee grounded Dominic, drawing him back to the present. Glancing over, he saw his own grim determination mirrored in Christian's eyes. They would unravel this mystery together.

Soon the rolling hills gave way to an ornate wrought iron gate. The grounds beyond had an eerie loveliness, frosted in moonlight. Dominic suppressed a shiver as they approached the imposing manse.

Powerful wards prickled across his skin. Adrian's magic kept even greater security measures dormant, allowing them passage. Inside, Dominic stayed close to Christian amidst the shadowed opulence.

They soon reached a study, its leather chairs and shelves of arcane tomes contrasting sharply with the sleek minimalism downstairs. Adrian conjured refreshments as they all took seats around the engraved table.

"First, allow me to express my gratitude for your aid against the creature," Adrian began solemnly. "Without your collective efforts, I fear none would have left that clearing alive."

Murmurs of dismissal followed, but Adrian's words chilled Dominic's blood. How close had they truly come to annihilation today? And how much worse did Ciaran imply this threat would become?

Speaking of the druid, all eyes turned to him.

"Dark times loom," Ciaran pronounced finally. "Willowbrook's magic grows tainted, corrupted from within."

"Corrupted?" Ben leaned forward intently. "But the ley lines have provided life and stability for generations untold. What could affect them so?"

"Unto that very question, I have devoted these last moons. And unearthed troubling answers." Ciaran's eyes were grave. "The ley lines' convergence, your Wellspring, has been compromised. Its Light fouled by an emerging Shadow."

Unease rippled around the table. Dominic stared down at his clenched fists. The Wellspring was essential to Willowbrook's existence. If its magic faltered...

Adrian broke the ominous silence first. "Forgive me, but how could any elemental Shadow withstand the Wellspring's power? Its Light has ever kept darkness at bay."

Ciaran sighed heavily. "In eras past, you speak truth. But arrogance has bred complacency of late. And now ambition stirs in one who would risk all to claim the Well's might."

Dominic tensed. If Ciaran had no leads on this mysterious Shadow Figure, how could they stop the darkness spreading through Willowbrook's magical veins?

As if reading his thoughts, Ben spoke up hesitantly. "From my research, a designated coven has always safeguarded important ley line convergences like the Wellspring. Have your investigations uncovered which guards Willowbrook's?"

A small meow made them all jump. Padding into the study was a familiar black cat, staring right at Dominic.

Dominic blinked at the cat in surprise. "Jimmy? What are you doing here?"

Ciaran smiled and approached to scratch Jimmy behind the ears. "Well hello there, it's been some time, old friend."

Jimmy arched into the scratching happily. "Ciaran! About time you came around again. Thought maybe you'd forgotten about little old me."

Ciaran laughed. "Never that, though clearly someone has gotten even more demanding in their old age."

Jimmy swatted at him playfully. "Look who's talking! How many centuries has it been now, you old oak?"

"Mind that sass, I can still turn you into a toad," Ciaran threatened lightly, eyes twinkling.

"You know the tail always wins with us," Jimmy retorted, swishing his long furry appendage smugly.

Ciaran just chuckled. As one of the most ancient and powerful familiars, Jimmy had always delighted in giving even respected druids like Ciaran a hard time. And their friendship went back countless generations.

"In all seriousness my friend, it's good to see you awake again," Ciaran said more solemnly. "We'll need your help and wisdom for the trials ahead."

Jimmy looked at everyone and sat back, "Apologies for intruding. But I overheard your dilemma." His yellow gaze took in each of them before settling on Dominic again. "Guarding the Wellspring has always fallen to mortals. A great honor."

Merin leaned forward curiously. "Do either of you know which coven was designated as its protector?"

Ciaran and Jimmy exchanged a somber look. Dominic tensed, and felt Christian squeeze his hand comfortingly under the table.

"From what I learned, your witch coven was charged with safeguarding Willowbrook's ley lines," Ciaran said, turning back to Dominic.

Shock reverberated through Dominic as Ciaran's words sank in. His family had been the sworn guardians of Willowbrook's magical heart, yet he'd had no idea.

Christian's steady presence beside him kept Dominic grounded. He gave Christian's hand a grateful squeeze in return.

"Why was I never told any of this?" he demanded, emotions churning. "Why keep these duties secret from me if I was to inherit them?"

Christian took his hand, grounding him. "Were any in your coven known to dabble in dark magic?" he asked gently. "Could they have obscured things deliberately?"

Dominic shook his head firmly. "No, never. They took our role seriously, I'm certain of it."

Though they had treated him poorly at times, he couldn't conceive of his family betraying their sacred responsibility so profoundly.

Adrian watched him closely. "People can do terrible things in pursuit of power, as I well know," he said heavily. "But I pray that is not the case here."

Ben's expression was thoughtful. "Is there any way you can uncover more about their activities in recent years? Any records or contacts who might know?"

Blowing out a shaky breath, Dominic hesitated. Probing those painful memories held little appeal. Yet if it could expose the source of the Wellspring's decay, he owed it to Willowbrook to try. "I...I can make some inquiries. But I won't promise answers."

Christian gave his shoulder a reassuring squeeze. "No one expects miracles. Just follow the path, wherever it leads."

Adrian inclined his head. "There is time yet to unravel this mystery. We will proceed carefully." He addressed Ciaran. "Please, remain here as our guest. Your wisdom has proven invaluable."

Ciaran dipped his head in thanks as the others began gathering their things. Dominic felt drained down to his bones. He wanted nothing more than to retreat home with Christian and leave these revelations behind, at least for the night.

As the manor study emptied, Dominic felt a nudge at his leg. Looking down, he met Jimmy's inscrutable yellow gaze. The cat beckoned with his tail for Dominic and Christian to follow.

"You two, follow me." Jimmy said.

Exchanging curious glances, they trailed Jimmy through the maze of corridors to the manor's vast library. Jimmy sat primly beside a carved chair, clearly expecting them to sit as well.

Settling cautiously, Dominic folded his hands in his lap. "Did you want to speak with us about something, Jimmy?"

The cat considered them both silently for so long that Dominic fought not to fidget. Finally Jimmy replied, "In truth, I merely wished to see how you fared after this troubling night."

Dominic tensed, old pain welling, but Jimmy continued gently, "Yet you bear fresh burdens now for Willowbrook's sake. I know you will face them with courage, as your mother did."

Dominic's throat tightened with emotion. Jimmy had known his mother? He ached to ask for stories or memories, anything to feel closer to her.

"You knew my mother?" Dominic muttered.

Sensing his inner turmoil, Jimmy gave a sympathetic rumble. "Some tales keep better shelved a span longer," he rasped wisely. "Their time comes when the soul is prepared." He blinked up at Dominic. "For now, nurture the seeds planted this night. From them shall hope's blooms spring."

Dominic released a shaky breath and nodded. "You're right. Thank you, Jimmy."

Dwelling on the past brought only pain. He needed to stay focused on the future—and helping Willowbrook any way he could.

Jimmy eyed him with approval. But as Dominic made to stand, the cat's tail shot out to block his path. "A moment more, if you would."

Jimmy stood and padded over to a shadowed corner, returning with a musty tome in his jaws and depositing it at Dominic's feet expectantly.

Bemused, Christian picked up the book, brow furrowing as he turned it over. "It has no title. What is this, Jimmy?"

"Open it and see for yourself," the cat replied mysteriously.

Exchanging a curious glance with Dominic, Christian cracked the leather cover. His eyes widened as he scanned the first pages.

"These are…personal journals." Christian's tone was hushed with awe as he traced a finger down the faded ink. "Quite old by the script. But how did you come by such a rare artifact?"

Jimmy's eyes took on a faraway look. "In my long travels, I have acquired a number of singular texts. That one found its way to me many centuries past." He focused intently on Dominic and Christian again. "Its contents reveal many secrets…including accounts of the very first witch and vampire true mates."

Dominic's breath caught. He and Christian were the first in centuries to rediscover that profound bond. Jimmy's words hinted at vital knowledge within reach. He met Christian's equally intense gaze.

"What became of them?" Dominic asked.

Jimmy's tail swished agitatedly. "They shared a glorious, albeit brief, union. You see, never before or since have the apex of light and dark magic combined so powerfully." His tone turned grim. "Many feared what they could achieve together. The journal was smuggled to me before they were…executed."

Horrified understanding sank into Dominic's gut. If even fellow magic users had turned on those fated mates out of baseless fears, untold darkness awaited him and Christian, centuries later. His hands clenched at the thought.

Gently, Jimmy stepped between their tense forms. "Peace. I did not show you this to foster despair." He nudged the journal closer. "Study it well. For contained within are also secrets to unlocking the full potential of your bond." His yellow gaze was piercing. "You will need that strength for the trials ahead."

Unease skittered down Dominic's spine. "You believe Christian and I will face similar persecution?"

Jimmy sighed heavily. "The currents of history have strange eddies. But your magic entwined is unique in this age. There will always be those who fear the unknown." His eyes softened. "Yet the bond you share can overcome much. Let it be your compass."

Dominic hesitated. "Why show us the tragic past, if not as a warning?"

Jimmy moved front of them and sat back on his haunches. "Because you must fully bond, and quickly," he rasped urgently. "Your lifeforce will drain otherwise."

Christian tensed. "What do you mean? How is this the first I'm hearing of such a curse?"

Jimmy's gaze was solemn. "Witches long ago enacted it on any of their kind who bonded as a vampire's mate. A cruel trick to avoid dirtying their hands."

Horror washed over Dominic. "Is there nothing to be done?"

"There is hope yet." Jimmy flicked his tail. "Christian, you must seek guidance from your sire. He descended from the vampire in the journal."

Christian looked thoughtful. "It's possible. I know little of my lineage." His expression firmed with resolve. "But I will seek answers, if it saves my Dominic."

Dominic's legs nearly buckled in relief. Christian would find a way, he had no doubt. They only needed time.

Dominic and Christian walked out of the library, their minds swirling with unanswered questions. The revelation that Dominic's life force could potentially drain away if they didn't complete their bond soon weighed heavily, though Dominic tried not to let it show. He suspected Christian could feel his anxiety anyway.

They said their goodbyes to the others, promising to share any updates, then headed to Dominic's car for the ride home. The silence in the vehicle was deafening, Dominic's thoughts almost audible in the stillness. He needed to break it before he spiraled into overthinking.

"What did you make of what Jimmy said? About me dying?" Dominic asked solemnly.

Dominic noticed Christian's grip on the steering wheel tighten briefly before he responded. "I didn't anticipate that being a risk. I wasn't aware your life force could drain away."

"I'm not sure what to make of it either. But I know you won't let that happen to me," Dominic said, trying to be strong for them both.

Christian tenderly removed his right hand from the wheel and grasped Dominic's left, giving it a gentle, reassuring squeeze. "We'll figure this out together. I promise."

The remaining drive back to Dominic's place was quiet but less tense after their talk, the earlier unease dissipated.

"Let's stop at the bakery first so we can get my keys from Lyra," Dominic remembered.

Christian lifted Dominic's hand to his lips, kissing it softly before turning towards the bakery.

When they arrived at the bakery, Dominic checked in with Lyra to see how business had fared that day. She cheerfully updated him as she handed over the keys, and he thanked her sincerely for holding down the fort. He urged her to head home and get some well-deserved rest.

Before locking up for the evening, Dominic had an idea. He turned to Christian. "Come with me into the kitchen for a minute - I want to make something special."

Christian arched an eyebrow curiously but followed as Dominic led the way.

Once in the warm, fragrant kitchen, Dominic grabbed an apron and gestured for Christian to take a seat. "I've been working on developing some new recipes using magical ingredients. I think your coven will enjoy them."

As he moved about the kitchen gathering ingredients, Dominic spoke over his shoulder to Christian. "Baking has always been an escape for me. Everything else fades away, and I can lose myself in the process. It's soothing, even meditative in a way."

He began mixing and measuring, deftly combining aromatic spices and enchanted herbs. "Feeling the dough take shape under my hands, watching the alchemy as simple components meld into something wonderful…it gives me a deep sense of satisfaction."

Dominic glanced up to see Christian watching him work with a small, besotted smile. He felt his cheeks warm at the open admiration in the vampire's dark gaze.

"What inspired you to start baking?" Christian asked.

Dominic considered the question as he rolled out pastry dough. "I'm not really sure where my passion for baking came from. As you know, I never knew my mother - she passed away giving birth to me."

He was quiet for a moment, focused on cutting the dough into neat shapes. "Growing up, baking was a way for me to feel some connection to her. Imagining she might have enjoyed it too, that it was maybe even in my blood."

Dominic carefully placed the pastries on a baking sheet. "It started as a way to feel close to the mother I never met. Over time it became my own passion. Experimenting with recipes, discovering how flavors pair together - it's been incredibly rewarding. Now opening my own bakery has made a lifelong dream come true."

He glanced up at Christian with a small smile. "So in a way, baking has allowed me to feel closer to my mother's memory. But it has also helped me discover who I am, and what truly brings me happiness."

"Your passion is inspiring," he murmured. "I can tell how much joy baking brings you. Thank you for sharing that part of yourself with me."

Dominic turned in the circle of Christian's arms to face him, touched by his words. "Of course. I feel like I can be totally open with you." He tilted his face up for a sweet kiss.

When the timer dinged, Dominic pulled the fragrant pastries from the oven, giving Christian a playful swat when he tried to sneak one prematurely. "Patience! We have to let them cool or you'll burn your ancient vampire tongue," Dominic teased.

Christian stole a quick kiss instead, flashing a grin. "Worth it."

Dominic carefully packaged an assortment of magical pastries, tying them up in a nice box for Christian to take back to the coven. He carried the gift box with him as they made their way outside.

After locking the bakery door, Dominic presented the box to Christian with a flourish. "A little taste of sweet magic for you and your vampire friends. I hope you all enjoy!"

Christian accepted the gift with a smile. "How did I get so lucky to find someone as thoughtful and talented as you?" he murmured, pulling Dominic close again.

Under the moonlight, they exchanged a long, slow kiss, savoring the simplicity of being together.

After closing the bakery, they drove to Dominic's house. As soon as they approached the front door, excited barks could be heard from inside.

When they entered, Dominic's dog Vale bounded over, tail wagging eagerly. "Hey boy, did you miss us?"

Dominic greeted him affectionately, filling his food and water bowls. He and Christian took turns petting and fussing over the ecstatic dog.

Their eyes met over Vale's furry head, soft and full of longing. In a flash, they were in each other's arms, lips locked in a passionate kiss. Still embraced, they moved wordlessly to the bedroom and slowly undressed one other.

Dominic drank in the sight of Christian's chiseled pale form as his clothes fell away, raking his fingers appreciatively over the smooth marble skin. He trailed kisses down Christian's neck, feeling the steady pulse beneath his lips. Christian made quick work of Dominic's remaining garments, gaze roaming hungrily over his exposed body.

They tumbled onto the bed together in a tangle of limbs, kissing feverishly. Dominic sighed blissfully as Christian moved down his body, trailing warm lips along sensitive skin. He nipped teasingly at Dominic's collarbone with blunt teeth, careful not to pierce the delicate skin.

Dominic tangled his hands in Christian's dark locks, back arching off the bed as Christian took him in his mouth. Waves of pleasure coursed through Dominic's body. He moaned Christian's name desperately like a prayer, fingers twisting in silky hair.

After bringing Dominic to gasping completion, Christian claimed his mouth in a searing kiss. Dominic could taste himself on Christian's tongue as they explored each other deeply.

"I need you, Chris," Dominic whispered against his lips urgently.

Christian positioned himself at Dominic's entrance, onyx eyes boring intensely into emerald green. He entered Dominic in one smooth motion, pulling a low moan from his parted lips. They found an easy rhythm, bodies undulating together in sublime harmony.

Dominic clawed at Christian's strong back, urging him deeper, harder. Christian complied enthusiastically, commanding Dominic's body masterfully. Dominic cried out in ecstasy, the rest of the world falling away until nothing else existed but their union.

They climaxed as one, the wave crashing over them simultaneously. Dominic trembled in Christian's arms from the force of his release, panting and spent. Christian held him close, peppering his face with tender kisses as they floated back down to earth together.

After, they lay tangled in the sheets catching their breath, hearts thudding in tandem. Dominic nuzzled into the crook of Christian's neck contentedly.

"I wish we could stay like this always," Dominic murmured. Christian's arms tightened around him.

"Soon, my Dominic." Christian's voice was rich with promise. "After the bonding, we'll have eternity."

Dominic smiled dreamily at the thought. But the nagging unease from Jimmy's warning crept back in, the blissful high ebbing. He tensed involuntarily.

Sensing the change, Christian shifted to meet Dominic's eyes, brushing a hand through his tousled curls. "Talk to me. What's wrong?"

Dominic chewed his lip anxiously. "What if...what if we can't complete the bond in time? What if your bite ends up hurting me somehow instead of helping?"

Christian shook his head firmly, cupping Dominic's face in both hands. "I would never do anything to harm you, you must believe that. We'll take things slow, figure this out together. I'll speak with my sire again, consult the archives for more information. There has to be a safe way."

Dominic searched Christian's face, finding only sincerity and love reflected back. He felt foolish for doubting.

"You're right, I know you'd never intentionally hurt me. We'll work through this." Dominic tilted his chin up for a kiss, tension dissolving.

They exchanged languid kisses until Dominic's eyelids grew heavy with drowsiness. He settled against Christian's chest with a content sigh.

Christian stroked his hair soothingly. "Rest now, my sweet witch. You're safe in my arms."

Reassured, Dominic let his eyes drift shut, comforted by the steady thrum of Christian's heartbeat. The last thing he recalled before sleep claimed him was the tender press of lips to his forehead.

12

Hidden Truths

Christian

Christian lay awake watching over Dominic as he slept. Earlier, Dominic had been restless, in the throes of another nightmare. Christian hadn't been able to drift off since. He needed to ensure his mate was alright.

Mate. Christian smiled at the thought. He still could hardly believe Dominic had accepted him. Though challenges lay ahead, he knew in his core they would face them together.

Christian longed to keep vigil at Dominic's side, but he had urgent matters to see to, answers to uncover. Careful not to disturb him, Christian pressed a soft kiss to Dominic's forehead before rising.

At the motion, Dominic stirred, blinking sleepily. "Where you going?" he mumbled.

Christian chuckled at the adorable, drowsy question. "Back to sleep, sweetheart. I have to return home, get started finding solutions so we have some answers."

Dominic merely pulled the blanket over his head with a grumble. "M'kay. Call me later."

"I'll make breakfast first," Christian promised. This got Dominic's attention, and he emerged from his cocoon with an endearing pout.

"Eggs and bacon?"

Christian smiled, leaning in to steal a kiss. "Your favorites, of course."

After changing clothes, Christian headed for the kitchen, Vale shadowing him eagerly. He bent to give the dog's head an affectionate rub before continuing on.

Entering the sleek, modern kitchen, Christian took in the cozy surroundings. Sunlight streamed in from the window above the sink, giving the room a cheerful glow. Vale's food and water bowls sat in one corner on a cute dog-themed placemat.

On the refrigerator, a corkboard displayed photos of Dominic smiling with friends, his arm slung around their shoulders. Christian's gaze lingered on a "Found Dog" poster front and center.

The counters were gleaming granite, free of clutter save for a small knife block and fruit bowl. A vase of fresh daisies from the garden brightened up the space. The appliances were all stainless steel and looked barely used.

Opening cabinets, Christian located Vale's kibble and filled his bowl. As the dog crunched away happily, Christian gathered ingredients for Dominic's breakfast. He smiled to himself, imagining Dominic baking in this cheery kitchen, music playing as he whipped up tasty treats for the bakery.

Christian cooked the eggs and bacon in a cast iron skillet, the sizzling and aroma making his mouth water. The entire kitchen felt so warm, welcoming, and full of life, just like Dominic himself.

Covering the plate to keep Dominic's breakfast warm and safe from Vale's begging gaze, Christian did a quick scan for the leash, spying it hanging on a hook by the door. "Want to go for a walk, boy?" At the word "walk" Vale bounded over eagerly, tail wagging excitedly.

While clipping on the leash, Christian took in more details of

Dominic's cozy house. The furniture looked worn but comfortable, covered in plush blankets. Houseplants of all sizes lined the windowsills, soaking up the morning light. The air smelled faintly of cinnamon and vanilla.

On the living room wall, Christian noticed several framed photos. One in particular caught his eye - a beaming young Dominic with his arm slung around an older man who must be his father. Both had the same kind smile and bright green eyes. Christian wondered what had transpired between them since. He made a mental note to ask Dominic sometime.

Trailing his fingers over the plush couch as they headed for the door, Christian imagined curling up there with Dominic to watch movies, safe in each other's arms. Vale's enthusiastic bark at the door broke him from his daydream. After one last glance around the cozy space, they stepped out into the sunshine for their walk.

The park down the street was quiet this early, just a handful of fellow dog walkers out. Dew still clung to the grass, sparkling under the morning sun. Tall oak trees dotted the landscape, their branches rustling gently in the breeze.

A walking path wound through the park, past a duck pond and playground. Vale strained against his leash excitedly, eager to explore every inch. Christian let him lead the way down the path, taking in lungfuls of fresh air and soaking up the sunshine.

The playground was empty at this hour - no children yet to scale the climbing walls or swoop down the slides. A pair of ducks paddled lazily in the pond, rippling the surface. The only sound was birdsong and the occasional jingle of a dog tag.

It was peaceful, almost serene this early with just a few meandering people and dogs. Vale paused to sniff curiously at a patch of flowers, tail wagging happily. Christian gazed up at the cloudless blue sky, feeling calm wash over him. Starting the day with this walk had been a great idea.

Though risky, being out in the daylight invigorated Christian. He gazed up at the trees, watching birds flit from branch to branch. It was astonishing how many small moments of beauty existed in the world, so easy to overlook. Having Dominic in his life made Christian more attuned to them all.

Christian explained how the enchanted ring Dominic had gifted him made him feel almost human again. "I'd forgotten the simple joy of walking through the park on a sunny day, surrounded by people. It's nostalgic."

Vale's leash pulled taut as the dog investigated a nearby bush. After selecting the perfect spot, Vale circled and squatted to do his business.

Straightening up from affixing the waste bag, Christian noticed a woman approaching on the path. She smiled kindly at Vale.

"What a handsome fellow!" She scratched behind the dog's ears. "You must be very proud, he has a wonderful temperament."

"Thank you, he's a special one," Christian replied politely.

Though the comment was innocuous, something about the woman's presence felt oddly significant. Christian was certain he didn't recognize her, yet an aura of depth surrounded this stranger.

"Treasure each moment with your soul's companion," the woman advised cryptically. "As the Awakened Ones, they hold the key to the coming battle."

Christian's brow furrowed, perplexed. Before he could ask what she meant, the woman turned and meandered away down the path. Christian watched until she disappeared from view, uneasy feelings swirling.

Clipping the leash back on Vale's collar, Christian murmured "Let's get you home, boy."

The dog trotted along contentedly, oblivious to his master's disquiet. What had the woman's strange message signified? Christian's instinct told him her words held some deeper meaning, if only he could decipher it.

Back at Dominic's house, Christian refilled Vale's food and water bowls. "Guard the place, okay buddy?"

Vale responded by licking Christian's hand happily.

After leaving the note for Dominic, Christian locked up and headed out. His encounter with the mysterious woman still troubled him as he drove back to Dawncreek. Who was she, and what had she meant about him being the "Awakened One"?

Arriving home, Christian quickly showered and changed out of his suit - much as he disliked the restrictive garments, vampires were oddly fond of formal wear. He just didn't understand those antiquated customs. Shaking his head, Christian donned a fresh suit and headed out to the coven house to consult his sire.

Checking the dashboard clock, he knew Augustus would be awake by now. As one of the rare vampires able to tolerate sunlight, his sire often rose early. Christian envied his freedom to roam in the daytime without fear of burning. Some vampires really did have all the luck.

Pulling up to the gothic coven house, Christian had just entered the foyer when he nearly collided with Eros emerging from a side hall. Eros' handsome face broke into an unsettling grin that was likely intended to seem friendly. Christian tensed warily - this vampire had made past attempts on his life, though his motives remained cloudy.

"Christian, fancy running into you here," Eros purred in his peculiar accent. His amber eyes glinted with malice. "Do be careful. Accidents can happen so easily these nights."

Christian tensed, unnerved by the thinly-veiled threat. "What exactly is that supposed to mean, Eros?"

Eros tapped his chin in mock thought. "Oh, just that a lone vampire could easily find himself in peril. Particularly one lacking allies." His smile didn't reach his cold eyes.

"If you're planning something against me or my mate-" Christian began heatedly, taking a step towards the other vampire.

Eros held up his hands in faux innocence. "Now now, don't be so suspicious. I merely worry for your safety, old friend." The endearment dripped with sarcasm.

"We are not friends," Christian spat. "Stay away from Dominic."

With an inscrutable smile, Eros brushed past him and out the front door, leaving Christian shaken. That vampire was unpredictable, but Christian knew to be on guard for when he finally pounced. Shaking off the uneasy encounter, he continued on to the library in search of his sire.

Christian found Augustus seated in a leather armchair near the fireplace at the far end of the cavernous library. Tendrils of fragrant cigar smoke wreathed his head, accentuating his distinguished and timeless features.

Though Augustus did not turn to look at him, he greeted Christian in his refined tone, "Back so soon, my childe?"

Christian's footsteps were muffled by the thick Persian rug spanning the space between towering oak bookshelves. The shelves rose two stories high on either side of the room, crammed to overflowing with leather-bound tomes and ornate scrolls. Christianity inhaled the scent of parchment, old paper, and seasoned wood that permeated the space.

Above, the ceiling was dominated by an exquisite mural depicting mythological scenes of vampire lore - pale figures locked in combat with winged beasts and other supernatural creatures. The paint had cracked and faded over untold centuries, but the images yet retained their power.

As Christian drew nearer the fireplace, its warmth washed over him, chasing away the perpetual chill that lingered in the underground manor. The only other light came from an ornate candelabra resting on a long table, its wavering glow barely making a dent in the cavernous gloom. Heavy velvet drapes blocked out any natural light.

Despite the library's imposing grandeur, the space had a comforting intimacy. Generations had sought refuge here among the accumulated wisdom of ages past. How many hours had Augustus himself passed in this room, Christian wondered, perusing ancient texts or reflecting in solitude? The armchair where he now reclined looked indented by centuries of use.

The sheer quantity of books was overwhelming. Volumes were crammed horizontally atop those already lining the shelves, making the stacks extremely precarious. Scrolls bound in ribbons spilled from baskets on the floor. No orderly cataloging system was discernible. It would take eons to simply read every title.

Yet somehow Augustus could instantly locate any desired work within the teetering literary labyrinth. Christian imagined him passing long nights ensconced here poring over some crumbling manuscript, searching for hidden kernels of knowledge. Though windowless and cavernous, this library was a sanctuary - the heart of the coven's ancestral home.

Now Christian stood at its center, searching not for written wisdom, but for secrets harbored in Augustus' long memory. The answers he sought would not be found on parchment or in leather-bound volumes, but in his sire's ancient heart. Words passed in this room would reshape Christian's understanding of his lineage and illuminate the path forward.

This hallowed chamber had witnessed centuries of vampire history unfold. Soon it would witness the next chapter in that enduring saga. With measured steps Christian approached the fireplace, waiting for Augustus to unburden the long-shrouded truth of his past. Though centuries had elapsed, this place would remember.

"Yes, I was hoping you could provide some guidance," Christian began, moving closer.

"Let me ask you something first," Augustus interjected, gaze still on the flickering flames. "Were you to regret my turning you all those years ago, what would you do?"

Christian blinked, surprised by the sudden serious inquiry. But he answered honestly, "I could never regret it. You saved me from the grip of the plague. My human life was fading - you gave me a second chance."

Finally facing Christian, Augustus gave a small smile. "Just as I thought. You have a good heart. Now then, tell me what brings you here today." He gestured for Christian to sit.

Christian removed an old leather journal from his bag. "I was hoping you could provide some insight about this."

He explained it contained the writings of the first witch and vampire true mates, and how their story might relate to his own bond with Dominic.

Augustus stood abruptly, eyeing the journal with sudden intensity. "May I examine that book?"

Christian hesitated, unsettled by his sire's intense reaction. Augustus was not one to show uncertainty. Ever. Reluctantly, Christian passed the journal over.

As Augustus pored over the aged pages, his stern expression softened. Christian thought he spotted a glimmer of wetness in the ancient vampire's dark eyes.

"Did you know them?" Christian prodded gently. "The two who wrote this?"

Augustus simply nodded, seeming lost in memories. Then, wordlessly, he left the room, returning minutes later with an ornate necklace dangling from his grasp.

Sitting beside Christian, Augustus spoke solemnly. "The witch and vampire bonded pair from this journal were named Anna and Henry Driscoll. And yes, I knew them very well. Henry was...my brother."

Christian's eyes widened at this revelation. Augustus rarely spoke of his human life.

"Anna was the most powerful witch of her age," Augustus continued. "Henry, a respected vampire scholar. Despite the taboo, they fell deeply in love. I did not care about outdated traditions - I supported their union. When Anna conceived, I was overjoyed at the chance to be an uncle."

His voice grew pained. "But the Covens discovered the pregnancy and relationship. They accused Anna and Henry of heresy for defying convention. I tried to protect them, but the Covens were determined to make an example."

Augustus paused, clearly still haunted. "They were captured and executed publicly - beheaded before my helpless eyes. It nearly destroyed me. Before she died, Anna entrusted me with two things: this necklace, and the task of protecting their child."

Christian sat in stunned silence, moved by this heartbreaking history. Gently, he asked, "What became of the child?"

Meeting Christian's gaze tenderly, Augustus answered, "He grew up safely, hidden away in the human world. Until he was a man grown and fate delivered him to my doorstep once more."

As comprehension dawned, Christian's fingers closed around the necklace, mind reeling. "Me? I'm...I'm their son?"

Augustus grasped his shoulder with sudden fierceness. "Anna and Henry loved you more than life itself. They wished only for your safety and happiness. As do I."

Overwhelmed, Christian asked how any of this was possible, given the circumstances of his human upbringing and turning.

Patiently, Augustus explained, "After your birth, Anna and Henry made the wrenching choice to surrender you to me for safekeeping. I in turn gave you to a kindly mortal family, far from here. It was necessary to conceal you, though it tore me apart to do so."

He went on, "I kept watch over you from afar your whole childhood. And when plague befell your village, I turned you not solely to save your life, but to finally reunite family. Your true lineage had to remain secret until now."

Reeling from these profound revelations, Christian looked down at the necklace - the only remnant of the parents he never knew. "I wish I could have met them," he said quietly.

Augustus tilted his chin up firmly. "In a way, you still can. Anna and Henry yet live."

Christian's head jerked up in shock. "How is that possible? You said they were executed!"

"Not permanently destroyed," Augustus clarified solemnly. "The Covens believed Anna and Henry were executed that day. But it was not truly them."

He went on, "With a necromancer's aid, they created decoys - corpses imbued with traces of their life essence to pass as them. While the decoys were beheaded publicly, Anna and Henry escaped into hiding."

Christian's head spun with this new information. "Where have they been all this time? Are they even still alive?" he asked urgently.

Augustus grabbed a piece of parchment, scribbling something down. "I have finally discovered their location after all these years. But we must take care - the Covens remain suspicious, and likely have spies everywhere."

He pressed the paper into Christian's hand. "Memorize this, then burn it. Tell no one except your mate. The necklace is yours now - keep it safe always."

Christian's hand closed tightly around the precious jewelry. He committed the address to memory before setting the parchment alight with a quick incantation.

Augustus gripped his shoulder, expression grave. "Finding your parents will be dangerous. But you possess great courage and strength, qualities befitting Anna and Henry's son. Trust your instincts."

As Christian turned to leave, a troubling thought halted him. "Wait. There is more I must ask."

He hesitated before continuing delicately. "When a witch bonds with a vampire, I've learned their lifeforce can begin draining away. Dominic may be in danger from some ancient curse. Do you know anything of this?"

Augustus' expression turned grim. After a weighty pause, he spoke. "You refer to the Witches Coven's retribution against vampiric mating. Yes, I know of it, though have scarce wisdom to undo such powerful magic."

Christian felt a spike of fear for Dominic, but pressed on. "Is there nothing to be done? Some means of delaying the effects perhaps?"

Augustus considered for a long moment. Finally he replied, "There may be a way to slow the draining, buy some precious time. But the knowledge lies solely with Anna and Henry."

Seeing Christian's crestfallen look, Augustus gripped his shoulder firmly. "Take heart. My brother and Anna will surely help you and your mate. They will be overjoyed to know their son has found love, despite all opposition."

Christian clung to this scant hope like a lifeline. Still, uncertainty gnawed at him. "What if we are too late?"

Sensing his desperation, Augustus met his eyes steadily. "Have faith. You possess a power beyond your knowing, passed down from two peerless bloodlines. Trust in your destiny."

With immense effort, Christian calmed his fraying nerves. Augustus was right - he had strength enough for this task. And Dominic was no helpless maid. Together they would uncover the knowledge needed to preserve their bond.

Still, the sooner he freed his parents, the better. Each passing hour heightened the peril to Dominic's lifeforce. Steadying his resolve, Christian embraced Augustus once more.

"I will find them," he vowed solemnly. "And once our family is whole again, we will lift this wretched curse."

Augustus clasped his shoulder tightly. "Of that I have no doubt."

With a final determined nod, Christian hurried out the door into the fading afternoon light. The path ahead would be fraught with dangers untold. But the time had come to confront his destiny. For Dominic's sake, and for the family he had only just discovered, he could not fail now.

13

Change of Heart

Dominic

Vale happily licked Dominic's hand as they stood outside the imposing iron gates of the coven house, his leash held loosely in Dominic's grip. They'd just come from the veterinarian's office where, thankfully, Vale got a clean bill of health.

Dominic had been on the verge of posting "Found dog" flyers for Vale around town. But no one had come forward looking for him, and the dog had happily settled into life with Dominic. It seemed meant to be.

The late morning sun beat down unrelentingly. A trickle of sweat ran down Dominic's neck as he stared up at the Gothic style building that loomed before them. He still wasn't sure why he felt compelled to come here again seeking answers, but some instinct had drawn him. They needed to find solutions, and their coven held knowledge passed down through generations.

Vale panted up at Dominic, tongue lolling. With a deep breath, Dominic gave the leash a gentle tug. "Come on boy, it's all or nothing now."

Vale barked as if in agreement and they made their way up the winding path to the imposing double doors. Dominic's heart pounded, but he ignored his nerves. Answers were inside somewhere, he just had to be brave enough to seek them out.

The cool shade of the covered entryway was a relief after the hot exposed walk. Dominic raised a shaking hand to grasp the ornate door knocker, its dull metal shape like a roaring dragon's head. The sound of it echoed through the stone chambers within.

Dominic noticed dark circles under Lee's eyes. "Hey, you alright? You're not looking too good…"

Lee started to reply then stopped, shaking his head as if to clear it. "Nevermind. Did you need something?"

Dominic decided not to push it. "Are Father and Lina around? I need to speak with them."

Lee stepped back, nodding reluctantly. As Vale entered, his melancholy seemed to lift and he bent to pet the dog affectionately. Dominic was struck by this uncharacteristically gentle behavior from Lee.

"I'll leave Vale with you while I talk to Father," Dominic offered, sensing they could both benefit from the dog's calming presence right now. Lee just nodded, not taking his eyes off Vale.

Back then, Lee had been like the big brother Dominic always wanted, bringing him snacks while gaming and letting him feel included. They'd drifted apart over years of simmering resentment on Lee's side. But seeing him just now, Dominic felt hopeful they could mend things.

Dominic made his way through the achingly familiar house to his Father's home office. As he passed the living room, he remembered nights playing video games there with Lee, before bitterness took over him due to Lina's influence.

Dominic felt an odd chill in the air that hadn't been there on his last visit. The hairs on his arm prickled uneasily. It was as if the very magic was being drained out of his body in this space - the energy felt wrong, tainted somehow.

Unease stirring in his gut, Dominic quickened his pace down the hall. The warm nostalgia that had gripped him earlier rapidly slipped away, replaced by a cold sense of wrongness. This was not the home he remembered.

The playful laughter of no longer seemed to echo from these walls. No more lingering scent of fresh-baked cookies or comfort. Only a bone-deep sense of something vital missing hung in the air now.

Dominic shivered, the change suddenly so acute. It was like the soul had been hollowed out from the house itself. Try as he might, Dominic could not pinpoint the source of the shift. But every instinct screamed for him to grab what he needed swiftly, and flee this increasingly oppressive place.

Resisting the urge to glance back over his shoulder, Dominic strode purposefully onward. He would get the information he came for, and then not return here again if he could help it. This cold shell was no longer a home - it was merely a structure housing dark secrets he intended to uncover, before making his escape.

Dominic hesitated outside the office door. Raised voices filtered out - the shrill tone of his stepmother mixed with his father's lower rumble. This had become an all too common sound in the coven house.

Steeling himself, Dominic knocked firmly and entered.

His father sat behind the heavy oak desk, looking haggard. Dark circles ringed his eyes and his face had a grayish cast. Lina stood over him, hands on hips, berating him in a grating voice. At Dominic's entrance, they both cut off and turned to him in surprise.

"Dominic?" His Father's eyes flickered with wariness. "To what do we owe the pleasure?" His words dripped sarcasm.

Dominic's gut twisted. The father he knew would have greeted him with a smile, maybe a lame joke. This weary stranger made him want to turn and flee the room.

Instead he took a deep breath. "I heard you guys arguing. Figured I should check it out."

Lina gave a nasal laugh. "Don't play dumb. We both know you were eavesdropping." She shook her head, the motion setting her dangling earrings swinging. "Nosy as always."

Dominic bit back a retort, his gaze shifting to his Father who at least had the grace to look abashed.

"Lina and I were just…discussing family business." His father said sternly.

"Family business?" Dominic raised his eyebrows. "Meaning coven business? Something you've apparently been keeping from me?"

He didn't bother hiding the bite in his tone. His father winced.

"Now you listen here, young man," Lina snapped. "You lost the right to know confidential information when you went against the coven. Cavorting with vampires? Have you forgotten who our enemies are?"

Dominic bristled. "Christian isn't my enemy. I don't care what ridiculous vendetta you have against his kind." He crossed his arms. "And last I checked, the coven was about protecting people. So I think I deserve to know what you're hiding, since it could impact the whole community."

His father and Lina exchanged a look. She pursed her lips, eyes flashing, and gave a slight nod.

Sighing, his father passed a hand over his face. "You're right. You should know." He sat up straighter in his chair. "There are dark forces gathering, Dominic. The ley lines in this area have been disturbed. Lina and I were tasked with reinforcing the protections on them."

Dominic acted surprised, pretending this was the first he was hearing about it. Still, he wanted to hear the truth from his father and Lina directly.

"What happened to the lines?" he asked, layering innocence into his tone. "And who put you in charge of guarding them?"

His father shared another glance with Lina, whose face remained stony. Turning back to Dominic, he continued. "The ley lines were damaged by an outside force. We don't know the specifics yet…only that the energy flow has been disrupted. It's our job to repair the wards and restore balance."

"So you let the Wellspring be compromised?" Dominic accused.

Lina sneered at him. "You gave up the right to know. This duty falls to the next heir now."

Dominic clenched his fists and turned to his father. "I don't understand why you didn't just tell me in the first place."

"It wasn't your concern anymore," Lina said coldly.

Dominic looked between his father and Lina, suspicion rising. "Do Lee and Austin know about the issues with the ley lines?"

Lina spoke up before his father could respond. "Of course they do," she said sharply. "As potential future leaders of this coven, they have every right." She shot his father a pointed look that Dominic didn't miss. "In fact, the boys have been integral to maintaining the wards thus far. It's vital preparation for whichever one of them ultimately inherits control."

Dominic felt like he'd been punched in the gut. He turned on his father angrily. "Is this true? You've brought them into this, are grooming them to take over, without ever telling me?"

His father held up a placating hand. "Son, please try to understand. Your destiny was here once, but you turned away from that path. We did what we felt was best…"

Lina cut in. "Yes, and now the duty falls to your brothers. One of them will make a fine leader someday." Her tone left no doubt who she favored.

Dominic felt his anger swell. "I'm not against them being heirs," he responded. "But you both need to know - I'm the rightful person to lead here." He turned to Lina, eyes flashing. "I won't let you tarnish what my mother and father built over the years. This is my legacy."

Lina clicked her tongue derisively. "I see that vampire of yours is already corrupting you. We warned you against continuing to fraternize with him."

"I know all about your curses and threats," Dominic shot back. "But nothing can make me turn my back on Christian. It won't work."

"Dominic…" His father started.

Dominic turned to his father, heart heavy with disappointment. "I don't even recognize you anymore, letting her poison our family this way. But I hope someday you'll remember who you truly are."

For a brief moment, his father looked stricken, regret plain on his face. Perhaps there was still hope of reaching the man buried beneath Lina's machinations.

Without another word, Dominic turned and strode out of the office, refusing to waste any more time or breath. He had said what needed saying. All that remained was to walk away with his head held high, leaving their schemes and negativity behind.

His true destiny lay elsewhere now.

Exiting the house, Dominic nearly collided with Lee lurking right outside the office door. Dominic suppressed a groan - he was in no mood for his step-brother's nonsense right now.

"What do you want, Lee?" he asked wearily.

Lee held up his hands in a placating gesture. "I'm not here to mess with you, I swear. Just listen - meet me at your bakery later tonight, okay? I've got some stuff I need to tell you."

Dominic eyed him warily. "Is this another of your stupid pranks with Austin? Because I'm not interested."

"No tricks this time," Lee insisted, tone sincere. "Please, just meet up with me. I know I've been a crap step-brother, but…" He trailed off meaningfully.

Taken aback by Lee's uncharacteristic vulnerability, Dominic found himself relenting. "Alright, fine. But this is your only chance - if you stand me up, we're done for good."

Lee nodded. "Fair enough. And...thanks. It's all I can ask." He stepped aside so Dominic could pass.

Collecting Vale, Dominic stepped outside, emotions still churning. As he took a deep breath, dark clouds swirled ominously overhead.

Dominic froze. Usually his own moods influenced the weather patterns, being the only weather witch in town. But he hadn't consciously summoned this storm. If anything, he felt his magic depleted after the confrontation.

The wind picked up speed, leaves swirling wildly around him. Vale whined and pressed close as lightning forked the gloom. Dominic's unease grew - his power had never manifested like this before. He could predict storms, but not create them fully formed.

Focusing inward, Dominic assessed his magic. To his shock, it felt charged, thrumming with power. This went against his sense of being emotionally drained.

Vale nudged Dominic's hand with his snout. At the contact, Dominic gasped as the energy surge instantly dissipated. The winds calmed and the dark clouds evaporated unnaturally fast, sunlight peeking through.

Bewildered, Dominic looked down at Vale. "What did you just do, boy? What are you?" The dog just barked, tail wagging as he licked Dominic's hand. As bizarre as it seemed, Vale had somehow absorbed the magical overflow.

Dominic shook his head in disbelief. First the uncontrolled storm, now this. His magic was behaving in ways he'd never experienced before. Where had that sudden influx of energy come from?

Glancing around warily, he saw no obvious cause. For now, the crisis seemed to have passed. But Dominic remained rattled. Between the ley line issues and this new magical instability, everything felt off-balance.

With Vale happily trotting beside him, Dominic continued on to the bakery, keeping his metaphysical senses alert for any further anomalies. But nothing seemed amiss now.

He had no clear answers, only worrisome questions. Dominic sighed, shoulders slumping. For the moment, all he could do was remain vigilant and hope the strange storm was an isolated incident. In the meantime, he'd be keeping a close eye on his canine companion. Vale clearly had hidden depths.

Arriving at the cheery bakery, Dominic was greeted by the comforting bustle of customers chatting over steaming drinks and pastries. He spotted his trusty staffer Lyra seamlessly toggling between taking orders at the register and frothing up lattes behind the counter.

Lyra glanced up and a smile lit up her flour-smudged face when she saw Dominic. He waited for a lull in the morning rush before waving her over.

"You're doing amazing holding down the fort, Lyra! Why don't you take your break?"

"You sure you don't need help first?" Lyra asked. "It's been non-stop all morning!"

Dominic placed a hand on her shoulder. "I've got this. You deserve a breather."

Noticing Vale peeking out from behind Dominic's legs, Lyra gasped. "Oh my gosh, who's this cutie?" She immediately dropped to her knees to scruffle the dog's fur affectionately. Vale soaked up the attention happily.

"Lyra, meet Vale, my new roommate," Dominic said, laughing at her reaction. "Go ahead and take fifteen minutes to get acquainted."

Looking up with a brilliant smile, Lyra threw her arms around Dominic in an effusive hug. "You're the absolute best, you know that?"

Dominic gently extracted himself from her grip. "It's you that's the superstar employee here. In fact, I'm giving you a raise for all your hard work!"

Lyra's eyes went wide. "Are you serious? Oh my god, thank you!" She looked ready to tackle him in another jubilant embrace before remembering she was on the clock. With an excited little squeal, Lyra hurried to grab her lunch from the back, Vale following at her heels.

Chuckling and shaking his head, Dominic headed to the kitchen to assess supplies. The morning rush had depleted the baked goods. He did a quick inventory of what needed replenishing.

Dominic decided some fresh loaves of his famous Winter Flower Bread were in order. It was a beloved recipe incorporating juicy berries harvested by Mr. Lidel, infused with the elve's own subtle earth magic as he kneaded the dough. The result was a fluffy, fragrant loaf that sold out daily.

Donning his favorite apron, Dominic swiftly laid out the necessary ingredients - flour, yeast, salt, and a touch of honey for sweetness. The smooth wooden work surface had been generously dusted with flour. Dominic inhaled deeply, the very scent transporting.

With practiced motions, Dominic combined the dry ingredients in a large bowl, making a well in the center before incorporating the wet. As he mixed and kneaded, feeling the dough become elastic under his fingers, Dominic softly recited a magical incantation, focusing his energy on infusing the bread.

Once the dough was smooth and no longer sticky, he set it in a warm place to rise, draping a clean towel over top. During the resting period, the yeast would produce air bubbles, making the dough light and airy. This was Dominic's favorite part of the process. The alchemy never ceased to amaze him.

While the dough proved, Dominic washed the bowls and utensils, leaving his work station pristine for the next steps. He hummed quietly, movements fluid and unhurried. Baking required patience, but the slow rituals centered him.

After the allotted rise time, Dominic turned the dough out onto a floured surface. He divided it into portions, gently shaping each into a taut round. The distinct floral scent of the magical berries now permeated the dough. Dominic inhaled their delicate perfume as he worked.

He placed the rounds in oiled loaf pans, then covered them once more for the second rise. As they plumped up, Dominic prepared the oven, allowing it to fully preheat. Once the loaves had doubled in size, they were ready to be baked, the yeast having created air pockets that would expand in the heat.

Dominic slid the fragrant loaves into the hot oven, setting a timer. The bakery's kitchen was filled with the comforting aroma of freshly baking bread. The familiar scents and motions of his craft brought calm after the day's turmoil. Here in his element, Dominic felt soothed and grounded.

By the time Lyra returned, looking refreshed, Dominic had replenished the bakery's stock just in time for the midday rush. He greeted customers while Lyra manned the counter, marveling again at her cheery efficiency. The girl really deserved that raise.

As the lunch crowd filtered out, Dominic retreated to the kitchen with Vale snoozing happily nearby. He had a couple hours before Lee was set to arrive. Time enough to prepare himself mentally for whatever revelations lay ahead. The answers were still elusive, but Dominic felt certain he could handle what came next. Centered in his sanctuary kitchen with Vale at his side, he was ready.

As evening approached, Dominic kept one eye on the bakery's clock. Lee was due to arrive soon, if he actually showed. At five minutes to closing, there was still no sign of him.

Dominic sighed, hoping Lee wouldn't stand him up. He started closing procedures, sending Lyra home with his thanks for another great day. After cleaning the kitchen and shutting off the lights, Dominic flipped the sign to "Closed" and settled at a table with Vale to wait, phone in hand.

With a few minutes to spare, Dominic decided to call Christian, missing the sound of his mate's voice. Christian picked up on the first ring, bringing an instinctive smile to Dominic's face.

"Hey you," Dominic greeted warmly. "We never got to have our date last night, everything got so crazy…"

"I know, love. Rain check for tonight?" Christian asked hopefully.

Dominic grimaced. "Actually I'm waiting on my step-brother Lee. He wanted to talk, said it was important."

Christian's tone turned concerned. "Do you need me there? Given your history, I don't like you meeting him alone."

"I appreciate the offer, but I should handle this myself," Dominic replied. "Lee promised he has information about the something. It could prove useful."

"If you're certain…" Christian still sounded reluctant. "Call if anything feels off, and I'll be there in a flash."

"I will, don't worry." Dominic glanced up as the bakery's door chimed. "Speak of the devil, he just walked in. I'll call you later!"

Dominic ended the call and pocketed his phone as Lee approached the table apprehensively. Up close, Dominic noticed again how unwell his step-brother appeared - face drawn, shoulders slumped in fatigue. Pity stirred in him.

"Have a seat, Lee. Can I get you a coffee or pastry?" Dominic offered gently. Lee shook his head, perching stiffly on the chair.

"N-No. I am good, thank you." Lee said who and Dominic heard the uncertainty in his voice.

An awkward silence stretched until Dominic prompted, "You wanted to talk?"

Lee nodded, not quite meeting his eyes. He seemed to be gathering courage. Finally he spoke, voice low and urgent.

Lee took a deep, shaky breath before speaking in a hushed tone. "A couple days ago, mother had Austin deliver some package to another coven, like he was just a delivery boy. But he hasn't come back, and she's being all weirdly cryptic about it."

Dominic's brow furrowed. "What does that have to do with me though?"

"I got worried, so I went to check out where Austin was supposedly going that night," Lee explained. "Near the old clearing, I felt some seriously dark magical vibes. Like a soul sacrifice had happened there."

Dominic's eyes widened in surprise. He hadn't realized Lee was sensitive to such things. "Are you saying you're a…a necromancer?" he asked carefully.

Lee hesitated before giving a slight nod, not quite meeting his gaze. "Never told anyone before. But with Austin missing, I had to use my abilities to try picking up clues."

Being discovered as a necromancer had severe consequences in their community. Necromancy was viewed as unethical, a perversion of natural magic. Those found practicing it were harshly punished and shunned.

Dominic knew there would be dire repercussions if Lee's abilities were revealed. Their society allowed little room for understanding with certain gifts. Lee would be exiled at best, if not worse.

It was a heavy secret to bear alone. Dominic understood why Lee had concealed his power, though it must have been painful and isolating. Their world was often unforgiving of those seen as different or dangerous.

Dominic hoped in time attitudes could shift, that a spirit of openness and acceptance could emerge. But for now, secrecy remained Lee's only security. It was a burden Dominic now shared, and he took the responsibility seriously. This knowledge could ruin Lee's life if it got out.

Dominic understood the risk Lee had taken confiding something so taboo. "Your secret is safe with me. I'm glad you felt you could trust me after...everything between us."

Lee's shoulders lost a fraction of their tense set. "Thanks. That means a lot. Anyway, the sacrificed soul wasn't Austin's - we're twins, so I'd know if he was dead. But something messed up is going on."

Dominic nodded thoughtfully. As twins, Lee and Austin shared a profound soul bond. If Austin had been killed, Lee would have felt it deeply.

"I'm sorry for how things went between us growing up," Lee said gruffly. "Resenting you for dad remarrying so soon after your mom passed...I somehow took it out on you unfairly. Truce?" He extended a hand hesitantly.

Dominic considered for a moment before shaking Lee's hand. If he was telling the truth about Austin, they would need to work together. "Truce. But no more lies, or the deal is off," Dominic warned. "Now, let's make a plan to find Austin..."

14

Blood Ties

Christian

Christian drove to meet Dominic, feeling anxious about the revelations he needed to share. He knew discussing it over the phone was too risky with the Council possibly listening in.

As he made his way to the diner, Christian reflected on his immortal life. Centuries of being despised and mistrusted for what he was had hardened him. But he recalled his parents' words, "No matter how dark life becomes, light still finds a way through."

That flicker of light had been elusive for so long. Until Dominic rekindled that spark in his soul. His mate made Christian feel accepted, loved, and hopeful - feelings long forgotten. Dominic was a ray of sunshine in his shadowed existence.

Now, with danger looming, Christian clung to cautious optimism. Whatever they might face together, Dominic would stand steadfastly by his side. And Christian would protect the life and love they were building, no matter the cost.

For the first time in forever, Christian felt part of something real and good. No matter how hard and dark the coming days, that guiding light would endure. Dominic had awakened parts of his battered heart Christian thought forever lost. He would fight with his last breath to keep that tentative light from being extinguished.

Christian's thoughts turned to the parents who had raised him, so lovingly. They had shaped him profoundly. It was their kindness and wisdom that buoyed him through long lonely years.

Now, Christian would finally have the chance to know his real parents, Anna and Henry. The revelation had left him reeling. After endless time apart, he still yearned for that connection.

It would not be easy - centuries separated them now. And awakening old wounds could bring more heartache. Yet something in Christian longed to understand where he came from, this missing piece of himself. He hoped to find even an echo of belonging with them.

His parents would forever hold a cherished place in his heart. But Anna and Henry also deserved the chance to reclaim their son, however late. Christian was ready to let them in, to discover together what still could be.

Perhaps it was a fool's hope. But Dominic had taught him wishes can come true, against all odds. With his mate's steady strength, Christian felt braced to withstand whatever awaited in this reconcilement. For too long, his true lineage had been denied. It was time to reclaim that lost heritage, in all its messy humanity. The past was prologue - now Christian would write their future.

He parked his car in front of the quaint diner, its windows emitting a warm glow in the early morning light. Stepping out onto the sidewalk, Christian took in the inviting facade - chalkboard sign out front boasting fresh pie and daily specials, flower boxes overflowing with cheery petunias.

Despite the early hour, customers already bustled in and out, keeping the small space lively. The scent of sizzling bacon and roasted coffee beans wafted through the open door as Christian entered. His sensitive hearing picked up the clink of cutlery and murmur of lively conversations beneath the jaunty music piping through speakers.

"Christian, over here!" He spotted Dominic waving eagerly from the bar area where patrons waited to be seated.

Christian's face broke into an instinctive smile as he crossed the room in a few quick strides to sweep Dominic into a passionate kiss, heedless of the public setting. Their joyful laughter mingled, a soothing balm to Christian's earlier unease.

"Ready for some breakfast?" Dominic asked, eyes dancing.

Though vampires subsisted on blood, Christian enjoyed sharing meals with his mate, savoring food's flavors and textures even if its nutritional value was lost on him.

A kindly waitress named Gem who clearly knew Dominic as a regular stopped by their table.

"The usual spot, Dom?" At his confirming nod, she led them to a booth beside the sunlit front windows.

After the waitress left, a comfortable silence settled between them. Christian cherished these quiet moments with Dominic, simply being together. Before diving into weighty topics, they lingered over coffee and breakfast, chatting lightly about plans for the weekend.

Eventually Dominic asked, "Did you uncover anything new on your end?" His tone was casual but gaze intent.

Christian set down his coffee mug. "I did. My sire revealed some startling information about my parents."

He went on to briefly explain his biological parents, Anna and Henry, may still be alive.

Dominic's eyes widened in surprise, then softened with empathy. "That's wonderful you could reunite, though surely complicated. I'm happy for you, Christian." His sincerity warmed Christian's heart.

"I'd like you there when I attempt to find them, if you're willing? I confess, the thought rather daunts me," Christian admitted.

Dominic covered Christian's hand with his own. "Of course, I'll be by your side. We're in this together now."

His simple vow meant the world to Christian. With Dominic, any feat felt possible.

After a pause, Christian asked about Dominic's own search for answers with his family. Dominic sighed heavily, updating Christian on the dead-end visit and Austin's troubling disappearance.

"I'll help however I can, we'll get to the bottom of this," Christian assured him. Dominic gave a small grateful smile at the offer.

After discussing Austin, Dominic asked, "Have you decided when you'll go check out the address your sire gave you? To find your parents?"

Christian considered. "I was thinking perhaps today, if you're free to join me?" He wanted Dominic's steady presence for courage.

Dominic nodded. "The bakery's closed on Sundays anyway. Where is this place located?"

"A town called Moonriff, a couple hours drive from here," Christian replied. He'd done thorough research on the remote area.

Dominic's eyes suddenly lit up. "Or we could portal there, if you're open to magical travel? It's fast and direct."

Christian quirked an eyebrow, intrigued. "Is that within your abilities?"

"Not me, but my friend Roan is an incredibly gifted fae. He could get us there instantly," Dominic explained with a grin.

Now Christian was even more fascinated. "You've never mentioned a Roan before. I look forward to meeting this talented friend of yours."

Dominic laughed. "Finish your oatmeal, then we'll swing by Adrian and Ben's place to pick up Roan. He'll be our ride to Moonriff."

After settling the bill, they headed out into the golden morning light. Christian felt bolstered by their easy rapport - with Dominic by his side, he could accomplish anything. Even face the ghosts of his distant past.

Dominic directed Christian to drive to Ben and Adrian's imposing but cozy manor house. Along the way, Dominic called Ben to give a heads up.

"Hey Ben, is Roan around? We could use his help," Dominic said casually.

Christian easily overheard Ben's response with his heightened senses.

"Oh really? What do you need him for this time?" Ben asked, tone laced with concern.

Dominic just chuckled. "I'll explain when we get there, don't worry." After they hung up, he turned to Christian. "Ben gets anxious whenever someone requests Roan's skills. He's overprotective."

Christian nodded in understanding. "What exactly is Roan's gift? I know he's a fae and all that." He was very curious to meet this new friend of Dominic's.

"You'll see. Let's have him explain," Dominic replied mysteriously.

Christian's interest was truly piqued now.

They soon pulled up the winding drive to Ben and Adrian's sprawling manor house. Ben stood waiting on the front steps, breaking into a grin and wave at their approach. After warm greetings, Dominic inquired about Roan.

"He's out back practicing with Jimmy and Merin," Ben explained, ushering them inside.

"Where's Adrian?" Dominic asked as they walked inside the manor.

"Checking out a vision lead with Margaret," Ben explained. "One of Merin's visions had revealed another potential seer near Willow-brook."

Stepping into the massive backyard, they spotted a lean, muscular man with jet black hair wielding an ornate spear, sparring against

Merin's glowing bow. Jimmy lounged nearby, casually grooming his fur.

"Roan!" Ben called. The dark-haired man turned, revealing handsome features and warm brown eyes.

Dominic introduced him as Roan. Christian stepped forward to shake Roan's hand in greeting.

"We were hoping to talk with you about something," Ben explained. "Let's chat in Adrian's office."

Roan nodded agreeably. "Sounds good, just let me grab a quick shower first and change. I'm all sweaty from training."

"Of course, take your time!" Dominic said.

They made their way inside while Roan went to freshen up. Christian settled into one of the plush leather chairs in Adrian's study to wait. Soon Roan would return, and they could explain their request for his mystical assistance.

Christian drummed his fingers impatiently - answers were so close now. Yet a bit longer patience was required before their journey through the past could commence.

After a while Roan showed up and grinned, deep dimples flashing. "I've been told that you need my services, what can I help you with?"

Dominic took a deep breath before speaking. "There's a remote town we need to get to without being seen. It's important I accompany Christian there, but we can't risk taking main roads or public transport."

Roan nodded thoughtfully. "So you need some mystical interstate action. What's so special about this place anyway?"

Dominic and Christian exchanged an uneasy look. There was risk in revealing too much.

"Let's just say…it holds some answers about my past I've been searching for," Christian explained carefully. "We only recently learned of its significance."

"It's sensitive information," Dominic added. "Please know we wish we could share more, but for now discretion is paramount."

Roan held up a hand. "Say no more, I understand. We all have parts of our story that are private." His expression grew serious. "I promise not to pry or speak of this to anyone. You can trust me."

Dominic smiled in relief. "Thank you, Roan. We knew we could count on your discretion. Now, can you get us there quickly and unseen?"

"With my powers, absolutely." Roan cracked his knuckles dramatically. "I won't let you down."

After Dominic explained their need for secrecy, Christian spoke up. "The town we need to reach is called Moonriff."

At the name, Ben gasped loudly. "Moonriff? But that area is notorious for having a large wolf pack rumored to be utterly ruthless."

Christian and Dominic exchanged a glance. This was the first they'd heard of such a threat.

"Ruthless in what way exactly?" Christian asked warily.

Ben leaned forward, voice low. "They terrorize the region's remote villages. Steal livestock, sometimes people too they say. Anyone crossing into their territory…" He drew a finger across his throat ominously.

"We appreciate the concern, Ben," Dominic replied. "But this trip is necessary. We'll just have to be cautious."

Christian nodded solemnly. "I'm willing to take the risk."

After waiting so long for answers, wild wolves wouldn't deter him.

Sensing his determination, Ben relented reluctantly. "At least take something with you."

"We'll be fine, Ben. You worry too much." Dominic said.

"So how can we open this portal?" Christian asked.

Roan cracked his knuckles. "I don't need materials, just some hand gestures…" He waved his fingers dramatically, brow furrowing in concentration. Before them a shimmering portal swirled open, as if tearing through the very fabric of reality.

Christian stared in awe. Roan's magic was incredibly powerful to summon a portal with just raw will and hand motions. His fae intuition and stubbornness made him uniquely gifted.

"There, all set!" Roan dusted off his hands. "Just step through whenever you're ready, and you'll arrive in a flash."

Christian shook his head, still impressed the portal required no arcane tools or rituals. Christian made a mental note never to get on this easygoing but formidable friend's bad side.

"Shall we?" Dominic extended his hand with a smile. Christian clasped it tightly, as they turned together to face the miraculous gateway and the secrets it promised to finally reveal.

As they prepared to step through the portal, Roan suddenly said, "Hey, mind if I tag along? Could be handy to have your ride stick close, in case you need to make a quick exit."

Dominic glanced at Christian, who nodded agreeably. "Of course, we'd welcome an extra set of eyes and ears," Christian said.

Roan grinned, cracking his knuckles. "Awesome! Not gonna lie, I'm wicked curious what secret mission you two are on. Let's do this!"

He stepped up to the portal's shimmering surface, waving them over. "Just stick with me, I know how to navigate these mystical highways. Wouldn't want you taking a wrong turn to, like, the demon realms or anything."

Christian and Dominic exchanged a nervous laugh, hoping he was joking. Hand in hand, they followed Roan into the magical doorway. Christian felt energy crackle over his skin as they passed through the dimensional veil.

In a flash, their surroundings changed to a deeply shadowed forest. Christian blinked in surprise at the sudden darkness - it had been mid-morning when they stepped through the portal.

"Shouldn't it still be daytime here? The town wasn't far…" Dominic voiced the same confusion.

Roan smiled sheepishly. "Oh right, I may have woven in a time spell without mentioning it. Wanted to get you guys there under cover of night just to be safe."

Christian's eyebrows rose. "That was clever thinking. But perhaps a warning next time?"

"Yeah my bad, portal travel etiquette - always disclose any time bending!" Roan laughed. With a flick of his wrist, he conjured a glowing orb that cast everything in an eerie bluish light.

Dominic glanced around uneasily. "Uh, where exactly are we?"

Roan studied their dark, unfamiliar surroundings. "Looks like we're in some abandoned stretch of supernatural woods."

Though caught off guard by the abrupt nightfall, Christian was impressed by Roan's quick spellwork. The darkness would provide added concealment as they sought answers in this unfamiliar place.

Looking around, Christian shook his head. He wasn't sure what he expected, but an empty forest wasn't it. As they moved deeper, the dense trees seemed to continue endlessly in every direction.

Dominic looked to Roan uncertainly. "Are you sure you brought us to the right place?"

"My portals never miss their mark," Roan replied confidently.

Just then, Christian halted, every sense on high alert. "We're being watched. Show yourself!" he called out sharply.

In response, three wolves emerged from the shadows ahead, their eyes flashing in the dim light. Dominic and Roan instantly readied defensive spells as Christian placed himself protectively in front of them.

"State your purpose here," Christian demanded, muscles coiled to attack. In a blur, the wolves shapeshifted into naked human forms - two powerfully built men and one lean woman. Shifters clearly, unconcerned with clothing.

The trio stared them down fiercely. "We should ask you the same question, trespassers," the woman spat. "What brings outsiders to these woods?"

Before Christian could respond, Roan stepped forward, puffing out his chest importantly. "Good people, we merely seek Moonriff. If you would kindly point us in the proper direction…"

Sensing the tension, Dominic intervened gently. "We mean no harm, only looking for two residents of Moonriff. Perhaps you know them - Anna and Henry Driscoll?"

At the names, the shifters exchanged a loaded glance, aggression melting. After a silent exchange, the woman said gruffly, "Follow us. No tricks, or you won't live to regret it."

As the shifters loped ahead in wolf form, Dominic whispered, "Think we can trust them?"

Christian considered carefully. "Let's hear them out, but stay alert." Weapons still ready, they trailed after their lupine guides.

The wolves lead them on for what seemed like forever but the wolves suddenly stopped and they all looked around to see that there was nothing different around the area.

The wolves threw back their heads in a synchronized howl. In response, a vibrant purple glow suffused the air around the settlement.

Before Christian's astonished eyes, people emerged from dwellings to mill about dirt roads. He took in the lively scene - children laughing and playing, some partially shifted, residents chatting amiably.

Lanterns and candles suspended from intricate ironwork cast a warm, welcoming glow across the community. Christian took in the rustic wooden buildings adorned with carvings of forest creatures and intricate knots. Each unique facade reflected the resident family's craftsmanship and ancestry.

As the wolves led them down packed-dirt roads, villagers paused their errands to smile curiously at the unfamiliar faces. The scent of meat pies and fresh bread wafted from a cozy tavern passed along the way.

In the town square ahead, a gurgling stone fountain was surrounded by children laughing and playing tag. Some were fully shifted into pup form, yipping playfully. The peaceful scene was a jarring contrast to the sinister rumors about this hidden village.

Clearly this was no dangerous den of ravenous beasts. Residents young and old alike exuded a calm happiness and harmony with nature. Flowers spilled from window boxes in vibrant displays. Strands of glowing crystals were strung between buildings, illuminating the community with their delicate light.

Their guides led them to an impressive two-story home of weathered timber and stone at the heart of town. Without the villagers' warm welcome, Christian would have assumed this was their destination regardless - the alpha's dwelling was clearly the pack's communal hearth and gathering place.

Pausing outside the carved double doors, Christian felt a sense of kinship with this sanctuary so similar to his own hometown. Their fears had proven unfounded. With relief, he let the last lingering tension drain away. They had found potential friends where they expected hostility.

Shifting back to human, their guides ushered them inside. Christian marveled at the spacious interior, adorned with plush rugs and fresh wildflowers. This must be the alpha's residence.

"Wait here, the alpha and his mate will greet you shortly," The female wolf informed them. The wolves departed deeper into the house.

Dominic let out an impressed whistle. "Not what I was expecting at all. This place is incredible!"

Christian nodded thoughtfully. "There's clearly more to this pack than rumors suggest. I look forward to hearing their side of the story."

He studied the spacious home with curiosity. Christian didn't fully understand how an alpha could come to rule over an entire remote village of shifters and humans alike. It was an unusual arrangement - but those questions could wait for another day.

For now, their priority was securing safe passage to this sanctuary. There would be time later to learn the history behind this secretive community and its leader.

Glancing around the spacious entry hall, Christian took in the fine craftsmanship evident throughout the stately home. A massive hearth of hand-cut stone was set into one wall, currently cold and swept clean. Above it hung an oil painting depicting a regal-looking couple - likely the current alpha pair.

Polished wooden beams crossed the high ceiling, which was decorated with intricate carvings of forests, rivers, and wildlife. The floors were covered in plush pelts rather than rugs. It gave the home a natural, earthy feel while still retaining an air of rustic grandeur.

Along one wall, a sweeping staircase led to the upper floors. The banister was expertly carved into howling wolves and winding vines. Large picture windows flooded the space with natural light. Christian glimpsed more buildings through them - this impressive home was clearly the pack's communal hub.

Potted plants and fresh wildflowers adorned tabletops and corners. Yet there was no clutter or mess. It felt lived-in while remaining tidy and welcoming. Signs of prosperity without excess or ostentation.

This blend of refined taste with unpretentious warmth must reflect the alpha pair currently leading the pack, Christian mused. He was eager to meet them and satisfy his growing curiosity about this place, and how they had come to create this sanctuary.

Heavy footsteps heralded the alpha's arrival. Through an arched doorway emerged an imposing, muscular older man. He stood well over six feet tall, with broad shoulders and bulging biceps. Yet his weathered face held a kindly expression.

"Welcome, travelers. I am Alpha Ulrich, and this is my mate, Anka," he rumbled in a deep, gravelly voice. At his side stood a petite woman with streaks of gray in her long raven hair. Her sage green eyes were sharp but not unfriendly.

Despite Ulrich's intimidating physical presence, his gentle demeanor immediately put them at ease. He regarded the visitors with an air of quiet wisdom rather than hostility. Up close, his sheer size seemed to match the magnitude of responsibility he bore for his pack and territory.

Yet he moved with a limber grace that belied his muscular bulk. And Anka's diminutive frame was not fragile either - she exuded a subtle strength and poise. Her piercing eyes took their measure shrewdly.

This alpha pair complemented each other beautifully, Christian observed. Ulrich provided raw power and protection, while Anka lent cunning and intuition. Together they presented a united front of courage tempered by caution.

Christian glanced at Dominic, seeing his own awe and respect reflected back. They had found more than just willing guides here - these two elder shifters could teach them much about leadership, and the wisdom of balancing might with compassion. Their quest was taking on new dimensions.

15

Alpha

Dominic

Dominic had awoken that morning with a slight headache and feeling a bit off, but it hadn't seemed like anything major at the time.

But now as they trudged down the forest path, a bone-deep exhaustion was setting in that Dominic hadn't felt in a long while. He probably had a nasty flu coming on, but he couldn't let Christian know. His mate already had enough on his mind with this visit to see his estranged parents. Christian didn't need to be worrying about Dominic too.

So Dominic swallowed back the nausea rising in his throat and forced his feet to keep moving. He focused on the beauty around them anything to distract from the pounding in his head.

When they stepped through the town of Moonriff, Dominic felt the breath leave his body. He stood gaping at the quaint village nestled amongst the hills and woods. log cabins with smoke curling from their brick chimneys, a bubbling stream winding through the main street, solitary lamp posts ready to cast a warm glow come dusk. The very air seemed imbued with tranquility and comfort.

This place was special, Dominic could sense it immediately. Powerful magic had been used to conceal Moonriff from unwanted eyes. Yet now they had been granted access to this sanctuary, this lovingly crafted home.

But even the joyful welcome they received couldn't entirely distract Dominic from the unpleasant sensations wracking his body. As they followed the wolves deeper into town, it was all he could do to stay standing. Strange flashes of heat and chills coursed through him in waves. He discreetly leaned on Christian for support.

Finally they arrived at an impressive two-story cabin. Dominic gulped back another swell of nausea as he took in the finely crafted home. This must be the domain of the Alpha pair they were to meet.

Heavy footsteps sounded from within, and a moment later the largest man Dominic had ever seen emerged onto the porch. Well over six feet tall, with muscles upon muscles, this shifter practically radiated authority and strength. Yet his weathered face held a kindly expression that immediately set Dominic at ease.

"Welcome travelers, I'm Alpha Ulrich," the man rumbled in a deep gravelly voice. He gestured to the petite woman now standing at his side. "This is my mate, Anka."

Anka inclined her head in greeting, sharp green eyes studying them intently. There was an uncanny wisdom in her gaze that seemed to pierce right through Dominic. He shivered, though whether from her stare or his escalating fever he couldn't tell.

They made for an intriguing pair—raw might tempered by sharp intuition. Dominic hoped fervently that the couple would lend their guidance to him and Christian. Their quest for knowledge had taken on new meaning in this tranquil haven.

If only he could focus through the encroaching haze in his mind. Dominic blinked slowly, struggling to track the conversation flowing between Christian and the Alpha pair. Their voices seemed oddly muffled, as if he were hearing them from underwater. His vision began to blur around the edges.

Not now, he pleaded internally. *Just a little longer.* He had to power through, to be strong for Christian. His mate deserved answers from his family, and Dominic would not be the one to take that away.

So he clenched his jaw against the tremors wracking his frame, and tried desperately to quell the roiling in his stomach. He could get through this. He had to believe that, even as his traitorous body screamed otherwise.

Christian noticed his discomfort and asked gently, "Are you okay, Dominic?"

Dominic quickly plastered a smile on his face. "I'm fine, don't worry," he said, willing his voice to sound steady. He got his shit together and acted like nothing was wrong.

Christian looked worried still but relented with a nod. The Alpha pair then led them to a spacious kitchen where a hearty meal was already laid out. Despite his nausea, Dominic forced himself to nibble at some bread, not wanting to offend their gracious hosts.

The couple exuded quiet authority and power, yet their hospitality was genuine. Once seated, Christian explained that they meant no harm - they were simply trying to find his biological parents, Anna and Henry.

"We don't want any trouble," Christian assured them earnestly. "We only seek answers about my past, and guidance moving forward."

Dominic smiled proudly at his mate, despite his ongoing inner turmoil. Christian was overcoming his own trepidation to take control of their quest. Dominic would do whatever it took to support him, no matter how awful he felt.

"We can sense that your intentions are true," Anka replied in her lilting voice. "You have no malice in your hearts."

Roan's eyes widened. "You can sense that? Do you have some kind of magic?" he asked curiously.

Anka smiled. "My mother was a soul reader. I inherited some of her abilities."

Dominic was intrigued. He didn't know such gifts existed. Even after all this time, he was still learning about the diverse skills different supernaturals possessed.

Ulrich regarded Roan thoughtfully. "And I can tell you have shifter blood in you too, son. What kind of animal form do you take?"

"I'm part bear," Roan explained. "But I didn't know until later in life. My shifting abilities didn't manifest until I was older. I never knew my real parents."

Ulrich nodded in understanding. "We have some bear shifters here in Moonriff. If you're looking to learn more about that side of yourself, we'd be happy to help."

"Thank you," Roan said sincerely. "I'd like that."

Eager to get back to the matter at hand, Christian turned toward Anka. "So Anna and Henry Driscoll still live here? We were hoping to speak with them."

"Yes, the two immortals are still here," Anka replied, pouring them all more tea. "May I ask why you are seeking them out?"

Immortals. So Anna had been turned at some point over the centuries. Dominic wondered if that was her choice, or if she'd been forced into it. He knew Christian wrestled with the same uncertainties about his own turning long ago.

Dominic thought about his own mortality. One day he would have to make the choice to turn as well, if he wanted to stay by Christian's side. But that was a matter for another time. Right now they had more pressing issues.

"Anna and Henry are…they're my biological parents," Christian explained hesitantly. "I'm hoping to get some answers about my past from them."

Anka nodded sagely as understanding dawned on her face. "I see. They reside on the east side of town, not far from here."

Ulrich gestured at their unfinished plates. "Eat up first, regain your strength. Then we will take you to them."

The warm meal and tea did help revive Dominic somewhat, though he still felt weak and shaky. He kept as much discomfort as possible off his face. This was Christian's moment, and he wouldn't jeopardize it.

At last they finished eating. Dominic leaned subtly on Roan as they followed Ulrich and Anka back outside into the crisp evening air. The sun was starting to sink below the horizon, casting elongated shadows across the village.

They didn't have to walk far before coming to a stop in front of a modest cabin nearly identical to the others around it. Ulrich stepped forward and rapped firmly on the wooden door.

It swung open, revealing a petite, dark-haired woman with a vaguely familiar bone structure. She stared at them in surprise. Dominic guessed this was Anna. She appeared around early thirties, but her eyes seemed ancient.

"Alpha Ulrich, is everything alright?" she asked worriedly. Her posture grew tense as she took in the unfamiliar faces on her doorstep.

"All is well, Anna," Ulrich soothed. "These folks just have some questions for you and Henry, that's all."

Anna glanced between them warily. Dominic tried to look as non-threatening as possible in his weakened state.

Finally her gaze settled on Christian. She stared at him hard for several moments. Dominic could pinpoint the second she realized - her eyes blew wide, lips parting in shock. One hand flew to her mouth.

"It can't be," she whispered. "Christian?"

Christian nodded hesitantly. "Hello, mother."

Tears shone in Anna's eyes. Without warning she surged forward to embrace him tightly. Christian stood stiffly for a moment before melting into the hug with a broken sigh.

Watching the emotional reunion, Dominic had to blink back a few tears of his own. He couldn't imagine the turmoil Christian must be feeling right now.

Anna finally pulled back, holding Christian at arm's length to look him over. She shook her head wonderingly. "My son…I never thought I'd see you again. What are you doing here?"

Before Christian could respond, footsteps sounded from within the house, followed by a masculine voice calling out, "Anna? Who is it?"

A tall, sandy-haired man joined Anna in the doorway - presumably Henry. His eyes landed on Christian and immediately widened in recognition.

"It can't be," he murmured, an echo of Anna's earlier shock.

Christian offered Henry a tentative smile. "Hello, father."

Henry looked positively thunderstruck. He moved forward on autopilot to embrace his son. Christian returned the hug gently. Dominic could read the cautious hope dawning on his face.

When they separated, Anna quickly ushered them all inside. "Come in, come in! We have so much to discuss."

The cozy cabin interior enveloped them in warmth. Dominic sank gratefully onto a plush sofa beside Christian. Just being off his feet brought immense relief. He still couldn't fully relax, not when they had many difficult conversations ahead, but it was a start.

After the emotional reunion, Roan, Ulrich and Anka quietly excused themselves to give the family privacy. They were going to visit with the bear shifters around town while Christian talked with his parents.

Anna and Henry led Dominic and Christian into their cozy living room, urging them to take a seat on the plush sofa. Dominic sank gratefully onto the cushions, relieved to be off his feet. Anna settled beside her mate, clasping Henry's hand tightly for support.

After a few moments of awkward silence, Anna spoke up. "How did you find out we were still alive, Christian? And how did you know to come here?"

"Someone gave me your old journal," Christian explained. "And my sire Augustus told me you both lived in Moonriff now."

Anna nodded slowly. "Do you still have the journal?"

"It's back home in Dawncreek. But I can show it to you next time."

Henry leaned forward curiously. "And how is Augustus faring these days? It's been many years since my brother and I have spoken."

"He's doing well," Christian assured him. "Still the same old Augustus."

Henry smiled faintly. Then his expression turned serious. "What happened that caused Augustus to turn you? Were you given a choice in the matter?" Worry clouded his eyes. "We never wanted you to go through this life without consent."

Anna gripped her mate's hand. "We hoped you would grow up normal and safe," she added softly. "Not caught up in the chaos we brought down."

Dominic gave Christian's hand a supportive squeeze, sensing his mate's inner turmoil. The circumstances around Christian's turning were still a painful subject.

Christian gave Dominic a grateful smile before turning back to his parents. "There was a plague in the village where I grew up," he began slowly. "It took the lives of those close to me, just as it did to those who raised me. Augustus made me an offer I couldn't refuse - immortality in exchange for my service." His voice held no accusation, only resignation. "I didn't have much left with everyone gone. In those circumstances, it felt like the only choice."

Henry's face was etched with sorrow. "Son, we're so sorry for what happened. Please know it was never our intention to leave you alone."

Anna clasped his hand tightly. "The situation was out of our control. But that doesn't excuse the pain we caused you." Her eyes shimmered with regret. "Can you find it in yourself to forgive us one day?"

Christian considered her words. "I know now why you did what you had to," he said at last. "The full truth from Augustus helped me understand, even if I can't fully reconcile it all yet. But I want to try."

Anna searched her son's face hesitantly. "Does this mean you want to have a relationship with us? Even after everything?"

Christian gave a small but sincere smile. "The parents who raised me taught me to give second chances, no matter what. So here I am, doing just that." He squeezed Dominic's hand. "Now that I've found my mate, we'll need family around us."

Henry turned his gentle gaze on Dominic. "You're Christian's mate then?" At Dominic's confirming nod, a welcoming grin split Henry's face. "Well, welcome to the family, son. I hope we can get to know you better."

Dominic already felt accepted by these two kind souls. "Thank you, si- I mean, dad." Henry's pleased chuckle made warmth bloom in his chest.

The conversation flowed easier after that. There was still much confusion and hurt to work through, but Dominic could see hope dawning in Christian's eyes. This was a start - a chance to heal old wounds and forge new connections.

"If you don't mind me asking, how did you come to live here in Moonriff?" Christian questioned. "Augustus wasn't sure of the details."

Anna and Henry exchanged a somber look. "After we fled the covens, we wandered for a long time trying to evade pursuit," Anna explained. "As a witch mated to an Elder vampire, our union was forbidden."

Henry picked up the thread of the story. "The covens saw us as a threat for defying their rules. We made mistakes trying to escape that only made us bigger targets."

"One day we stumbled upon an ancient enchantress, living alone deep in the forest," Anna continued. "She could see how desperate we were for sanctuary from those hunting us."

"The woman told us of a hidden village warded by powerful magic," Henry said. "A haven where we could find peace, if our intentions were true. Moonriff would be invisible to our enemies."

Christian leaned forward, intrigued. "How did you gain entry then?"

"The enchantress herself escorted us to the boundary," Anna revealed. "Her magic allowed us through the protective barrier and erased our trail. We've been safe here ever since."

Henry nodded gratefully. "She gave us a second chance, though we hardly deserved such grace." His voice wavered with emotion. "We owe her a debt we can never repay."

Dominic could see the toll those haunted years on the run had taken. But finally they had found sanctuary, and each other. Now Christian was back in their lives, giving them hope again. It was a powerful redemption story.

"We understand how blessed we were," Anna said solemnly. "Not a day passes that we don't thank the powers above for guiding us here, where we could build a life and home."

Christian reached out to squeeze his mother's shoulder. "I'm grateful you finally found peace," he said sincerely. "Perhaps everything unfolded as it should."

Anna gave a watery smile at her son's absolution. Dominic was amazed by the empathy Christian showed, despite their past betrayal. His resilience and goodness filled Dominic with admiration.

Hours slipped by unheeded as the family talked. Dominic was enthralled listening to them reconnect after centuries apart. Christian's obvious joy learning about his origins made any discomfort worthwhile.

But eventually, Dominic could no longer ignore his body's weak protests. He shifted uncomfortably as cold chills wracked his frame, breaking out in a light sweat. The bone-deep exhaustion from before returned with a vengeance.

Of course, Christian noticed right away. He pressed a cool hand to Dominic's clammy forehead, concern furrowing his brow.

Anna and Henry exchanged a solemn look. "It must be the curse taking hold," Anna said gravely. "Your life force is starting to drain away."

Christian's head whipped toward them, alarmed. "The curse - that's part of why we came," he explained. "We were hoping you could help break it."

Henry leaned forward intently. "Have you two blood-bonded yet?"

Christian shook his head. "We haven't exchanged blood."

"You must, to start the bonding process that will counter the curse," Anna said urgently.

Henry was already on his feet. "Let's get Dominic to the guest room so he can rest."

Carefully, Christian lifted Dominic into his arms. Dominic felt limp and weak as a newborn kitten. His head lolled against Christian's chest as he was carried down the hall.

Gently laying Dominic on the bed, Christian perched next to him, cradling Dominic's feverish face in his hands. "Just hold on, my heart. We'll get you through this."

Dominic's mind was foggy with exhaustion. He watched dazedly as Christian bit into his own wrist, blood welling up.

"Drink, sweetheart," Christian murmured, pressing the wound to Dominic's mouth. Warm, metallic liquid coated his tongue. At Christian's reassuring nod, Dominic swallowed instinctively.

Dominic drifted off clinging to the solid anchor of his mate.

Darkness, thick and suffocating, surrounded Dominic. He peered in vain through the inky void, searching for any pinprick of light, but was met only with more darkness. It was if he floated in an endless abyss.

A bone-chilling silence pressed down on him. He strained to hear anything at all - the rush of wind, the drip of water, even the beating of his own heart. But only an eerie, unnatural quiet filled the space. The lack of sensation was more terrifying than any physical torment could be.

Time lost meaning in the depthless dark. Had he been adrift for mere moments, or eons? Dominic called out in desperation, but the void swallowed his voice, leaving no echo behind.

When the sinister words finally came, they pierced through the nothingness like a blade of ice. "Dominic...you never fail to amaze me." The voice slid sinuously around him - deep, gravelly and laced with cruel mirth.

Every instinct screamed at Dominic to flee from that bone-chilling presence, but there was nowhere to run, nowhere to hide from the malicious intent focused wholly on him. He fought back the only way he could. "Come out and face me!"

He tried to summon his magic, to wield the power of storm and wind against this evil, but nothing happened. No spark of lightning, not even a wisp of cloud answered his call.

Another chilling laugh echoed from the darkness. "Your magic is useless here, weather witch. In this realm, I control everything." Dominic shuddered at the overwhelming malice carried in that disembodied voice.

"Who are you?" he demanded, proud that his own voice did not quake. "Show yourself!" Only mocking laughter answered.

"We will meet in due time," the presence purred, each word dripping with menace. "For now, you're going to play along."

Dominic strained against the suffocating gloom, seeking any way out. But there was no escape. He was trapped - a helpless specimen under the gaze of some ravenous beast toying with its prey. Chest constricting in panic, Dominic prayed someone would wake him from this nightmare...

Just when he thought the terror would crush the breath from his lungs,

Dominic heard it - the faintest echo of his name, called in a beloved voice. Christian! He clung desperately to that lifeline, using his mate's distant call to pull himself from the brink of despair.

Summoning his last ounce of strength, Dominic surged toward the sound of Christian's voice. The darkness seemed to recoil from that point of light and hope. Brighter and brighter it grew...

Until finally awareness rushed back in, and Dominic awoke once more to blessed sunlight and his mate's comforting presence.

16

Ephemeral Gale

Christian

Christian watched over Dominic intensely, never leaving his mate's side. It had only been a few hours since their first blood exchange, but Christian was already fraught with worry.

He sat in a rustic wooden chair beside the bed, clutching Dominic's limp hand in both of his own. The small guest room was cozy but sparse - log walls hung with colorful wool blankets, a brick fireplace with a few sputtering embers, and the bed piled high with quilts.

A vase of wildflowers on the nightstand tried to lend some cheer, but nothing could distract from Dominic's pale, feverish countenance. His breathing came in faint, uneven rasps as his body fought the curse raging within.

Morning light streamed through the room's single window, though the world outside felt far removed from this tense vigil. Beyond the cracked glass, the sky was ominously overcast to match Christian's mood. It seemed the very weather responded to Dominic's anguish.

Dominic's skin still held an unhealthy pallor, and he thrashed fitfully in restless sleep. Christian pressed a hand to his clammy brow, wishing he could siphon away the sickness.

They were running out of time. If the bonding ritual wasn't completed soon, the curse would continue draining Dominic's life force away. Christian couldn't bear the thought of losing his heart's beloved so soon after finding him.

Gazing out the window, Christian noticed the weather taking an ominous turn. Dark clouds were rolling in, replacing the previously sunny sky. The wind picked up, lashing the trees violently.

Christian turned back to the bed with mounting concern. Dominic was twitching more violently now, face contorted in fear. His head thrashed against the pillow as he mumbled incoherently.

Alarmed, Christian gripped Dominic's shoulder, trying to rouse him. "Dominic, wake up! It's just a dream, Dominic. Come back to me."

But Dominic remained trapped in the throes of his night terror, oblivious to Christian's pleas. The wind howled more fiercely outside, mirroring the inner turmoil. Thunder rumbled in the distance.

The door suddenly banged open, making Christian jump. Anna strode in, her expression grim as she read the burgeoning storm outside.

"What's happening?" Christian asked anxiously.

"Dominic is one of the Gifted," she said. "This is no ordinary dream." At Christian's baffled look, she elaborated. "A weather witch - his magic makes him a target."

"What do you mean? And I can't let suffer like this." Christian said.

"You have to let this play out. I must inform the Alpha. Stay with Dominic - keep trying to reach him." With that cryptic order, she hurried out.

"This is insane." Christian muttered to himself anxiously.

Christian turned back to the bed, more frightened than ever. He tried shaking Dominic harder, with no response. The wind screamed against the windows as if seeking entrance.

"Come back to me, my heart," Christian pleaded. "I'm right here waiting for you."

For untold minutes he kept calling desperately to his mate. Finally, blessedly, Dominic's eyes flew open with a gasp. The storm outside calmed as quickly as it had risen.

Christian gathered Dominic into his arms. "Thank the ancestors," he breathed.

Dominic clung to him tightly, still getting his bearings. Christian felt him slowly relax as the nightmare's hold receded.

When Dominic seemed more settled, Christian pulled back to search his face. "What happened?"

"It was pitch black all around, like I was suspended in a void," Dominic began uneasily. "I couldn't see or feel anything. It was suffocating."

Christian smoothed a hand over Dominic's tense shoulders. "It's alright, you're safe now."

"It felt like that evil presence was crushing the life from me," Dominic whispered, eyes haunted. "Like a predator toying with helpless prey. I thought I might go mad from fear."

Christian wrapped protective arms around Dominic. "It's over now. But we'll figure this out, I promise."

Dominic finally relaxed into his embrace. The lingering unease remained, but with Christian holding him, the terror of that nightmare retreated.

"Thank you for pulling me out of there." Dominic said.

Christian smoothed back his hair tenderly. "You should rest more, my heart. Regain your strength."

Dominic nodded, the ordeal clearly having drained him. Christian stayed by his side, providing a soothing presence until Dominic's eyes drifted shut in healing sleep.

Only once he was sure Dominic was settled in restful sleep did Christian silently slip from the room, closing the door behind him. As he made his way down the hall, the savory aroma of stew greeted him, beckoning warmly.

Stepping into the cozy kitchen, flickering lantern light cast a homey glow over worn wooden counters and a large brick hearth. Iron pots bubbled invitingly over the fire, filling the space with comforting scents of garlic, thyme and smoky meat.

Despite the mouthwatering meal awaiting, an air of unease lingered in the room. At the scarred oak table, Anna and Henry looked up wearing matching expressions of parental concern. Christian's heart swelled at their care, even after so long apart. Roan was in the back, a silent confidence emanating from the man.

Anna wordlessly handed Christian a steaming mug as he sank into a chair. The mint tea soothed his frayed nerves. But tension still lined his shoulders, echoing his parents' own worry.

"How is Dominic?" Anna finally asked, breaking the pensive silence that had fallen.

Christian stared into the fragrant tea, wishing he had reassuring news. "Resting for now."

Anna nodded. "Come and have a seat with us."

"What's going on?" Christian asked as he sat. "Why did Dominic's dream affect the weather?"

Anna and Henry exchanged a tense look. Roan stood by silently, brow creased in concern.

Finally Henry gestured them all to take a seat. "There are things we must tell you now, before it's too late."

"You mentioned Dominic is 'Gifted,'" Christian said slowly. "What did you mean by that?"

Anna clasped her hands together. "It began long ago, before your father and I even met. A great seer prophesized that a malevolent being would one day seek to wreak havoc in this realm."

Roan's eyes widened in surprise. "I know of this prophecy. Moriganna warned us of the same threat."

Henry raised an eyebrow. "Moriganna is still around? That little sprite was a menace when I knew her, still learning to control her magic."

"She's now Queen of one of the In-Between realms," Roan informed him. "But please, tell us more about this prophecy."

Anna nodded gravely. "The seer didn't name the evil, only that it would be a man of great power and cunning. But she also foretold that gifted individuals would arise to counter him."

Christian's brow furrowed. "But how can we defeat this faceless threat? We know nothing about it."

"The prophecy said these 'Awakened Ones' would gain abilities to stand against the coming darkness," Anna revealed. "Their powers would awaken when the time was right."

Roan's eyes lit up in understanding. "Like my friend Ben! Since his magical talent emerged, we've speculated there may be more Awakened ones out there."

"Yes, though the exact number remains unclear," mused Anna. She focused intently on Christian and Dominic. "But now I believe your mate may be one such gifted soul."

Christian looked down at Dominic's sleeping form, a mix of awe and fear welling up. "You think he's meant to stand against this great evil?"

Anna smiled softly, knowingly. "The seer told me my child would one day be matched with a gifted mate. It was why we had to protect you at all costs."

Christian shook his head, trying to process it all. "So what happens now?"

Henry leaned forward, expression grave. "For now, you need to focus on completing the bonding ritual. Dominic has taken your blood, but the curse will only be halted when you fully bond. This is just a stop gap."

Despite the questions swirling in his mind, Christian knew his father spoke wisdom. Their spirits had to be fully joined for Dominic to withstand whatever lay ahead.

After speaking with his parents, Christian went to check on Dominic again. But he found the guest room empty, the bedsheets rumpled. Moonlight streamed through the open window. Where had his mate gone?

Worry spiking, Christian quickly searched the small cabin until he discovered a concealed side door left ajar. It led onto a cozy wooden balcony overlooking the surrounding forest. There he found Dominic leaning on the railing, staring distantly at the view.

Christian took a moment just to look at his mate, awake and on his feet again. Dominic's dark hair shone in the morning sunlight, the healthy color returned to his handsome face. He seemed lost in thought as a light breeze ruffled his shirt.

Christian let his gaze linger on Dominic's strong profile - the straight nose, sculpted jawline, the tiny furrow between his brows. He was breathtaking, inside and out. Christian's unbeating heart swelled with love and protectiveness.

Unable to resist, he moved up behind Dominic and wrapped his arms securely around his mate's waist. Christian nuzzled against Dominic's neck, breathing in the earthy scent of herbs and pine that was uniquely his. It filled him with comfort and longing.

Dominic gave a contented hum at the contact, the furrow smoothing from his brow. He clasped their hands tightly together and leaned back into Christian's embrace. For a peaceful moment they stood chest to chest, simply existing together.

Christian followed Dominic's gaze out at the stunning vista surrounding the secluded cabin. From their vantage point on the balcony, they could see for miles in every direction.

He pressed a feather-light kiss below Dominic's ear. "Talk to me, my heart," he murmured. "Let me help shoulder your burdens."

Dominic sighed and leaned more heavily back against him. His voice was solemn when he began to speak...

"I've been having nightmares on and off since I was attacked by a man named Gary at my shop a while back." He shuddered. "The assault left me feeling so weak and useless. I snapped at everyone, isolated myself...even resorted to drinking for a time." Dominic said.

Christian focused intently on each word, providing the support Dominic needed to open up. And he silently vowed to protect this precious man with everything he had. The darkness would not claim Dominic's radiant spirit - not as long as Christian drew breath.

Rage ignited in Christian's chest at the thought of anyone harming his mate. "What became of this Gary?" he bit out.

Dominic quickly turned in his arms. "I honestly don't know. Ben and Adrian got him away from me. I haven't seen him since."

He cupped Christian's face gently. "Let me know if you want him dealt with."

Dominic smiled at him. "I can fight my own battles, love. The past is done."

The sincerity in Dominic's eyes cooled Christian's anger. He would respect his mate's wishes, though his protective instincts raged at the thought of this warlock still living freely.

Taking a deep breath, he simply said, "If you ever need me, I will come. Your battles are mine as well now."

Dominic's eyes shone with unshed tears as he leaned up to kiss Christian tenderly. "I know," he whispered against his lips. "We look after each other."

When Dominic pulled back, his expression was solemn again. "But this recent dream…it felt different. Like some dark omen." He shivered despite the warm sunlight.

Christian wrapped him in a fierce embrace, wishing he could shield Dominic from all harm. "Whatever comes, we will face it together," he vowed. "You don't have to be strong alone anymore."

With a last lingering kiss, he led Dominic back inside. But Christian knew the shadows would not be banished so easily. Still, having his mate safely in his arms again was enough for now. Each moment of light was a treasure.

They returned to the guest room, and Dominic recounted more of his past trauma at Gary's hands. Christian listened intently, arms tight around his mate as he trembled through the painful memories.

"I've never felt so violated and afraid," Dominic admitted. "If Ben hadn't shown up when he did…" He shook his head, unable to continue as tears slipped down his cheeks.

Fury surged within Christian again, but he tamped it down, focusing only on offering Dominic comfort. "That monster had no right to hurt you, my love. But he will never lay a hand on you again, I swear it."

Dominic clung to him. "Afterwards I shut everyone out, thinking I could handle things alone. But the nightmares just got worse." He looked up at Christian beseechingly. "I don't want to push you away too. We protect each other from now on."

Christian kissed him desperately. "Never again, my heart. I will stay by your side, always." He wiped away Dominic's tears, wishing he could erase the pain just as easily. "We are one now."

Gradually Dominic's tears ceased under his gentle care. Though shadows still haunted him, Christian hoped his comforting presence brought some small measure of peace to his mate.

Curled together on the bed, Christian tenderly stroked Dominic's hair and back, wanting to soothe away his pain. Dominic clung to him like a drowning man to a raft, pressing desperate kisses across Christian's chest and shoulders.

As their mouths met again, an intense passion overtook them both. A primal need to reaffirm their bond, to reconnect and share breath and skin and soul. Hands roamed fervently, followed by lips worshipping every inch they could reach.

Their lovemaking took on a feverish urgency, a wordless affirmation of the devotion flourishing wildly between them. Christian poured everything he had into worshipping his mate's body and spirit. Dominic matched him touch for touch, kiss for kiss, until nothing else existed but their joined forms.

Time itself ceased to hold meaning; there was only this perfect union of souls. The outside world with its dangers and demons faded away. Here in their shared passion, they found sanctuary. A haven where only light and pleasure and their love for one another held sway.

Afterwards, Dominic gazed up at Christian pleadingly. "Please, my heart - drink from me."

Christian hesitated, worried about hurting him. "Are you certain, my love? I don't wish to cause you any more pain."

But Dominic gripped his hand tightly. "I've never been more sure of anything," he insisted. "Make me completely yours, in body and soul."

Seeing the trust and need shining in Dominic's eyes, Christian could only nod reverently. He tilted Dominic's head back, exposing the smooth column of his throat. Dominic sighed encouragement.

As Christian's fangs pierced tender flesh, Dominic's rich blood filled his mouth, the taste ambrosial. But beyond the physical ecstasy, Christian was overwhelmed by an influx of emotion - joy, comfort, absolute belonging.

For the first time in centuries, the gaping loneliness inside him was filled. This remarkable man had come into his life and made him whole again. Dominic was the missing piece of his soul.

When he finally, reluctantly pulled back, licking the marks closed, Christian was shaken to his core. He gazed at his mate, heart full to bursting. "I love you," he whispered fervently. "My heart, my life, my everything."

Dominic gave a wondering smile, eyes bright with tears. "And I love you," he breathed. "My soulmate, my home."

They clung together as waves of euphoria washed over them. Christian had never felt such a profound connection. At long last, he was no longer alone. They had found in each other the belonging they craved.

Whatever darkness tried to intrude on their newfound joy, Christian was certain their light would overcome it. Their union was unbreakable now. The future shone brightly for them both.

17

Veil of Shadows

Dominic

Dominic awoke slowly, warm rays of morning sun spilling across the bed. For a moment he kept his eyes closed, simply basking in the feeling of comfort and safety. He couldn't remember the last time he'd slept so peacefully.

Finally blinking open his eyes, he turned to see Christian's sleeping form next to him. His mate looked utterly relaxed, lips curved in a hint of a smile. Dominic's heart swelled with love.

They were tucked cozily under the quilts. After last night, they'd drifted into sated and dreamless rest still locked in an intimate embrace.

Dominic studied Christian's handsome features - the strong jaw, straight nose, the mussed golden hair falling over his forehead. Even at rest he seemed to radiate strength and vitality. Dominic sighed, unable to resist brushing a soft kiss over his lips.

At the contact, Christian's eyes fluttered open. Their gazes met and Christian gave him a drowsy grin that made Dominic's stomach do flips. "Good morning, my heart," Christian murmured, voice still

201

husky from sleep.

"Morning, love," Dominic replied, smiling helplessly in return.

Christian drew him in for a longer, languid kiss. Dominic sank into it, marveling that he could have this - lazy morning affection with the man fate had made for him alone.

When they finally separated, Christian gazed at him intently.

"How do you feel?" He reached out to brush Dominic's hair back, as if checking for any lingering sign of fever or chill.

"Better than I have in years," Dominic assured him honestly. For the first time he felt wholly himself, healthy and strong. He grasped Christian's hand and brought it to his lips for a fervent kiss. "Thanks you."

Christian's eyes shone with relief and joy. But any further conversation was interrupted by Anna's voice calling loudly from outside. "Rise and shine, boys! Breakfast is waiting."

They both laughed at her motherly summons. Dominic's heart swelled realizing this was his family now too. After one more long, heated kiss, they reluctantly left the cozy nest of blankets to get dressed.

Christian and Dominic used the same clothes as they didn't expect to stay the night. They took turns cleaning up in the washroom attached to the bedroom. Dominic wished they had time to share the shower for more amorous activities, but the enticing aroma of sizzling meat and fresh bread urged them on.

Soon they were seated at the kitchen table beside Roan, who was already enthusiastically tucking into a heaping plate of food. Anna bustled about pouring coffee and pressing second helpings on them all. Even Henry, the imposing vampire, was all smiles this morning.

Dominic glanced at Christian to find a soft, contented look on his face that made something inside Dominic click into place. This was what his mate had been missing for so long without even realizing -

the warmth and liveliness of family, being surrounded by people who loved him.

Well, now he had that unconditional love and support again. Dominic silently vowed to make sure Christian never spent another day feeling alone.

The lively meal passed enjoyably, full of lighthearted chatter and banter between them all. Dominic could have lingered forever in this homey kitchen. But the outside world eventually came calling.

Both his and Christian's phones began buzzing insistently from the bedroom. With apologetic looks, they excused themselves to take the calls. Dominic's heart sank when he saw it was Lee.

"Dom, where are you? We need to meet," Lee said without preamble. "I found a promising lead on Austin but we have to move quickly."

Dominic glanced at Christian, seeing his own reluctance reflected back. "I'll be back as soon as I can."

"Understood. I'll be there soon…" Christian said before hanging up.

He trailed off as Christian ended his own call, features clouded with concern. "What is it?" Dominic asked.

"Some of the younger vampires have gone missing from Dawncreek," Christian revealed grimly. "Augustus needs my help to track them down."

They stood in unhappy silence for a moment, the real world intruding on their idyllic bubble. At last Dominic squeezed Christian's hand. "Duty calls. But we'll come back soon."

Nodding, they returned to the kitchen to relay the news. Anna and Henry's faces fell, but they understood.

"Here, take these," Anna said, pressing wooden amulets into their hands. "They will allow you entrance whenever you wish to visit."

Dominic closed his fingers around the gift, heart brimming with gratitude. After farewell hugs, they gathered their things to depart. But this was not a permanent goodbye - only a temporary parting.

They had family waiting for their return.

Christian glanced back wistfully at the cozy home as its door closed behind them, severing them once more from the haven inside. Sensing his sorrow, Dominic wrapped an arm around his waist.

"We'll see them again soon," he murmured. "And we'll always carry the warmth of this place with us."

Christian turned to him then, eyes glowing with so much love it stole Dominic's breath. "Anywhere with you feels like home," he said simply, and kissed Dominic deeply.

Hand in hand, they walked down the path away from the cabin. The world called, but they would face it together. And someday, they would return here to the family who would always welcome them with open arms.

When they reached the edge of the protective wards around Moonriff, Dominic turned to Roan. "Could you open two portals for us? One for Christian back to Dawncreek, and one for us to Willowbrook."

Roan nodded agreeably. With a swipe of his hand, two shimmering gateways appeared before them. Christian's parents had followed to see them off, smiling softly.

Dominic embraced Christian tightly. "I'll come as soon as I can," he promised. "Stay safe, my heart." They shared one last lingering kiss before parting.

With a final goodbye to Anna and Henry, Dominic and Roan stepped through the portal back to Ben and Adrian's manor. They emerged into the cozy living room where Ben and Adrian sat cuddling on the couch, Jimmy snoozing contentedly in their laps.

The couple started in surprise before carefully setting Jimmy down and hurrying over to give hugs.

"You're back! We were so worried," Ben exclaimed, checking them both for injuries.

Dominic smiled reassuringly. "All is well, I promise. The trip went amazingly." He glanced regretfully toward the front door. "But Lee is waiting for me about a lead on Austin. I can't stay to chat."

Ben's brow furrowed in concern. "Do you need me there with you?"

Dominic shook his head. "I should handle this alone. But thank you, my friend."

After heartfelt goodbyes all around, he headed out front.

In the driveway, Dominic paused by Christian's car. "Actually, I'll take this back for Christian. No use leaving it stranded here." Adrian agreed easily.

Soon Dominic was settled in for the drive home, his mind spinning over Lee's urgent message. He watched the manor fade in the rearview mirror, already missing the sanctuary he'd found within its walls. But the memories of his time with Christian and their families would sustain him in the days ahead.

When he arrived at his house, Lee was already waiting on his doorstep looking anxious. He jumped up when Dominic arrived.

"There you are! I've been trying to reach you," Lee said in a rush. "We have a real chance at finding Austin, but the window is closing fast…"

He glanced curiously at Dominic's clothes as they headed inside. Dominic just shook his head wryly. "Long story, I'll explain later. Just tell me what you found out."

As they entered the apartment, Dominic said, "Give me a sec to change, then we'll talk."

In his room, he quickly shed Christian's borrowed clothes for a comfortable shirt and jeans. Vale, his husky, padded over for ear scratches which Dominic happily provided.

"Hey boy, were you good while I was gone?" Vale licked his hand in response. Dominic gave the dog fresh food and water before heading back out.

He shot his mate a quick text that he was home safe. Just contacting Christian eased some of his tension.

Back in the living room, Dominic sank onto the sofa across from Lee. Vale curled up contentedly at his feet. "Alright, tell me what you found out," Dominic said, absently petting the dog.

Lee pulled a sealed envelope from inside his jacket. "I discovered this hidden under Austin's pillow when I was searching his room again for clues…"

Dominic tuned in intently as Lee explained the mysterious letter. Having Vale nearby brought him comfort and familiarity after the stress of recent events. Some semblance of normalcy was returning.

Dominic picked up the envelope almost reverently. His name was scribbled across it in Austin's familiar scrawl. Hands shaking slightly, he opened it and unfolded the letter inside. Clearing his throat, he began reading aloud.

Dominic and Lee,

If you're reading this, then I'm already gone. I'm so sorry to put you both through that pain, but I didn't have a choice. Mom gave me some kind of potion that forced me to obey her commands against my will. I tried to resist, but her magic was too strong.

She's sending me away to protect our secrets, or at least that's her excuse. But I think she just wants to isolate me for some bigger purpose. I wish I could explain more, but the compulsion prevents it.

Dominic, I know Lee and I have bullied and tormented you since we became stepbrothers. But underneath it all, you're still my brother and I love you. That's why I've spelled this letter - Lee can use it to track my location with a locator spell. You two are the only ones who can find me.

Please know I never wanted to abandon you both. Despite our past, you're the best brothers I could ask for. I'm so sorry for the pain Lee and I have caused you, Dominic. If I come back from this, I promise to make things right between us.

Lee, take care of our brother. I know you'll look out for each other. I love you both and pray we'll be together again soon.

Your brother,

Austin

After reading the letter, Dominic looked at Lee curiously. "What did Austin mean about you tracking him?"

Lee hesitated before explaining. "Since we're twins, I can tap into his magic a little using my own necromantic abilities."

"What is Austin's magical affinity?" Dominic asked.

He didn't even know what type of magic his brother wielded.

"Well…he can communicate with souls," Lee revealed. "We realized it when we were young and Austin was always chatting with his invisible 'friends'."

Dominic's eyes widened. He'd never heard of such an ability. "How did you figure out what his power was?"

"At first I thought it was just an overactive imagination," Lee admitted. "But over time we realized the spirits were real. Austin had been talking to the dead since childhood."

Dominic shook his head in wonder. He'd had no his stepbrothers held such rare gifts. It made Austin's disappearance somehow even more tragic.

Lee carefully picked up the letter, brow furrowed in concentration. He held it delicately between both palms and began chanting under his breath. At first nothing happened. Then the paper started glowing with a deep violet aura, rising to hover unsupported in the air.

The temperature in the room dropped sharply, their breath fogging. The lights flickered as energy was drawn to fuel the spell. Eyes closed, Lee increased the cadence of his incantation.Complex symbols manifested across the letter in fiery violet script, casting an eerie glow.

Shadows crept up the walls, swaying in time with Lee's voice. The veil between worlds was thinning. This was primal necromancy at work. Dominic watched in awe, skin prickling from the power thrumming in the air.

Lee's eyes flew open, blazing with violet intensity. He made a tearing motion with his hands and the envelope split cleanly in half, pages floating apart. An image began to take form, blurry at first but gaining clarity.

The temperature plunged further. Dominic's exhale came out in frosty plumes. The image solidified into a scene - Austin unconscious and haggard, slumped in a dim room. His wrists were bound, clothes filthy and torn.

Dominic's heart clenched at the state of his brother. Austin's chest barely seemed to move with breath. Was he still alive? Dominic reached out instinctively but his fingers passed through the phantom projection.

Lee wavered on his feet, face drawn and pale. The spell was taking an immense toll. But his eyes blazed with triumph through the strain. After months of fruitless seeking, finally they had found a glimpse of Austin.

Letting the image linger a moment more, Lee released the letter. It floated gently back to the table as the shadows retreated up the walls. The violet aura faded, warmth returning to the room. But Lee looked utterly drained, panting heavily…

Dominic lurched forward in concern. "What's happening? Is he okay?"

"He's trapped somewhere in the deep woods," Lee grated out, still focused on maintaining the spell. Sweat beaded his forehead from the effort. "But alive for now."

Before Dominic could ask anything more, Lee withdrew a silver ring from his finger. With a few arcane words, he bound the tracking magic into the metal. The letter drifted back to the table.

Seeing Dominic's questioning look, Lee held up the ring. "Now we can use this to lead us to him. Here…" He slid the ring onto his own finger, then slowly turned in a circle with his arm extended. A faint violet trail manifested in the air pointing toward the balcony.

"It works like a compass focused on Austin," Lee explained. "Wherever he is, this will show us the way." Hope and determination blazed in his eyes.

He gripped Lee's shoulder tightly. "Then let's go bring our boy home." With the ring as their guide, he knew they would succeed.

Dominic kept glancing at the silver ring on Lee's hand as they worked. Their brother had trusted them to find him. Failure was not an option.

Soon they were ready to depart, with backpacks stocked for a trek into the remote mountains. The ring glowed more intensely as they headed out, as if sensing Austin growing nearer.

The silver ring glowed brighter as Dominic and Lee hiked into the remote forest mountains. It tugged them along like an invisible tether bound to Austin.

Eventually they reached a familiar clearing - the site of the dark magic infection Dominic had investigated before. But as they stepped into the open space, he instantly sensed the vile corruption was much worse now.

The inky tendrils had spread outward from the focal point, tainting the surrounding trees and earth. The air felt heavy and foul, laden with unnatural malice. It pressed down on their skin like a humid shroud, making each breath a struggle.

No birds sang, no animals rustled in the underbrush. The clearing was deathly silent except for a distant, high-pitched hum at the edge of hearing. The unearthly noise set Dominic's teeth on edge.

His magic roiled inside him, reacting to the wrongness saturating the area. Every instinct screamed to get away from this unhallowed place. It felt like the darkness was watching them, reaching for them with grasping, malevolent intent.

Dominic shuddered as they passed the afflicted patch. "This place feels wrong. The dark is growing stronger."

Lee nodded uneasily. "Let's keep moving. We shouldn't linger here." Consulting the ring again, he led them toward a secluded ridge.

Dominic and Lee quickly moved toward the far side of the clearing, hurrying to leave the oppressive atmosphere behind. But Dominic could still sense that vile presence, its unseen eyes following their progress. He shuddered as the tainted brush tugged at their clothes like ghostly hands.

They wouldn't linger here a second longer than necessary. The sooner they found Austin and escaped this evil place, the better. Jaw clenched against the dark forces pressing down upon them, Dominic focused on putting one foot in front of the other.

Just a little farther and they'd be free of this living nightmare. He repeated that to himself like a mantra as they plunged deeper into the infested forest. Austin was waiting. They had to reach him before the darkness did.

Nestled against the mountainside sat a small, rundown house surrounded by iron fencing. Dominic realized with a start that the building was made entirely of cold iron, glinting dully in the moonlight.

"It looks a like something is hidden inside," he murmured. Austin had to be trapped inside.

They cautiously approached the entrance, a heavy iron door barred from the outside.

Lee held up the silver ring, its violet glow intensifying. "He's here. I can feel my brother's spirit."

Dominic grasped the handle and turned with all his might, but it refused to budge. Frustration mounting, he stepped back. "Stand clear," he warned Lee.

Drawing deeply on his magic, Dominic made it surge inside him like a gathering storm. Lightning crackled in his palms, the energy almost too great to contain. With a roar, he directed the fulmination at the door.

The metal exploded inward with an earth-shaking boom, torn fragments screeching as they ripped free. The raw display of power shocked them both. Dominic stared at his smoking hands in disbelief.

"Where did that come from?" Lee asked, eyes wide.

Dominic shook his head uncertainly. He didn't know if it was the mate bond with Christian, but this felt like power far beyond his normal capacity. Yet now was not the time to wonder over it.

"No time to analyze it. We need to get Austin now," he said urgently.

Whatever dark forces inhabited this place, he could feel them gathering in response to the intrusion.

Dominic pushed down his questions about the seemingly new depth of his magic. Austin was here fighting for his life. That took priority over everything else. They had to save Dominic's brother before it was too late.

With smoke still curling from his fingertips, Dominic led them quickly inside. The power thrumming through his veins was unfamiliar, but he would use it to protect his family. They would face the coming darkness together.

Moving quickly, they swept through the small house, finding nothing of note until Lee stepped on a creaky floorboard. Prying it up revealed a trapdoor and ladder leading down.

Below was a cramped earthen tunnel ending in a heavy iron door. An ominous chill hung in the stagnant air. Dominic steeled himself and blew the cell door off its hinges with another concussive blast.

Rushing inside, their flashlight beams fell on a hunched figure chained to the far wall - Austin. Dominic's heart clenched at the sight. His brother was filthy, bruised, and far too thin, but alive.

"You found me," Austin rasped as Lee frantically freed him from the manacles.

"Always, brother," Lee said firmly. "Let's get you home."

With Austin leaning heavily on them, Dominic and Lee emerged from the foul iron prison. Only once his brother was safe in the open air did Lee finally let his composure crack, pulling Austin into a desperate hug.

Dominic turned away, throat tight with emotion. They had found their missing brother against all odds. But a sniffle from Austin pulled Dominic from his thoughts - they weren't safe yet.

As they moved away from the house, Lee suddenly halted. "Do you feel that?" he asked tensely.

Dominic focused his senses and nausea rose within him. A dark wave of magic surged toward them, impossibly malignant. "Lee, when I say so, shield yourself and Austin," he instructed urgently.

Lee started to argue, then simply nodded. They continued on, muscles coiled in anticipation. The forest had gone deathly still around them - no insects buzzed, no leaves rustled. Only the sound of their own hearts pounding.

Then, as one, the trees and plants started rapidly decaying, browning and withering before their eyes. The stream running nearby turned foul, fish floating lifelessly on its surface. Dominic's mouth went dry at the unnatural blight.

"Shield, now!" Dominic yelled. Lee immediately summoned a shimmering violet barrier around himself and Austin.

None too soon - as the plant life rapidly decayed before their eyes, an emaciated wraithlike being rose from the withered ground. Empty, cavernous sockets blazed with sickly green fire fixed malevolently upon them. This was no mere undead, but a powerful lich.

Dominic instinctively called on his magic as the creature rushed them, talons outstretched. He'd heard lore of liches - sinister necromancers who chained their cruel souls to the earth through dark magic - but never seen one himself. Whoever had summoned this horror possessed forces beyond reckoning.

Catching the lich's jagged claws on a gale force wind, Dominic struggled to hold it at bay. The malevolent power rolling off the undead was staggering. Fighting it alone would quickly sap his strength.

The lich pressed closer against the howling winds, tattered robes whipping violently around its skeletal frame. Glowing green energy coruscated along its bones. Wherever that cursed radiance touched, plants instantly blackened, fracturing into ash.

Seeing the damage, Dominic realized just one brush of those claws could rot the flesh from his body in seconds. He desperately wove walls of wind and lightning to keep the lich contained, but its power ate away at his buffers like acid.

Soon it would break through. Sweat ran down Dominic's face from the exertion. He pulled harder on the well of magic inside him, determined to hold out as long as possible. Lee and Austin were depending on him.

The lich seemed to sense his weakening, grinning madly and increasing its assault. Sickly verdant light seared Dominic's vision as the last wind wall disintegrated. He braced for the end, when suddenly...

Roots erupted from the ground beneath the lich, entangling its limbs and halting its advance. Dominic risked a glance back to see Ciaran kneeling amid the vegetation, hands pressed to the soil, face set in concentration.

"The binding won't last - finish it off now!" Ciaran gritted out. "Aim for the core!"

Trusting his friend, Dominic focused the last of his magic into a concentrated lightning blast directly at the lich's center. It let out an unearthly wail before disintegrating into dust.

The adrenaline left Dominic in a rush and he sank toward the ground, utterly spent. But Ciaran was there in an instant, grasping his arm to steady him.

"Well done," Ciaran said, with a proud smile. "I knew you had power in you."

Dominic shook his head in disbelief. "How did you know to come?"

Ciaran's green eyes glinted knowingly. "I'm a druid, I sensed your plight. Let's get you all home."

With Ciaran's help, they made it through the portal and back to Dominic's apartment without further incident. Austin was safe at last, cradled between his brothers as they hurried him inside. The explanations could wait - tonight called for joy and relief, not words.

No matter the cause or who had sent these forces against them, Austin was free from that prison. Together they would unravel the rest of the mystery. Tonight their fractured family was made whole once more.

18

Nocturnal Convergence

Christian

Dread settled like a stone in Christian's stomach as he stepped through the portal into his house. His sire's message had been brief - several young vampires were now missing from the coven. No details on who or how, only a terse summons to return immediately.

Changing quickly into a suit, Christian tried to temper his spiraling concern. Dominic's text pinged, a brief reassurance that his mate had made it home safely after their ordeal. Christian clung to that bright spot amidst the turmoil. He sent a quick reply before steeling himself and heading for the coven.

Approaching the sprawling mansion, an ominous chill swept over him. The wards that usually thrummed with power were disturbingly silent. Their magical protection had been stripped away somehow without triggering any alarms. Impossible, unless...

Pushing down his unease, Christian entered the foyer. Too quiet. The whole place felt lifeless in a way that raised the hairs on his neck. A living tomb.

Voices echoed faintly from his sire's office. Christian hurried toward them through the unnaturally still halls. If Augustus was with someone, maybe they had answers about this unsettling situation.

He froze in the office doorway, shocked to see his best friend Elvira perched on the leather couch next to Augustus' desk. Elvira seldom visited anymore since she had her own quarries with Eros.

Dread coiled tighter in Christian's stomach. Her presence here did not bode well.

Elvira stood gracefully to embrace him. "Christian. I'm sorry we had to meet again under such circumstances." Her eyes were solemn, lacking their usual playful light.

"What's going on?" Christian asked, returning her hug fiercely. "Why are you here?"

Augustus rose from behind the desk, his expression grim. "All will be explained, son. But the missing young ones take priority now." He gestured for Christian to sit.

Settling into an armchair, Christian struggled to reconcile the lifeless halls and missing fledglings. The coven was supposed to be safe haven, impenetrable. Now everything felt off balance, ominously uncertain.

Augustus folded his hands before him, emitting a heavy sigh. "As I'm sure you guessed, someone dismantled the wards and took the youngest vampires directly from their quarters. I don't know how yet."

Christian shook his head in disbelief. "But how? That magic was unbreakable."

Elvira's eyes flashed with anger. "We believe a dark mage assisted from within. There may be a traitor among us." Her tone left no doubt of the culprit's fate when discovered.

Augustus nodded gravely, the temperature in the room chilling further with his displeasure. "Nobody invades my home and family unchallenged. We will find answers." His ancient eyes bored into

Christian, who forced himself not to shrink back.

"Do we know who was taken?" he asked, almost dreading the answer.

In response, Augustus slid photos across the desk. Christian's heart clenched. There were five faces, all young - the newest additions to their coven family. And one he knew very well…

"Matt," Christian whispered, a fist squeezing his heart.

The shy young vampire had been under his personal guidance for the past year. Christian had hand-picked him for mentorship, promising to keep him safe in these early delicate years. Now he was gone.

Christian stared at the photo, guilt and self-recrimination crashing through him. He had vowed to protect Matt, to help him gain confidence and control over his new abilities. But he had failed utterly.

Matt had trusted him, relied on him for guidance. And Christian had let him down in the worst possible way. Anything could be happening to the gentle fledgling right now. The possibilities ate at Christian like acid.

Elvira grasped his hand tightly as anguished fury crossed his face. Her emerald eyes reflected the torment in his own.

"We'll get him back, Christian," she insisted vehemently. "Him and all the others taken. I swear to you."

But her promises couldn't pierce the miasma of guilt enshrouding Christian's heart. He should have been there, should have protected them. He was one of the oldest vampires in the coven, yet he'd had no inkling anything was amiss. Some mentor he turned out to be.

If anything happened to Matt or the others because of his negligence, Christian knew the shame would haunt him forever. But wallowing in self-blame wouldn't help now. He had to act.

Christian hardened his resolve. He would make amends by doing everything in his power to bring their lost family home again, no matter the personal cost. It was the only way to lance the festering regret inside him.

Augustus came around the desk to grip Christian's shoulder. "We will find the perpetrator and recover our lost ones," he said with quiet certainty. "But we must act swiftly and with care."

Christian looked up at his sire, seeing the vengeance barely leashed behind the stoic facade. Augustus would tear the world apart to protect their family. Steeling himself, Christian rose to his feet. If cunning darkness threatened them, he would answer with fury and light.

But Augustus held up a hand, expression contemplative. "There is another matter we must discuss first, before investigating the missing young ones."

Christian cocked his head curiously. What could take priority right now?

Augustus moved to sit again. "I've been considering this for some time, but recent events have cemented the decision. This coven should leave Dawncreek."

Christian jerked back in surprise. "Leave? But what about maintaining order here?"

"Elvira's coven will take over our role," Augustus explained calmly. "We've already discussed it."

Elvira nodded. "Your club will remain under your authority, so we'll retain some presence. But a change of leadership was overdue."

Christian's mind spun. He couldn't wrap his head around such sudden upheaval. "Where will we go? And when?"

A small smile crossed Augustus's face. "I was thinking Willowbrook. It seems fitting now that you've found your mate there."

Understanding dawned on Christian. "I know you intend for me to lead the new coven someday." It was not a question.

"You're ready, Christian. Past ready," his sire said solemnly. "Once matters settle, I will step down and name you my successor."

It was a lot to process, but Christian couldn't deny the rightness he felt. "Have you told the others yet?"

Augustus shook his head. "Only we three know for now, until arrangements are finalized." His expression grew serious once more. "But first, our lost family must be recovered."

Christian nodded thoughtfully. "What about Eros? Is he aware of the planned move?"

Augustus' brow furrowed. "No. We must keep this quiet until preparations are complete, in case there are spies waiting to exploit any vulnerabilities."

"Let me know if you need anything from me," Christian said resolutely.

Augustus gave him a grateful smile and gripped his shoulder. "For now, I want you two to investigate these missing vampires. You have my full authority to use any resources here or in town that may help." His ancient eyes bored into Christian's. "Move swiftly and bring our family back home."

Christian straightened with renewed sense of purpose. "We will uncover whoever is responsible for this offense," he vowed. "You have my word."

Satisfied, Augustus dismissed them to begin the search. Christian's mind raced with possibilities as he walked briskly beside Elvira. Together they would leave no stone unturned, no dark corner unexposed, until their missing loved ones were safe once more.

Christian silently swore to protect them all, now and forever. Never again would harm come to his coven family. This he promised upon his very lifeblood.

As they strode briskly down the hall, Elvira asked "Where should we begin the search?"

"The missing fledglings' quarters," Christian decided. "We may find clues the perpetrator left behind."

Elvira nodded sharply, her expression promising retribution. "I'll take two rooms. You check the other two and Matt's room."

With that, she veered left down another corridor.

Christian made his way to the fledglings' wing, heart heavy. When first turned, all new vampires were offered sanctuary here to safely navigate the volatile transition period. He knew that trauma intimately.

After Augustus had turned him all those centuries ago, Christian had been brought to a similar coven house, completely disoriented. The enhanced senses, bloodlust, and unpredictable power surges had been terrifying at first.

He vividly remembered lying alone in his windowless room, overwhelmed and afraid of this alien new reality. The isolation ate at him, even as the tempting scent of human blood called like a siren song.

Augustus had been endlessly patient, guiding Christian through the darkest days and nights. Slowly he learned to control the urges, channel the magic thrumming in his veins. His sire stayed by his side, providing a pillar of strength when Christian felt utterly lost.

Over many difficult months, the mansion went from feeling like a prison to a true sanctuary. Christian had emerged reborn, welcomed into the coven family. Augustus had given him a gift by sharing this sheltered space to safely transition.

The missing fledglings were just beginning that precarious journey into immortality. Vulnerable, scared, completely dependent on their elders' protection and wisdom. Instead, their refuge had been ruthlessly desecrated.

Fury simmered in Christian's chest. He intimately understood the trauma inflicted upon these youths. Unforgivable. He would find them and bring them home, no matter the cost. On his life, he silently vowed it again.

Christian steeled himself as he approached the first door. This fledgeling, Lucas, was usually quiet but charming, beloved by the coven for his gentle spirit. Entering the small bedroom, however, nothing seemed amiss. The space was tidy, bed neatly made. No signs of struggle.

Perplexed, Christian moved on to Devin's quarters with similar results. No upended furniture, no torn curtains or bedding. It was as if the two had simply vanished into thin air while relaxing in their rooms. Impossible - he would have sensed a magical transportation.

His disquiet growing, Christian came to the last door. Matt. The shy, artistic vampire had flourished under his patient tutelage this past couple of years. Christian dreaded what he would find within.

Taking an unneeded breath, he turned the handle. At first glance, only darkness greeted him. But vampiric sight soon adjusted to reveal chaos. Bed overturned, shelves smashed, pages ripped and scattered across the floor. Dried blood splattered one wall.

Matt had fought back. Fierce pride mixed with agony inside Christian. If only he had been here. He carefully righted a fallen chair, heart fracturing at the violence visited upon this gentle soul.

Searching for any useful evidence, his eye caught a metallic gleam beneath the bed frame. Christian retrieved the object, inhaling sharply when he recognized the fine silver filigree work. More concerning was the powerful magic that thrummed from the metal, stinging his fingertips.

This was no ordinary silver, but a relic infused with ancient spells. Silver's mystical anti-vampiric properties made it a common tool amongst the fanatical covens who saw Christian's kind as abominations.

The potent magic worked into the precious metal could weaken and constrain even elder vampires, burning vampire flesh on contact. Its discovery here implicated the fanatics immediately.

Rage rapidly overtook Christian's grief. The mark on this crime was unmistakable now. They were zealots who would stop at nothing to punish Christian and his people for the perceived sin of existing.

He wrapped the silver carefully in a monogrammed cloth and slipped it into his pocket to show Augustus later. This was solid evidence of the coven's infiltration, likely by someone internally allied with their enemies.

The cowards had waited until the mansion's vulnerabilities were exposed, then stolen away Christian's vulnerable charges in the night. It was a profound violation of coven law and customs.

They meant to send a message - that nowhere was safe from their judgment. Christian's fury hardened into cold resolve. For Matt and the others, he would tear the those who took them piece by bloody piece, no matter how long it took.

This insult would not go unanswered. He swore it on his very lifeblood and magic.

After thoroughly searching the fledglings' rooms, Christian and Elvira reconvened in the mansion's spacious living area to share findings. Elvira regretfully reported no clues or signs of struggle in the two rooms she'd checked.

Christian revealed the enchanted silver artifact he'd found discarded under Matt's bed.

"This implicates a lot of things," he explained grimly. "They must have had inside help."

Elvira's expression darkened as she examined the elaborate filigree silver piece. "Only high-ranking members could access these banned relics now. The Council tightly restricts them."

"Which means there's a traitor among us," Christian concurred. He shook his head, anger and betrayal vying within him. "But who?"

Elvira's mouth thinned to a grim line. "I think it's time we checked the security footage. Maybe our spy got sloppy."

Nodding sharply, Christian led the way to the basement control room. A lone human named Bernard manned the monitors, tasked with overseeing the property's supernatural security. Part of his contract was immortality in exchange for service.

Bernard looked up in surprise as they entered. "Mr. Christian, Ms. Elvira. How can I help you?"

"We're investigating a security breach involving missing vampires," Christian informed him without preamble. "Have you noticed anything unusual on the cameras lately?"

Bernard paled slightly but shook his head. "Nothing I can recall. But you say there are fledglings unaccounted for?" Distress tinged his voice.

"Five taken from their very rooms just last night," Elvira confirmed grimly. She leaned over the control desk, tone brooking no argument. "We need to review the footage immediately."

Nodding, Bernard quickly set to work scanning through the previous night's recordings. Meanwhile, Christian asked, "Who else was on duty here last night?"

Bernard's expression turned thoughtful. "Let me think - only one of our new hires, Leo. Quiet lad." He glanced down at the camera monitoring, then back to Christian. "Would you like Leo's contact information?"

"Yes, thank you. I'd like to question him about anything he might have noticed," Christian decided. Someone had to know what happened here.

However, once Bernard finished reviewing the footage, his confusion was evident. "That's very odd - there are several hours missing from the tapes when Leo was on shift. Almost like they were erased."

A chill ran through Christian, his suspicions all but confirmed. "It seems we have our traitor then." He met Elvira's equally enraged gaze. "Time to pay this Leo a visit and get answers."

No one harmed Christian's people and lived. This Leo would deeply regret ever trespassing on their family. Christian and Elvira would ensure it, once they pried the fledglings' location from the turncoat's miserable hide.

But first, they had a hunt to conduct. Christian would track his prey to the ends of the earth if needed. The oath upon his blood and magic remained unbroken. For his lost loved ones, he would let nothing stop his vengeance.

Christian and Elvira left the mansion, Leo's address in hand. Elvira recognized the location - one of the more run-down parts of Dawncreek's supernatural district. As they drove, Christian reflected sadly on the stubborn pockets of shadow that persisted even in their peaceful home.

Though the coven tried to bring light to all, some still embraced darkness willingly. And now it had invaded their family.

"I know the area," Elvira remarked as they pulled onto a main street. "It's seen better days."

Christian gazed out at the changing scenery, heart heavy. Overall Dawncreek was a welcoming haven, but certain neighborhoods had fallen into disrepair and crime. Despite the coven's outreach efforts, many there still rejected aid, preferring to languish in shadow.

As they drove on, the cheerful shops and flower boxes lining the sidewalks gradually gave way to derelict buildings with boarded windows. Graffiti marred the crumbling brick walls. Broken glass and trash littered the streets. The few residents they passed walked quickly with heads down, avoiding eye contact.

It pained Christian to see parts of their community mired in such darkness and hopelessness. The coven provided resources for all, but they could not force help on those determined to refusal. And so pockets of decay persisted, fertile ground for the wicked to take root if given the chance.

But never had Christian imagined one of their own would collude with these dark forces, betraying family to abduct innocents. It went against their most sacred codes of honor. Unprecedented. Intolerable.

Elvira's voice broke his brooding thoughts. "So tell me, how are things with Dominic? Have you visited your family yet?"

Christian smiled softly, the mere thought of his mate chasing away some shadows. He summarized their emotional journey to meet his biological parents in Moonriff. Elvira listened keenly, asking questions and seeming glad for Christian's newfound joy.

"It was good. I didn't think that after so long that I would have another chance of having a family again." Christian mused.

"I am happy for you, darling." Elvira said and Christian appreciated her.

The casual conversation soothed his nerves during the short drive. But unease returned full force as they pulled up to the dilapidated row house. Rotted wood, crumbling brick and overgrown weeds surrounded the dismal place. Its bleak facade screamed condemned.

"Be on guard," Christian cautioned as they approached the front door. His instincts blared warnings of potential danger. Elvira nodded, emerald eyes scanning their surroundings warily.

Their sharp knocks elicited no response. Christian's sense of foreboding grew. Fearing the worst, he directed a focused blow at the locked door, snapping it open.

They were met by darkness and the overpowering stench of blood. Christian quickly told Elvira to cover her nose and mouth with a handkerchief before she could inhale the visceral odor. Breathing shallowly himself, he searched for the source.

They moved cautiously through the gloomy house, Christian in the lead. In the dingy kitchen, a flashlight beam illuminated a body lying prone in a pool of red. Christian rushed over, carefully turning the man onto his back.

It was Leo, his face a mass of bruises and gashes still oozing dark blood. His eyes were shut, skin clammy and white as a corpse. Christian felt for a pulse, fearing the worst. But a faint, fluttering heartbeat still echoed under his fingertips. Leo clung to life, however tenuously.

The wounds told a vicious story - Leo had been viciously beaten, presumably for his earlier cooperation. But by whom?

Elvira returned with towels to staunch the bleeding, her quick thinking and field medicine training kicking in. Christian was grateful - his rage threatened to overwhelm reason at the callous assault perpetrated here.

Who could do such violence upon their own ally? The absolute cruelty turned his stomach. But Leo might still hold vital clues to the fledglings' whereabouts and captors. They had to rouse him before it was too late. Time was running out for all of them.

"What do you know about the missing fledglings?" Christian demanded, shaking Leo roughly. When that got no response, he slapped the man's battered face, hard. "Talk, or I end your treachery here!" he snarled, letting rage take over.

Leo's eyes flickered half open, glazed with pain. "Was just… following orders," he slurred, choking on blood. "One of the…elders… "

Christian's insides turned to ice. "Where did he take them?"

Leo mumbled incoherently, fading fast. Christian resisted the urge to simply end him. Finally Leo choked out "…heard them talking. The woman and the elder. More tonight…at the club Midnight…"

His head lolled back, the effort having depleted his last reserves. But Christian had heard enough. This Elder was foolishly brazen if he thought to openly take victims under Christian's nose. He would soon regret severely overplaying his hand.

But Leo had slipped back into delirium. Christian barely restrained himself from snapping the prone man's neck. Finally Elvira pulled him back, emerald eyes blazing.

"He's not worth sullying your conscience," she said sharply. "We need to warn the others now." Her eyes softened, seeing Christian's inner conflict. "Killing the pawn won't stop whoever is doing this."

Christian released a harsh breath, knowing she spoke truth. With effort, he turned his fury inward. They had one lead to follow - the Elder would be at Midnight tonight. The traitorous elder had much to answer for.

Back outside in the relative fresh air, Elvira placed a steadying hand on his shoulder. "What now?"

Christian's jaw tightened with resolve. "Inform Augustus. I'll go to Midnight and end this." If this vampire thought to hurt more under his protection, he would learn his terrible mistake this very night.

The missing fledglings were running out of time. But Christian would tear down the heavens themselves to save his people if demanded. Upon his blood oath, this injustice would not stand.

19

Second Chances

Dominic

Dominic sighed, leaning on the counter. It had been a long night caring for Austin after finally rescuing him. Dominic and Lee had stayed up waiting anxiously for their little brother to wake, but he remained deep in magical healing sleep.

Around midnight, Ciaran came downstairs from where he'd been working on Austin in the guest room.

"How is he?" Dominic asked urgently, rushing over.

Ciaran gave a tired smile. "I've done all I can for now. His physical wounds are mended, but whatever dark magic was used on him runs deep." His expression turned solemn. "It may take time for him to find his way back."

Lee gripped Dominic's shoulder, fear in his eyes. "But he will wake up fully, right?"

"Have faith," Ciaran advised gently. "Austin needs to heal at his own pace. Stay by his side and call if anything changes." He squeezed Lee's arm. "Your brother is strong. He'll come back to you when he's ready."

After Ciaran left, Dominic and Lee returned to Austin's bedside to resume their vigil. Dominic clutched his little brother's limp hand. "You're safe now, Austin. We are here. We'll be waiting right here when you wake."

Lee brushed Austin's hair back tenderly. "Take all the time you need. We're not going anywhere."

They sat in silence for a few minutes just watching the steady rise and fall of Austin's chest. Finally Lee spoke up quietly. "That lich in the woods…I've never seen anything like it." He looked at Dominic. "But who has the power to summon something so evil?"

Dominic shook his head grimly. "I don't know. But Austin might, when he wakes up. He's the only one who knows what's been going on."

Lee nodded. "We'll get answers soon hopefully." He squeezed Austin's hand. "Just focus on healing, little brother. We can handle the rest."

Exhausted as he was, Dominic couldn't rest not knowing if Austin would truly recover. So they kept watch as the night stretched on, holding out hope that Austin would wake up with the answers they desperately needed.

Now Dominic stood in the bakery kitchen, headache pounding relentlessly as he worried about his little brother still comatose at home. He desperately hoped Austin would open his eyes again soon…

The oven timer buzzed, jolting Dominic from his thoughts. He blinked blearily, trying to recall what he'd been baking before getting lost reminiscing about the long night.

Right, the croissants for the morning rush. He quickly pulled the trays out, sighing in relief to see the pastries were perfectly golden brown. The comforting scent helped ground him.

He set the croissants out to cool before starting on kneading more dough. As he rhythmically worked the pliable mass, Dominic rubbed gingerly at his temple. The vice-like migraine pressure was worsening by the minute.

Usually staying busy kept the curse's headaches at bay, but today not even the familiar work could distract from the relentless pain. He winced as a particularly sharp spike lanced through his skull.

Lyra breezed back into the kitchen balancing empty mugs and plates. She paused seeing Dominic's tense expression. "Hey, you doing okay?"

Dominic attempted a weak smile. "Yeah, just a little headache. I'll be fi-"

He broke off as another wave of nauseating pain hit. Lyra set her tray down and came over to peer at him critically.

"Nope, you are clearly not fine," she decreed, crossing her arms. "You're white as a sheet. When's the last time you took a break?"

Dominic tried to think through the haze of pain. He'd gone nonstop since arriving at the crack of dawn.

At his silence, Lyra nodded firmly. "That's what I thought. Time for you to get off your feet for a bit. We've got plenty stocked up already."

Dominic started to protest, but Lyra fixed him with her no-nonsense doctor's gaze. "Not up for discussion. Go sit down and rest while it's slow." Seeing him hesitate, she softened. "Just for a little while? For me?"

Between the genuine concern in her voice and his skull feeling ready to split open, Dominic finally relented. "Okay fine, you win. I'll take five minutes."

"Fifteen minutes minimum," Lyra countered archly. "Doctor's orders. Now go on and relax, I'll bring you a coffee."

Too worn down to argue, Dominic simply nodded and turned to untie his apron. The strings blurred in his vision for a second. Maybe he did need a quick break.

He washed up and splashed some cool water on his face, which helped marginally. The cafe's cozy warmth enveloped him as he emerged from the kitchen's controlled chaos. It was late morning, the earlier rush over. Only a few tables were occupied by lingering regulars.

Sinking gratefully into a cushioned chair by the window, Dominic had to admit it felt good to be off his feet. The sunlight streaming in calmed his throbbing head slightly. He closed his eyes and focused on taking slow, even breaths.

True to her word, Lyra soon appeared with a steaming mug. "Here you go. Drink up." She set down the coffee and squeezed his shoulder. "Take all the time you need. I can handle things here."

Dominic managed a small but genuine smile. "Thank you, Lyra. I'll just be a few."

Nodding approvingly, she headed off to cover the counter. Dominic watched her go, gratitude for his steadfast friend swelling in his chest. The cafe was emptying out now as lunchtime neared. For a little while, he could steal some peace.

Sipping the fragrant drink, Dominic turned his face back to the sun and just breathed…

When his phone buzzed, Dominic instantly smiled seeing Christian's name. He answered quickly, "Hey you."

"Hello my heart," Christian replied, though his voice sounded subdued and tired.

Dominic's brow creased in concern. "How are you holding up?"

Christian heaved a weary sigh. "Well enough, now that I hear your voice." He went on to summarize the lack of progress finding the missing vampires. "We thought we had a solid lead, but they must have realized we were coming. It was another dead end."

Dominic's heart ached, hearing the pain and frustration in Christian's tone. "I'm so sorry, love. I wish I could help somehow."

"Just having you here for me is help enough," Christian assured him, soft sincerity returning to his voice.

After chatting a while longer about lighter topics, he asked gently,

"How are you feeling today?"

Dominic considered downplaying it, but answered honestly. "My whole body is sore and I've had a splitting headache all day. Feels like the curse is getting worse again."

Christian made a worried sound. "Do you need me there? We could do another blood exchange, see if it helps."

It was a tempting offer, hearing the concern in Christian's voice. Even just listening to him lessened Dominic's discomfort slightly. Their mating bond truly was a marvel, if complex.

"I'm managing for now, but will let you know if it gets bad again," Dominic said, not wanting Christian to rush over and neglect his own pressing duties. "Just hearing you helps more than you realize."

Christian hummed thoughtfully. "This distance is difficult, but together we'll figure it out. I hate to cut this short, my heart, but there are some new developments here I must see to. But I'll call again soon."

"Of course, go do what you need to do," Dominic said supportively. "I'll be here when you have time. Stay strong, my love."

Lost in thought about their connection, Dominic's gaze wandered idly around the cafe. Then his blood ran cold. Gary, his warlock tormentor from months back, had just entered and was approaching the counter, laughing loudly with his companions.

Gary…here. The nightmare Dominic thought he'd escaped stood in the flesh, just as sadistic and controlling as he recalled. Panic clawed up Dominic's throat.

"Dominic? What's wrong?" Christian asked urgently.

"I'll call you right back," Dominic said tightly, ending the call with Christian. Eyes fixed on Gary, he sagged back in his seat, praying the man wouldn't notice him. But luck wasn't on his side.

Gary glanced over casually, then did an astonished double take. A grin spread across his face and he strode toward Dominic's table.

Dominic tensed, ready to flee or fight.

But as Gary approached, Dominic sensed something different in his demeanor and emotions. The arrogant superiority was gone, replaced by uncertainty. This wasn't the same taunting bully who had tormented Dominic before.

Gary stopped a few feet away, hands raised unthreateningly. "Hey Dominic. I don't want any trouble. Just hoping we could talk." His tone was subdued, conciliatory.

Dominic remained wary, but nodded cautiously. "I'll hear you out." As an empath, he discreetly assessed Gary's emotional state. This wasn't a magical talent per se, but simply being attuned to others' feelings. Dominic's empathy was heightened slightly by his magic.

Focusing on Gary, beneath the surface anxiety, Dominic sensed genuine remorse and guilt. None of the malicious glee or haughty arrogance from their past encounter. This was a very different man standing before him.

Still, Dominic stayed on guard, not fully ready to trust what his instincts were telling him. But he would give Gary a chance to speak. Everyone deserved an opportunity to redeem themselves, if they truly sought to make amends.

Dominic met Gary's uncertain gaze steadily, willing to hear him out. But words alone wouldn't be enough - Gary had much trust to rebuild through actions. For now, Dominic would remain cautiously open, hoping despite past pain that change was possible. It was a fragile hope, but one he nurtured as Gary began to speak...

Gary gave a tentative smile. "Could we get some coffee maybe?"

Dominic studied him a moment more before nodding to Lyra at the counter. As she went to get their drinks, Dominic focused wholly on Gary. "Go ahead and talk then."

Gary clasped his hands on the table, unable to meet Dominic's eyes fully. "First off, I...I'm so sorry for what I did that day. I wasn't myself, but I know that's no excuse." His shoulders hunched, ashamed. "I'll never forgive myself for hurting you and Levi."

Dominic took a slow, steadying breath as memories of that trauma resurfaced. "You have no idea the effect your actions had on me," he began quietly. "For weeks after, I couldn't sleep from the nightmares. I'd wake up screaming, feeling like your hands were still on me." Dominic's own hands shook with the echo of remembered fear.

Gary paled, but nodded for him to continue. "You took away my sense of safety," Dominic went on, voice husky with emotion. "I shut everyone out, stopped trusting people I'd known for years. My relationships suffered." He locked eyes with Gary. "So no, it being the Malachite's influence doesn't erase what you did. Those memories will haunt me for a long time."

Gary seemed to fold in on himself. "You're absolutely right," he rasped. "I destroyed so much that day. I know no apology or amends could ever be enough." His eyes shimmered with restrained tears. "But I swear I've changed, Dominic," Gary implored. "That monster Malachite created is gone. I'll spend my whole life trying to become someone who deserves forgiveness."

Dominic studied him intently. The remorse pouring off Gary seemed genuine. With time and effort, redemption was possible. But the road would be long for them both.

"It's a start that you're here acknowledging what you did," Dominic said finally. "Keep making that effort, and we'll see where it leads."

Gary nodded, looking cautiously hopeful. Dominic felt the first small sliver of peace since that horrific day. They had a difficult road ahead, but the chance to walk it together.

Against his better judgment, Dominic felt his anger begin softening. "Is that where you've been all these months then? Trying to outrun your actions?"

Gary shook his head. "No, Larry and Steve...they helped me recover my mind and conscience. I've been in therapy working through what I did." He met Dominic's gaze sorrowfully. "I'm so sorry for the pain I inflicted on you and those you love. I don't expect your forgiveness, but I hope to someday earn back your trust."

Dominic saw the sincerity in Gary's eyes. Real change was difficult, but not impossible. "Apology accepted, for my part," he said finally. "But it will take time to move forward as friends again. You have much to make amends for."

Gary nodded, looking cautiously hopeful. "Thank you for hearing me out. I know I don't deserve it." He extended a hand tentatively across the table.

After a moment's hesitation, Dominic reached out and shook it. Gary's relief was palpable. It would be a long road, but everyone deserved a chance at redemption if they sought it out.

Their coffee arrived then. They talked more, the conversation coming easier. Maybe this could be the start of healing old wounds. The past still cast shadows, but the future held light if they walked toward it together.

After an emotionally draining talk with Gary, Dominic was relieved to get back to the comforting familiarity of work. He felt lighter, the headache that had plagued him all morning finally abating after speaking to Christian.

Dominic missed his mate fiercely, but he knew Christian had duties to his own family right now. They would reunite soon enough. For today, Dominic took solace in the memory of Christian's voice.

Closing up the bakery that evening, Dominic remembered he needed to restock Vale's dog food and grab a few groceries. Lee and the still-recovering Austin were staying at his place, so he wanted to cook up something nourishing.

The grocery store was only a few blocks over, so Dominic decided to walk and enjoy the fresh air after being cooped up all day. But as he strolled along, the hair on the back of his neck prickled unexpectedly. Glancing around and seeing no one, Dominic shrugged it off and raised a subtle protective ward just in case.

Inside the brightly-lit grocery store, Dominic grabbed a basket and headed for the pet section first. He smiled browsing the diverse treats and toys, making a mental note to spoil Vale soon. His dog had been so well-behaved while he was away.

The Willowbrook Market was beloved by the locals. Dominic nodded greetings to familiar faces as he shopped. Despite the size, it retained a cozy, friendly ambiance.

Mouthwatering aromas filled the air from the bakery and deli sections. Dominic's stomach rumbled as he passed displays of fresh-baked breads and cakes. The produce section overflowed with colorful fruits and vegetables, some from local farms.

Upbeat music played softly over the speakers as customers chatted and laughed while perusing the aisles. Kids trailed after parents, begging for snacks and candy from the rows of tempting shelves. It was a microcosm of the warm community spirit Dominic cherished.

Distracted, he accidentally bumped carts with a woman passing by.

"Oh I'm so sorry!" she exclaimed brightly, steadying his basket. Her strangely intent gaze made him tense instinctively.

Then his magic flared in warning an instant before her hand shot out like a viper toward his chest. Dominic dodged just in time, adrenaline spiking. Giving her a wide berth, he rushed to grab the last few items and get out of there.

Bursting out the automatic doors, Dominic was startled by a blood-curdling scream nearby. Reacting on instinct, he called up a weather shield to encapsulate the store and civilians inside. Thunder rumbled ominously as he scanned for the threat.

There - the woman from before floated several feet off the ground, human facade melting away to reveal a spectral horror. Lank hair writhed around her skeletal face and empty eye sockets as she opened her maw and released another glass-shattering screech.

Dominic dropped his groceries, hands clamping over his ears in agony as the wraith's screams shredded the air. Gritting his teeth, he countered with a gust of wind that blew her backwards but failed to do real damage. He couldn't risk going all out so close to the store full of people.

The creature recovered quickly, her empty eyes fixing malevolently on Dominic as she pressed her assault. Dominic could only defend and evade, her sinister magic too powerful and otherworldly. He was tiring fast. Who had summoned this monster?

Just as he was flagging, Dominic heard someone shout his name. He turned to see Gary sprinting toward them, face set with determination.

"Do you know what that thing is?" Dominic yelled over the banshee's furious screeches.

"It's a banshee!" Gary called back. "One of the deadliest spirits from the hell dimensions!" He eyed the wraith warily. "Someone must have summoned her here!"

Dominic ducked another shrieking blast. "Got any ideas how to defeat it? I can't keep this up!"

Gary gave him a reckless grin. "Lucky for you, I'm from the hells too. It'll take a demon to beat this bitch." Before Dominic could respond, Gary shifted into his true diabolic incubus form.

With a challenging laugh, Gary launched himself at the banshee. She turned her fury on this new foe, skeletal claws swiping. But Gary evaded her blows with ease.

"That's right, come to papa," Gary taunted. As she dove for him, he opened his fanged mouth impossibly wide. With a horrible sucking sound, the screeching spirit was drawn completely inside him.

Silence fell, broken only by Dominic's harsh breathing. As Gary gently floated back down, reverting to human form, Dominic staggered.

His strength had fled abruptly.

Gary caught him before he could fall. "I've got you," he soothed, letting Dominic lean against him.

When he could stand on his own again, Dominic gripped Gary's shoulder. "Thank you. I owe you."

Gary shook his head. "I'm just trying to make amends." He glanced around warily. "But this doesn't seem right."

20

Harbinger

Christian

Christian approached the secluded forest gravesite slowly, flowers in hand. Even after relocating the ashes here to Dawncreek, this site remained his sacred place of solace and reflection.

He was still thinking about how abruptly Dominic had ended their call earlier. Christian hoped nothing was wrong and that Dominic would share the reason soon. Their relationship was still so new. Navigating separation was a learning process.

When Christian had relocated to Dawncreek from England a long time ago, he'd brought his adoptive parents' remains to re-inter them here. Their old burial site across the sea had begun feeling too conspicuous as more people encroached on the remote estate grounds.

Leaving England had been difficult, but It stopped feeling like home. So his coven had sailed for America, his parents' ashes safely in tow.

Now they rested in this tranquil forest on the outskirts of Dawncreek, isolated and undisturbed. Christian liked to think they would have enjoyed the wild natural beauty of this land they'd never seen…

Kneeling before the twin granite headstones, Christian gently placed the lilies he'd brought - his mother's favorite. The inscription was simple: "Here lie Karina and Ludwig Picard. Beloved Parents."

Christian traced the engraved names, overcome with bittersweet emotion.

Long after Karina and Ludwig had passed on, Christian still missed them fiercely. They had given him a true home again when he was adrift, nurtured his wounded soul back to joy. He owed them so much.

Christian rested his palms atop each gravestone. He still spoke to his adoptive parents often, updating them on his immortal life. They were always listening somehow.

"Hello Mother, Father," he began softly. "I'm sorry it's been a few weeks. Things have been...eventful." He huffed a quiet laugh, picturing their reactions.

"You always said everyone deserves a second chance at family. Well, I've found mine. My real parents are still alive after all this time." Saying it aloud still felt surreal.

"I know you never told me I was adopted to protect me," he went on. "But I understand why now. And I forgive any hurt it caused. You gave me everything - love, guidance, a home."

Christian's voice grew thick with emotion. "I'll never stop being thankful you took me in. You made me the man I am today. I hope I've made you proud."

Wiping his eyes, Christian steadied himself to continue. "There's someone special I want you to meet. His name is Dominic." Just saying his mate's name warmed Christian's heart.

"He's my true match, the one you always said was out there waiting for me," Christian confessed, smiling softly. "I can't put into words what Dominic means to me. With him I'm finally whole."

The shadows of leaves dancing in the sunlight caught his eye. Christian imagined it was the spirits of his adoptive parents expressing their joy at seeing him happy.

"I wish you could have met him," Christian whispered. "You would have loved Dominic's kind heart and unconquerable spirit. But I know you're watching over us."

For a time Christian stood there in tranquil silence, taking comfort from the whispers of wind through the trees. His family - past, present and future - enveloped him in their love. He would make them all proud.

Finally Christian bid his farewell. "I'll come visit again soon," he promised. "Take care of each other."

With lighter steps, he headed back down the forest path. But after only a few paces, the air turned abruptly frigid. The scent of ozone permeated the atmosphere - the herald of powerful magic nearby.

Christian halted, instantly on guard. Then, from behind him, an ethereal female voice spoke.

"They have done their job well, protecting and guiding you." The voice was melodic, seeming to resonate through Christian's very soul. "Your parents are so very proud of the man you've become."

Christian whirled around. Floating several feet away was a radiant woman with flowing silver hair and luminescent skin. Impossible magical energy swirled around her. Christian's jaw dropped.

"Who are you?" he managed to ask. "How do you know of my parents?" If this being meant him harm, he was unsure he could defend himself against her ancient power.

The woman gave a benign smile. "I have many names - Queen, Enchantress, Goddess. But you may call me Moriganna." She inclined her head graciously. "Be at ease, Christian. I mean you no harm."

Christian's eyes widened. From what Roan told them she was the mythical Queen of Magic herself, and she stood before him. Her mere presence seemed to cause the very air to vibrate with power.

She summoned a glistening crystal staff and waved it through the air.

An orb manifested and began glowing, then familiar faces appeared within - Elizabeth and James.

Christian gasped, overcome with emotion. Though only images, seeing his adoptive parents' kind eyes and warm smiles again felt like coming home.

"We hear you, Christian," they said in unison. "We are so very proud of the honorable man you've become. Take care of your new family now." Then they faded away.

"No, wait!" Christian cried out desperately. But the orb dissolved, images winking out. They were gone again.

Moriganna regarded him with ancient empathy. "Worry not. Their spirits rest in the realm of the souls, at peace." Her expression turned solemn. "But dark times are coming. I come with a warning."

Christian refocused on her warily. "What warning do you bring?" If a being as powerful as her was concerned, the danger must be grave.

"Evil stirs, threatening this world," Moriganna intoned. "No matter what comes, you must stay strong. Do not break, or all could be lost."

Before Christian could question her further on this ominous prophecy, Moriganna vanished in a flash of light. The forest was silent once more, but her words echoed hauntingly in Christian's mind.

What terrifying darkness was awakening that troubled even the Queen of Magic? Fear gripped Christian, but also determination. With his family and friends beside him, he would answer this evil with light.

Moriganna's warning hung heavy, but Christian clung to hope. They would face the shadows as one and emerge stronger for it. Together, united by bonds of loyalty and love, the coming darkness did not stand a chance.

Stepping into his office at the back of the Midnight, Christian took a moment to appreciate the luxurious space he'd crafted for himself.

As owner, he'd designed it as an oasis of comfort and elegance.

The first thing that struck him was the rich, smooth scent of leather and mahogany. The walls were paneled in the deep reddish wood, giving the office a refined masculine ambiance. One entire wall was taken up by built-in shelves full of leather-bound books and curiosities collected over centuries.

Plush blood-red carpet cushioned his footsteps as he walked past the stately wooden desk toward the sitting area. A leather couch and two wingback chairs provided a welcoming space to relax or entertain guests. The furniture was an insanely comfortable leather that perfectly molded to his body.

Overall, the office exuded an atmosphere of understated refinement. During the often chaotic nights at the club, Christian enjoyed retreating here to regroup and handle business in civilized comfort. It was his own personal bastion of tasteful luxury.

Standing at the wet bar cart to pour himself a drink, Christian nodded in satisfaction. He'd designed the space to fulfill his every need and desire. Surrounded by fine wood, leather and expensive liquor, he could focus his mind and energies completely.

Settling into the plush desk chair with his crystal glass in hand, Christian took a deep breath, letting the familiar scents soothe him. He was ready to handle anything awaiting his attention tonight. His domain gave him strength.

Christian reviewed CCTV footage from the night the fledglings disappeared, searching for any clues. Moriganna's dire warning still echoed in his mind, but for now he forced himself to focus on the task at hand.

He was doing paperwork while observing the security feed, looking for anything out of the ordinary the night they lost Matt and the others. Most cameras showed nothing unusual. Until one outside caught Christian's protégé Matt leaving after his evening shift.

Christian gripped the desk tightly as a nondescript black van followed Matt down the street after he'd waved goodbye to friends. Christian's fury boiled up. How dare these monsters stalk one of his own right outside his territory.

Before he could put his fist through the monitor, a knock interrupted his dark thoughts. Taking a deep breath, Christian called for the visitor to enter. It was Igor, one of the oldest vampires in the coven...

Moriganna's prophecy still lingered, but Christian couldn't lose himself to fear. He had to stay focused on the immediate threat and getting his people back. One battle at a time. The coming darkness would not find him broken. Christian had tasked him with investigating the enchanted silver artifact's origins.

Igor sank into the leather chair across from the desk, expression grim. "Any developments on the silver?" Christian asked without preamble.

"Nothing concrete yet," Igor replied. "But I've heard whispers of unusual activity out at an abandoned warehouse deep in the forest." He held up a hand as Christian leaned forward intently. "Could be nothing. But worth looking into."

Christian's mind raced. A promising lead at last. "Have you done any reconnaissance there yourself?"

Igor nodded, withdrawing some photos from his coat. "I did a brief sweep of the perimeter. Here's what I found."

Christian quickly shuffled through the images - the crumbling warehouse, clearly long deserted. It had probably gone unnoticed until now, tucked far off any main roads. One photo made his undead blood run cold.

There, parked outside the warehouse doors, was a black van identical to the one that had stalked Matt. Rage and fear warred inside Christian. These fiends were operating right under the coven's nose. No more.

Christian met Igor's gaze sharply. "Contact Elvira immediately and have her meet us here. Then you'll take us to this warehouse." His voice allowed no argument. Igor simply nodded and left to make the call.

Fingerprints embedding in the sturdy oak desk, Christian stared unseeing at the damning photo. Whatever these monsters were doing with his people, it ended tonight. He would lay waste to their whole operation if he must.

While waiting for Elvira, Christian and Igor went to the bar to have a drink. Christian took it upon himself to mix up some cocktails for them.

As he slid a glass over, Igor remarked, "So you're mated now, huh?"

Despite the grim circumstances, talk of Dominic still made Christian feel lighter. "Yeah, it happened when I least expected it."

Igor patted his shoulder. "I did some digging on your man after I found out. Just wanted to be sure." At Christian's raised brow, he added, "Don't worry, I didn't find anything worrisome. His step-mom was in some witch group apparently, but that's it."

Christian filed away that tidbit for later. He wasn't bothered - Dominic had nothing to hide. Their conversation moved to lighter topics as they waited.

Soon Igor stiffened, his advanced senses detecting Elvira approaching. As a scout, he had preternatural awareness of temperature changes. Igor could perceive even minute fluctuations in body heat from great distances.

This unique ability allowed him to literally sense life forces moving around him. It gave Igor a critical advantage when hunting or tracking. He could pinpoint prey precisely even in pitch darkness.

Igor's thermal sensing talent made him an invaluable asset to the coven. No one could evade his notice or sneak up on them with Igor on watch. He was their first line of supernatural defense.

That's why Christian relied on him now to help uncover this latest threat. Igor's singular skills would sniff out their hidden foes. Between his thermal tracking and Elvira's combat expertise, the coven had a potent strike team assembled.

Right on cue, Elvira strode in looking ready for action. The latex cat suit she wore suited her perfectly. "Damn, girl, you clean up nice," Christian teased.

Elvira laughed. "You know it takes time to look this good!" She took the drink Christian offered and he quickly updated her.

"So what's the plan?" she asked, eyes intense.

Christian leaned forward. "We take both our cars separately as decoys. Igor will go on ahead first. Once he gives the all-clear, you and I follow and hit their operation hard."

Elvira nodded sharply, tightening her gloves. "Sounds good. Time to hit these bastards where they live."

Christian's answering smile was cold and feral. The monsters had poked a sleeping dragon. He would rain holy fire upon them for daring to steal from his nest. By his blood oath, they would pay dearly this night.

With his allies at his side, Christian headed out into the darkness. His formidable powers simmered just below the surface, hungry for vengeance. Before this night ended, his foes would learn why vampires were creatures to be feared.

The hunt was on. By the time he was through, they would have no doubt who ruled this territory. Christian had been merciful for too long. That ended today. His wrath would be a chilling reminder to all who thought to violate his family.

They executed their plan flawlessly. Igor went on ahead as decoy while Christian and Elvira followed covertly in separate vehicles. The entire ride was tense, the only sound the growl of the engines. Christian's mind raced with what they would discover at this mysterious warehouse.

As they drove deeper into the remote forest, the landscape grew increasingly ominous. The friendly lights of town faded away behind them, swallowed by writhing shadows. An icy wind howled between the dark trees lining the winding dirt road.

Up ahead, Christian spotted Igor's taillights turning off the main path. Their destination lay just ahead now. Christian tensed, ready to unleash fury upon these monsters who had taken his people.

They arrived to find Igor already scouting the perimeter. His thermal senses would warn of any lookouts or traps. So far the place seemed deserted.

Exiting the cars, they convened for final preparations. Pale sunlight still filtered through the canopy - they had maybe an hour before full dark.

"Will the sun be an issue?" Christian asked his companions. Protected by magic, it didn't affect him. But the others were more vulnerable now.

Elvira shook her head, leather outfit creaking. "I've got another hour or so before it becomes a problem." Her eyes glinted with anticipation.

Christian nodded. "Igor, keep watch out here. Elvira, go invisible and search inside. I'll breach straight through the front." He grinned fiercely. "Let's remind them why vampires are feared."

Elvira vanished from sight with a savage smile. Her invisibility made her the perfect infiltrator. Christian felt a swell of gratitude for his loyal friends. Together they would conquer this evil.

Igor's brow furrowed. "Oddly, I'm sensing no body heat inside. But stay alert." He melted into the shadows around the crumbling warehouse.

Drawing on his ancient power, Christian approached the bolted door. His first blow dented the thick metal. The second blow tore it completely off its hinges, crashing inward. Through the dust, he strode inside ready to face hell itself.

The massive front doors were locked tight. Circling the perimeter, Christian spotted a broken window along the side that provided access. He slipped inside, immediately on high alert.

The cloying stench of silver infused the stale air. Christian quickly pulled a scarf from his pocket to cover his nose and mouth. Prolonged exposure to the toxic metal could weaken vampires. He called out a warning to invisible Elvira to do the same.

Using his phone for light, Christian explored the cavernous interior. The main space was empty except for sinister evidence of dark rituals. In the center lay a half-finished summoning circle surrounded by melted candles and chalk sigils. Dried blood completed the macabre scene.

Christian closed in on the circle cautiously. Violent scorch marks and toppled equipment indicated someone had interrupted the ritual. But who? And for what vile purpose?

Spotting an engraved silver amulet on the floor, Christian instantly crushed it under his boot. The less of the hateful substance left, the better. He continued searching for clues to what evil had transpired here.

In a far corner, his light revealed a pile of desiccated corpses drained of life force. Christian's stomach twisted. Whatever malice had festered here, it bore only contempt for mortal life. Destroying it would be a mercy.

Elvira materialized next to him, scowling at the carnage. "I found a whole stockpile of silver weapons downstairs, and cells like a prison." Her eyes roamed around again and scowled. "Who the hell is behind this?"

Before Christian could speculate, movement caught his eye. A familiar figure lingered at the edge of the shadows, watching them with a cruel smile, before vanishing from sight.

"Eros," Christian bit out. The traitorous elder had played his hand at last. Christian had allowed his former mentor's dissent for too long. That ended tonight.

Elvira's gasp echoed his shock. "That bastard? I'll kill him myself!" Her fangs glinted as she growled.

Before Christian could respond, Igor's shout rang out from outside - "Incoming!" Seconds later, the floor shook violently. The summoning circle began glowing neon red.

A massive ogre wielding a spiked mace materialized within the circle, beady eyes fixing on them. It threw back its head and bellowed furiously before charging straight at Christian.

"Hold them off out there!" Christian yelled to Igor. To Elvira he shouted, "Get ready!" Then the ogre was upon him.

Christian dove aside, the mace crashing down where he'd stood and shattering concrete. The ogre wheeled with shocking speed, swinging again. Christian blurred out of reach, landing blows to its thick hide that barely slowed the brute.

Circling warily, Christian searched for a weakness while evading the devastating strikes. Elvira launched herself at the creature from behind, clawing viciously at its eyes to distract it.

The ogre roared in pain and rage, arms flailing blindly. It clipped Elvira, sending her skidding across the floor. Sunlight streamed onto her prone form from the broken window. She screamed as her skin started smoking.

Seeing Elvira's peril reawoke Christian's fury. He rushed the staggering ogre, pounding it with all his might. But its hide seemed impervious, and his blows grew desperate. Elvira was running out of time!

As the ogre turned for a finishing blow on Elvira, something snapped in Christian. He sprinted and leaped onto its back with a primal roar. Icy energy surged down his arms as he gripped the ogre's head.

The brute froze mid-motion, skin cracking with frost spreading from Christian's hands. He leapt off as the ogre toppled like a felled oak, shattering on impact.

Panting hard, Christian helped Elvira to shelter. "Are you alright?" At her weak nod, he asked in wonder, "How did I do that?" He stared at his hands still steaming with cold vapor.

"No clue, but it was epic!" Elvira rasped before collapsing against him. They had survived, somehow. Now to finish this and go home.

Outside, Igor had dispatched a handful of rogues trying to flee. "Got a phone off one," he reported. "It may provide clues."

Christian's expression hardened. "Let's move out."

21

Dark Secrets

Dominic

Dominic *found himself standing in an endless field of gently swaying lilies that stretched as far as the eye could see. A serene azure sky arched overhead, dotted with puffy white clouds. The floral scent infusing the soft breeze calmed his spirit.*

Glancing around in wonder, he noticed a lone woman standing amid the delicately nodding flowers some distance away. Dominic called out a hesitant greeting that seemed to hang crystallized on the still air.

The woman turned unhurriedly, an expression of profound love blossoming on her delicate features. "Hello, Dominic," she said softly, his name on her lips ringing like a long forgotten but familiar melody.

Dominic approached her slowly, confusion giving way to dawning recognition. Though only seen previously in faded photographs, he knew that gentle face instantly in his heart. "Mom?" he asked, voice breaking on a sob.

"Hello, my son." His mother's beatific smile shifted into something radiant and joyful at the maternal title from his lips.

Overcome with emotion, Dominic closed the distance between them and

251

swept her up into a crushing embrace. She felt solid and real in his arms, warm and vibrantly alive. He buried his face against her floral-scented hair and wept. "How are you here?"

His mother stroked his hair soothingly, just as he'd always imagined she would. "This is but a dream, my love. A gift from benevolent powers." She pulled back, her brown eyes so like his own growing solemn. "We only have a short time together."

Dominic clung to her, wishes and regrets tumbling out in a fervent rush. "There's so much I want to tell you, ask you...I don't want to lose you again."

Taking his hands in her smaller ones, his mother said earnestly, "I cannot stay, but came with a purpose. You face grave danger, and must believe in your inner strength." Her sage gaze bored intently into his. "You must accept all that you are, or risk being lost."

Before Dominic could ask her meaning, she pulled him close once more and tenderly kissed his cheek. "I love you always, my precious son," she whispered fiercely against his skin. "Never forget..."

Then the peaceful floral vision dissolved, his mother's final words echoing as darkness engulfed him...

Dominic woke with a gasp, tears wet on his face. Morning sunlight streamed through the curtains of his bedroom. With a shaky hand, he reached up to touch his cheek where phantom lips had grazed it.

The beautiful dream was already fading, details slipping through his grasping fingers like wisps of smoke. But her voice seemed to linger, musical and beloved, whispering "I love you..."

He clung to those precious words like a lifeline as he rose to start his day. Their veracity resonated in his very soul. Whatever trials awaited him, Dominic carried his mother's enduring love with him always now. It would give him strength.

Dominic paused in surprise when he entered the kitchen. Lee stood at the stove gracefully flipping pancakes and scrambling eggs, looking utterly comfortable in the domestic role.

"Morning," Dominic said, impressed at the hearty spread of food.

Lee glanced over with an easy smile. "Hey bro, grab a seat. Grub's almost ready."

Dominic settled at the small kitchen table as Lee brought over piping hot plates loaded with fluffy pancakes, crispy bacon, scrambled eggs, and roasted potatoes. "Man, this all looks amazing!" Dominic said as his stomach rumbled loudly.

Chuckling, Lee sat across from him and passed the syrup. "Well dig in before it gets cold."

They ate in contented silence for several minutes, enjoying the meal. Eventually Dominic commented, "I honestly had no idea you could cook. These are restaurant-worthy."

"Thanks," Lee said, looking pleased by the praise. "Someone had to pick up the culinary skills. Lord knows Mom was useless in the kitchen." He took on a mock-serious tone. "Big brothers have to be masters of many arts, you know."

Dominic laughed at Lee's antics. It was nice seeing his step-brother relaxed and joking around. Usually magic and family drama overshadowed everything between them.

As they continued chatting and eating, Dominic realized how little he actually knew about Lee's interests and goals for the future outside of spellcraft. They spoke more in this one morning than the past ten years combined.

"What do you enjoy doing, besides magic?" Dominic asked after they'd finished and were nursing mugs of coffee. "Any hobbies or projects?"

Lee leaned back thoughtfully. "I love photography actually. There's something about capturing a beautiful or meaningful moment in time that speaks to me." His eyes took on a wistful look. "I'd like to publish a book of photos someday. But lately there's been little time for it."

Dominic smiled, intrigued by this creative ambition he'd never guessed Lee harbored. He found himself hoping their tentative truce continued, if only to get to know the man behind the magic…

They rushed into Austin's room, following the worrying thump. Instead of sitting up awake, Austin was thrashing around on the bed clearly in the throes of a violent nightmare.

Dominic's heart sank. He'd worried something like this might happen given all Austin had endured. The psychological torment would leave deep scars not easily healed.

"Austin, wake up!" Lee called, trying to restrain their flailing brother without hurting him. "You're safe now, it's just a dream!"

But Austin remained trapped, head tossing as he whimpered. Dominic helped Lee try to rouse him gently but firmly. Finally Austin's eyes flew open with a gasp.

Seeing his brothers, he went limp with relief. "Dominic…Lee…" he rasped weakly.

"We're right here," Dominic soothed, grabbing a glass of water. Austin's panicked thrashing had reopened partially healed wounds.

When he returned, Austin seemed more aware, though shaken. Dominic helped prop him up against the headboard to drink.

"I'll make you something gentle to eat," Lee said after checking Austin over for serious injuries. He gave Dominic a meaningful look before leaving them alone.

A heavy silence fell. Eventually Austin said with a weak, bitter laugh, "You're probably thrilled to see me taken down a peg or two after everything."

Dominic sighed. "No one deserves what you went through, no matter their past actions." He took Austin's hand tentatively. "I can't say it'll be easy to forget, but if you're truly sincere about making amends, I'm willing to try."

At that, tears began leaking down Austin's bruised face. "I'm so sorry," he choked out. "I know it's not enough, but I swear I'll spend my life making up for the harm I caused you."

Unsure how to respond, Dominic simply held his brother's hand, letting him cry it out. The road would be long, but if Austin was committed to changing, Dominic would offer a second chance. It was all they could do - walk forward with hope.

Lee returned then with a tray of food, casting a concerned look between them. But he didn't pry, for which Dominic was grateful. There would be time to talk, and heal. For now, having his family together was enough.

Once Austin had eaten, Dominic gently asked if he was up to explaining what had happened before they found him imprisoned. Austin hesitated, then nodded slowly.

Dominic and Lee pulled up chairs to listen attentively as Austin gathered himself to begin the tale.

"It started a couple weeks ago when Mom asked me to deliver a package to a coven across town," Austin said quietly. "I refused - I'd heard dark rumors about them."

He took a shaky breath before continuing. "A few days later, Mom invited me for tea. We were just talking normally when I started feeling lightheaded. Things got hazy after I drank the tea..."

Lee's brow furrowed. "So she drugged you? But how'd you write us the letter then?"

"It wasn't outright mind-control," Austin explained. "More like an obedience spell. I couldn't refuse her orders, but still had some agency." His hands fidgeted anxiously in his lap.

Dominic chose his next words carefully. "Do you know what was in the package she wanted delivered?"

Austin shook his head helplessly. "I couldn't even open it to see. After I was compelled to take it to the coven house, a witch and vampire intercepted me. They took the package and that's when things get dark…"

His voice broke as he relived the memory of his brutal abduction. Dominic grasped his hand supportively, signaling he needn't continue just yet if it was too painful.

"I'm so sorry we didn't find you sooner," Lee said regretfully. "But you're safe now."

Nodding, Austin wiped his eyes and sat up straighter. "I know. Thank you both for coming for me when no one else could." He looked between his brothers with sincere gratitude that gave Dominic hope for their reconciliation.

There were still missing puzzle pieces about Lina's motives and who had orchestrated Austin's imprisonment. But those mysteries could wait until Austin was stronger. For now, Dominic was simply grateful to have Austin home.

The road ahead would be long, but together they would walk it as a family. Their bonds had been tested, bent but never broken. As long as they still drew breath, Dominic would fight to protect what they were rebuilding.

After a thoughtful silence, Dominic asked carefully, "In your letter, you mentioned having information about your mother, Lina. Will you share what you discovered?"

Austin hesitated, then gave a resigned nod. Lee and Dominic scooted their chairs closer, giving him their full attention.

With a heavy sigh, Austin began. "Mom's kept huge secrets, especially about her past. A year ago I started investigating and learned some disturbing things."

He glanced between them nervously before continuing. "She was part of a cabal of witches who practiced very dark, prohibited magic. Blood rituals, demon summoning, and other bad things you could think of - awful things."

Dominic paled at this news of Lina's illicit activities. Austin went on, "I had a friendly ghost keep tabs on her movements. And she's been…controlling Father in subtle ways, magically influencing him."

Lee cursed vehemently. But Dominic just felt cold dread pooling in his gut at Austin's revelations.

All his suspicions about Lina manipulating his father from the shadows were apparently true. Dominic thought of his kind, gentle dad who had welcomed both him and his mother into the family. The thought of Lina mistreating him made Dominic feel ill.

"Do you think Father's life is in danger from her?" he asked Austin shakily. Just saying the possibility out loud made his chest constrict with fear.

"I'm not certain of her exact endgame," Austin admitted regretfully. "But removing you as the heir and your father as the leader seems part of it. And she's mentioned a big plan that's almost ready for execution."

Dominic felt lightheaded with panic. He should have acted on his misgivings sooner. But he'd never imagined the depth of Lina's treachery. Now his inaction may have doomed his dad.

No more standing idly by while Lina destroyed their family. He would confront her and get the full truth. If she had harmed a hair on his father's head, there would be no mercy this time.

Jaw clenched with resolve, Dominic strode for the door. One way or another, Lina's web of lies and deceit ended today. Whatever she was scheming, Dominic would not allow it to come to pass. Far more than their family hung in the balance.

Lee stood and began pacing, clearly disturbed. "This ends now. She's our mother, but this has gone on long enough." He turned to Austin urgently. "We must stop her before she can enact whatever madness she's devised."

Austin nodded, then hesitantly met Dominic's gaze. "There's one more thing you should know. She's been magically influencing Lee and I against you all these years. I managed to break my control, but

Lee…"

Lee froze mid-step, face stricken. "Wait, she's the reason for my misplaced hatred of Dominic?" At Austin's confirming look, Lee sank into a chair, head in hands. "Hell's gates, all this time I thought it was my own failing…"

Dominic placed a comforting hand on Lee's shoulder, sensing his stepbrother's remorse was genuine. "The past is done. We must focus on Lina's next moves."

Just then Vale padded into the room and jumped up next to Austin, tail wagging. Austin's face lit up as he hugged the affectionate husky.

Dominic smiled softly. Trust Vale to know just when some comfort was needed. The charming dog never failed to lift spirits with his fuzzy face and boundless warmth.

Turning serious again, Dominic said, "Lee, can you look after them while I'm gone? There's some unfinished business to handle."

Lee hesitated, then nodded. "Whatever you decide, know we support you," he said solemnly.

Dominic was touched by this show of solidarity from the stepbrothers he'd considered enemies up till now. He certainly hadn't foreseen gaining their backing. If he'd had a bingo card for unlikely events, their trust would merit eating a dozen cupcakes.

After a final encouraging hug, Dominic headed to his room to gear up mentally and physically. He donned a durable outfit and his favorite leather jacket, feeling like the old battle-ready version of himself.

On his way out, he spotted Christian's sleek car still parked outside. Well, those keys were his to use for now. He had a feeling the flashy ride's speed would come in handy.

The drive to the coven house was tense and unnervingly quiet. Dominic didn't know what awaited him there. Had Lina already hurt their dad? Was he walking into a trap? He could only pray his father was safe for now.

The closer he got to that imposing mansion, the heavier Dominic's sense of foreboding grew. His hands clenched the wheel till his knuckles whitened. Loose gravel crunched under the tires as he pulled up the long drive. Time to face the tempest head on.

Jaw set with determination, Dominic marched up to the imposing double doors. Lina would answer for her lies and betrayals. He would see justice done, no matter the cost...

Dominic approached the mansion cautiously. The ornate front door hung ajar, a dark omen. Strengthening his magical shields, Dominic stepped inside the eerily silent entry hall.

Immediately the cloying miasma of dark magic pressed down on him. The very air was choked with lingering corruptive energy - someone had been conducting foul rituals here recently.

Glancing around nervously, Dominic took in signs of struggle and disarray that painted a grim picture. Scorch marks blackened the walls, broken furniture littered the floors. Even some blood stains marred the once pristine white marble.

The whole place reeked of malice, making the hair on Dominic's neck stand on end. This was no longer the welcoming family home he'd known. Some malevolent presence had taken up residence in the hollowed-out remains.

With growing dread, Dominic hurried toward his father's familiar suite. All the doors lining the hallway stood ajar, the rooms within darkened and ravaged. More blood dripped an erratic trail along the carpet.

Fighting back panic, Dominic rushed into the study. Books and shattered glass crunched under his feet. The whole space had been torn apart, as if by a frenzied search. What horrors had played out here while he was away?

Heart in his throat, Dominic followed the scarlet stains until he froze in dismay at the study doorway. The scene of destruction that greeted him was worse than his darkest imaginings…

His father lay prone on the soiled carpet, deathly still and covered in his own blood. Crouching next to the limp form, Dominic desperately felt for a pulse.

"Father, it's Dominic. Stay with me," he urged desperately. Unfocused eyes flickered open at his voice.

"D-Dominic?" his father rasped in confusion, clearly clinging to consciousness by a thread.

Dominic squeezed his hand. "I'm here, just hang on."

His father gripped his arm weakly. "Behind…you…" he choked out before passing out.

Whirling around, Dominic saw Lina standing casually in the doorway, a sphere of pulsating dark energy floating above her palm. Her eyes were cold and void of humanity. This was not his stepmother anymore, but something twisted and evil wearing her face.

"Well, well, look who's come to die," Lina purred sinisterly. "Don't worry, I'll reunite you with daddy soon."

Dominic stood swiftly, shielding his prone father with his body. "Your games end here, Lina," he declared. "I know the truth now."

Lina let out an awful, grating laugh. "Oh child, you know nothing of true power. But you will learn respect before the end."

With that, she flung the corrupted orb of dark energy straight at them. Acting on instinct, Dominic called up a powerful gale force wind that halted its momentum inches from impact.

The pulsating sphere hovered menacingly, pushed back by the howling winds but still inching closer. Sweat beaded Dominic's brow from the intense effort of holding it at bay. The corrupted magic throbbed threateningly, seeking to consume their life forces.

With a shriek of rage, Lina added her own violet flames to the orb, bolstering its sinister magic. The air sizzled with reddish black lightning as it collided with Dominic's wind wall.

He grit his teeth, fighting to maintain the protective barrier around his prone father. But Lina was stronger than he expected, hammering his defenses relentlessly. She pressed the assault like a woman possessed.

The study lit up with blinding flashes as their magics clashed. The flaming orb crept forward slowly but inexorably, corrupted power fueled by Lina's manic hatred. Dominic slid back step by step across the carpet as he struggled to stand his ground.

This couldn't be his stepmother's unaided strength - she must be channeling some darker force. Its foul essence leaked through, eroding Dominic's concentration. He had to end this soon, before the evil consumed them all.

Gritting his teeth, Dominic poured all his will into summoning a howling typhoon inside the confined space. Papers, furniture, even shards of drywall went flying under its power. The winds whipped and screamed around Lina's body, threatening to shred flesh from bone.

For a moment the gale seemed to swallow her orb entirely. But then violet flames re-ignited within the storm, battling back the cutting winds. Their dueling magics filled the study with fiery destruction, neither witch willing to yield any ground. The room tremored under the clashing forces.

Panting harshly, Dominic dug deeper than ever before for reserves of power. He would not fail his father. The raging tempest responded to his desperation, redoubling its efforts.

Then his father, barely clinging to consciousness, grabbed Lina's ankle causing her to stumble. The lapse allowed Dominic to channel the last of his power into one consuming lightning blast.

Howling rage, Lina collapsed, rendered immobile by the damage. "You may have won this battle, boy," she hissed vehemently. "But the corruption cannot be stopped now..." Then she vanished.

Breathing hard, Dominic hurried to gather his father's limp body in his arms. Lina was defeated for the moment, but her ominous words lingered. He had to get help before she could regroup and attack again

Breathing hard, Dominic hurried to gather his father's limp body in his arms. Lina was defeated for the moment, but they weren't safe yet.

As he stood, his father stirred weakly. "Dominic...you have to leave me," he rasped. "The dark magic...it's too late..."

"No!" Dominic said forcefully. "I won't give up on you. We'll find a way to help."

His father gave a sad smile. "Always so stubborn. Just like your mother." He coughed harshly, fresh blood staining his lips.

Dominic wracked his brain desperately for a solution. Then it hit him - Larry and Steve. Surely the celestials could help counteract Lina's foul magic.

Keeping his father supported with one arm, Dominic fumbled for his phone. Ben picked up on the second ring.

"Ben, are your dads there? It's urgent," Dominic said without preamble.

"They're here, what's going on?" Ben asked, sounding worried.

Dominic quickly explained the situation. "Have Roan portal us to the manor, now! We're running out of time."

"On it!" Ben said. Dominic heard him shouting to the others before the call cut off.

Moments later, a shimmering gateway opened before them. Cradling his father close, Dominic hurried through to the manor's warmly lit foyer.

Larry and Steve were already rushing forward, visually assessing the dire situation. Roan and Ben hovered anxiously behind them.

"Bring him this way, we have a room prepared," Steve said, expression grim but focused. Together, they moved swiftly to get Dominic's dad stabilized...

22

Traitor

Christian

Christian hurried over to Ben and Adrian's manor in Willowbrook. He got a call from Ben saying that Dominic was there and it looked like he needed him - his mate.

Arriving at the large house, Ben greeted him at the door.

"Hey Christian, thanks for coming so quickly," Ben said, letting him inside. "Dominic is in one of the spare bedrooms resting."

"Is he okay?" Christian asked worriedly.

"I think so, just pretty shaken up it seems," Ben replied. "My dads are with him and his dad right now. Come on, I'll take you to him."

Christian followed Ben up the ornate staircase and down a long hallway. Ben stopped in front of a door, nodding for Christian to go inside.

Taking a deep breath, Christian turned the handle and entered the room. He immediately saw Dominic asleep on a sofa next to the bed. In the bed was an older man who appeared to be Dominic's father based on the resemblance.

Two other men Christian didn't recognize were in the room as well. They introduced themselves as Larry and Steve - Ben's fathers. Christian could sense power emanating from them. He shook their hands politely.

"Dominic is going to be alright, as will his father," Steve said kindly. "We were able to heal their external and internal injuries."

Christian glanced worriedly at Dominic's torn clothing. "What happened to them?"

"I think it's best if Dominic shares those details himself," Larry replied. "It's not our story to tell."

Ben and his fathers left the room, leaving Christian alone with Dominic and his sleeping dad. Christian took a moment to really look at Dominic. His clothes were badly shredded and he had some lingering bruises. It was clear some kind of altercation had occurred.

Christian knelt down next to the sofa where Dominic rested. He gently brushed a lock of hair from Dominic's face and caressed his cheek.

"Dominic, sweetheart," Christian said softly. "Can you wake up for me?"

Dominic's eyes fluttered open slowly. He looked confused for a moment before focusing on Christian.

"Christian?" he said hoarsely. "You're here."

"Of course I'm here," Christian replied. "Ben called and said you needed me. Are you alright?"

Dominic sat up with a pained expression. Christian helped prop him up with some pillows.

"I'm okay I think," Dominic said. "Just really sore and tired."

"What happened?" Christian asked. "It looks like you were in some kind of fight. And who hurt your father?"

Dominic took a shaky breath, fresh tears pooling in his eyes. Christian grasped his hand supportively.

"It was my stepmother Lina," Dominic explained. "She ambushed us at home. I barely got my dad out in time."

"Why would she attack you both?" Christian asked, shocked.

"She's insane," Dominic said bitterly. "Ever since she married my dad, she's been trying to get rid of us so she could have full control of the coven. I think she was planning on killing us tonight."

Dominic choked back a sob. Christian wrapped his arms around him comfortingly.

"It's okay, you're safe now," he soothed. "Just take your time telling me what happened."

Dominic explained how he arrived at the coven to find it tainted by dark magic, with signs of struggle everywhere. He described following a trail of blood to his father's demolished study, where he found his dad grievously wounded. Lina then appeared, surrounded by corrupted power and barely human. She attacked mercilessly, forcing Dominic to realize she was channeling some evil magic. The study was destroyed as they battled, but Dominic's father managed to trip Lina, allowing Dominic to strike her down.

Christian comforted his shaken mate, praising his resilience and courage throughout the harrowing encounter. Though reliving the traumatic memory caused Dominic immense distress, Christian's supportive presence helped reinforce that the ordeal was over and could no longer hurt him

Dominic gave a faint smile. "I just did what I had to do. But we're both still here thanks to all of you."

"I'll always be here when you need me," Christian reaffirmed. "We'll get through the rest of this together."

Dominic lifted his head to meet Christian's gaze. "What about you though? How are you holding up with everything else going on?"

Christian sighed, touched by Dominic's concern even after his own ordeal. "I'm alright, just worried about the missing vampires from my coven. We thought we had a lead but it turned out to be a trap."

"A trap?" Dominic asked with concern. "What happened?"

Christian's jaw tensed at the memory. "We were ambushed by an ogre. Barely made it out intact. The false trail feels like a deliberate taunt from whoever took the vampires."

Dominic placed a comforting hand on Christian's cheek. "I'm so sorry. But I know you'll find them. You're strong and determined, and you have the whole team supporting you."

Despite the dire situation, Christian couldn't help but smile softly at his mate's faith in him. "Thank you, love. Having you by my side makes me believe I can face anything."

He placed a gentle kiss on Dominic's forehead. They sat in comfortable silence for a few moments, simply drawing strength from each other.

Eventually Dominic spoke up hesitantly. "Can I tell you something that might help? It could be connected to the missing vampires."

Christian straightened with interest. "Of course, anything you know could be useful. What is it?"

"Well, my step-brother Austin said a vampire attacked him recently," Dominic explained. "And that the vampire was working with a witch. Do you think it could be related?"

Christian's brow furrowed thoughtfully. "Possibly. Did Austin describe the vampire who attacked him?"

Dominic shook his head. "No, he was pretty shaken up about the whole thing. But if it is connected, we need to find them."

Christian nodded thoughtfully. "You're right. I can't be certain it's related until we learn more about what the rouge elder is up to."

If he was involved in the disappearances, things could be even more dangerous than Christian realized.

Dominic regarded him curiously. "Do you have any pictures of the Elders of your coven? Maybe I can help a bit."

"Good idea," Christian said, pulling out his phone. He brought up a photo of him and the other Elders and handed the phone to Dominic.

Dominic took the phone, his eyes widening as he visibly tensed. Christian noticed the reaction with concern.

"What's wrong?" he asked. "Do you know him?"

Dominic nodded slowly and pointed at the face of Eros. "I've seen this vampire before. He was at our coven house not long ago, meeting with Lina."

Christian went very still, gears turning rapidly. "Are you absolutely certain it was Eros you saw with Lina?"

"Without a doubt," Dominic said seriously. "I only caught a glimpse but I'd recognize that face anywhere now."

Christian's mind raced at the implications. Eros working with Dominic's stepmother, right before she attacked the coven? It was too coincidental given the other events unfolding.

"Did you happen to overhear what they were discussing at all?" Christian asked intently.

Dominic's face fell apologetically. "No, I'm sorry. I wish I could be more help."

Christian tipped Dominic's chin up, meeting his eyes sincerely. "You've given us a critical lead already, love. Any information about Eros is invaluable right now."

Dominic still looked uncertain and Christian was not having it.

Christian pressed a kiss to his temple. "Truly, this could be the breakthrough we've needed. You've done more than enough, sweetheart. I love you."

Dominic finally relaxed, reassured by Christian's words. Christian held him close, infinitely grateful to have someone to share the burden with.

Exhausted from recounting his trauma, Dominic soon drifted off to sleep in Christian's arms. Christian tucked a blanket around him before settling back, Dominic's head pillowed on his shoulder.

Christian's mind churned as he kept watch over his sleeping mate. The implications of Eros working with Dominic's stepmother were deeply troubling. What could a dark witch and a rogue vampire hope to achieve together? Surely nothing good.

Christian longed to stay right here with Dominic, keeping him safe. But he knew he couldn't ignore his responsibilities to his own coven, especially with vampires still disappearing.

His troubled thoughts were interrupted by a soft knock. Ben poked his head in, gesturing for Christian to join him in the hall.

Moving carefully so as not to disturb Dominic, Christian eased out from under him and tucked a pillow in place of his shoulder. He pressed a feather-light kiss to Dominic's forehead before slipping out.

"What is it?" Christian asked Ben quietly, pulling the door mostly shut.

"There's a vampire here asking for you. Said his name is Igor," Ben replied.

Christian tensed in surprise. Igor wouldn't show up unannounced unless it was urgent business.

"Did he say what he wants?" Christian asked.

Ben shook his head. "Only that he needs you to return to Dawncreek right away."

Christian glanced back at the room where Dominic still slept. The last thing he wanted was to leave his mate so soon. But duty called, especially if it concerned the missing vampires.

"Please let Dominic know where I've gone when he wakes," Christian requested. "I don't want him to worry."

"Of course," Ben agreed readily.

With a resigned sigh, Christian followed him downstairs and out the front door where Igor was waiting. Ben tactfully gave them privacy.

"What's happened?" Christian asked without preamble. "Why are you here?"

"My apologies, but there's been an...incident," Igor said delicately. "We require your immediate return and counsel."

Christian's stomach dropped. "The missing vampires?"

Igor's grave expression was confirmation enough. After a tense beat, Christian nodded.

"Let's go then. We've no time to waste."

Heading inside, Christian quickly explained the situation to Ben, asking again that he assure Dominic of his return soon. Ben promised to relay the message.

After hastily taking leave of Ben and Adrian's manor, Christian and Igor made haste back to Dawncreek. Igor informed him that Augustus urgently required his presence in the recovery room.

Christian's mind raced with trepidation as he rushed there. Why would his sire summon him to the infirmary now of all times? Only dire circumstances came to mind.

Bursting into the recovery room, Christian froze at the sight meeting him. There lay Matt - Christian's own protégé - battered and unconscious in one of the beds. Augustus kept vigil at his side.

"What happened?" Christian demanded, shocked.

"He came back here rushing and was already bleeding heavily," Augustus said grimly. Upon closer inspection, Matt's wounds suggested concentrated silver exposure - lethal to their kind. Yet somehow, he still clung to life.

"How has the silver not killed him?" Christian asked, stunned.

"It appears to have no lasting impact," Augustus mused. "His advanced healing remains intact. Highly unusual..."

They exchanged troubled looks. A vampire immune to silver was unheard of - and would certainly draw unwanted suspicion. Matt had to be kept safe until they understood more.

Christian approached the bedside and gently grasped Matt's hand. "Can you hear me? What happened?"

Matt's eyes fluttered open weakly. "Elder Christian...forgive me, I tried to fight..."

"Hush, just rest," Christian soothed, although his thoughts raced. As Matt's attacker, he may hold vital clues.

But Matt struggled to sit up, wincing in pain. "Please, you must know...it was Eros," he rasped urgently. "I heard him mention his partner, some woman..."

Christian nodded. "Thank you. We'll take it from here, Matt."

Gently urging Matt to recover his strength, Christian conferred privately with Augustus. His true agenda remained maddeningly unclear.

For now, they could only increase security around their most vulnerable. Their one concrete lead was Dominic's intel linking Eros to his stepmother.

Leaving Matt in Augustus' care, Christian made for the door, but his sire's voice gave him pause.

"Tread carefully, my son."Augustus said.

Christian nodded, resolving to end this threat.

Striding down the hall, Christian fished out his phone. It was time for direct confrontation - he dialed Eros' number. To his surprise, Eros answered right away.

"Took you long enough," Eros drawled casually.

Christian fought to control his fury. "You'll pay for your actions, Eros. I know you're working with a witch."

Eros merely chuckled. "Oh please. Why don't you come prove those accusations?"

Clenching his jaw, Christian pressed the point. "Release the captives, then we can settle this face to face."

"Come to me within the hour or they die," Eros stated coldly, and ended the call.

Moments later a location pinged Christian's phone - Eros was laying a trap, clearly. But with lives at stake, Christian had no choice but to confront him on his terms.

Walking briskly outside, Christian steeled himself for the coming confrontation. Win or lose, this ended tonight. He would get the truth from Eros, by any means necessary.

"Going alone against him is foolish, you know," a wry voice spoke up.

Christian turned to see Elvira leaning casually against the wall, looking unimpressed. "How long have you been lurking there?" he asked.

"Long enough to know you're about to do something stupidly reckless, per usual," she retorted, falling into step beside him.

Christian bristled. "I don't have a choice. If this is the only way to free the captives…"

"There's always a choice," Elvira interrupted firmly. "Rushing into Eros' clutches blindly helps no one."

When Christian stayed stubbornly silent, she tried again. "Look, you know it's a trap. At least let me watch your back covertly."

Christian hesitated, then nodded grudgingly. "Fine, but stay hidden unless absolutely necessary." Having backup couldn't hurt.

Elvira gave a wry salute and vanished from sight. Christian felt the subtle shiver in the air that indicated she still followed.

Together they made their way toward the waiting car. The coordinates Eros provided were on the outskirts of Dawncreek. Christian's hands tightened on the steering wheel as he drove, his passenger invisible but ever present.

After several tense minutes of silence, Elvira's voice sounded again, seemingly from the backseat. "So what's your plan for when we arrive, oh fearless leader? Please tell me it extends beyond 'storming the castle.'"

Christian's jaw tightened. "I'll assess the situation first, then confront Eros directly to force answers about the captives. Whatever trap he's laid, I can break through it."

"Uh huh, sure. And what if it's a trap you can't break through?" Elvira challenged. "Rushing in blindly could get us both killed, and then who would rescue the others?"

Christian's hands clenched in frustration on the wheel. "You think I don't know that? But Eros hasn't left me any options. And I will not abandon our people to him."

Elvira sighed heavily. "Look, I know your heart is in the right place. But you also have a recklessness problem when it comes to playing hero. So just…promise you'll be smart about this. The clan needs their leader alive."

Christian glanced over where she supposedly sat. Elvira always could call him out bluntly when no one else dared. "I am not a leader yet, but I promise I don't have a death wish, if that helps," he muttered.

"It's a start," she replied. "And hey, we've faced worse odds before and lived to tell the tale."

Despite himself, Christian huffed a small laugh. "True enough." Elvira made an unlikely voice of reason, but she had a point. He needed to be smart and cautious in facing Eros.

The abandoned manor soon loomed out of the darkness ahead. Time to see what trap Eros had prepared. With Elvira as invisible backup, Christian felt ready to face whatever lay within those shadowy walls and finally get some real answers.

Christian tensely approached the decrepit manor, wary of traps. Inside, unfamiliar vampires greeted him, saying their master awaited in the throne room. Christian bristled at the implication of Eros believing himself their king.

Entering the imposing chamber, Christian saw Eros lounging arrogantly upon the throne. "I'm here. Now release the captives," Christian demanded.

Eros smirked, signalling his cronies to bring out four weakened, abused vampires. Christian recognized them as recently missing clan members.

"Why are you doing this?" Christian asked sharply, stalling for time.

Eros rose and prowled nearer. "Come now, isn't it obvious? I mean to take the throne for myself. And for that, you need to die."

Sensing Elvira hovering nearby, Christian told the prisoners to flee while distracted. Once they'd escaped, he nodded almost imperceptibly, signaling Elvira.

A floating silver blade suddenly pressed to Eros' throat - Elvira revealing herself. But Eros just chuckled. "Predictable as always."

He snatched Elvira's concealed arm and used her own dagger against her. Christian shouted as Eros flung her out the window.

Christian launched himself at Eros with preternatural speed, a blur of movement even to vampire senses. Eros reacted instantly, meeting him blow for blow as they traded strikes at blistering velocity.

Christian went for a crushing overhead punch, but Eros spun aside with uncanny agility, raking his claws toward Christian's throat. Christian in turn contorted his body at an impossible angle to avoid the deadly swipe, then kicked out Eros' knees in a crippling sweep.

Momentarily grounded, Eros bared his fangs and tried to get at his neck. Christian jerked his head back just in time. He followed up with a devastating axe kick straight down toward Eros' chest, but Eros rolled away and was on his feet in the blink of an eye.

The ancient vampires clashed again and again, exchanging hundreds of blows per second, any one of which could maim or kill a normal being. Christian's muscles burned with the exertion of matching Eros' ferocity and speed. He knew he couldn't keep this pace forever.

Sensing an opening, Christian feinted left then spun right, getting inside Eros' guard. He grabbed Eros in a crushing bear hug, simultaneously sinking his fangs into his shoulder. Eros roared in rage and pain, writhing like a wild animal.

Summoning all his preternatural might, Christian hoisted Eros overhead and hurled him straight through a stone pillar with earth-shaking force. Dust and debris exploded outward on impact.

Christian moved in swiftly to press the advantage, but Eros burst from the rubble in a explosion of movement. His fist smashed brutally into Christian's gut, folding him over with an agonized wheeze. Eros' knee crashed up into his face next, dazing Christian and sending him reeling backwards.

Before Eros could land another punishing blow, they both sensed magic roiling nearby. Lina stalked into view, dark energy swirling around her hands. With a sinister grin, she hurled the corrupted orb straight into Christian's back.

The malicious sorcery exploded against him, sending Christian crashing to the floor in agony. As his vision went dark, the last thing he saw was Eros and Lina gloating over his defeated form, their alliance unbreakable. How could he have faced such combined power alone? Despair clutched Christian as oblivion took him.

Dazed, he looked up to see a woman lowering her glowing hand, malicious satisfaction in her eyes. "What took you so long, Lina?" Eros said.

Their gloating voices sounded warped and distant as black spots flooded Christian's vision. He had sorely underestimated their combined might. Now he was at their mercy.

Christian drifted in and out of consciousness, only catching snippets as Eros argued with Lina. "Take him, now and his apprentice. We don't have much time. The ritual must be completed before the full moon."

23

Sacrificial Blood

Christian

Christian regained hazy consciousness, his vision blurred and head throbbing. As his sight slowly focused, he recognized the forest clearing where he and Dominic had investigated recently. But the once inviting glen now felt heavy with foreboding.

Blinking hard, Christian scanned his surroundings, trying to get his bearings. The full moon filtered down through the canopy in ethereal beams, casting the enclosing woods in silver-blue light. An unnatural stillness permeated the area - no sounds of wildlife stirred the night air, as if the forest held its breath anticipating danger.

Attempting to rise, Christian realized his hands were tightly bound behind his back. Thrashing against the restraints proved useless, the ropes refusing to give. A foul taste filled his mouth and Christian recognized traces of mystical sedation keeping his vampire strength suppressed.

Swiveling his head, Christian spotted Elvira unconscious and tied to a thick oak tree across the clearing. He tried calling out but only managed a strangled croak through the haze of drugs. How had they both come to be captives here? His mind struggled to piece together fractured memories through the dizzying fog.

A snapped twig jerked Christian's attention over his shoulder. Heart lurching, he beheld Eros and Lina watching him like vultures scoping dying prey. The predatory anticipation in their eyes pierced through Christian's muddled thoughts - he was in mortal danger here.

Renewing his struggles, Christian tried summoning his powers to tear free of the mystic bonds, but the sedative coursing through his veins left him weak as a mortal. He thrashed wildly anyway, desperate to loosen the ropes before his captors approached. It was no use, the restraints refused to give even an inch.

Chest heaving, Christian collapsed back in exhaustion and turned a venomous glare up at Eros and Lina.

"Why have you brought us here?" he spat, hideously reminded of being caged earlier.

Eros gave a sinister smile. "All in due time. We require your... cooperation, for a special ritual." Beside him, Lina began laying out strange implements - the purpose for them fraught with dark implication.

Christian tasted bile, sensing where this was headed. "If you think I'll submit to being your sacrificial pawn, think again," he growled defiantly.

Eros chuckled, clearly unconcerned. "Come now, let's not get ahead of ourselves." He leaned down and roughly grasped Christian's chin. "We have ways of securing your participation, willing or not."

Christian tried to jerk away but Eros' grip was iron. His claws extended slightly, drawing pinpricks of blood across Christian's jawline.

"We could start by viciously killing your little friend over there while you watch, helpless to intervene," Eros suggested lightly with a nod at Elvira. "That might help persuade you to cooperate."

Dread pooled in Christian's gut but he kept his expression stony. Elvira began to stir, looking around in bewilderment. Christian had to find some way to free them both before these monsters could enact their vile schemes under the moon's watchful eye.

But bound and suppressed, what options did he have? Perhaps stalling for time and waiting for any opportunity or lapse in their guard. Anything could provide the key to turning the tables. He simply had to endure and bide his time…

Christian eventually got out of his chains and snarled "Don't touch her!"

Christian hurled himself against the invisible enclosure, only to be harshly repelled. It was like slamming into a wall of solid steel. The air shimmered briefly with a glowing sigil at the point of impact, revealing the barrier's magical origin.

Looking closer, Christian could perceive a domed perimeter enclosing him on all sides, defined by faintly glimmering runes. Eros must have had this containment spell prepared specifically for him. No matter how Christian pushed or punched the mystical walls, they would not yield.

Frustrated, he scraped at the dirt around the edges, seeking any weakness. But the sorcery extended underground as well, the sigils forming an unbroken sphere. Digging underneath would be useless.

Studying the enclosure, Christian recognized symbols of binding, suppression and isolation. Together they created an impenetrable metaphysical prison, cut off from any outside magical aid. The emerald glow of the runes indicated the caliber of spellcaster involved - this was powerful witchcraft indeed.

Snarling in mounting anger, Christian unleashed an ear-splitting roar and struck the barrier with all his prodigious might. The resulting shockwave blew back trees at the perimeter, branches and leaves flying violently. But the magical walls stood firm, unaffected.

Chest heaving, Christian probed every inch seeking some flaw to exploit. But the witchcraft was watertight - no gaps or weaknesses existed. Eros had come maddeningly prepared.

Clenching his fists, Christian turned a burning glare on his captors. Trapped by such immutable sorcery, he stood little chance of breaking free by force. His only option was to stall for time and wait for an opening.

Eros just yanked Elvira's head back further, placing a clawed hand at her exposed throat. "Her life depends on your choice, Christian. Willingly take her place here, and she goes free."

Elvira's shouts were unintelligible through the gag. Eros ripped it away impatiently. "Let them take me!" she pleaded desperately. "You can't give them what they want!"

Eros backhanded her viciously. "Silence! Well, Christian? Decide before I rip her throat out." His claws dug in enough to draw blood.

Christian froze, agonizing over the impossible choice. He could never sacrifice Elvira, but to willingly die and fuel their dark ritual? Either way, evil would win tonight.

Unless…their overconfidence might provide the key. Buying time and watching for any opportunity was his only play now. He had to keep them talking long enough for a miracle.

"Enough!" Christian shouted raggedly. "I'll do as you ask, just don't hurt her." Defeat laced his tone.

Eros grinned triumphantly and shoved Elvira aside. Lina began making preparations for the ritual.

Eros shoved Elvira aside and Lina began ritual preparations. Seeing a chance to disrupt their plans, Christian called out "Face me in single combat, Eros! When I win, we walk free."

Eros glanced at Lina amusedly. "Let me have some fun before we finish him."

Lina shrugged. "Make it quick."

Eros grinned menacingly at Christian. "I'm going to enjoy this. Like when I killed your parents."

Christian saw red at the admission. "You took them from me? I'll end you for that!" he raged.

"I'd like to see you try, whelp," Eros taunted.

With a feral roar, Christian launched himself at the barrier containing him. It shuddered under the crash but held firm. Snarling, Christian struck it again and again, heedless of self-harm.

Laughing, Eros made a gesture and the mystical enclosure vanished. Christian immediately barreled into him with crushing force.

They traded earth-shaking blows, the very ground cracking under their clashing might. Christian fought with reckless fury, but Eros matched him casually, toying with his prey.

"Is vengeance all that drives you?" Eros mocked, evading Christian's wild strikes. "You'll have to do better than that."

Christian felt himself tiring already under Eros' onslaught. As a last resort, he reluctantly drew on his deepest well of power - an ability that sapped his lifeforce. Immediately his strength and speed amplified exponentially.

Now Christian went on the offensive, landing punishing hits that drove Eros back step by step. But Eros just laughed, clearly enjoying himself.

"Yes, show me your true potential! It will make snuffing out your life all the sweeter."

To Christian's shock, darkness erupted around Eros as well, granting him a tremendous boost in power. They collided again with earth-shattering force, craters forming beneath their feet. Christian knew he couldn't sustain this prolonged clash.

Then Eros summoned his killer fog, letting it flow toward Elvira's helpless form. "Let's see you save the girl while fighting me," he challenged cruelly.

Cursing, Christian flashed to Elvira and swept her to safety in the blink of an eye. But the distraction cost him - Eros' fist smashed into his spine, hurling Christian to the ground.

Before he could rise, Eros' booted foot stamped down, pinning him by the throat. "A valiant effort, but it ends here," Eros pronounced, raising a spear-like hand to deliver the death blow.

Christian desperately sought any way to turn the tables against Eros. But he was simply outmatched by the ancient vampire's raw power. Christian's own ability was rapidly draining his life force to dangerous levels.

Sensing his foe's weakening, Eros pressed his advantage ruthlessly. He landed a series of merciless blows that Christian was too slow to deflect in his weakened state.

A final crushing strike hurled Christian violently to the ground at Lina's feet. Eros planted a foot on his back in triumph.

"It's over, little lord. You never stood a chance against true power," Eros mocked.

Lina clicked her tongue impatiently. "Enough playing. The moon is waning - put him in the ritual circle so we can begin."

"Of course, my queen," Eros said obsequiously. He dragged Christian's semi-conscious form over to the glowing sigils Lina had prepared and cast him down inside.

The mystical runes flared ominously at Christian's presence, their light intensifying into malevolent violet flickers. The ground began to shudder in response. Christian struggled weakly, but his drained body refused to respond.

Lina's arms rose as she began her dark incantations, face exultant. The shaking earth groaned louder, the circle burning Christian's prone form where he made contact with it. He was utterly trapped, at the mercy of their malicious sorcery.

As searing pain wracked his body, Christian's thoughts went to

Dominic. He exhaled a shuddering breath and whispered "Forgive me, my mate. I've failed you."

Eros and Lina's chanting reached a thunderous crescendo. The circling sigils suddenly compressed, constricting Christian's body agonizingly. He choked back a scream through clenched teeth.

24

Witch's Familiar

Dominic

Dominic awoke to find Christian gone. He looked around in confusion - where was his mate?

The other side of the bed was cold and empty. Dominic placed a hand on the indent where Christian had lain, missing his comforting presence already. Their time together had been cut short.

Ben sat nearby reading, and noticed Dominic stirring. "Hey, sleepyhead. Christian got called back to Dawncreek but said he'll be back soon."

Dominic felt a pang of disappointment in his chest. He had hoped to wake wrapped in Christian's strong embrace. The vampire's abrupt departure left an ache of absence that put Dominic on edge.

He understood Christian likely had urgent coven matters to see to, especially with the recent chaos. Still, Dominic couldn't help feeling somewhat hurt he had left without a proper goodbye. The few nights they'd shared had not been nearly enough time together after the trauma they had endured.

Dominic sighed, trying to shake off his melancholy. Christian would be back as soon as he was able - he knew his mate would not abandon him unless absolutely vital circumstances demanded it. Their duties to their people had to take priority, despite Dominic's wishes to simply lay low with Christian awhile longer.

Still, he hoped all was well in Dawncreek and this separation would be brief. Christian's stalwart presence had become a pillar of comfort and strength for Dominic. The looming threat of his stepmother also weighed heavier without Christian's reassuring influence.

But Dominic had his own role to play in unraveling Lina's schemes. He would be ready when Christian returned, hopefully with new insights to share. Until then, he could only have faith their time apart would pass swiftly. He already yearned for his mate's arms around him again.

Just then, Dominic's dad made a faint sound. Dominic rushed over as his father's eyes blinked open weakly.

"D...Dom?" his dad murmured.

Dominic's breath caught - his dad hadn't used that childhood nickname in years. He nodded, taking his father's hand. "I'm here."

His dad gave a faint smile and Dominic had to steady his emotions. After everything, his father was going to be okay.

Ben quietly fetched some water before tactfully excusing himself, sensing they needed time alone. Dominic helped his dad take small sips, then settled back, simply holding his hand.

After a few moments, his father spoke again, voice rough. "I'm so sorry, Dominic. For all of it - for not protecting you from her." His eyes glistened with tears.

Dominic shook his head firmly. "You have nothing to apologize for. This was all Lina's doing. Lee and Austin told me how she manipulated everyone."

At the mention of his stepbrothers, Dominic's dad grew concerned. "How are Austin and Lee? Are they safe?"

Dominic quickly reassured him. "They're okay, don't worry. Austin got roughed up by a vampire, but Lee is taking good care of him while he recovers at home."

His father relaxed slightly hearing they were out of harm's way for now. Still, regret clouded his expression.

"I should have realized much sooner the kind of malice Lina harbored," he said, voice thick with emotion. "Maybe then I could have shielded all of you from her treachery."

Dominic gave his hand a comforting squeeze. "You can't blame yourself. None of us saw through her act until it was too late."

His dad's face was pained. "You warned me about the changes in her aura when you first came home. I should have trusted your instincts."

"It's okay, Dad," Dominic said gently. "Lina fooled all of us. What matters now is stopping whatever she has planned next."

Nodding, his father continued solemnly. "By the time I uncovered her interest in harnessing the ley lines, it was too late to intercede. She moved against us that very night."

Dominic tensed. "Do you know what exactly she wants with their power?"

His dad shook his head. "My investigation was cut short. But based on the dark materials she had gathered, I fear she means to use the ley lines for a ritual sacrifice of some kind."

Dominic paled at the implication. His stepmother was clearly playing with forces beyond her control. They had to find and stop her before she could unleash calamity.

Gripping his dad's hand tighter, Dominic said "Try to rest for now. We'll figure this out and protect the coven, I promise."

His father managed a faint smile. "I know you will, son. You're stronger now than you realize." With that, he drifted back into a healing sleep.

Dominic sat vigil a while longer, thoughts churning. He had to warn

Christian about this new threat from Lina. Together, surely they could prevent disaster and bring her to justice.

After his father drifted off, Dominic quietly left the room. He headed to the kitchen, finding Ben, Adrian, Roan and Merin seated around the table chatting while Jimmy groomed himself contentedly.

Ben spotted Dominic first and drew him into a warm hug. "Hey! How's your dad doing?"

"Much better, he's awake and talking now," Dominic said with relief as he took a seat beside Merin.

Ben slid him a steaming cup of tea. "That's great news."

Dominic smiled softly. "I never properly thanked your dads for healing him. I'm not sure he'd have made it otherwise."

Ben waved it off. "You don't need to thank us, they were happy to help."

Sipping his tea, Dominic asked, "Where's Ciaran? Has he found anything monitoring the ley lines?"

"Out tracking disturbances again," Merin supplied. "Hopefully he turns up something useful soon."

Adrian leaned forward intently. "Did you manage to learn anything more from your father about the ley lines?"

Dominic quickly relayed what his dad had revealed about Lina's interest in harnessing them for some sinister ritual sacrifice. The reactions around the table made it clear they all grasped the potential severity of that threat.

"A sacrifice using that much power is surely a dangerous prospect," Adrian said grimly.

Before they could discuss it further, the room began to shake. Dominic clutched the table to steady his tea as the others looked around in alarm. Picture frames rattled on the walls.

"Earthquake?" Roan wondered out loud. But Dominic felt an ominous prickle on his skin - this felt supernatural in origin.

Jimmy hissed and arched his back as the tremors intensified. Mystical turbulence was definitely the cause. Dominic shared an anxious look with the others, afraid what destructive forces might have been unleashed.

Suddenly a windblown Ciaran burst into the kitchen, looking wild-eyed. "It's the ley lines!" he exclaimed. "Their power is being violently tapped - we have to hurry!"

Exchanging ominous glances, they all hastily followed Ciaran outside. Dominic's gut twisted with dread. Whatever Lina was attempting, it appeared to be reaching fruition. He could only pray they weren't too late to stop it.

They all hurried just to see an ominous dark fog enveloping the surrounding forest. The origin was undoubtedly supernatural.

Dominic asked Ciaran urgently, "Is there any way to stop this?"

The druid's expression was grim. "We must eliminate the source. It will continue draining the Wellspring until there's nothing left."

Before they could discuss further, a car pulled up carrying Lee, Austin, and Vale. Dominic was surprised to see them.

"How did you know to come here?" he asked.

Austin explained, "Vale refused to stop freaking out until we got in the car. It's like he knew exactly where to lead us."

Lee regarded the encroaching fog warily. "What the hell is happening?"

Dominic quickly outlined the situation - Lina tapping the ley lines for a dangerous ritual. Likely what Vale had sensed.

Just then, Jimmy sauntered over to Vale. "Well, well, if it isn't Valen. It's been a while." He began nonchalantly grooming himself.

Vale gave an excited bark and licked Jimmy, who recoiled. "Stop that this instant, Valen!"

Dominic was confused how they knew each other. "Wait, you two know each other?"

"But of course," Jimmy replied. "Valen here is one of the most powerful familiars around. I see he's chosen you as his new master."

Dominic looked down at Vale in surprise. The dog whined and bumped Dominic's leg persistently. Then he nosed at the pendant around Dominic's neck - a gift from Mr. Lidel.

Puzzled, Dominic asked Jimmy, "What's he trying to tell me?"

"He wants you to use the necklace to return him to his true form," Jimmy explained. "It can serve as a conduit for your magic."

Still uncertain, Dominic removed the pendant and held it up, clutching the chain tightly. He focused his power into the simple piece of jewelry, willing it to become a conduit for the magic thrumming through his veins.

The pendant grew warm in his grip as it began soaking up Dominic's mystical energy like a sponge. The metal took on an inner glow, pulsating with the cadence of a heartbeat as energy coursed through it.

Dominic felt a slight drain on his own reserves fueling the necklace, but he gritted his teeth and pushed more power into it. The pendant was almost too hot to touch now, throbbing urgently with unrestrained magic begging for release.

With an encouraging nod from Jimmy, Dominic aimed the pulsating beam of light issuing from the glowing pendant directly at Vale. As the energy made contact, Vale became enveloped in a dazzling aura of his own.

Vale's small canine body began levitating off the ground as the magic suffused his very cells. He shone brighter and brighter within the mystical cocoon, features blurring as the energy triggered his transformation.

They all watched in awe as Vale's shape grew larger and shifted within the blazing light. Two majestic spiraling horns took form atop his head as his squat legs elongated into powerful haunches.

Shimmering feathers of deepest onyx sprouted along his spine, rippling in an ethereal wind.

With a final flare, the blinding glow exploded outward. Dominic raised an arm to shield his eyes. When he was able to look again, Vale's glorious true form stood revealed - a mystical dark unicorn.

Vale shook out his wispy, star-flecked mane and stamped one shining hoof. His coat was the endless black of a moonless night, marked here and there with glimmers of distant galaxies. A very emblem of ancient magic woven into flesh.

Dominic could only stare in awe, staggered by the wild beauty of the celestial creature his familiar had become. The others looked equally dumbstruck by the stunning transformation they had witnessed.

Vale dramatically shook out his wispy mane and spoke directly to Dominic. "Well it's about time, Master. Honestly, I was starting to think you'd never figure it out."

Dominic reeled at the voice. "Wait, you can talk?"

Vale let out an exaggerated sigh. "Uh, yeah? All familiars can, once back in our true form. Do try to keep up, human."

Dominic blinked, taken aback by Vale's abrupt sass.

"Now can we get a move on here?" Vale continued impatiently. "In case you hadn't noticed, your deranged step-mommy dearest is about to destroy the world. Priorities, people!"

Dominic shook off his surprise. Vale was right - whatever Lina planned, they had to act quickly. Still, he shot his familiar an amused look.

"Well aren't you suddenly full of opinions and attitude?"

Vale tossed his mane haughtily. "Don't blame me for being impatient. You have no idea how boring it is being stuck as a mute dog all this time. Mama's got centuries of sass to make up for!"

Dominic had to laugh despite the circumstances. He already found himself growing fond of this new cheeky side to Vale. And the unicorn was correct - they could marvel over his wonders later. For now, lives were at stake.

With his fabulously opinionated new ally at his side, Dominic felt they finally stood a real chance against his stepmother's evil. Come what may, he and Vale would face the storm together.

Adrian quickly took charge, issuing orders. Dominic instructed Lee and Austin, "Stay here and watch over Dad."

The twins immediately protested. "We want to help!" Lee argued.

Dominic stood firm. "It's too dangerous. I can't risk you two getting hurt."

"We can handle it!" Austin insisted.

Dominic placed a hand on each of their shoulders. "I know you can. But please, let me keep you both safe this time. Guarding Dad is crucial too."

The twins shared an unhappy look but reluctantly nodded.

Adrian cut in decisively: "Ben and I will fly ahead. Roan, portal yourself and Merin to the forest's edge. Ciaran, you too. Dominic, ride with Vale." He made urgent shooing motions. "Move out, people!"

They swiftly split up to follow Adrian's directives. Swinging atop Vale, Dominic chuckled as the unicorn huffed "Well it's about time, human! Let's get moving already."

Despite the danger ahead, Dominic grinned. "Pretty sassy for a mythical creature."

"You have no idea, honey," Vale tossed his head. "Now hang on tight, we've got a deranged witch to stop!"

With that, he broke into a brisk gallop. Dominic laughed and stroked Vale's silky coat as they raced toward the looming forest.

They regrouped at the misty treeline as planned. Adrian immediately instructed, "We need to cover ground quickly, so we'll split up. But be cautious - no telling what lurks within."

Dominic asked, "Any idea where exactly to search first?"

"Trust your instincts," Adrian advised. "Ley lines converge in places of power - your magic should guide us."

Nodding, Dominic and Vale took the left-hand path into the shadowy woods. Adrian's guidance proved accurate, as an intuitive pull soon directed their route...

25

Stormweaver

Dominic

Dominic and Vale charged forth to intercept the dark beings emerging from the mist. But these were no mindless constructs - each monstrous form appeared sapient, glowing eyes fixing hungrily upon the pair.

"Be cautious, Master," Vale warned. "The fog empowers them - do not underestimate their might."

Dominic nodded grimly, magic flaring around his hands. The first twisted creatures attacked in a savage wave.

Vale reared with a piercing whinny, driving them back with blasts of celestial light from his horn. Dominic wove watery shields around them, deflecting claws and venomous spines.

They fought in flawless sync, neither straying far from the other's side. Vale struck with precision, purging the unnatural decay riddling each body. Dominic supplemented with defensive spells and fiery strikes.

But the darkened horde was endless - for each creature destroyed, two more emerged from the shadows. "There's too many!" Dominic shouted over the din.

In answer, Vale's horn flared even brighter, wreathing them both in a sphere of protective light. Safe within it, they could catch their breath.

"Well this is certainly bracing, isn't it darling?" Vale quipped, though he looked drained. Holding the barrier was taxing.

Dominic quickly uncorked an invigorating draught, sharing half with Vale to bolster their reserves. "We can do this - just hang on."

Nodding, Vale dissolved the shining shield. Immediately the spidery fiends swarmed them anew. Back to back, Dominic and Vale weathered the assault.

But the potion's effects were already fading. Dominic could feel his power waning under the relentless malice flooding the woods. If they didn't end this soon, the darkness would swallow them whole.

A colossal spider-like horror erupted into their midst, scattering lesser creatures before it. Vale bugled a warning - this was no mindless monster. Red eyes brimming with cunning intelligence focused on Dominic, razor mandibles clacking greedily.

"You will make a fine host, boy," it rasped wetly.

Dominic stood his ground, though his heart quailed at the giant's aura of festering malevolence. "I bow to no one," he declared boldly.

It let out an awful screeching laugh. "Brave words. Let's see you defend them!"

Its disturbingly humanoid arms shot forth blindedly fast to seize Dominic. He only just barely dodged, the claw tip shredding his shirt. Vale struck back instantly with a searing blast of magic, but the demon shrugged it off.

They exchanged a dismayed look - its hide seemed impervious to their attacks. But they had no choice but to fight on.

The frenzied battle carried them throughout the clearing, neither side able to gain advantage. Dominic used the terrain to outmaneuver his massive foe, buying time for Vale to seek weaknesses. But the demon matched them blow for blow.

Exhaustion threatened to overwhelm Dominic as the fight dragged on. He was struck by a reckless idea - it was their only chance. Whispering urgently to Vale, he sprinted straight toward the looming spider.

Just before impact, Dominic slid feet-first between its legs. As he passed beneath, Vale struck the demon's vulnerable underside with a concentrated beam.

Howling in agony and outrage, their foe thrashed wildly. Dominic rolled clear, peppering it with fiery darts to keep it distracted.

With another piercing blast, Vale finally pierced its exposed core. The demon convulsed, then crumpled into viscous smoke. The remaining creatures quickly dispersed without its influence.

Breathing hard, Dominic leaned against Vale in exhaustion. "We make a pretty great team," he panted. Vale bumped him affectionately with his horn. Together, they turned toward the ritual site - ready to end this.

Dominic and Vale continued fighting corrupted constructs as they pushed deeper into the mist-cloaked woods.

"Any idea where these foul things are coming from?" Dominic asked, blasting one back to viscous smoke.

"If I had to guess, your stepmother is opening a portal to the demon realm," Vale posited grimly. "That would explain the infestation."

Dominic felt icy dread trickle down his spine at the implication. A gateway to actual Hell? Just how far had Lina fallen into madness and evil? The scope of her ambitions shook him to his core.

This confirmed she had to be stopped immediately, before she could unleash literal hell upon the earth. Dominic refused to let his stepmother bring such catastrophe down upon them all.

If she tore open a portal between realms, the demon hordes would pour forth in limitless numbers. Their world would become engulfed by an eternal nightmare from which there was no waking.

Dominic quickened his pace, desperate to reach the ritual site in time. With a gateway to Hell at her fingertips, Lina would become nigh unstoppable. Only together could he and his friends stand a chance at stopping her now.

The further they went, the stronger the stench of decay and sulphur. It was as if the forest withered away wherever the hellish fog drifted. Lina was meddling with forces far beyond her control or comprehension.

Dominic only prayed they could seal the breach before it was too late. All that mattered was stopping whatever destruction Lina intended to unleash from the pits of Hell itself. He had to end this nightmare, no matter the cost.

With Vale stalwart at his side, Dominic steeled himself to face the fire and fury ahead. For the sake of everything he held dear, failure could not be an option.

They finally reached the perimeter of the familiar clearing. Peering from the trees, Dominic's blood turned to ice. At the clearing's center lay Christian's lifeless body, trapped within a spell circle steadily draining his essence.

Lina and Eros stood nearby, attention focused on the swirling portal behind them. Its violet light marked it a gateway directly into the depths of Hell.

Dominic trembled with rage and anguish at the scene. He had to stop this immediately, protocol be damned.

"Stay hidden for now," he whispered to Vale. "I don't want to reveal our position unless necessary."

Vale hesitated, but nodded reluctantly. Keeping low, Dominic crept as close as he dared, then channeled his magic.

With a bolt of lightning, he blasted the focal point of Lina's spell circle. It cracked violently, breaking the ritual. Acrid smoke billowed up, shielding Dominic as he sprinted forward to pull Christian's limp body from the damaged ring.

Dominic dragged Christian's limp body from the shattered ritual circle, calling his name frantically. To his immense relief, Christian's eyes fluttered open with a weak groan.

"That's it, stay with me," Dominic urged, cradling Christian's head. "You're going to be okay."

Christian managed a faint smile. "Knew you'd come..." he rasped.

Their reunion was cut short by an enraged scream. Lina glared at Dominic with maddened eyes. "How dare you interfere, you wretched boy!"

Dominic stood swiftly, shielding Christian with his body. "It's over, Lina. Whatever you're planning ends here."

She let out a grating laugh. "Oh I have what I need from your vampire. Now there is but one final piece to collect."

Her gaze turned to Eros with sinister purpose. His eyes widened in sudden apprehension. Too late, he tried to flee.

Lina made a tearing motion with her hand. Eros let out an agonized wail as ghostly tendrils ripped forth, wrenching the life essence from his body. Dominic watched in horror as she absorbed the stolen energy, leaving Eros a withered husk.

"You're a monster," Dominic accused, nauseated by her brutal callousness.

"No, I have become a goddess!" Lina declared fervently. Closing her eyes, she beseeched the swirling portal. "I call upon the powers of Hell - come forth and grant me your strength!"

To Dominic's dismay, a huge raven-like specter emerged from the vortex. With a shriek, it flew straight into Lina's willing body. She convulsed, back arching and limbs twisting unnaturally as the demonic spirit fused with her.

Christian struggled upright to witness the transformation. "What have you done?" he whispered.

Lina's body crackled with violet energy, levitating off the ground. Her eyes became endless voids. Great shadowy wings unfurled from her back.

The others arrived just in time to see her shift into an ethereal wraith-like form. A cruel smile stretched too widely across her gaunt face.

"Behold true power," Lina - or the thing she had become - rasped. "All shall tremble before me."

Dominic turned to the others urgently. "Get Christian to safety. I'll try to hold Lina off."

"Are you insane?" Ben argued. "She'll destroy you!"

"It's my responsibility to stop her," Dominic said resolutely. "Just protect yourselves."

Before Ben could protest further, Adrian pulled him back. "He's right, this is his fight." Though his eyes were full of concern.

As the group shielded Christian behind mystical barriers, Dominic faced the swirling dark spectre alone.

Lina's fathomless eyes fixed hungrily on him. "Let's end the chatter. I have a world to conquer."

Dominic called on his magic, sparks dancing across his skin. "I won't let you spread your evil."

Lina's wings sliced the air, sending razored discs of shadow magic at Dominic. He deflected them with a whirlwind shield.

"Pathetic tricks," Lina scoffed. Her jaws unhinged grotesquely, expelling a writhing sphere of black energy.

Dominic flung it back with a thunderous crackle of lightning. But Lina absorbed the attack effortlessly. They exchanged blow after blow, the clearing quaking under the magical barrage.

Though evenly matched at first, Dominic felt his power steadily waning against her demonic strength. He panted harshly, limbs leaden and trembling.

Lina pressed her advantage, striking with renewed ferocity. She slammed Dominic with an umbral blast that sent him skidding through the dirt.

Looming over his dazed form, Lina summoned a spear of crystalline dark magic, angling it toward his heart. Dominic threw up a hastily woven shield, but it only slowed the spear's creep.

"Now you die alone and forgotten," Lina gloated. The spear's tip pierced Dominic's weakening barrier, inching closer...

A searing beam of light suddenly collided with Lina's side, hurling her away with a shriek of agony. Vale galloped to Dominic, horn smoking.

"Thought you could use a hand, darling," the unicorn quipped. Together, they turned to face Lina's fury anew. Perhaps they stood a chance united.

Dominic managed a weary smile as Vale blasted Lina back. "Nice timing. Shall we finish this together?"

The unicorn nodded resolutely. Side by side, they faced down the raging wraith.

Lina came at them in a frenzy, demonic power fueling her strikes. Vale wove shields of light to blunt her attacks while Dominic countered with lightning and wind.

But their combined strength only enraged Lina further. She lashed out viciously, forcing them onto the defensive. Dominic could feel the dark magic behind each blow - she was still growing stronger.

Cackling madly, Lina tore open a dozen portals around them. Horrors from the depths of Hell spilled out, surrounding Dominic and Vale.

"Get ready!" Dominic yelled to the others. The team joined the fray, engaging the demonic invasion. But the hellspawn just kept coming.

Spying an opening, Dominic focused his efforts on Lina again. But his reactions were sluggish, magic weakening. A brutal backhand sent him crashing earthward.

Suddenly Christian was there, hauling Dominic to safety. But even that taxed his depleted strength - the ritual had drained him to the brink of death.

In desperate inspiration, Dominic offered his wrist. "Feed, it will help restore you," he urged.

Christian hesitated only a moment before sinking his fangs in. As he drank, some color returned to his pallid skin. He straightened with fiery purpose. "Let's end this."

Together they charged Lina amidst the chaos. She cackled and rose to meet their challenge. The clearing shook with the force of their colliding powers.

As Lina raised her shadowy axe for the killing blow, a blinding light enveloped Christian and Dominic. When it faded, they found themselves alone in the familiar clearing, restored to its former tranquility.

"What happened?" Dominic asked in confusion. "The others need our help!"

"Peace, young one. Time is frozen for the battle," spoke a melodic voice.

They turned to see the enchantress Moriganna regarding them solemnly. Dominic demanded she return them so they could fight beside their friends.

Moriganna shook her head. "There is something important we must do first, to unlock your full potential against what is to come."

Christian met her ancient gaze steadily. "Why have you brought us here?"

"Your destinies are intertwined in vital ways. But your bond must deepen further, if you are to prevail," Moriganna explained cryptically.

Comprehension dawned on Christian. "A true soul merging ritual. It's the only way."

Dominic looked between them anxiously. "What do you mean? Can this help us defeat Lina?"

Taking Dominic's hands in his, Christian said gently, "To complete our bond, we must open our souls to each other fully. But it will turn you immortal as well."

Dominic's eyes widened, but he did not hesitate. "I've wanted that gift from you for awhile now. I'm ready."

Christian embraced him joyfully. Grinning, Moriganna gestured for them to sit across from each other. "Let us begin."

As they clasped hands, Moriganna began to chant in lilting ancient tones. Christian and Dominic closed their eyes, focusing inward. They visualized their essences as glowing orbs of light.

Responding to Moriganna's spell, the orbs floated toward each other until they touched. Heat flooded both men at the contact. The orbs began to merge, light intertwining.

Christian and Dominic gasped as they felt their minds fuse, heartbeats falling into sync. Souls laid bare, memories and emotions flowed freely between them. Two became one.

When it ended, their eyes opened, now glowing silver. They regarded each other with intimate new understanding. The ritual was complete - they were truly and forever united.

"We don't have much time," Moriganna urged. "Go now with my blessing, and finish what has been started this night."

Nodding, the newly Bonded pair grasped hands once more. As Moriganna returned them to the chaotic fight, Christian and Dominic shared a determined look. Together, their strength would be unstoppable.

The battle raged on. But this time, when Lina attacked, Christian and Dominic moved as mirror images. Back to back, they wove elemental magic in flawless tandem.

Dominic narrowly dodged Lina's savage strike, strength renewed after the soul bond. He and Christian exchanged a determined look and nod.

In a blur, Christian spun away to assist their friends against the demon horde. Lina shrieked in outrage and tried to stop him, but Dominic drew her fury back to himself.

"You're not getting away that easy," Dominic challenged. He could feel his magic thrumming just under his skin, amplified by their merged souls.

Closing his eyes, Dominic channeled the well of power within. His whole body crackled with energy longing for release. This must be the awakened strength Moriganna promised.

When Dominic opened his eyes, they glowed with azure fire. Gazing skyward, he raised both hands. The air grew heavy, clouds blackening and swirling overhead in response to his call.

With a thunderous boom, arcs of lightning rained down around Lina. She barely threw up a shield in time to absorb the blows. Snarling, she counterattacked viciously.

But Dominic was ready. He punched the air, and a battering gust slammed into the wraith, driving her back. With sweeping arms, Dominic summoned a barrage of wind, rain, and hail to pummel his foe without mercy.

Lina responded with umbral fire and venomed crystal. But Dominic held his ground, weather magic protecting him. Their battle shook the heavens - neither witch willing to yield.

Sensing an opening, Dominic clenched his fists. The dark clouds compressed, sparking with power. An earsplitting thunderclap heralded a blinding column of lightning that engulfed Lina entirely.

She let loose an unearthly wail, writhing and convulsing under the unrelenting electrical onslaught. When it finally ceased, she collapsed smoking to the ground.

Wary of tricks, Dominic cautiously approached her still form. But sudden fissures split the earth, spewing sulfurous smoke. Coiling shadow tendrils erupted to drag Lina's body down into the fiery chasm.

Dominic rushed into Christian's arms. They clung together desperately, the pent up terror and adrenaline melting into relief. Breaking their fervent kiss, they turned as one at the sound of galloping paws.

"Vale? But how…" Christian stared at the excited unicorn in shock.

Dominic just laughed giddily. "I'll explain everything later, I promise!" Hand in hand, they went to join their weary but triumphant friends.

Adrian clasped Dominic's shoulder. "You did it. We can't thank you enough."

"I couldn't have done it without all of you," Dominic said earnestly. They had faced the storm as one.

Ben spoke up hesitantly. "Is she really gone for good though? That felt too easy…"

Ciaran shook his head gravely. "Great evil leaves wounds not quickly mended. But thanks to Dominic, we have time now to prepare."

"What matters is we have each other," Christian said, squeezing Dominic's hand. "Together, we can overcome anything."

Merin surveyed the corrupted clearing anxiously. "Think we can cleanse this place eventually Ciaran?"

The druid closed his eyes, chanting under his breath. The earth shuddered in response. Ciaran slammed glowing fists down and brilliant tendrils spread outward, returning life and light.

When he finally stood, the clearing was restored to its former serenity. They all exchanged awed looks.

Dominic turned to Christian, emotion welling up. "I love you. None of this would have been possible without you at my side."

Christian caressed his cheek. "I'll be beside you always now, in this life and the next." They kissed softly.

The long night was over, but their journey stretched onward. Side by side, they would see it through together.

26

The Deal

The Deal Maker

The Deal Maker watched events unfold in his scrying crystal with great amusement. Lina's spectacular downfall was entertaining, though not unexpected. He'd known she would fail, but allowed it to proceed anyway.

"Retrieve her before she is lost completely," he ordered Malachite in his usual imperious tone. The warlock obeyed, though his hatred simmered just below the surface.

The Deal Maker knew Malachite chafed under his command. But the warlock also valued his life enough to serve dutifully, for now at least. In time, Malachite's inevitable betrayal would provide some sport.

For the present, the Deal Maker would use Lina's hunger for power to control her. She could still further his own grand schemes, properly leashed. He would not waste this opportune new pawn.

When Malachite returned through a sulfurous portal with Lina's unconscious body, the Deal Maker appraised his fetching prize. Yes, much potential still lingered here, ripe for molding.

The Deal Maker prodded Lina with one polished shoe. "Wake up, my dear. We have much to discuss."

Lina stirred weakly, eyes focusing on her mysterious rescuer. "Where am I? Who are you?" she rasped in confusion and fear.

"I am the Deal Maker, and I have saved you from oblivion," he proclaimed, savoring her unease. Nothing sweeter than fresh mortal terror to whet the appetite.

"But why?" Lina asked warily.

The Deal Maker grinned, revealing sharp teeth. "Let's just say I saw potential in you, despite your abject failure tonight."

He began slowly circling where she sat tense. "You require guidance to reach the heights your ambition envisions. I can provide that…for a price."

Lina's eyes followed him mistrustfully. "And if I refuse your offer?"

At a snap of his fingers, Malachite opened a portal to the hellish domain beyond. Lina recoiled at the monstrous shapes lurking hungrily.

"Then you may take your chances there, among devoted fans of your previous work," the Deal Maker said lightly.

Visibly quailing, Lina turned her gaze away from the nightmarish vista. "Very well. I agree to serve you, my lord." The words were bitter acid on her tongue.

The Deal Maker smiled in satisfaction. With a flourish, he produced an ancient contract. "Just sign here, to make it official." A blood quill materialized in Lina's hand.

Once she had carved her name unwillingly, the Deal Maker rolled up the scroll. "Perfect. I do so look forward to our partnership." Lina shivered, unnerved by his shark-like grin.

"What is your bidding, Master?" she asked quietly.

"All in good time." The Deal Maker rose to depart his new pupil to Malachite's cruel tutelage. The game was afoot once more, on grander and more chaotic scales.

About the Author

Introducing Ken Sanchez, the visionary behind spellbinding M/M romance-fantasy worlds where love and magic entwine in a mesmerizing dance. With a heart devoted to the art of LGBTQ+ romance and an unbounded imagination, Ken is your guide to immersive realms he's painstakingly crafted. A dreamer who infuses passion into every stroke of his ink, he's conjured tales that not only enchant with fantasy but also stir the deepest emotions of love, taking readers on a spellbinding journey through his vivid narratives.

Also by Ken Sanchez

Enchanted (Willowbrook Book One)
In the mystical town of Willowbrook, secrets are written in the whispers of the wind, and magic hides in plain sight. A gifted young man named Benjamin, with the power to breathe life into stories, embarks on a journey of love and mystery. His path converges with a reclusive, cursed Beast named Adrian, and their destinies become enigmatically intertwined.

"Enchanted" unveils an enigmatic, gay retelling of a timeless legend, where every word holds hidden power. As their story unfolds, the heart of Willowbrook stands on the precipice of a chilling, unending winter. A fading enchantment, veiled truths, and a love as mysterious as the tale itself will rewrite the destiny of a town and its inhabitants.

Unlock the Magic Within, and Let Love Rewrite the Story. Journey into a world of mystery, where secrets and enchantments await your discovery.

Echoes Of Destiny (Shadowguards Book One)
Eryx, a gifted musician, channels melodies that bridge the realms of the seen and unseen. Little does he know that his haunting tunes are echoes of his godly lineage, a connection he's yet to unearth. When a sinister encounter alters his reality, he finds solace in an enigmatic guardian named Alex, whose presence sparks a connection that defies explanation.

Unbeknownst to Eryx, Alex is Hades, the lord of the Underworld, and a sentinel between the mortal realm and the divine. Possessing an air of danger and allure, he battles malevolent forces threatening to tip the balance. As he guides Eryx through the labyrinth of their intertwined destinies, an undeniable attraction forms between them, challenging the very fabric of their worlds.

Amidst the backdrop of a contemporary New York City tinged with ancient mystique, Eryx and Alex's love story unfolds. With the looming resurgence of ancient prophecies and an encroaching darkness, their bond becomes a beacon of hope. As Eryx's godly ancestry awakens and their love deepens, the duo embarks on a quest that will test their resolve, unravel hidden truths, and determine the fate of humanity itself.

"Shadowguards" is a spellbinding gay urban fantasy that marries the ordinary with the extraordinary. In a world where shadows hold untold power and love defies all odds, this novel explores the complexities of destiny, self-discovery, and the unbreakable ties that bind us. Prepare to be captivated by a tale where music and shadows converge, and where the line between the mortal and divine blurs beyond recognition.

Soul Reckoning (Shadowguard Files Book 1.5)
Leo Rodriguez, a powerful necromancer with a dark past, works for the Human Investigation Bureau (HIB), maintaining the delicate balance between the living and the dead. But when his own necromancer coven summons him home, Leo is forced to confront his past and the unresolved conflicts that haunt him.

Dr. Finn Sloane, a compassionate healer with a hidden gift, is dedicated to protecting and helping others. So when Leo, a man shrouded in mystery, seeks his assistance, Finn is drawn to him despite the secrets he keeps.

As they delve deeper into the paranormal mysteries of their world, Leo and Finn are drawn together by a powerful force beyond their control. But their newfound love is tested when they uncover a malevolent entity threatening Leo's coven and the entire city.

In a world where the line between life and death is blurred, Leo and Finn must rely on their love and unique abilities to face an unknown darkness that threatens to consume everything. Will their love be their salvation, or will they be consumed by the mysteries that lie ahead?

No Matter What

In the vibrant heart of London, amidst iconic landmarks and hidden gems, two lives collide in a tale of unbreakable bonds and unwavering love. When David's memories are stolen by a violent attack after a promising date, his best friend Ryan steps up to mend the shattered pieces. As they navigate the city's playful quirkiness and emotional depths, David and Ryan's friendship blossoms into something unexpected. Guided by a series of heartfelt letters, signed with the promise 'No Matter What,' they embark on a journey of self-discovery, tracing their shared past and forging a future full of hope and passion. Amidst the backdrop of playful banter, stolen glances, and the rich tapestry of London, they unveil the truth about their connection and embrace a love that transcends memory.

'No Matter What' is a heartwarming and witty novel that captures the magic of friendship, the power of resilience, and the joy of finding love where you least expect it."